A Map of the World
(With All Faults)

a novel by
Edward R. Weingold

HP

Hawkeye Publishers

A Map of the World (With All Faults)

© Copyright 2019
All Rights Reserved Edward R. Weingold

For more information, please address Hawkeye Publishers
HawkeyePublishers.com

Los Angeles, California

Library of Congress Control Number: 2019912123

Paperback: 978-1946005311
Hardcover: 978-1946005328
Ebook: 978-1946005335

For Rina, Maya, Martí, Arlin, Ian, and Bettina.

Keep in mind...

A Map of the World (With All Faults*)
is a work of fiction.

It includes several individuals whose words and actions
are based on historical records, but whose interactions and
dialog with other characters are purely speculative.

Please refer to the Dramatis Personae at the end of this
novel to orient yourself as necessary.

* With All Faults refers to the auction house term for as-is.

"What human affairs can seem important to anyone who keeps all eternity before their eyes and knows the vastness of the universe?"

— Cicero: Tusculanae Disputationes

CHAPTER 1

Duchy of Brabant, Spanish Netherlands, Early Spring, 1564

Do not give in. Numb fingers make his work a misery. *Do not give up.* Needle-like rain stitches eleven-year-old Jonas Hoen, who grasps the stiff canvas on the uppermost windmill blade. He grits chattering teeth to ward off the ache in his fingers as he reefs and lashes sailcloth flailing in the wet wind. Four fields away, a gang of peasants works in desperation to shore up the earthen dike.

"Should have got out there two days ago," his father, the miller, complains. "But it won't be like last time." Instead of consolation, however, his father's attempt at conjuring hope strikes a well of pain in Jonas' heart. He was five years old when a similar storm surge had burst the loamy dikes and washed most of the village away. His family lost their eight-year-old daughter, Jeltje, in that flood. His parents and he had escaped a watery death only by hauling themselves atop their thatched roof as it rafted inland.

Today, he and his father fix worried eyes on blackened skies to the west. His father slaps the boy's sopping back. "Good thing you're so strong." Jonas feels quite the opposite, weak in the knees and shivering, thankful to be done. They climb down the wind-whipped ladder and scramble to their hastily rebuilt cottage. The miller pushes hard against the door to latch it. His mother frets but lays out fresh clothes and towels her son's skin raw.

"He did well," his father says. "No faint heart in the boy."

She pats Jonas on his rump. His coloring is similar to hers, more bronze than fair like his father. His eyes are deep brown, also like hers. But Jonas sees in her eyes that she cannot hide fears of the floodwaters that swell the rivers and roll in from the angry North Sea. He wishes he could wipe her anxiety away, but he cannot squelch his own dread. He hunches his shoulders as winds whistle noisily through the skeletal arms of the mill house.

"He's all we have," says his mother, a hand on Jonas' damp hair. "We must go to higher ground. The rivers are swollen. Your cousin in Dordrecht—"

"No," his father protests. "Not a week ago, we took in fourteen cartloads. The barley will rot in this wetness."

"Grinding it does not make it dry. And if we all die in a flood?" Vrouw Hoen argues.

"Do not invite the devil to sup, woman."

His parents' bickering drips like acid in Jonas' ears. The miller turns his back on his wife. Jonas looks away, knowing how the miller disguises his alarm. "If we don't mill his grist, we won't see another cartload from Donkervoort. We must protect our reputation. The dikes will hold." His father speaks with finality.

The rain does not relent. Supper that night is sullen as unspoken reproach crackles like static above the rude table. His tight-lipped mother serves her husband, whose face glowers in the candlelight. Winds swirl; bursts of howling create a noise-scape of warnings. Even the livestock in the pen become eerily silent.

His mother prays and his father ruffles Jonas' ginger hair. His mother hugs him especially hard and utters, "Christ keep us safe."

"Mama," he says, "they were repacking the dike. This time it will be different."

Her hand trembles on Jonas' face. They creep into their beds, and listen to the now bawling goats huddled in their pen. Jonas tugs on his nightshirt, blots out the fierce sounds and drifts into a troubled sleep, disrupted by a recurrent dream that confuses and bedevils him. A mournful cry in Spanish, a language of which Jonas has no understanding. *Me llamo es Eduardo Orellano. Dios es mi testigo, cuando yo digo, yo soy un Cristiano.* The voice ends in despair and Jonas covers his ears with his pillow to shut out the temporal world, an ear-splitting tumult. The cracks of thunder are so loud that he never hears the bell tolling atop the village church, or rushing waters that breach the dikes. A massive surge tears across the fields, slams into the Hoens' cottage. Walls collapse. Jonas' severest fear spills him awake. He tumbles in the cold, wet debris of bedding, splintering wood, and drowning livestock. His mother reaches for him and he thrashes to meet her fingers but the rush of water tears him from her grasp. Over and over he tosses in the roiling maelstrom.

"Mama! Vader!" He coughs up brackish water—only to be sucked down again. Water chokes his throat and lungs. He panics, reaches for something, anyone to grasp. *Mama?* He surfaces and water explodes from his lips and nose. But like a sea monster toying with him, the water sucks him under again. *Just open my mouth and drink it all.* He fights a wish to embrace such a death, join his departed sister, gulp in the water and succumb. *Do not give in.* He flails to find the air, to defeat a ravenous beast bent on swallowing him whole. *Do not give up.* He struggles to the surface and kicks to finally spread the jaws trying to crush him.

Time itself has drowned. Exhausted, he floats face up on a river where none was before. *Mama, Vader!* Through the sheeting rain, lightning flashes like tentacles across angry skies. The surge pulls him far from home, far from the familiar. He is in the watery hands of fate. With stunner force, his shoulder strikes something hard and he is in the clutch of bare branches, leafless twigs, frigid in his torn nightshirt.

Jonas awakens under a gray overcast. Recognizes nothing. He closes his eyes against the pale light and fades from consciousness. Later, a searing ache in his left shoulder jars him awake. The taste of blood is on his lips. He shivers. Knife-jabs shoot through his shoulder again. He cries out to still the ache. *Voices!* He tries to shrink, become tiny so they will not see him in the leafless tree. *Hooded demons below!* But it is too late. Arms reach up from a skiff.

He quakes in the grasp of one of these black-cloaked beings. He is surely being carried off to hell. His father often repeated the priest's warning: *unworthy souls go to the devil.* Jonas tries to read the expression of whomever is carrying him.

"Brother Thomas," a rumbling voice behind him calls. "Who have we here?"

What's your name boy?" The mouth moves below a shock of carrot-hued hair surrounded by the black woolen cowl.

"J—Jonas, son of Joachim Hoen, the Miller," he rasps.

The man holding Jonas stifles a laugh and tosses back his hood. A copper-fringe monk's tonsure dances with his chuckle. "Jonas? Escaped the whale? Safe now."

"My mother, my father?" Jonas asks. Nothing more is said. He breathes shallow draughts to calm his bruised shoulder. Finally the skiff comes aground on a low upland. An afternoon haze hovers, a mist of gloom.

"Can you walk, Jonas?" Brother Thomas asks.

Shakily, he finds his land legs. "My mother, my father…." Jonas trails off. Monks emerge from a monastery on a rise near a wood. In the distance he sees steeples of a walled city. "Antwerp," Brother Thomas says. "You are far from your hamlet. It is drowned." Another monk speaks in mournful tones. "Your village is gone, young Jonas. We are Brothers in Christ. We care for orphaned boys."

The monk's words clap like thunder. *An orphan—motherless—fatherless. How could this happen in one dark moment?*

"You were spared," the Brother says. "Use this gift in God's service."

CHAPTER 2

Eindhoven, Netherlands, 3 March 1944

Herman Dijkstra's pencil point hovers above the entry on the onionskin sheet. *Housekeeper—I don't trust her. I'm afraid for Hetty.*

Herman regards the centuries-old book of maps open atop a low lectern centered on the sideboard, a gift from his wife's family on their marriage. His notes, a way of confiding to his dead wife, are tucked behind the end pages of the antique atlas.

Unwelcome warmth flushes his face. Emma Berghuis—hired after Marthe's remains were shipped home. Marthe—gone to Rotterdam to help with a cousin's birth, May 1940. Herman's throat tightens; he waves a hand weakly before him trying to dispel a recurrent image of his wife, crushed, burnt in the blitzkrieg. He squeezes back the lump in his throat and tries to focus on Emma as a godsend, cooking meals and cleaning for him and his two sons. Even with the shortages, Emma has uncanny abilities to prepare a table, arriving with pails of coal, while neighbors go cold and hungry. When the boys were stripped of their jobs at the Philips light bulb factory and shipped off to a German labor battalion, she was steadfast and reassuring. After the unexpected arrival last year of the terrified girl, Emma accepted his explanation, "An orphan niece from Rotterdam."

He hates what he has said about Emma Berghuis and reaches for an eraser to rub out his suspicion. But the single cough of a Daimler engine, followed by a backfire on the street outside, stops him. He hastens to the study window. Two Nederlandsche SS step out of the Standaard V black sedan adjusting their holsters and peaked caps. *Not prepared! What first?* Panicked, he shoves the onionskin indictment of the housekeeper between the back cover and the last leaf. He flips the atlas leaves to display the map of the world, *Typvs Orbis Terrarvm*. The boots of the SS men scrape the worn stone stairs. Herman turns toward the kitchen, but whirls, and races to the sideboard. He opens the drawer and feels about quickly.

"Hetty." Herman stifles his voice as he calls her name. The first knock on the door spurs his urgency. But he slows. No need to alarm her. She will be awash in fear soon enough. With deliberate steps he enters the kitchen. The brown-haired girl with intelligent eyes is drying dishes. She looks up and smiles. His brow is furrowed. Her smile freezes. He tries to make his voice conversational. "Hetty? They've come, as I said they might one day." The joy drains from her face. "Go quickly to the hiding spot, stay completely quiet." He pauses. "And do not come out until I call you."

"But—but, no. Stay with me, please." She strangles the dishtowel.

"They will go away, but you must hide." Herman implores. The knuckles rapping on the front door become more insistent. He forces a grin and nods. "Courage. It will be fine, Hetty, like a game of hide and seek," he whispers. She tries to mask her face with the dishtowel. It betrays her hurt at a promise broken.

"But you said—" she stops, turns away, and crawls through a cupboard into a spider-webbed passage built five centuries earlier as a precaution against Spanish mercenaries.

"Quiet as you can be," he hisses. Herman sniffs the stale odor of the secret passage and closes the cupboard door. "Dear Jesus," he mutters; he traces Hetty's muffled sounds inching down the wall. The pounding rattles the front door.

"Open up!"

"Coming. What's the big racket?" He unlocks the door, feigns surprise.

"Where is she? Where is the Jew girl?" The odors of boot polish and gun-oil suffuse the air.

"What? What are you asking? There's no—"

The thick-necked SS man pushes a stubby finger into Herman's chest and backs him into the hallway. "Herman Dijkstra, yes?"

"Yes, of course," Herman says.

"It will go hard if you don't turn her over directly," the other snaps. He looks familiar. Where has he seen the weak chin and off centered eyes?

"Do I know you?" he asks, backing toward his study.

"No stalling," the crooked faced SS man snaps.

"I have a niece from Rotterdam staying here, Dutch Reformed, naturally, not—not Jewish." He laughs, fooling no one.

"Diederik," says the thickset partner, "this is already taking too long." He pushes past Herman toward the stairs.

"Diederik?" Herman repeats.

"Produce her now," demands the man Herman cannot exactly place. Diederik looks up the stairs. Herman searches his memory, was he the butcher down the street, a salesman trying to get him to buy new stitching machines? The factory!

"She is on an errand." Herman lies. "Did you once work at my linen factory?"

Diederik tilts his head like a cat pawing a wounded a bird.

"If my housekeeper were here I would offer you a coffee—we may still have a little—but she is—"

"Yes, yes, we know. The girl!" Diederik unclasps his holster.

Then Herman is certain—an upsetting meeting in his office eight years before—he had sacked this man for stealing three bolts of linen.

He sees Diederik relish the upper hand. "You know, of course, Mr. Dijkstra, the edict against Jews entering the home of a Christian."

"But that is not the case—" Herman objects.

Diederik interrupts, "Those who are complicit—your boys already serve in Germany. But they are free. Doing their duty. You will be treated exactly like the one you have harbored unless—come, come. There is no niece from Rotterdam."

Diederik's partner has been tapping on the wall by the staircase with thick knuckles. "Ah, these old canal houses." He thuds solid plaster until he hits the boards near the stairwell. "What do we have here?"

They know everything! Herman imagines Hetty in the darkness, hearing the SS man inches from her face.

"Look!" Herman raises his voice. "I have her papers." He hurries to the sideboard in his study, hoping they will follow. Herman yanks open the drawer. "Her baptismal certificate, her—" He pulls out a fistful of papers. "My niece, from Rotterdam. Not back for hours." Too late, his anger has won the battle. He grasps the Belgian pistol. You traitors." He turns, and levels the small caliber gun. "Get out! Find yourselves real work."

"Henk!" Diederik shouts. Henk fires. Herman cries out, more in surprise than pain as the bullet tears into his chest. But he jerks the trigger of the Melior automatic, is amazed at its kick and shocked to see blood spurting from Henk's neck. Diederik shouts again, and Herman fires wildly, one shot shattering Diederik's kneecap. He shrieks a stream of profanities.

Herman loses his footing. His torso twists onto the book of engraved maps. He grasps the lectern. His fingers linger at the edge of the hastily hidden onionskin sheet. Then his knees buckle. Two more bullets pierce his back. The last thing he sees is his blood smear across the map of the world. *Oh, the times I warned my sons—and the little girl—'Be careful to never to spill anything on these special pages.'*

CHAPTER 3

Walnut Creek, California, Early March 2016

"Be careful, Michael! Don't spill even a drop." His father's words form in his mind. *Words from when?* "Seven or eight years old," he sniffs, "well before the mad times."

Michael Dijkstra scans the poorly lighted basement through watery eyes. He had helped develop the brightest, longest lasting light ever, but can barely see under the glow of a 25-watt tungsten bulb in his sour-smelling cellar. But, as he stoops his gaunt body, stiff with age, to avoid a joist, he clips his forehead. "Fu-uh," he grunts, and almost decides to go back upstairs, forget the quest that troubles him so. One hand on his stinging brow, he moves dusty cartons to locate the discolored corrugated box. He tamps down a wry sense that he has found what he had buried in the darkest corner of the basement, and a fury, harbored since the Nazis imperiled his very existence. He had shipped the heirloom book from Eindhoven when Philips Electronics put him in charge of LED developers in Silicon Valley.

After another registered bank letter arrived yesterday, he searches for anything left of value to sell that might stave off foreclosure on the house he has lived in for twenty-five years. Online, he makes startling discoveries about atlases published by Flemish cartographers, Mercator, Hondius, de Jode, Ortelius. *Was his family's antique atlas…?* Early editions could sell for over sixty thousand dollars. A few maps with original hand coloring commanded over a hundred thousand.

The heft of the box ignites a memory of carrying the atlas safely home on a bicycle through war-blasted streets of Eindhoven. He carries it up the stairs, clears the dining room table, and uses a paring knife to slice the aging paper tape that he had moistened in 1992 for the shipment to America. He had wrapped the book in the *Eindhovens Dagblad*. The front page for that October day carried news of a plane crash which decimated an apartment building in Amsterdam killing many. "The worst tragedy to befall the Netherlands since the Second World War," the prime minister said. He lingers over the yellowing newsprint to recall the tragedy. A moment later, he is engulfed by roars and flashes of exploding bombs as he and his brother, Pim, run from the forced labor munitions factory under Allied bombardment. He leans on the table, brought back yet again to the imagined crushing of his mother in the bombing of Rotterdam. He shakes his head to cease the memory of when he was fifteen, and tears the protective newspaper away to reveal the scarred brown leather. He lifts the old tome but drops it as though it were on fire. His heart pumps at what he had seen the first time seventy years ago—the pages partially sealed by the blood of his father, shot by the SS in his home on the Keizergracht in 1944.

"Be careful, Michael! Don't spill even a drop." He traces the bloodstained edge of the book. His breathing normalizes and he removes the book from its box as though disinterring a sacred relic. The atlas had belonged his mother's Rotterdam family, owners of commercial seagoing vessels for centuries. An inscription on the inside front cover reads: "To Ship's Master Jacobus Vandeven: With deepest gratitude for your aid now and in the past. J. Hoen, November 1567." The book floods Michael with sadness *and* anticipation." He turns the first leaf to the expertly colored title page. "ABRAHAMI ORTELI ANTVERP" confirms his great hope.

"I have an antique map to sell," Michael says. He brushes the sleeve of his brown thrift-store suit. "Or consign it for auction, if it could happen soon," he adds, consulting the business card he has been handed, "Mr. Pinkham." A voice buzzes in his head. *Don't do this. This Pinkham is a shark.* The ashen-faced auction house manager, also elderly, squints through rimless glasses.

"Let's have a look, Mister—?" Pinkham, eyebrows raised, nods toward the man's makeshift container, a flattened corrugated box.

"Dijkstra," Michael says. He pronounces it *Doikstra*. "Michael Dijkstra."

Pinkham peers over the counter as Michael slips the antique map from its cardboard housing. "Not a nice way to treat— Hardly pristine, is it?"

"Yes, that's why I'm here and not at Christie's," Michael snaps. "I need a net of five thousand dollars." Michael's tone sounds shrill to his own ears. A voice keeps repeating *don't do this, Michael.* He says with resolution, "And I need it to go into your next auction, or, if you buy it outright, I would take the reserve. Maps like this have fetched ten times—"

"Never in this poor condition," the old auctioneer raises his hand. Michael recognizes that he is a practiced angler who easily plays the would-be consigner. "Our experts need to see it, of course." Pinkham smiles through bucked teeth. "I'll write you a receipt, but it is not a guarantee of acceptance. We can discuss a reasonable reserve for April. In the fall, when we have our prints and graphics—"

"How soon could you know for April?" He struggles to get his words out, at war between his need for quick cash and, seeing the dull cinnamon-colored stain, a nagging desire not to part with the map.

"Three o'clock tomorrow." The auctioneer interrupts Michael's slippage into the past. He sees that Michael is irresolute and rattles on. "If we can accept it, you are extremely lucky." He accelerates his pitch. "Tomorrow is the cutoff for the next catalog. I need your particulars."

Michael hesitates, but passes a 3×5 card to the auctioneer.

"Ah, this will do, Mr. —Ah, Didg—?"

"Dijkstra, Michael." Nausea churning, he watches the auctioneer fill in a Consignment for Auction form with the Fleming Auction Galleries imprint. On the line marked Item(s), Pinkham writes: *Engraved, hand-tinted map, possibly 16th C—distressed.*

CHAPTER 4

East Palo Alto, California, April 11th, 2016

Patricia Spencer looks over her fourth grade class writing their essays about the Camino Real. She knows the missionary route of the Franciscan friars and Spanish army in the 16th Century holds minimal interest for most of the class. She fixes her gaze on Esperanza Reyes, whose dark eyes scowl at the words she has written. *Poor girl.* Patricia recalls her principal's cold assessment of the girl's predicament, her parents deported following an ICE raid three months earlier. "A crying kid in class is a distraction." Patricia cannot shake her melancholy over the unfairness of a child born in California who suffers a separation for her parents' undocumented status. To quell her gloom, she surveys the students and stops, jarred by the slack-mouthed stare out the window by the class clown, Mario Kinsella.

Another damaged kid, this one abandoned while still with his parents. A painful parent teacher-meeting with the Kinsellas: Mom, a doughy blonde who shook her head in disbelief that Mario is disruptive in class; Dad, ruddy-faced, doused in shaving lotion that does not quite mask the odor of liquor. "Not a peep outa' him at home," he insists. "You must'a got our kid mixed up with some other. Let a kid be a kid," Mr. Kinsella advises. "He ain't goin' on to no college. Gonna join up anyways, once he's old enough."

Patricia tries to dim the memory of Mario's parents as their son slips deeper into sullenness. Her eyes travel to a world map at the side wall of her classroom; a shadow runs north to south in a diagonal line. She looks to the windows of her room to see one of the shades hung up on its track; the afternoon sun pours through the unfiltered panes of the window and emblazons most of the map to create an oblique shadow. For reasons she cannot quite fix, the world map disturbs her in this lighting.

She casts her eyes back at Mario Kinsella as he too gazes at the hung-up window shade. Her eyes return to Esperanza who holds her face in her hands and presses exhausted shreds of facial tissue against her tears.

Patricia averts her eyes. She looks to Mario but is shocked to see, not the troubled 11-year-old-boy, but Owen, her 48-year-old husband, crammed into the desk. She snaps her head away again to take in first the shadowed map, then the skewed window shade. Her neck aching, she slowly turns toward Mario's desk and is relieved to recognize the scowl on the face of the boy who struggles to answer a question about the labor that built the adobe missions. Patricia peers out the window toward the bay. Her eyes fix on a sailboat heeled over in the afternoon wind. *How does it keep from sinking?*

Twenty minutes west of her gaze, Owen Spencer ends a phone attempt to dissuade a rich client from chasing a fake contemporary Gutenberg portrait. His mood sours. He ruminates darkly over a snapshot of Patricia and him, both smiling broadly from a peak in Yosemite. The photo, taken by a passerby on the Sentinel Dome ten years earlier, peeks out behind art magazines, gallery circulars, and a stack of *The New York Times* Art and Design sections. His desk is a repurposed door atop file cabinets in his garage office behind their faux Spanish cottage. Owen's thoughts slip to his recurrent dream life. Lately, he conjures Hieronymus Bosch and Pieter Bruegel the Elder—horrific scenes, gruesome enough to wake him from fitful sleeps. His attempts to fall back asleep by envisioning the work of Magritte fail to ground him and turn all this Belgian weirdness into a lark. Instead, he is at a peasant-wedding, food and drink slobbered on him by drunken revelers farting and belching. His ringing phone cuts short his mood over Patricia's and his off-kilter relationship.

"Maurice Bregmann, here," the deep voice intones in accents from east of the Hudson River.

"Ah, yes, Dr. Bregmann." Owen smiles recognizing the Jewish Studies scholar, curator of Western Judaica for the UC Berkeley Bancroft Library. His last transaction had been a year earlier, a set of architectural drawings for a synagogue near Union Square in the 1880s.

After an exchange of greetings, Bregmann asks, "Can you make time to check an item in the Fleming Galleries' auction? A world map that has caught the attention of Yad Vashem in Jerusalem." Owen recalls Yad Vashem's focus. *Holocaust and the Nazis.* "They want to know its provenance and get a firsthand view of the condition," Bregmann continues. "The catalog entry is a bit vague."

"Is this a Judaica item?" Owen asks.

"Strictly speaking, no. It's a piece of Ortelius cartography, Lot 256."

Owen riffles through the mound of circulars teetering on the corner of his desk. He fears that he has not been attentive enough to this lower-tier auction house. Ortelius maps were often easy to turn over. He had not bothered to open the latest when he had read the catalog title, "Miscellaneous Literary Treasures."

"Actually, Owen, we need you on this by tomorrow. Thursday is the last of their open preview days."

Without locating the needle in his haystack of mail, Owen accepts the request as he spies two brown paper-wrapped Mucha lithographs leaned against the garage wall. "I'll be in The City tomorrow to deliver some prints. I can swing by for Fleming's preview. Lot 256, yes?"

"Give me a call with anything you learn and how this map comes to be auctioned. Thanks for doing this on such short notice," Bregmann concludes.

As Bregmann ends the call, Owen finally fishes out the catalog. The cover shows a color photo of dust jackets for a handful of signed first editions. He flips through the pages to Lot 256 and sees a black and white reproduction showing a damaged specimen of the world map titled *Typvs Orbis Terrarvm*.

Copper plate map, Antwerp, Contemporary hand-colored folio sheet, 546×431 mm (21.5"x16.9")

The map looks authentic. But its condition is awful.

Circa 1571, world map engraved by Frans Hogenberg for Abraham Ortelius' first (ever) world atlas, Theatrum Orbis Terrarum. South America disproportionately defined; ill-charted west coast. California coast misshapen. Southern continent labeled Terra Australis Nondum Cognita.

If the date is accurate, this is a later printing from a first-state copper plate.

Decorated with sailing ships, sea monsters, and strapwork cartouches for the title and a quotation from Cicero. Dutch text on verso.

Dutch text! A twinge of excitement puts Owen on alert. This plate might be extracted from the first Dutch language printing of Ortelius' atlas.

Condition: Minor foxing, margins yellowed, darkening along vertical centerfold, dark dampstain right side of plate. Offered W.A.F.   1500-2000

"W.A.F., With all faults," Owen translates the initials aloud, the insiders' version of *as-is*.

He scans his diary for Thursday and decides to deliver the pair of Mucha lithographs to his customer first, then head to the financial district to preview the map in the gallery showroom. He wonders why Yad Vashem has taken an interest. He goes online to view the digital version of the upcoming auction catalog. After zooming in on the color image of the world map and panning across possible "Judaica" sites, Owen finds nothing remarkable about the treatment of the areas near modern-day Israel. He scans the lands that make up the Russian Pale of Settlement—declared by Catherine the Great a legal area for Jews, well after the Ortelius map was engraved. Again, nothing stands out. Online, Asia looks like it had been sadly spattered by rusty water.

Nevertheless, glad that an old client has called him for a consultancy, Owen shuts down his laptop and casts his eye on the two lovers atop Sentinel Dome. The light of love dances in both their smiles. His eyes crinkle in a grin as he remembers the light-hearted, top-of-the-world trip with Patricia when their love still had the radiance of newlyweds, even after a decade together. Then, Owen would have scoffed that his marriage, now twenty years on, could become so fragile. *Since the death of her mother—has it already been half a year—so tightly wound—like a stranger lately.* He scratches at his graying temple and feels gratitude that he is sitting in the converted garage from which he runs his business. He recalls Patricia, steadfast, even defiant of her mother's wish that she not move to Palo Alto.

"So who needs an MBA jerk when a starving artist named Owen is who I love?"

"And if I make it big?"

"Hit the road, Jack."

Owen often returns to the banter from the infancy of their relationship. His masters in art history had led to short turns as an adjunct lecturer at three community colleges before he became a fulltime print dealer fifteen years ago. Patricia's teacher's salary has carried them through lean stretches. But now, returning from frazzled school days, she offers none of her carefree bonhomie. Eager for distraction, Owen revisits the unexpected call from Bregmann and the intriguing antique map. Rereading the catalog entry for the stain-damaged Lot 256, he doubts that any of his work today will result in accounts receivable.

He snaps to as he realizes the time. Wednesdays are his night in the kitchen. "Hump day cuisine" he has christened this routine. He snatches up the paper copy of the Fleming's catalog and pauses in the kitchen to assess his marinade-smothered rack of ribs in the electric slow cooker. The aroma makes him smile as he uncorks a bottle of Pinot Noir. *Why is Yad Vashem interested in a damaged map?*

CHAPTER 5

Benedictine Monastery, Near Antwerp, 1564

Soon after his arrival, Jonas chokes back his tears and spirals inward, as he adjusts to life at the Benedictine Brothers abbey. He says little, protecting the kernel of himself deep inside, lest it be ripped from him like his family. As the waters recede after his rescue, swarms of flies create buzzing canopies above drowned livestock and people. Oddly, these clouds give him momentary hope. But if Jonas' mother and father had been found, they were never named. Untold hectares of land were rearranged; buried under ocean sand, silt from the rushing rivers, liquefied fields. Jonas tries to harden his heart. *It is only a bad dream.*

The Brothers see a boy who rarely smiles. He leaks rather than cries.

"What shall we do with you until you regain use of your arm?" Brother Thomas asks the first week—and answers his own question. "Light duties in the cookhouse until you can do more hardy work." Jonas joins an eight-year-old as an assistant to the woman who prepares meals and does a myriad of chores looking after the monastery's monks and the orphaned boys.

"If he could shed tears, his days would be happier," Maria de Vries confides to Brother Thomas who stares at her uncomprehending. The plump mother to the Brothers and orphans finds moments to touch Jonas' forehead or tousle his hair as she bustles from the kitchen building to the dining hall.

Jonas spends three hours a day in catechism class and he adapts quickly to lessons in Dutch and Latin. He is given a pencil and papers to begin declension lessons in the language of the Mother Church. He learns quickly, but finds the droning teacher, Brother Cornelius, uninteresting. His mind wanders to memories of his family, still unfound. He thinks of his sister, Jeltje, and is shocked to realize he cannot recall her features. He becomes lost in memory because it is painful not only for the loss but it triggers a miserable guilt, for they had argued the morning of her drowning. Five-year-old Jonas had stalked off into a neighboring field in the steady rain and then made a game of it, running away. Tasked with taking care of him, she follows, but in a mischief-inspired moment, he circles back to their cottage while his sister searches deep into a second pasture, moments before the surge turns the field into a lake. She is found half buried in the mud, not far from the washed out levee.

At seven years of age, Jonas infuriates the village priest when he confesses through his tears that he was responsible for his sister's death. "That is the sin of pride," the priest sputters. "Stop that blubbering. How dare you think you can create a flood? Go home and wipe such thoughts from your mind."

Later that day, Jonas struggles with what "Confession" means while he assists his cursing father in dressing the primary millstone with a mallet and cold chisels. He ruminates on the unjustness of the accusation that he was prideful. His father snaps his commands as the distracted boy tries to pass the proper chisel. The door to the mill house opens and the red-faced priest reports Jonas' arrogance. His father bids the priest a "good afternoon, and many thanks" as he drops the tools on the partly sharpened stone. He picks up a wooden rod and whips Jonas severely.

"Never—never again bring your mother or me to notice of the priest. Do you understand?" Jonas nods through salty tears, but he understands only that his buttocks sting from the whipping. Thereafter, he keeps his own counsel.

In Brother Cornelius' classroom he tries to recapture a memory of how his sister looked by sketching from his remembrances, but her features elude him. He leaves the young girl's face blank. Driven to keep the memory of his parents alive, he sketches his mother and father with more success. He captures the faint smile lines of his mother's face, and the piercing eyes of his father on separate attempts to put their visages down on paper.

"Jonas!" Brother Cornelius hisses. He covers his sketches under his declensions of Latin verbs. But the teacher has seen the breach of class decorum and he snatches the drawings. Jonas barely stifles his urge to snap them back. A pall comes over him. The world is intent of robbing him of his family. He seethes as Brother Cornelius harangues and uses Jonas' shame and suppressed fury as an example to the other pupils of how ungrateful some orphans can be for their deliverance.

He returns to the cookhouse to help prepare the evening meal, head down, his healing shoulder aching with tension. He is brought up short when he sees a beautiful young woman of twenty, flaxen hair peeking from her white cap, conversing with Maria de Vries.

"Hah, Jonas. This is my daughter, Godlieve."

He stills his shame at the rebuke of Brother Cornelius, and smiles in greeting.

"Jonas came to live with us two weeks ago. The floods…." Maria says with a sad shake of her head. Then she changes her tone. "Look! Lieve has brought us fresh chanterelles. With all the wetness, these mushrooms didn't know the time of year and they are going to make delicious soups for the next week."

A reed basket heaped with red and tan mushroom caps sits on the worktable.

"Hello, Jonas," the young woman brings a blush to his face. "Mother says you are a help sent from heaven. Please keep her young by minding her words." Her smile shows white teeth and bits of green in her eyes that make his cheeks tingle.

Maria de Vries says, "Jonas, put those mushrooms in that crock so Lieve can take her basket." He does as he is bidden and the women return to their conversation. He steals looks at Maria's daughter, and his day brightens.

After the young woman leaves, a melancholy returns at having become an orphan after the merciless storm.

That evening, following Jonas' chores, Brother Thomas calls him to discuss the disrespect he has shown Brother Cornelius. The monk holds the pencil drawings the teacher had confiscated.

"I finished my classwork," Jonas says in a fearful voice. I was only just trying to remember."

"You made these drawings?" Brother Thomas asks, his voice softening.

"Yes," Jonas admits. "My mother. My father. But my sister's face, I cannot recall."

"Hmmm," Brother Thomas mutters, with no reproach in his tone. "Never in Brother Cornelius' classes." He begins to return the drawings to Jonas, but pauses over the one of his mother. "Did you get teaching in how to draw, Jonas?"

"No. I was trying to remember how they looked."

"Would you like to learn more how to draw?"

Jonas shrugs, winces as his left shoulder shoots a reminder of his loss.

"Perhaps we can help." Brother Thomas nods to say their discussion is done.

The next week, Brother Thomas guides Jonas to the scriptorium door. There, Brother Uwe, thin, taciturn, leads Jonas past four Brothers who copy texts, ecclesiastical and secular, to new sheets of paper and parchment made from sheepskin. Brother Uwe is the precentor, the librarian whose primary duty assures order and security to the monastery's collections and works in progress. He walks Jonas to a wizened monk who peeks through folds of skin tabs that hang from his eyelids. "Brother Bernardus," Brother Uwe mumbles, as his attention shifts to the precarious position, half hanging off the writing table, where one of the copyists has placed a rare manuscript on loan from a French monastery. The Brother lectures the careless monk who hangs his reddening head.

Jonas looks sideways as the cadaverous Brother Bernardus regards him.

"They have sent you to me...." the palsied monk in his black habit begins. Jonas stealthily shifts his weight as the monk searches for his words. Jonas strains to hear because the parched lips barely move to produce intelligible words. "To learn!" The blurted sounds, like constipated stools, shoot through an orifice. "Watch!"

Jonas sits nearby on a high stool in the scriptorium. The aged illuminator selects an oft-used sheet of pasteboard with a rectangle cutout. He masks the Latin-inscribed page so that only the section he will illustrate shows. He grasps the stylus in his claw-like fingers. His arthritic knuckles are huge. With quavering hand, he applies a series of dots to the sheet of parchment. Jonas breathes shallowly, for the old man exudes an odor of mustiness. But the illuminator's intense focus enthuses Jonas as he watches him squint and will his hand to steady and create the outline of an ecclesiastical figure poring over a book in the enlarged D that begins the Latin text. Before he can calculate the time he has been watching the old man, Jonas witnesses half a dozen techniques applied to rough in the image of a scholar studying scripture. The subject does not impress as much as the old monk's craft as he readies the drawing for application of pigments.

The Brother's palsied hands are again made to obey his steel will as he scrapes a hillock of dust off a chunk of malachite to form a yellow trail of copper carbonate in a paint pot. The old man tips a jar of foul smelling liquid over the malachite dust and Jonas realizes it is urine. The monk's withered hand mixes the two elements until a smooth syrupy paint develops into a brilliant yellow. The bell tolls four times as the last of the pigment is applied. For the first time since Jonas has been ordered to sit and watch, the old monk's eyes contact his.

"Tomorrow you will get to practice," he croaks.

Jonas can barely wait.

In the weeks following, Jonas learns the rudiments of illustration following instruction from the difficult to understand the monk. When Brother Bernardus speaks, a tic makes his mouth snap open and closed before the words pop out. Jonas concentrates not to stare or avert his eyes in discomfort as the affliction takes on the guise of a stutter or stammer. Fortunately, old Bernardus is stingy with his words and Jonas is free to lose himself in his practice of drawing. When the artist leaves the scriptorium to relieve himself, Jonas steals looks at the tomes that fill bookshelves lining the walls. The white lambskin vellum bindings interest him most. The mottled white and gray book covers and spines seem richer than even the finely tooled gold and silver foil surfaces of the brown cowhide covers. As the precentor comes near Jonas' worktable, he asks if it were permitted for him to open one of the books.

"Only when I can supervise you," the librarian says, passing without stopping. Jonas continues to practice winding vines and grape leaves around an alphabet of capital letters on his practice sheets.

The days drift into months. Bernardus finally entrusts Jonas to decorate a minor treatise by Saint Basil. He glimpses the text and realizes that the church Latin reads as turgidly as it appears on the page. He is grateful that he can mask the copyist's rendition of the work and concentrate only on the initial letter, a mundane Q beginning the sentence in Latin, *"Quid ergo est, doctrina?"* He translates the Latin: "What then is our doctrine?"

Jonas roughs in the leaves like a twining vine of ivy, knowing that he must add an ornate cross as the central image in the Q, bearing the Savior. Jonas considers what it might be to suffer the passion of death nailed to a wooden T.

Disturbingly, he hears his daytime mind crying *"Me llamo Eduardo Orellano… Yo soy un Cristiano."* He chases the voice from his mind by beginning an illustration of the Savior on the cross. But he diverges from the sample drawing by adding a mallet grasped by a disembodied hand striking the spike into the right palm of the Christ. He draws agony onto the face of the Savior.

When Brother Bernardus returns and glances at the new artist's effort, he strikes his bony hand across Jonas' face, a slap that catches his left ear.

"D-don't ever ch-change my instruct-tion," Bernardus jeers in stinging rebuke. "Ob-obedience, obedience!"

As the buzzing in his ear recedes and his confusion and shame amplifies, Jonas removes the mallet and tormentor's hand from the window of creativity he abused. The old monk rants as Jonas works. "The-the b-boy knows noth-nothing of symb-symbols. He-he-e makes di-divine blood f-f-flow. Is he a Jew? Is he a blood-blood-lust Jew who relishes th-the Say-savior's agony? He knows nothing of symb-symbols." Jonas hears with one ear burning with shame, the other smarting from the blow. But he makes certain the nail is already embedded in the Savior's palm, and the face is changed to one of repose, accepting the punishment as His Father's will. The monk calms down after Jonas makes the corrections.

In the dining hall that evening, Jonas looks away from the table at which Brother Thomas sits. He glimpses the look of concern the copper-tonsured monk shoots in Jonas' direction. Jonas has no appetite. He stolidly awaits the end of the meal, never looking at any of the Brothers. He fixes his eyes on the surly Willem Booten, a boy a year older than Jonas who had arrived that week. The new arrival sparks Jonas' anger because he thrusts younger boys roughly out of his way. The boys dare not complain, but Jonas makes clear in his hard look that he does not take kindly to the bullying of the smaller boys. Booten's silent sneer challenges Jonas, who expects that they will soon settle their enmity with a fight. The Booten boy had been orphaned not by the storm and sea surge but the rash murder of his parents by a Spanish soldier. From the gossip of Maria de Vries Jonas learns the details.

"Minding their own affairs, his mother and father, farmers from a village near Leuven. I can't get him to utter a word," Maria de Vries complains. "The burghers who brought him here said that the Spaniard flew into a fury when he was told his stipend from the Duke of Alva would be delayed because the taxes were not yet collected. Killed Willem's mother and father with his slashing rapier." Maria's chin quivers. She makes a clicking sound with her tongue and teeth. "Willem becomes suddenly an orphan…with no words."

She takes hold of Jonas, as though he is her flesh and blood and presses him against her. She seems to take strength from him and straightens up, smiling. "But enough of sadness. Do you enjoy your tasks in the scriptorium? Is old Brother Bernardus a good teacher? Will you draw a picture of me when you feel able?" Her questions do not wait for answers. She touches Jonas ear, affectionately. "We count our blessings, eh?"

Jonas suppresses his desire to know if Maria's daughter, Godlieve, will visit again. The flaxen-haired young woman has been appearing before his closed eyes filling his mind with unclean thoughts.

CHAPTER 6

Benedictine Monastery, April 1564

A week later the same ear Maria touched with affection is painfully puffy with the cuffing Brother Bernardus gives Jonas that afternoon for his attempt at depicting the torture of the Savior. Jonas stares at Willem Booten who fixes his gaze on the plate of food he has barely touched. Booten and Jonas' eyes meet. The older boy's face turns into a sneer.

The next morning, as the boys file out of the chapel following morning prayers, Willem Booten grasps the hoe leaning against the chapel wall where he and the other orphans rest their tools. Only this morning, Willem swings the hoe over his shoulder, clips Jonas on his forehead, and sends him sprawling. Jonas scampers up and wrests the hoe from Willem's grasp. He flings the hoe into a patch of nettles and squares himself to fight the crimson-faced Booten. Willem advances on Jonas who crouches to spring. The other boys raise an excited ruckus and jostle each other to ring them for the expected fistfight.

But Brother Thomas strides through the knot of boys and holds the two apart before a fist is thrown. "I saw it all," Brother Thomas admonishes Willem. "You will never, never again use a farm tool to strike another boy here. Is that understood?" Willem glowers at Jonas. Brother Thomas shakes Willem until the boy nods to signify that he has understood. "Pick up your hoe. Brother Aristide, take charge of this boy and make sure he uses his tool properly." He addresses Willem again. "At the end of your workday you see me and we will discuss what Saint Benedict meant when he put *pax* first, the prime precept. We will see how you put peace first while you are under the protection of this abbey. As you work today, think about how to reach for an olive branch rather than a weapon."

When Brother Aristede and his crew leave for the fields, Brother Thomas checks the blow to Jonas' head. Wordlessly, he guides Jonas toward the cookhouse, pushes the door open and seizes a wide cleaver. Terrified, Jonas shrinks back. "This will stop the swelling, silly lad," the monk says, applying the cold flat of the blade against the knot that has begun to enlarge on Jonas' forehead. Maria dips a soft cloth into a bucket of water, wrings it out and presses the cooling cloth against the swollen knot. "Farm tool accident," Brother Thomas says to Maria. "One of the boys stepped on a hoe and smacked Jonas on his forehead."

Maria shoots a suspicious look at the monk.

"Something like that," Brother Thomas says, smiling. "He'll survive. We all will survive."

Brother Thomas leaves and Maria ministers to Jonas.

"Willem?"

Jonas tightens his jaw.

"That boy is a misery. Not to excuse him. But he is suddenly making everyone here dumb. Speak to me. What happened?"

"Accident," Jonas says, "As Brother Thomas said."

Maria smiles, not fooled for a moment. "You boys need to be more careful."

She turns the cloth over and applies the cool surface to his head. She smiles irrepressibly, and Jonas feels the warmth of his surrogate mother again.

Jonas detects little of the peace Willem Booten is expected to cultivate at Brother Thomas' command. For the rest of Jonas' time at the monastery, he is on guard against Booten's surliness.

He knows to never antagonize Brother Bernardus again and stifles his urges to modify any design that the old monk has authored. Meanwhile, he improves his drawing skills and discovers how to work with color to illuminate the manuscripts. He loses himself in the multiple crafts he practices to become an artist under the strictures of his old school instructor. Soon, he is entrusted to take charge of finishing several manuscripts in progress. Jonas notices, as time wears on, old Bernardus winces, holding his chest. He becomes more palsied than ever.

Months later, Brother Bernardus utters his last strangulated plosive when a massive heart attack takes his life. Brother Uwe looks toward Jonas, now fourteen and asks if he thinks he is ready to be the primary finishing artist for the copyists. Brother Uwe and Brother Thomas meet with the abbot of the monastery. Jonas learns that he will temporarily hold the post of illuminator. After six months, Jonas has a completely free hand in sketching and executing initial capitals for the work of the scriptorium. Elements of agony or joy begin to make their way into the features of the martyred saints. Without Bernardus to restrain him, Jonas explores how to translate emotion to the flat dimension of the page. He also taps into a well of rebelliousness. While thinking of his family in unmarked graves somewhere in the vicinity, and lamenting no record anywhere of their existence except in his memory, Jonas hides a "J" in the shrubbery of a garden scene that depicts Mary mourning for her son. Then he scatters the rest of the letters in his name, "O-N-A-S," disguised as foliage. As his work in the scriptorium proceeds, he adds his last name. His acts of insurrection go unnoticed by Brother Uwe, and soon, nearly every illustration Jonas draws has a secret life, an identity with letters of his name, his parents' and sister's names, secreted within his illuminated initial capital letters.

CHAPTER 7

Palo Alto, Late Afternoon, April 11th 2016

Patricia arrives in a flurry of kicked off shoes, briefcase tossed onto the sofa, and quicksteps to the bathroom, accompanied by "Gotta pee!"

Owen lights the gas barbecue on the rear deck, paints the meat-falling-off-the-bone rack of ribs with barbeque sauce, and sets a timer.

"Well I had a crappy day," Patricia says. She has changed from her school uniform of the day, gray wool suit, and white blouse with ruffled collar to loose-fitting jeans and a burgundy sweatshirt.

He brushes her brown bangs to one side and looks too closely at her eyes, surrounded by dark hollows.

"What? Why are you looking at me like that?" Patricia asks sharply.

"Whoa, didn't mean anything." He opts not to reply that her nights have been restive, awakening him with jerks and whimpers.

She softens. "Didn't mean to jump down your throat." Owen hopes she'll say more. She doesn't. He stifles his impulse to ask *what's going on, Patricia?*

As if on cue, the timer goes off and Owen brings in the sweet smelling rack of ribs and pours glasses of Pinot Noir. Over dinner they share their day.

Patricia's tone is indignant. "Esperanza? Who I told you about? Kid's parents deported? The brilliant Dr. Marge Bloom says"—she affects a mocking tone—"'don't spend too much time fretting about her, Patricia, dear. Lost cause. If she weeps in class, she's not learning. Give your attention to kids from more stable homes.'"

"Cold. Principal Bloom," Owen agrees.

"I could wring her neck."

Owen taps her wine glass. "I'll drive the getaway car."

He tells her how a possible commission in a Gutenberg print went south. Then he relates Bregmann's call, his need to go up to The City the next day to deliver some prints, and have a look at an Ortelius map.

She tells how, on a short essay, three kids spelled Junipero Serra's last name as S-A-R-A-H.

"I think you'd have to search pretty deep to find his feminine side," he quips.

"On Friday we have a field trip to Mission Dolores," Patricia reminds him. She chuckles ruefully. "When I was a kid in L.A., the Missions unit was taught so romanticized, like the Indians could barely wait to be colonized."

"I slept through California history in grade school," Owen says.

"You knew better."

"No, I just knew my future was going to be as a chef who made great ribs." She raises her brows in mild appreciation. Encouraged, Owen says, "Seriously, I wish I had you for a teacher back then. You'd have been in all my adolescent fantasies."

Patricia scowls. Only recently has she regarded his puerile humor as completely lame. *Not even a friendly eye roll.* They wash and dry dishes in silence. As they retire for the night, Owen picks up the auction catalog. "Oh, this is it," he says, passing it across the bed, open to the page with the map. Patricia recoils. Then she takes a closer look. Queasiness and a glint of terror shade her face.

"You okay?" Owen reaches to steady her.

"Ooof. Too much wine maybe."

She's only had one glass.

He sets the catalog on his nightstand. Patricia is already reaching for her novel. He is about to ask again, "You okay?" but intuits her annoyance, now a fixture in their relationship. Owen steps into the bathroom.

Patricia feels relief to be alone. Owen's presence is smothering. Her breathing quickens as she listens to the sounds of her husband preparing for bed, the clink of the electric toothbrush tapping the tile-top sink. She finds herself hating that, years earlier she agreed to move to Northern California, five hours from her mother's home in Santa Barbara. She becomes unexpectedly furious, silently blames Owen, who had assured her that the San Francisco Bay market in prints and graphics would prove fortuitous. Patricia's brow creases remembering her mother's unfiltered look of betrayal, when she informed her of their decision.

"You cannot. You must not go so far," her mother had beseeched.

Patricia's breathing stops, a panicked feeling familiar as a child when her mother clung too closely if either was afraid. In a sweat-inducing fear, she closes her eyes, clutches at the down comforter. She hears with dread her mother's feeble voice describing sounds through a wall. She opens her eyes, but imagines she is still in the pitch dark as the bathroom-sink tap turns on. *Dear, God, let me get a peaceful night's rest.* She removes the bookmark, breathes deeply, and tries to bore into the print on the page, hoping the young adult novel will exhaust her to sleep.

CHAPTER 8

Benedictine Monastery, October 1568

Jonas is awakened by the distressed coughing of a brother orphan. Hoarse attempts to dislodge phlegm from bronchial tissue are localized at first to three beds away. But the next night Jonas hears a cacophony of boys' fighting for their breaths as the night wears on. A monk comes into the dormitory holding a candle to determine if this is mischief by the spirited boys. Later, Maria de Vries is summoned to learn if she knows how to contain the outbreak of catarrh. Her solution is for each of the boys to wear a bag of crushed garlic around his neck. Now the hacking and coughing dormitory becomes malodorous.

In his fifteenth year, with his increasing regard by the Brothers, Jonas is afforded more favors in the library. He does not need permission from the precentor to examine the volumes that line the walls. Brother Uwe merely nods when Jonas pulls out the first of seven books copied from the manuscript written and illustrated by Hildegard of Bingham. From the precentor, he learns that Hildegard was a Benedictine nun, the abbess of a Twelfth Century convent, gifted in practical, scientific, and medical matters. The volume he has selected is written not in Latin, but the vernacular— Low German, similar to Dutch, a treatise on curing diseases with common herbs and flowers. Jonas reads about poultices that can be laid on the chests of sufferers of catarrh. He asks Brother Uwe to allow Maria de Vries to examine the texts.

The stern librarian sputters, "No—these are precious and must not be removed from the library for the cook"—he sneers—"the cook! A charwoman—to run her greasy fingers over."

In a dark frame of mind, Jonas makes his case to Brother Thomas. "The boys are suffering and it is not right that remedies should be kept from Maria." Brother Thomas consults the abbot and permission is granted for Maria. The illustrations of the plants with healing properties guide Maria de Vries to direct the collection of lobelia, oregano, peppermint, hemp, mullein, and sage. Jonas copies the desired plants after the illustrated versions in Hildegard's *Causae et Curae*. The healthy boys and several Brothers are pressed to find the wild-growing herbs using his drawings; the cookhouse becomes a minor manufactory of teas and pastes. Within a week, the outbreak subsides, and Maria gets access to all of the volumes authored by Hildegard of Bingham to help keep the orphans healthy.

This chilly November morning, Jonas is in the chapel with the other boys prior to dispersing for their assigned jobs. The eldest monk leads prayers in Latin:

"Gracious and Holy Father, Please give me: Intellect to understand You."

Jonas steals a glance about the chapel. The other boys are reciting dully, most not yet understanding what they are saying. Marius, only eight years old, fidgets, picks his nose, and mumbles the church Latin. As old Brother Theo intones the verses, Jonas translates them to Dutch to wrestle with the meaning.

"Reason to discern You."

What does that mean? He resolves to ask Brother Thomas who has taken the role of his mentor. The monk with the coppery fringe will try to explain what *discern* means in this context. But, as usual, Jonas will only hear: "You must believe, and then you will understand." If Jonas pursues, the Brother struggles, clenching his eyes to find a pathway to Jonas' getting a glimmer of the faith that sustains the monk.

"Diligence to seek You."

"Persevere. Persevere," Brother Thomas repeats. "You must labor diligently in seeking Him." Jonas sees Pietrus, two years his senior, eyes rolled back in his head, mindlessly intoning the phrase. Jonas can think of nothing diligent about Pietrus.

"Wisdom to find You."

Does that mean that only smart people could know God? It is unjust to Jonas, and so another sinkhole opens up in the catechism. A year before,

Jonas began despairing that he would ever find God. *Did I lose my ability to become wise and know God, too?*

"A spirit to know You."

Jonas shakes his head, bewildered, for "spirit" implies the Holy Ghost, a concept none of the Brothers have clarified to his understanding. He hears Jan, full-voiced, repeating the phrase, his eyes seeming to glisten. *Jan has the spirit to know God.* He is a newcomer, pockmarked and scarred, orphaned by the murder of his parents because they would not recant their conversion to the Reformed Church. Meanwhile, Marius has stopped moving his mouth and is in the middle of a long yawn. *No spirit there.* Pietrus peers dully before him, half asleep. In that moment, Jonas imagines himself drawing mouths, agape, yawning, and a tongue hanging from the side of two lips, as from an exhausted dog. *Spirit.* Jonas thinks. If spirit is imagination, an unseen guide, his spirit is to make pictures. A calm comes over him.

"A heart to meditate upon You."

Prayer, again. Jonas' mouth twitches in a rueful smile. He meditates on how a distance could be shown on paper by making an object smaller in the background, or larger in the foreground. He meditates on how foreshortening could show a being in motion. He accompanies such meditation with images he draws in his mind of hands and elbows, legs and feet in various angles to give the illusion of dimensionality. His breathing quickens with a pencil or quill in his hand. He owns this morning in chapel that this is the god he worships.

"Ears to hear You, Eyes to see You, A tongue to proclaim You."

Jonas hears his art in the countryside while his orphaned brothers till the soil on the monastery grounds, the birds chirping their songs of joy and terror, the dogs barking their stories. He hears the rote recitations in the chapel led by the Benedictine Brothers, in their black robes, speaking their fervent prayers. *I could never proselytize what I do not understand.*

"A way of life pleasing to You."

The monastic life, of course. If his impure thoughts are any indication, his way of life is far from pleasing to God. In his imagination he couples with the daughter of Maria de Vries, every night. His damp awakenings confirm that Jonas is more pleasing to himself.

"Patience to wait for You and perseverance to look for You."

Another sinkhole of contradiction. Patience to wait and a drive to search. Did not these qualities negate the other? By this verse in the Morning Prayer, he despairs. And lately he does not even mouth the words in Latin.

And then the coda:

"Grant me a perfect end, Your holy presence, a blessed resurrection and life everlasting."

Would he really want a life on a cloud under the watchful gaze of the heavenly father? Forever?

Amen

They file out of the chapel to their appointed jobs. As he walks to the library to continue illuminating the *Concordia Regularis*, a treatise by Saint Ethelwold on unifying practices of Benedictine monasteries, he sees Maria de Vries in the courtyard leaning over a wooden barrel of soapy water. In daylight she is the Dutch-capped, efficient, cheerful mother to the brothers and orphans, patching bruises and scrapes, warding off sickness with herbs and well-prepared food, and sewing tattered garments and gashes to the skin. By night, she is the mother of the siren who calls Jonas to be in touch with his base instincts. Under the Rule of Saint Benedict Jonas is expected to expunge carnal thoughts. Jonas struggles until he recalls sheep and lambs, favored images for a priest's flock. These woolly symbols of obedience and sweet chastity run into the grinding stone of Jonas' experience. As a farm boy, he watched fascinated by young rams mounting ewes in rut.

Maria de Vries waves at Jonas. He waves back. He has not a shred of remorse for his imagined liaisons with the sunny woman's daughter.

CHAPTER 9

Monastery, Outskirts of Antwerp, Late Autumn 1569

When Jonas is nearly sixteen, Brother Thomas draws him aside just before the midday meal and tells him that it has been arranged that he will go to work for the Boekprintere Scheldt. Jonas blinks in surprise and confusion.

"Master de Diest," Brother Thomas informs him, "has a commission from the cartographer, Abraham Ortels, for a large project. He is in need of apprentices."

A kernel of fear tightens his chest. "But—but this is not fair!"

"Jonas," the Brother says with emphasis and smiles, "this is the Boekprintere Scheldt, selected by Master Ortels, even over Master Plantin's printworks, to produce the first book of maps of the world. Where this can lead you, learning to be an engraver of cartography, is boundless!"

The pain Jonas feels is like being punched in the heart. He doesn't understand his visceral ache, as if leaving the monastery will result in him lost and adrift in the roiling flood. He has grown more and more accepting that his life will continue as a worker in the abbey. While he can only feign an interest in the rituals of the Church, he feels an allegiance to these men who rescued him. He feels safe when he loses himself in the ornamented initial capitals he designs and executes. "I will make you proud only if I can stay here."

Brother Thomas is blunt. "Obedience is a touchstone of our belief. Your defiant tone—" He breaks off his reprimand and takes another tack. "You must show your thanks for your time here by contributing in the secular world."

"But why do you send me away?" Jonas asks, raising his voice. Maria de Vries, across the dining hall, looks up from her serving tureen. She shakes her head to see Jonas in such distress. "Is my work not satisfactory?"

Brother Thomas smiles, nods. "Far better. But you are a young man now and we know that the monastic life is not your calling."

"But, Brother Thomas...."

The monk who had pulled him, barely conscious, from the beech tree speaks in somber tones: "'*Ora et labora,*' Saint Benedictus said in his *Rules*—prayer *and* work. You do not pray, Jonas, with the fervor with which you work. You have talents you must develop outside these walls. It would be sinful not to take the chance to work in the de Diest printing house."

Jonas clamps his mouth to contain the fury that burns in his breast. His anger scares him. He does not know why he has such a terror of making his way outside the monastery. But a grave sense of injustice gnaws within. He leaves the monks at their table, unable to meet their gaze. He feels especially betrayed by Brother Thomas, and stalks stiffly toward the doors of the dining hall. He glimpses silent Willem smirking from his seat at the long table. Jonas slows in front of the boy orphaned by the unpaid mercenary and imagines smashing his mocking face. The old abbot had threatened Willem Booten with expulsion for striking Jonas with the hoe handle, but the threat was empty, and Jonas continues to harbor vengeance. Try as he might to turn the other cheek, his raw fury almost makes him punch Willem Booten. Instead, he breaks off eye contact with Willem and returns to the scriptorium where he tries to quiet his mind by illustrating Jesus' Sermon on the Mount. *Brother Thomas is right. I do not belong here. I find no joy in prayer.* He dulls the quill nib by pressing too hard on the vellum sheet. In frustration, he blots the inked error and rubs the surface down to the translucent lambskin. He leaves his worktable and steps outside the library just as Willem violently pushes Marius out of his path.

Jonas intercepts Willem, pushes the bigger boy around the corner of the dining hall. He lands the first blow to Booten's face. A grunt of pain issues from the stricken boy, and Jonas flails his fists, quickly becoming exhausted. Booten, however, is muscular from his farm duties and in no time pummels Jonas to the ground. Only the shouts of the other orphans bring several Brothers into the fray to separate the boys. Jonas' nose drips blood. His right eye is swollen nearly closed. He is numb with pain but even more with grief that a safe haven is about to be pulled from underfoot. He needs to justify his own expulsion from the Benedictine orphanage. *Is that why I picked a fight with Willem?* Unaccountably, he begins to weep, and, like a thunderstorm, tears erupt more violently than ever before. He cannot find words to say why, but he cries unstoppably. Stinging tears spill from both his swollen eye and his good one. It is as if all the heartache of his short life has burst like a faulty dike. He is shocked to see Maria de Vries smiling kindly at him in his pain. He recalls the agony he drew on the Savior's face in the belief that anyone so mistreated would be beside himself, not wear a beatific mien. Jonas clamps his eyes shut and wonders why he has allowed himself to be engulfed in such pain. He has grasped a false belief with a clenched mind that the abbey is the completion to his life. In a flash of clarity, he recognizes his narrow perspective. *Desperate for a safe port in a storm—but it is not storming any more.* He sees what Brother Thomas knows—for his own good he must leave the nest. He recalls a Latin text that embedded in his mind. When a fledgling eaglet refuses to leave the nest, the parents dismantle the nest, every twig, until the young bird simply must take wing.

He feels embarrassed and quickly releases the false feeling that he will be annihilated if he leaves the safe port. Jonas' sobs subside. Brother Thomas, too, is smiling at him. Through the welt over his eye, he peers at the monk who had so encouraged him. He bows his head. "I beg forgiveness, Brother Thomas," Jonas says through blood-encrusted lips. "I—You…"

"You are pardoned. You have suffered punishment enough from Willem."

"I mean for not understanding," Jonas haltingly begins. "What you want for me—to draw what people will want to see. I will go with gratitude for your guidance, and try to bring respect to the monastery for having me here these years." Inwardly, Jonas wonders, *Will I be judged favorably by the printing house master, de Diest; by the master cartographer, Ortels?* As Brother Thomas nods in appreciation of his apology, Jonas feels a dull ache in his chest. *Could I have a future in the craft of illustration that I have come to assume in the scriptorium?* The dead Brother Bernardus' scowl appears in Jonas' imagination, nodding *"No."*

"Let us see to that eye," Maria de Vries urges. She puts an arm around his shoulders and takes him to the cookhouse. "You are a very brave young man." She stops him from shaking his head by holding his face between her palms. "Yes, you are, because you have a heart that is bigger than all the scripture, all those books in the library. You must know by now that bravery is *not* "not being scared"—but pressing on despite your fears. When you challenged Brother Uwe to grant me privileges to read the Abbess Hildegard's healing books, you were very brave. Many of the boys owe you a debt of thanks for pushing through your fears."

Jonas takes in her words. He recognizes that it is not his nature to accept praise. Deep in her eyes is a love that would not lie to him. "You are fearful about leaving the monastery for the unknown. But you are a brave young man, and your heart will always be true to you if you are true to it."

Maria begins to daub a lemon balm paste over his injured eye. "Look at how you have earned the respect of the Brothers here."

He frowns.

"Stop that," she snaps. "You know it is true. It is only natural to doubt, but give yourself a space, a short gap before you doubt yourself. Antwerp is a whole new world. Push through your fears; remain true to your heart. It will see you through."

Jonas slips into his habit of shaking his head.

"*That* is a lie of the mind," Maria says, punctuating her point by dotting his nose with a dab of the lemon balm.

CHAPTER 10

Palo Alto, 10:00 p.m., April 11ᵗʰ 2016

Patricia looks up from her novel when Owen emerges from the bathroom, smelling of peppermint toothpaste. Lately she barely notices him, but tonight she dabs her finger with her tongue and rubs the speck of white on Owen's chin. He smiles and kisses her lightly on the lips. He rolls to his side and turns off his light.

A few minutes later Patricia bookmarks her page and snuggles momentarily. He turns and kisses her lips, more forcefully this time; she draws back. She breathes a sigh and squeezes his fingers.

Sometime later, a buzzing horsefly circles in the room followed by another. Patricia had seen a group of these flies on Sunday moving leadenly about the windowpanes in the back bedroom. She had intended to open a window and shoo them out, but forgot while she corrected her fourth grade Friday quizzes.

Patricia wakens to a threshold consciousness. She hears Owen grunt, then turns away from the sound, and falls back asleep. The swirl above their heads changes from the beating of wings to stories that play in their unconscious.

The first time Owen falls asleep he is fixated on the catalog photograph of the copper plate map. He has seen and sold several specimens from the Ortelius atlases over the years. He has always been entranced by the practice of cartography engravers to decorate their oceans with seagoing leviathans. As the two flies buzz below his threshold of hearing, Owen falls into an unnerving sense of being dragged through a water funnel into the ocean depths by a sea beast. While Owen thrashes through his nightmare, Patricia slips into a dream of a ten year-old girl with wide eyes named Esperanza.

Patricia's mind speeds past Esperanza to the long-hidden story that her own mother told only on the evening she died nearly a half-year earlier. In her dream, Patricia sees vivid images of the frigid February streets leading to the Stationsplein, pandemonium of uprooted families clutching luggage, cries and shouts by the Dutch and German human machinery. Patricia, rigid, steps into her mother's body at age nine, exhausted from the long walk, cringing at the barked orders, hand grasped by her tight-lipped father. Without warning, a surging crowd of deportees is forced into their family at a run by club-wielding Dutch Nazis. Hetty's hand is wrenched from her father's. "Papa, Papa," the girl cries.

"That is the last time I see him or my mother," the 75-year-old woman, shrunken by cancer, tells Patricia as she leans in over the rented hospital bed. "I am lost, forced off to a side alley. It saves my life, I think." Patricia fitfully relives her mother's harrowing escape as the early hours wear on.

Another memory wells up in Patricia's unconscious. This one, a more frequent nightmare over the years, triggered by her mother's erratic behavior. She recalls an argument between her mother and her father, a soft-spoken accountant who encouraged Patricia to explore life boldly, unlike her mother who offered only tight, restrictive warnings. Patricia, in her fourteenth year stops in the foyer in their Fairfax district home as her father uncharacteristically shouts to quiet his hysterical wife. "Hetty, for God's sake, calm down," he implores.

"I don't want to move, is that so crazy?" Patricia's mother wails. "I could jump into the La Brea tar pits, you make me so scared."

"Dearest, it's less than a hundred miles," her father tries to placate. "We could come here from Santa Barbara in two hours. Maybe less. This is a promotion, Hetty. I would run the Santa Barbara office. Not so much traffic. Not so much smog. Right near the beach, too. A healthy place for Patty, for you, and me."

"You promised," her mother's voice had never sounded so bitter to Patricia. "You said this was my safe place. Here I know where to shop, I have my routines. I have my lifelines. A doctor, a drugstore that keeps my head on an even keel."

"Sweetie—"

"No, no more moves—"

"You're overwrought—you need to calm down."

"Calm? I'll show you calm—" Her mother's voice chills Patricia—and then the crash of a heavy glass object shattering—Patricia rushes into the living room. Her father is kneeling, bewildered and holding his foot. Chunks of the large amber glass ashtray that sat on the coffee table litter the parquet floor.

"Get out," her mother shouts at Patricia. Go to your room. Can't you see he's hurt? Get your things we must move. Be quick about it!" Patricia runs to her bedroom but hears her father's plaintive voice. "Hetty, why are you scaring her so?"

Patricia awakens in a sweat, realizes she is in her bed in the Palo Alto cottage and tries to return to sleep. But tumultuous thoughts make her attempts fitful at best. At four a.m., Patricia's dream begins anew. She is an eight-year-old holding her mother's hand, crossing a street when a unit of Los Angeles motorcycle police is first heard, then seen riding in formation down La Cienega Boulevard. Her mother's grip becomes a chokehold around Patricia's fingers.

"Not so hard," Patricia complains.

"Sh! Quiet! No talking. No complaining!" Her mother responds brusquely.

"But you're breaking my fingers!"

"I survived to hear this?" Mrs. Baron complains bitterly. Patricia has no idea of what her mother is talking about.

The motorcycles roar, abreast of them now. Patricia feels her mother pull them both closer and closer to the side of a building. They are well away from the roadway, but the urgency in her mother's grasp tingles in Patricia's left hand to a point of pain forty years later in her uneasy sleep.

The dream jumps in time to her mother's last moments, five months ago, the hospital bed set up in the front room of her cottage.

"She is slipping in and out, Mrs. Spencer," the hospice nurse says.

"The horse knew. The dog knew." Barely discernible, the old woman repeats the words.

"What does that mean, Mama?" Patricia implores.

Hetty, her frail arm attached to the morphine drip, fights to stay awake. She needs to tell Patricia something. Her daughter feels her mother's withered hand squeezing with all her reserves and speaking through her dying gasps.

"I caused my family' to be caught, to be rounded up, to die. When they come for us in Haarlem, the Black Police, they say 'Where is your papa? Where is your Jood star!' I show them my star sewn to my jumper hidden under my jacket."

"'I would be ashamed, too,'" the policeman says.

"All dead—mother, father, my two little brothers, Albert—Isaac, only three, who would be your uncles today, because I told them."

"Who?" Patricia prompts softly. Her mother had always squelched Patricia's curiosity with a single sentence, snapped with annoyance. "No one needs to know you have Jewish blood!"

"Who?" Patricia asks, as her mother's hand eases. It tightens as she speaks.

"The Black Police and the Germans on their motorcycles riding up and down in Haarlem. I told them where we live. And then, and then...." Patricia holds the glass of water near her mother's mouth as she sips on the glass tube.

"And near the Stationsplein, in Amsterdam, when I let go of Papa's hand, I cannot get back to him. If I can, they would maybe live. Instead, they are pushed into the railroad cars with the others. I hide behind the dustbins in the alley and the Dutch resisters find me. Gerdi hides me and cuts off the Jood star and says, 'never tell anyone,' and she puts me in a wagon and we go to Eindhoven."

Hetty's voice trails off weakly and Patricia must lean in to hear.

"The housekeeper. Mrs. Berghuis—she says if I stay, they will kill Mr. Dijkstra. And they do. I have his blood on my hands. Sticky blood. I hide like he says but they shoot him because they are looking for me. I am only alive because he is killed. Patricia. Never tell them you are Jewish. Never."

"I won't, *I won't*," Patricia cries, desperate to make sure her mother hears.

Owen is awakened by Patricia's cry. "I won't Mama, I won't tell anyone. Don't go. Please, don't die. Don't—"

"Shhhh," Owen whispers. "You're dreaming, sweetheart, no one is dying."

Patricia's eyes open wide. "Oh, my—my gown is soaking." She stumbles to the bathroom. Owen hears the tap turn on and then a towel pulled off the rack. In the darkness he hears Patricia open a bureau drawer and muffled sounds of her putting on a fresh nightgown.

She falls back into bed and whispers. "Her story on her deathbed—I can't stand these nights. I relive her terror, her crazy guilt." Owen puts a helpless hand on her forehead. "And I have a full load tomorrow," she says, frustrated and pushes Owen's hand from her.

He hears something like white noise in his ears, dares not inquire about her dream further. Awake in the darkness, he considers suggesting therapy, but better not to say anything like that now. Then, in his mind Owen catches a glimpse—the tiniest moment—of a snapshot when he was four or five, unearthed when he was going through a collection of early photographs shot mostly by his father. But the moment of remembrance is like a shock of seeing himself in a mirror under strobe light. Little Owen clutches a rubber horseshoe from a children's tossing game an aunt had given him for his birthday. *Clutches* is the operable word, for in this photo his four-year-old self presses—welds—the horseshoe into his side, as though to say, "you can't take this from me." His free hand is balled in a fist and his face— baleful, wretched, distressed, is a tightly worn mask to hold back his tears, eyes glaring at the photographer, his father. The little boy is a picture of helpless defiance. He stands no chance of being disobedient, and he hates that he has no power to be his own person. He is a mute objector to a heinous wronging of him. Patricia's rejection of his attempted consolation stirs this memory.

Soon it becomes chatter in his head and he drifts off, thinking about Pieter Bruegel the Elder. Within minutes, he is caught up in 16th Century Flanders.

In the half-light, only provided by LED numbers on her bedside clock, Patricia stares at the ceiling unable to escape the fraught night of her mother's dying.

CHAPTER 11

Antwerp, December 1569

Brother Thomas drives Jonas along the Mechelen-Antwerp road in a donkey-drawn cart. They are uncomfortably aware of the Spanish pike men, soldiers with swords and arquebus muskets, from the moment they enter the north gate and roll through the heart of the old city; Dutch and Walloon citizens avert their gazes, never meeting the eyes of the occupying forces. The Spanish crown, through dynastic marriages took the mantle of "protector" of the Holy Roman Empire against Protestant incursions in the once universally Roman Catholic walled cities of the German Lowlands. Much of the century was bloodied in the religious wars between the traditional Christians and the Protestant Reformation, which focused on biblical teaching, to replace the pope's Christianity as corrupt and self-serving. As religion and politics clash, Antwerp in 1569 is a Spanish military stronghold, with a large fortress, The Citadel, under construction to assure future control by the popes and cardinals of the Apostolic Palace in Rome.

When Jonas comes under the glare of a Spanish soldier, he quickly looks toward the Port of Antwerp's cityscape. It is compelling to the monastery boy as a commercial hub on the Scheldt River with its wharves, warehouses, bourses, guildhalls, tapestry workshops, fine arts studios, goldsmiths, print shops, and engraving houses.

The moment has arrived. Jonas stands before the arched doors of the Boekprintere Scheldt. Brother Thomas pushes gently on his back and Jonas enters a new world. Unlike the ordered monastery that had been his home for five years, the brick, stone, and wooden three-story house is chaotic, a dizzying warren of rooms devoted to printing and papermaking, bristling with noise. The odor of oily ink fills his nostrils, pungent and seductive.

"Wait here," a printer's assistant says, leaving the monk and Jonas to witness the spectacle as he hastens up the stairs and disappears on the second floor. Jonas watches gape-mouthed at the frenzy. The din pounds his ears— shouts, clacking friskets, creaking timbers as platens press ink to paper. He turns to Brother Thomas who smiles through his own unease in the noisy surroundings. Guild masters, journeymen, and apprentices crisscross the hall. A powerful man turns the massive wheel with both arms and a leg to operate the press. Printer's devils hang newly peeled sheets over drying racks. In one wing, typesetters draw letters from type cases and press Latin text into composing sticks. His eyes snap to an alcove where maps inked by copper plates hang from wooden pins. *Will I be drawing those?*

A towheaded apprentice and an obese, blotch-faced boy, not much older than he, eye him as if he is mortal prey.

Brother Thomas leans over to speak in Jonas' ear. "Noisy, eh?"

A man in his seventies with gray hair flying beneath his flat cap and an untrimmed beard, descends the stairs quickly and says to Brother Thomas, "Yes?"

"Master de Diest, I have brought the boy you said you needed."

"Ah?" de Diest asks, distracted by something he sees in the type-composing wing. "Oh. Oh, yes. He is approved by the Guild." He barely looks at Jonas, but calls to a printer's devil, an apprentice who has just completed a task at the large printing press in the center of the room. "You, what's your name?" he calls to the freed-up boy. "Jan Grens, Master de Diest."

"Show this boy to the empty dormer in the boys wing. Then bring him back down to Master Hogenberg...ach! Hogenberg is gone for the day. Bring him to Master Du Brul and then get back to work. Quickly, quickly, and return to your inking duties."

Jan Grens taps the newcomer's shoulder. Jonas turns back to say goodbye to Brother Thomas, but de Diest has already ushered the monk toward the door. Jonas follows the boy up the stairs to the third floor. The door to his room is pushed open and he leaves his cloth bag containing his change of clothes. He follows the rushing apprentice downstairs. Instead of returning to the large printing hall, Grens nudges Jonas down the hallway toward the back of the building and then into a hall with different odors, caustic soda, whiffs of soiled linen. "Master Du Brul, Master de Diest says the new boy should start here with you in paper-making."

Put to work immediately, Jonas has plenty of work and little time for contemplation, let alone prayer, which had marked his stay with the Benedictines. But his first work has nothing to do with illustration. He is thrust unexpectedly into helping to make rag paper. He is baffled as to why he was sent here. How will he learn what he needs to, here? The master papermaker, the red-faced Pieter Du Brul, oversees several girl apprentices who sort and help pulp the rag and linen into its fibers. Jonas spends his day pounding linen and woolen scraps with an apparatus of beating wooden mallets. When broken down to its fibers, the pulp is added to water-laden vats and stirred into a white soup. Finally, the master papermaker skims off the residue into the mesh-bottomed frames called *deckles* for drying.

The giggling girls are a wholly new experience to Jonas, and he steals glances at one, with black ringlets peeking from her cap, who Master Du Brul calls "Sofie." She smells of soap as she whisks by, and barely acknowledges him. He feels awkward around her. Still, her giggle when she is light-hearted with the other girls captures him, and he finds himself in a daydream in which the two of them converse. But he is tongue-tied and fights to maintain attention on his mind-numbing job of pounding linen fiber into pulp.

By the time his first day ends, he is exhausted. His old shoulder injury aches.

Night. Finally quiet. Still, his ears buzz with the beating of linen rags in the papermaking hall. Beneath the wool cover in his room atop the printworks, his body aches for sleep, but his mind jitters with the face of the girl with the black ringlets who darts in and out. He shuts out voices of the unwelcome dream that threatens to infiltrate his slumber. He opens his eyes wide to stay awake. The wintry moon sprays pale light through the small window.

CHAPTER 12

Santa Barbara, November 2015

The rented hospital bed overwhelms the living room of Hetty Baron's modest home. Patricia and Owen have arrived for the death vigil, Owen in an armchair in the corner of the room, Patricia in a straight-backed chair leaning in to her emaciated mother. The dying woman drifts in and out of wakefulness. A morphine drip trickles through plastic tubing. Her multiple stage cancers have won the battle weeks earlier, but her body hangs on following chemo and radiation therapy. Shrunken to barely 70 pounds,

Hetty passes water and blood into the bag strapped to the bed. The hospice nurse checks her vitals hourly.

Patricia's voice implores softly, "You can let go now, Mama. You can let go anytime you want. I love you. Owen and I love you and wish you Godspeed on your journey. You need not hold on any longer."

"You don't know," the old woman rasps in a voice that crackles like dry reeds in a gust of wind. "The horse, knew…. The dog knew." Her cryptic words fall on Patricia's ears and create confusion along with her throat-choking sadness. "You never knew. I made certain…. You never knew, Patricia."

"Knew what, Mama?"

Hetty's eyes are closed. Patricia looks uncertainly at Owen who leans forward in his armchair straining to make out his mother-in-law's gasped words. "Never knew what, Mama," Patricia's voice wavers, torn between wanting to know more and fearful that the effort for her mother to speak is too taxing.

"Never…let…them…know…." Hetty manages to say with finality.

"Mama? Never let them know…what?" Patricia asks. She leans in close because Hetty Baron is speaking in a child's voice.

"Mr. Dijkstra's voice goes loud. 'I have her papers.' Then the voices get softer again. They must be going into the front room, his library. Then he shouts, 'Get out! Find yourselves real work.' Gunshots! One, another, and another—yelling, bad words—then a body bangs on the floor. Footsteps now! Overhead…on the stairs—the cursing policeman finally stops climbing…and the steps…they go back down. I…I wet myself. My underwear is soaking. Will they smell me? My hands shake. I shiver in that darkness. I do not know what is going on. More cursing. The policeman yells, 'Henk. Henk. I will get you to hospital. My knee! He shot my knee, too.' Boots scrape across the floor. The front door slams shut; I hear the car engine finally catches outside. The tires screaming."

Patricia is constricted by her mother's childlike voice, her piping lucidity. She dreads what Hetty is speaking of. The effort parches her mother's throat. Patricia spoons ice chips to Hetty's lips. Owen leaves the armchair and presses Patricia's shoulder. Her mother speaks again, words labored, her adult voice now.

"And then the quiet…after the police car runs down the street. But no one comes for me. I have no idea how long I stay. 'Do not come out until I call you,' he tells me. So I stay. I stand and listen. But my knees—they can't stop shaking. My imagination sees kind Mr. Dijkstra, victorious over the Black Police. Would the housekeeper return and say, 'It was all a dream, you stupid girl?' Why doesn't he call out? Why doesn't he sing out, 'It's all right now for you to come out, Hetty.' How I blamed Mr. Dijkstra a moment before I hid! I feel terrible. But he promised it would be safe. He promised. And I hated how he broke his promise. I made it his fault. It was stupid. Finally, I hear Gerdi's voice! Is that my imagination, too? Then the pretty young lady comes. Gerdi—she saved me near the railroad station in Amsterdam."

Patricia's white-knuckled hand grips Owen's. A picture of her mother's life as a child unfolds for the first time, never talked about before, painstakingly avoided. Patricia realizes that Hetty has surrounded some raid on the Dijkstra house in a gauzy *never did happen* disguise. Her mother is whispering, child-like again.

"'Hetty? Hetty?' Steps on the stairs above my head, on the landing, her voice calls. Frantic. 'Hetty? Are you here?' My words freeze in my throat. No words, a little scream—but loud enough for her to hear. 'Hetty. I'm here.' Gerdi shouts, 'Come out. You can come out, now, please, sweet girl.' But through the wall her voice is shaking. 'Stay in the kitchen, dear, when you come out!' I try to move quickly through even more cobwebs—where do they all come from? When I crawl through the kitchen cupboard into the light, I see the smudges and scrapes on my arms, my grimy dress, and the dirt-rubbed dishtowel I'm still holding. Then, through the doorway to the library—Gerdi on her hands and knees tries to rouse Mr. Dijkstra. Blood on her palms, in her long blonde hair. Gerdi snatches up the pistol from his dead hand, puts it her coat pocket. I see the map of the world dripping with blood. 'I have to change, I—I have…I have soiled myself.' I say. So ashamed."

She stops speaking. Patricia holds a hand to her mother's forehead and looks at Owen, tearfully. She does not know what to make of her mother's words. Is she hemorrhaging? All of Hetty's fluids flow through a catheter. *What has she been through?*

"Gerdi kneels on the floor near his body. 'Gather your things, Hetty.' Gerdi's hands are red trying to stop the blood from the wounds. Flies. I see the flies. I see blood on the book of maps that the man loved. I see the map of the world dripping with blood. And the flies—buzzing around his body; puddles of blood up the stairs and then back down to the front door. Gerdi grabs my hand. Sticky. Sticky, with blood. 'Quickly, quickly,' Gerdi tells me. In my room, she picks up clothes and a hairbrush, frantic. 'My book, my book,' I cry. Once again my world is falling apart."

'Where is it?'

'I don't know!'

"Then the first whine of police cars on the Keizergracht. 'Hetty, we must leave now!' Gerdi pushes me downstairs with my pillowcase filled with clothes and out the back door. My book, 'The Mystery—Angora Cat,' and my horse and dog—in the book! 'Not now, sweetheart.' She drags me through the alley to the side street. 'I will come back and find them, I promise,' she says. But she never… She never…. Then the *waaWAAwaaWAA* sirens of the police. The sirens shoot urgency into Gerdi."

"Soon we race to the corner. Gerdi drags me to a flat three streets away—a young woman—Giselle, she lends a bicycle; miraculously, it still has tires that roll. With me seated behind, and my belongings in a basket across the handlebars, Gerdi pedals bumpy kilometers east to a farmhouse near Nuenen, the village. They tell me the farm is refuge for six other Jewish children and some adults who have gone to ground. I make no friends. I have a face people can see and a secret face, a mask, that I only wear when I pull the blanket over my head at night, like this."

Dying Hetty screws her ravaged face into a grotesque smile. Patricia nearly bursts into tears.

"But in my retreat from the house in Eindhoven, I lost another favorite picture, two children and a butterfly. All I have left from the apartment on Gasthuissingel across from the canal in Haarlem. In the Eindhoven house, I imagine the smiling faces of my brothers, Isaac and Albert. In the farmhouse, I have nothing."

"Ohhh," Patricia keens.

"Then Canadian troops come and liberate. Food is in pitiful supply. But living on a farm, I am nourished by fresh milk and eggs, potatoes, and root cellar stores. I barely remember anything of Eindhoven and Nuenen. A blessing to blot out those two years. Then the Jewish agencies—and I immigrate to America. I meet Jack Baron and we have our daughter."

Patricia hears the vivid details, but she has no context since her mother has never spoken of her survival before, except to say, "Oh, that was ancient history, nothing. I lived on a farm and the war was far away. What did you learn in school today?"

In the days and months that follow Hetty's death, Patricia relives her mother's unexplained nervous episodes as she was growing up. Details of Hetty's dying words inhabit Patricia's dreams: her mother entombed in the dark passage, her benefactor, dead of gunshot wounds, staining the map of the world.

CHAPTER 13

The Boekprintere Scheldt, Antwerp, Late December 1569

On Jonas' fourth day in the pulp-pounding alcove, Gilles Coppens de Diest, discovers him as if he was a misplaced stocking. "You, boy—are you the Hoen boy? From the monastery?"

His ears ring from the beating mallets. But he hears "monastery," and nods.

The master printer pulls him out of the papermaking rooms and apprentices him to Frans Hogenberg, the exacting engraver charged with reducing or enlarging in scale all of the maps to fit into the book. "Ah, finally," he says. "Sit there and I will give you plates to clean up. Burs, burs. Your work will be to remove the burs at first. Use those gravers." The master engraver points at the burins, small, finely knurled files, and scraping tools in a box on his worktable. "Above all, be very careful and see me if you have a question."

Slowly at first, Jonas discovers which tools work best for the finishing work on the incised copper. Two other engravers, the Arsen brothers, also work intermittently in the alcove reserved for copper plate inscribing, and Jonas finds them as self-absorbed as Hogenberg.

Within a few days, Jonas feels the resentment of several of the other apprentices, sons of printing guild craftsmen. The boys, aged eleven to eighteen, regard him through hooded eyes and unfriendly smirks. Jonas delivers a copper plate to the printer to be proofed. He is standing near a press in the main hall when the obese apprentice, named Ritsaert, spittle collected at the sides of his lips, demands: "What's your father's trade?"

"He was a miller."

Another boy, taller and older than Jonas, with wild straw hair, pushes Ritsaert aside. Joop Baldus is the unofficial warden of the apprentices. Three others arrange themselves for a show. Joop squares himself and looks down at him. Jonas folds his fingers into fists.

"Why are you here, when a mill is where you belong?" Joop says with scorn.

"I am where I belong."

"A miller's son. Will you grind a book into bread?" The baiting strikes Jonas with the same intensity as Willem Booten's sneer.

"No, but I can beat a Baldus pate into a jelly." Jonas stares into Joop's deep-set blue eyes and turns on his heel rather than continue to trade barbs.

"You'd better be careful, miller's son," Joop's voice calls behind him.

Jonas hears no more taunts that day, and he warms to his new work. He learns to apply a thin coat of heated beeswax on the copper surface. After several weeks, he is told to trace the outline of a country onto the hardened wax from the thin paper version that Hogenberg has drawn based on maps procured for the project by Abraham Ortels.

"Stop," Hogenberg says, wearily. "Do you really want to learn this craft?"

Jonas drops his shoulders with the master engraver's understated taunt. A moment later, however, he clears his throat and says, "Sir, I do want to learn."

Hogenberg says nothing. But he takes a rectangular mirror on a stand from his worktable and hands it to Jonas, who tries to suppress his confusion. The master engraver takes the drawing of the island of Sardinia and sets the mirror behind his drawing so the entire image is reversed left to right in the mirror. "If you were a bird looking down on the island from due south, what you see in the mirror is how Sardinia would look. Do you understand now what must happen to incise a copper plate?"

Jonas nods and discovers how to work directly on the wax veneer; and later, to modulate the pressure and never cut all the way to the metal surface, lest he impede the master engraver's process. He observes Hogenberg penetrate the wax layer through to the copper with engravers' tools: burins, pressed with the palm, awls, styli, and scrapers, called by their general name, *gravers*. The wax lubricates the cutting edge; the secrets of the art and craft are in the pressure and angle of the cut and the tool selected for the task.

After the master engraver completes several days of incising a map, place names, decorations, and Latin inscriptions, Jonas rids the plate of imperfections before he inks the metal for a proof sheet. He makes certain that all incisions in the copper are filled with ink and clears off the excess with cheesecloth infused with olive oil to polish the face of the plate. The rivulets of black ink in the declivities of the copper plate are transferred to dampened paper under great pressure by the screw press. This machine used for proof sheets, he learns, has been adapted from the presses that have squeezed liquid out of olives and grapes since ancient times. Most of the plates require multiple cleanups and repeated proof processes. Hogenberg silently points out flaws in his work which Jonas takes pains not to repeat.

He sees that the minuscule part he plays has value in Master Ortels' massive project, seventy different maps on fifty-three double folio sheets, all drawn by artists from cartography of other mapmakers and ocean navigators. Stern-faced Master Ortels is ever near, checking the work and spending many hours writing text to accompany the maps.

The boy is intoxicated by his apprenticeship. Jonas learns something new every day. Today, he puts finishing touches on the plate called *Americae Sivi Novi orbis*, the two Americas of the New World. On this map alone, he discovers how the engraver's stipple marks creates the illusion of vast waters surrounding the north and south New World continents. Every mark is the engraver's puncture and the depth of the incised dot must be struck with measured pressure throughout the entire map. *How does one learn that skill?* He looks more closely and sees patterns suggesting depths, currents, conceivably, shadows from overhead clouds. And look! *The decorative ships in the Pacific Ocean are clearly Spanish galleons off the coast of the Americas, befitting the primary explorers of those seas and the lands of Hispania Nova.* And see the four corners of the plate! *The ocean winds, personified by a classical figure's face with cheeks blowing zephyrs through trumpets!* And the hand-drawn place names, all the letters etched in reverse, of course. *Each easily read on a level line, thanks to the steel straightedge Hogenberg uses religiously.*

A month into his apprenticeship, by observation, Jonas has already absorbed a wealth of instruction, with barely a word spoken by Frans Hogenberg.

From his worktable, Jonas steals looks from afar when the black-haired girl with the easily flushed cheeks walks to the pressroom with trenchers of newly made paper. At nightfall, she occupies his thoughts in the tiny room on the third floor that looks out over the Scheldt River, three streets away. He falls asleep to the sound of squawking terns that bolt from the yardarms, and pennants fly from the port's cargo ships at every hour of the day.

The chilly New Year triggers a melancholic mood over the loss of his parents. Unlike his time at the monastery, however, his apprenticeship at de Diest's pulls him out of the depths quickly. As the activity below races toward the completion of the first edition, he is in the flow. The pace accelerates for the typesetters, the printers, and the engravers.

Early February 1570

A disturbing pattern develops, however. The tow-haired bully Joop Baldus runs his gang of sycophants. His favorite, the loutish, immense Ritsaert Mesman, will rudely bump the bench. At Baldus' instigation, other apprentices view Jonas as an interloper who has come through a back door to attain the status of apprentice in the Guild of Saint Luke. After all, only de Diest's *master* ranking in the guild enables him to bring on several apprentices to fill out the workforce for the publication of Abraham Ortels' undertaking.

Because Hogenberg has little interest in maintaining discipline in the alcove reserved for engraving, Jonas is on his own to hold his ground when the slovenly boy jostles his worktable or Joop impugns Jonas' origins.

To stay even-tempered, he thinks of Brother Thomas when his anger rises. "If you don't learn to control your passions, you will never enter the kingdom of heaven," Brother Thomas had warned, followed with a gentler observation: "Jonas. If you try to correct every slight, every wrong, you will never become your own master. Your gall and your spleen will rule you, and that will ruin your spirit."

He struggles to keep his temper in check, but he notices that, at his worktable, especially as a novice gaining experience, he becomes vigilant anytime Joop or one of his minions walks near. This Friday in February, while smoothing rough patches left by the master engraver's burin on a map of Africa, Jonas hears Ritsaert's heavy footfalls behind him. Instinctively, he lifts the burnishing knife he uses to smooth the surface. As expected, Ritsaert shoves his hip against the worktable. If the sharp-pointed tool had been touching, it would have gouged the copper. Enraged, Jonas leaps up and swipes the air to menace the boy. It erases the smirk from Ritsaert's face. Jonas suppresses his fury with the thought of Brother Thomas. When Ritsaert sees Jonas' tamping down his anger, he snarls a challenge accompanied by lip froth. "Hey, miller boy, come and try it. I will flatten you. I will do it just for fun when you are not so armed."

"Wipe your chin and watch where you walk, Pigface," Jonas retorts, softly.

Ritsaert lowers his head, ready to charge, but falters confusedly when Jonas deftly picks up the copper plate, turns his back, and walks with deliberate steps to the master engraver's workbench, where he calls Hogenberg's attention to a bur on the plate and asks, "Did you want this removed too, sir?"

When he turns back to his worktable, he sees Ritsaert's wide frame shuffle from the engravers' alcove into the printing hall. Jonas also sees Sofie watching from the archway. He has noticed that she makes detours on her rounds to the printers' hall and her eyes sparkle with mischief beneath her black ringlets. When she and Jonas lock gazes, her cheeks glow and she walks prissily by Jonas' workbench as the moment of connection fades, leaving Jonas with a much more pleasant memory to recall than the interaction with Ritsaert.

As February wears on, he feels secure enough in his skills that he relaxes during his work to hold her look as she pouts by his workbench. She tilts her head and glides with a self-conscious smile past him. This morning, Sofie walks briskly to the main printing hall, overloaded with quires of paper, and bumps into Jonas carrying a newly pulled proof.

"Careful!" They say, simultaneously. Each laughs; hers, a high-pitched giggle, his, a series of short snorts. Jonas reaches to support her armful of double folio-sheets, carried like a food trencher pressed against her cross-laced kirtle. He does not step out of her way this day, but smiles as her linen partlet rises and falls with each breath. He expects an indignant rebuke. Instead, she smiles and her eyes dance to a melody that they both seem to know. At length, he says. "Can I help you carry?"

"Not this time," she whispers, flushing her shade of rose. "But another, yes."

Jonas steps back, and she sweeps into the printing hall, her green skirt rising to show a calf. He tingles as his blood rises.

CHAPTER 14

Palo Alto, Thursday Morning, April 12th 2016

The front door slams and Patricia's car revs up for her trip to her school in East Palo Alto. Owen tries to clear his head of his troubled relationship. Remembrances of delirious phrases spoken the night Hetty Baron died filter into his thoughts randomly from Patricia's nightmare and vaguely familiar language from that night in Santa Barbara—"map of the world, dripping with blood." He dismisses them as ramblings of the dying woman, shaves and dresses for his drive to The City. If he didn't need to drop off the two Mucha prints, he would consider taking the train, but the framed packages are too fragile to bring aboard during rush hour. He begins to collect the prints when the catalog entry flies through his thinking. "1571" "Dutch text on verso." He checks Lot 256 in the catalog and logs on to his computer, searches and discovers a 1986 issue of *The Map Collector* noting that only 275 books were issued in the first Dutch edition and of that number merely five percent or 14 actual copies were believed to have survived. Centuries of floods, fires, and two World Wars in Holland and Belgium could account for such a low survival rate of these books. Owen adds this data to his mental cache of information about Ortelius cartography.

He loads the Mucha prints. The lithographs have enough wear to make them desirable to a lover of art nouveau prints contemporary to *fin de siècle* Paris where Alphonse Mucha created theater posters. They might easily have graced a Montmartre kiosk.

Owen shifts his thoughts to his unexpected commission to investigate the old map. As he takes the onramp for San Francisco, he reviews what he knows about Ortelius engraved maps, having researched and sold several from the multiple editions of the *Theatrum Orbis Terrarum*. These maps adorn dens, offices, and waiting rooms of his clients who have an affinity for antique cartography. The Antwerp print house, Christophe Plantin's Sign of the Compass, issued many of these editions. What fascinates Owen about the Ortels-Plantin undertaking is that these atlases had been printed during hostilities between Dutch-Flemish insurgents and the Spanish occupation armies in the early stages of the Eighty Years War. Due to its importance as a seaport and commercial center, Antwerp was a flashpoint.

Earlier research of Abraham Ortels, whose expanded name of "Ortelius" reflected the high esteem of his contemporaries, reminds Owen that the man responsible for the first true world atlas walked a thin line with his Spanish overlords. Born into a Catholic family, Ortels never married. He was, for a time, a member of the Family of Love, a sect that disowned Roman Catholic trappings and sought a gentler approach to being one with God than the heresy and terror tactics of the Spaniards under Philip II. Christophe Plantin had joined the Family—by night, a secret publisher of Family of Love literature—by day, the King's printer of Catholic treatises used to counter the Reformation. Ortelius and Plantin each evaded the Spanish Inquisition, prospering through Philip's patronage despite their repugnance of the Spanish boot on the necks of the Lowland burghers and nobility, alike. Philip II had even named Ortelius the king's geographer following publication of the *Theatrum Orbis Terrarum*.

As traffic slows near the airport, Owen recalls that the chief engraver was Frans Hogenberg, who began many of the plates in his Cologne studio, where many of the plates for the maps were begun. Only in the last months of the ten-year project, did Ortels and Hogenberg assemble the plates in Antwerp for final touches and printing.

As he crawls through morning rush hour traffic, Owen finds himself intrigued by the prospect of seeing another Ortelius map, even in its diminished condition. The complexity of the marriage between cartographer's craft and the printing arts of the late 1500s fascinates him. He is in the hunt now, and his difficulties with Patricia slip from his consciousness.

CHAPTER 15

Antwerp, Early March 1570

Jonas rarely strays from the job in front of him, but Gilles Coppens de Diest's son, Mark Anthony, provides an unexpected distraction to his long work hours. Jonas is given a sheet of text and told to take it to the proofreader. The master printer points up the stairs and Jonas knocks on several closed doors until an annoyed voice snaps, "Come in, and stop making a clamor!"

He enters a chamber lined floor-to-ceiling with printed and sewn volumes, but at first sees no one. A tabletop is littered with books, papers, quills, and ink. A young man occupies the upper rungs of a wooden ladder, two or three years older than Jonas, wearing spectacles, with a sharp-featured face reminiscent of his father—Gilles Coppens de Diest. The master printer's son peers over his narrow lenses. Mark Anthony Coppens' look intensifies when he sees the sheet of text in Jonas' hand.

"Aha," the young man grunts as he clambers down. Jonas holds out the paper, and Mark Anthony snatches it as though it contains hidden secrets.

"What's your name?" The proofreader asks, absently. He leans over the table, devouring the Spanish text.

Jonas does not reply immediately, as he feels barely addressed. "Your name," snaps Mark Anthony, now staring with interest at Jonas.

"Jonas Hoen, late of the Benedictine monastery on the Antwerp-Mechelen—"

"Ah, the apprentice given high marks for illuminating scripture by the Brothers—dying art—good to move ahead. So! You can read Latin. Do you read Spanish, too?" Mark Anthony waves the sheet at Jonas.

"No, sir."

"'Mark Anthony,' Jonas."

"No, Mark Anthony, only Dutch, and I have an understanding of the Latin."

"This is not good," the printer's son says, snapping fingers on the sheet Jonas has delivered. Jonas sees that the document, handwritten in Spanish, with an imprint showing a nobleman's family crest of checkerboard shield, filigreed leaves and scrollwork, is an official decree from the Duke of Alva, Governor of the Netherlands and feared enforcer of the Spanish Inquisition headquartered in Brussels.

"The Iron Duke's patent overrides all Brabant and Dutch laws as though they were dust in the wind," Mark Anthony says, agitated. He scowls in Jonas' direction and continues to read, but breaks off. "Oh, this grasp for power." Mark Anthony shakes his head, but interprets for Jonas. "His grandees already have full prosecution control over any accused of insurrection. This document installs a new secretary of the tribunal—Jeronimo de Roda, and the heresy trials—" He abruptly stops speaking. "Leave me now, Jonas. I need to turn this—this outrage—into French and Dutch. Tell my father I will have translations straightaway."

Jonas heads for the stairs, thinking about the Spanish property confiscations of those charged with following Calvinist rather than Roman Catholic doctrine. He is well aware that these measures chafe the burghers of Antwerp. Even the farmers at his father's mill, before the flood, spoke of the Inquisition in hushed tones. The yoke of Spanish rule and its grinding taxes were always in the undercurrent of conversation. As he descends to the first floor to find Gilles Coppens de Diest, Jonas recalls the violence done to Willem Booten's family by the Spanish occupiers. His sense of injustice makes him take on some of the publisher's son's upset at Alva's decree. He stops abruptly partway down the staircase. *This building is a place where resistance to the Spanish rule is in progress.* The message he delivers to de Diest takes on a grave importance.

Gilles Coppens immediately sends Jonas back to Mark Anthony with translation instructions: "Dutch first, then French. And then tell the typesetters in Room 14 to set up for a run using Garamond Roman."

Jonas takes the stairs by twos and knocks again on the translator's door.

"Yes," Mark Anthony barks.

Jonas repeats Gilles Coppens de Diest's message.

Mark Anthony sniffs. He sets aside the sheet with the beginnings of the French translation. "Dutch first. That's easy. Come by at noon and deliver it to the typesetters. I don't know which press my father wants to use."

"The one in Room 14," Jonas offers.

"We shall have a meal together soon," Mark Anthony says, by way of goodbye.

Jonas acknowledges his gesture of friendship with a nod and a smile. "Wait," Mark Anthony calls, tapping on the engraved shield, banners and mix of heraldry ornamentation at the top of the letter he will translate. "This Spanish noble's coat of arms—the Duke of Toledo—Alva. If you sketched this—same size—can you make up a replica of this in a copper plate? Same size?"

"With enough practice, I could, I believe." His face tingles at the prospect.

"When I am done, I want you to make your sketch," Mark Anthony says.

Jonas hastens to the east wing of the building and into Room 14, with its small press—there she is again, Sofie, emerging from the pressroom with a younger, sallow-faced girl who also works in the papermaking hall. Both girls slow their steps and suppress smiles. No words pass. He hears the girls behind him.

"*That's* him?" The younger girl whispers her question.

"Shh, Janine," Sofie says.

He steps into the room to deliver Mark Anthony's message to the pressman. He can barely hide his smile over the interest the girl takes in him.

Later, after he completes the tasks assigned by Master Hogenberg who leaves for the day, Jonas traces the coat of arms of the Duke of Alva. It is quite complex he discovers, and takes him several tries on copper. His first attempts are disasters, troughs gouged, etched too deeply or faintly. Finally, on his fifth bid, he transfers the illustration using finer strokes. He misses his evening meal, and for well over four hours, uses Hogenberg's gravers to etch the Spanish noble's family crest. The risk he takes energizes and excites him. By candlelight, at his worktable, he moistens a sheet of paper, inks the etching he likes best and removes all but the ink in the troughs. He strikes the plate face down on the paper with a wooden mallet. He holds his breath as he peels the copper from the indented paper. And there it is—a clean and reasonable replica of the Duke of Alva's family crest. He laughs aloud at the success of his maiden effort. He scissors out the paper proof copy of his forgery, and uses a fine-tooth saw to cut out the two-inch square copper plate. He replaces Hogenberg's gravers and tools, clears his worktable and ascends the stairs with the small plate, the paper proof, and the original document with intent to give these to Mark Anthony the next morning. However, he sees a faint light at the floor of Mark Anthony Coppens' door. He knocks and is admitted.

"Oh, yes," Mark Anthony whispers, conspiratorially, as a smile brightens his usually taciturn face. "Well, done."

That night, alone in his room, Jonas' thoughts center not only on Sofie, but also on Mark Anthony's confidence in his skill to create even a small copper plate—not to mention clarity, for the first time, of where his own sentiments lay in the matter of Prince Willem van Oranje's revolt to wrest the Lowlands from Spanish rule. Jonas bolts upright in his bed and ponders that he is not merely on the sidelines of a pitched battle, but in his way, much engaged. He has created a facsimile of the Duke of Toledo's crest for some as yet secret use by resistors to the Spanish occupation. His world has grown much larger and more complex.

CHAPTER 16

Engravers Alcove, Boekprintere Scheldt, Late March 1570

Abraham Ortels, Gilles Coppens de Diest, and Frans Hogenberg hold brief meetings around the master engraver's worktable, and Jonas becomes privy to parts of their discussions. A month and a half after he is apprenticed to Hogenberg, Jonas scrapes copper burs left in a portion of the Scottish coast. At Ortels' request, the engraver has scaled down a Mercator map of the British Isles and offshore Hebrides to fit across the double folio pages of the *Theatrum*. While Jonas removes the tiny shards of copper so the plate will print cleanly, he hears the imposing compiler of the maps for the *Theatrum*, in conversation with Gilles Coppens, saying, "So we must seem obsequious to el rey Felipe Dos."

Jonas sees Hogenberg look up from the cartouche he is etching, Ortels speaks with concern. "Frans, I have a post from Almeida in Lisbon."

"And?" The edge of irritation hides in his question.

"On the Lesser Germany map, do you include coats of arms?"

Hogenberg scowls. "What if I do?"

"Oh, Jesu," mutters Gilles Coppens de Diest.

"Jonas," Hogenberg snaps. "In the case of plates, fetch the one for Lesser Germania."

Jonas hears snatches of the continued conversation as he locates the plate.

"I knew it," Coppens de Diest complains. "The rebellious duchies will push us into the fire."

"You must have some idea of how long those family crests took to engrave." Hogenberg mutters to Ortels, who nods gravely.

Jonas immediately sees the problem on the plate. The four corners of the map named *Tio Germaniae Inferioris*, the territory of the Netherlands and Flanders, contain each of the stadtholders' crests. Several within the loose alliance of duchies and provinces are engaged in the undeclared war against the Spanish Crown.

Jonas gingerly places the plate on Hogenberg's worktable. From the hard looks, he senses the dangerous heat rising from the coats of arms in the corners of the plate. He retreats to his worktable, and resumes scraping copper burs from a section of Scotland near Edenborg. The gasps behind him rage in a torrent.

"They must go, of course," Ortels finally says in his deep voice. "Keep this quiet, please, gentlemen. We must take extra care not to jeopardize the collection."

"I didn't miss a one," Hogenberg complains. "The van Oranje—half a day to get right—four lions, two in mid-roar—and his shields, four of them— one with two powder horns."

Ortels tries to placate. "Frans. We don't want a visit from the Iron Duke's men."

Hogenberg is furious. "These maps have nothing to do with the Lutherans, the Calvinists, the Huguenots, and the god-forsaken Anabaptists."

De Diest slaps his hand on the worktable. "Every duchy north of Flanders is in rebellion against the Spanish *Rey* and his taxes to finance the occupation. The House of Oranje's crest, especially, is like a red flag before a bull. Abraham. Talk sense to your chief engraver."

"I'm sitting right here, Gilles," Hogenberg says testily. "Jonas! You need to heat a poker to put out the eyes of those subversive nobles." He turns to Ortels and de Diest. "This will leave gaping spaces in the four corners. If you want scrollwork done, assign it to the Arsens. Ferdinand does that treacle in his sleep."

"Yes, yes. Ferdinand will do the finish work," de Diest says, wearily. "Jonas. Come with me and I'll show you how to fire up the furnace to heat the pokers. Bring the Lesser Germania plate with you."

Jonas drapes a rag over the map of Scotland, takes up the plate, and races to catch up with the elderly de Diest.

Gilles Coppens de Diest opens the door to a narrow furnace room, and says, "Built to be a type foundry—until Christophe Plantin comes along and makes another type foundry unnecessary because his fonts at the Golden Compass are so superior." He throws up his hands and shrugs as though it were an old argument he had lost. Jonas notices a trace of envy for the French-born printer, successfully established and roundly respected in Antwerp.

Jonas is more interested in the pleasant warmth the room exudes from its glowing embers in the oven, a welcome respite from the chill February that permeates the entire building.

"But we always find uses for the furnace," de Diest continues, "like today, cleaning up Master Hogenberg's too enthusiastic promotion of the seventeen provinces' stadtholders."

Jonas pumps the handle of a bellows and adds several shovels of peat to the waist-high hearth of the room's brick oven. He places two rods in the fire and watches as the poker tips become ashen. Gilles Coppens taps Jonas on the back and turns, calling over his shoulder, "You will be fine. But use common sense so you don't burn completely through the copper."

Alone, Jonas adjusts the plate on a butcher's block table, scarred and seared by hot iron. The increased heat within the room warms him. When he notices the tips of the pokers glowing red. He reaches for one poker and drops it with a clang. The heat has traveled quickly to his fingers. He blows on the stinging burn and curses his own stupidity. He spies several soft chamois leather swatches and wraps his hands before picking up the poker. Gingerly, he touches the tip to the first coat of arms when he hears the door swing open behind him. Still grasping the smoking hot-tipped poker, he whirls at the sound and beholds wide-eyed Sofie van Alsing. She slams the door shut. After a confused moment, Jonas returns the poker to the hearth and opens the door. Sofie stands blinking, unsure of whether to bolt or hold her ground.

"Oh!" They say simultaneously. Jonas laughs nervously. "I—I didn't know who—I'm sorry I startled you. Sofie, yes?"

"Yes," Sofie replies.

"Come in, if you like," he says, unsure how to act. She looks about, sees no one in the corridor, and slips into the warm room. Jonas takes his hand off the doorknob.

"Don't let the heat out," she says.

He takes this to mean shut the door, and does so, softly.

"You are Jonas, yes?" He nods, at a loss for words.

"What are you doing?"

Grateful to have a question requiring a response, he says: "I need to gouge out the crests of the rebelling nobles."

She blinks in bewilderment. "What? Why?"

"Master Ortels says we must, because the Duke of Alva might send soldiers if the coats of arms are not made to disappear."

"Oh. The revolt," Sofie whispers.

Jonas squints his eyes and cocks his head. "The revolt, you know, Willem van Oranje. His mother is Sofie, too." She blushes.

"Pretty," Jonas says impetuously. Her face goes crimson. "I mean—it is a pretty name." He searches for words and gets in deeper. "You're pretty, too."

Sofie begins to bite at a fingernail. "You don't mock me, do you?"

"No. No. You are. Pretty."

She turns away and looks at the copper plate on the butcher's block. "What do you mean, 'gouge out the crests'?"

Relieved to change the subject, Jonas explains, "Master Ortels says the whole book is endangered if the maps show coats-of-arms from the stadtholders who are in rebellion. It saddens me, to be honest. It took many hours to create them."

"Can I watch?"

He tilts his head. "Yes, but no talking. I have never done this." Jonas wraps the soft leather around his palms and picks up a poker. He applies the hot tip carefully to a coat-of-arms, removes it quickly.

"Oh," she utters, touching his arm.

They watch the copper sizzling as the emblem is replaced by a smoking, darkened declivity. He is aware that Sofie has grasped his arm. He looks at her and she releases her grip. "I didn't know. That is, I didn't mean—That's good."

Surprised at his first results, he replies only, "Yes."

"Can I try, too?"

Jonas hesitates. "If you like, but you must be very careful. This poker is murderously hot." He replaces the rod he used on the first emblem and wraps her hands in the chamois. She is looking at his face. He sees her coloring up again. He guides her hand to the heating poker. She draws the iron rod out, but frowns at the weight. She pushes it back onto the hearth. "No. I don't have the skill."

"Here," Jonas says. "Practice on the table block first so you get the feel."

Sofie smiles at his thoughtfulness. She strains to hold the iron in one hand but must use two. She glides the tip onto the wood surface, which turns black.

"There, lightly. You've got it. Ready now? See those lions? Make them roar." Jonas points at the crest of Willem van Oranje.

"No. It is too beautiful. I can't do it."

"Yes, Master Hogenberg says he spent hours getting it right."

"I can't destroy that. I'm sorry." She lays the poker on the butcher block.

"Good that you have the choice. I don't." He unwraps the chamois from her hands and picks up the blistering-tipped poker. As he applies it to the sizzling crest, he hears the door open and close behind him. He feels very alone, and humiliated that he is carrying out the destruction of the excellent work of the master engraver.

"It is not fair," he says aloud. "Unjust that art must be sacrificed because the Spanish threaten the entire project." His face stings with heat, not from the furnace, but from the stunning realization that creating a work of art is trumped by political power and worse—he is the instrument of its destruction. His gloom deepens as he applies the poker's searing tip to each crest. He will have hours of work creating a flat, smooth surface for Ferdinand Arsen to engrave some kind of embellishment. The four corners of the Netherlands plate look like cannon-blasted battlegrounds.

CHAPTER 17

Boekprintere Scheldt, 20 May 1570

Full runs commence in mid-April for all but a handful of maps. By the second week of May, all of the copper plate cartography had been pulled—leaving only the map of the earth's surface based on Gerardus Mercator's projection, which Ortels has titled *Typvs Orbis Terrarvm*—Image of the Round World—the book's first map.

Frans Hogenberg finishes work on this plate a week early, and is satisfied with the proof sheet, enabling Gilles Coppens de Diest to schedule this map for its run to assure 325 usable copies. Jonas delivers it to the journeyman printer the afternoon before that scheduled run. After a frantic day for the printers and apprentices, an accident occurs—if indeed it was an accident. Five cartographers whose work is included in the collection meet late that afternoon. One of those cartographers, an intimate of Gerard de Jode—a rival to Ortels—either accidentally or with purpose, places a coin beneath a sheet of folio paper in the path of the heavy cylinder that rolls across the paper surface. An unknowing printer turns the wheel of the press, and the coin obliterates the engraving of an elaborate sailing ship decorating the Indian Ocean.

The frightful blemish to the plate is discovered early the next morning by the publisher, de Diest. He rushes to informs Ortels, who, sleepless, has been updating his *Catalogus Auctorum*, the pages that credit the many cartographers who provided the sources for his collection of maps. "It must be fixed immediately," he demands. Agitated, the publisher pulls on his street shoes as a yawning Jonas descends early to the first floor of the printworks to help wet and stack folio sheets for the printing of the image of the world plate.

"This is how you wake up, eh, Jonas?" Sofie whispers as he descends the stairs. Jonas turns and smiles through sleepy eyes. Sofie, her black hair wound in a headscarf, pushes past him on the way down to the ground floor. He is trying to think of something bright to say when the publisher bursts through the door to the main printing hall and strides to the press where the disaster had occurred.

"You, boy!" Gilles Coppens de Diest calls. "I need you to stoke the fire and heat the irons. We need to re-melt and re-engrave the damage on this plate. God, why *this* plate?" His eyes roll upward to an unknown deity on the ceiling. Jonas has never seen Gilles Coppens de Diest so agitated.

Coppens drops the ink-stained copper plate on Jonas' worktable with a smacking sound. Jonas' eyes fly straight to the damage—a gash the size of two fingers shows the form of a crushed circular blemish. Hogenberg's painstaking embellishment is now a dismasted shipwreck. If printed, the paper would display a black disk where the ship had been. Jonas finds it difficult to breathe. "Do it now while I go to wake Master Hogenberg."

Jonas sets to re-firing the furnace at the back of the building. He pumps the bellows and the cinders ignite. Inexplicably, he feels responsible for the damage to the plate. Absurd, but, he is convinced that it was his fault that the plate had been left on the press the night before. Part of his job is to clean and place the proofed plates in the rack of drawers at the back wall.

Shortly, the coals in the furnace glow red through their ashy skins, and he adds another shovel of peat. He pumps the bellows until the mound of fuel throws up flames. He thrusts the poker into the fire.

He considers that it *wasn't* his fault. The plates are always delivered to him by one of the pressmen or an apprentice. Hadn't he had repeated confrontations with Joop Baldus, who would carelessly dump a plate on his workbench? Jonas would sometimes need to flatten a corner due to such careless handling by Joop.

Jonas pushes the tip of the iron against the burning fuel. *Who had defaced the copper plate—the last map before the final press run?* He guides the hot poker to the destroyed section and sniffs as the copper melts and re-fuses into a flat oval that needs to be ready for the master engraver.

Gilles Coppens de Diest walks briskly in the pre-dawn to the master engraver's house. Vrouw Hogenberg, tugging on her wrap, opens the door. She crossly tells Gilles that Frans is in Mechelen, on a commission to engrave a view of the city walls, and adds, "Shame on you for rousing one at such an ungodly hour!"

De Diest apologizes and hurries to the house of his second most trusted engraver, Ambrose Arsen. He is greeted with a discouraging message: "He is at de Jode's shop," the elder son informs Gilles. "Hasn't been home for days."

"And his brother?" Gilles asks, in desperation.

"Uncle Ferdinand is also on Master de Jode's commission."

Gilles Coppens de Diest's shoulders collapse.

Jonas is back at his workbench, rubbing the copper plate surface with vinegar to loosen the ink. It takes several applications with cheesecloth to bring back the bright metallic sheen.

"You, there! Jonas!" Desperate, de Diest issues his order: "Run up an illustration of a ship under full sail. He points at the plate. Jonas' heart leaps and then sags when he realizes what the publisher wants.

"That defaced ship was magnificent, I have not got the skill, Master de Diest."

"Can you do a Leviathan, a sea serpent? One nothing like that one." The distraught publisher points at the fanciful sea creature etched on the damaged plate in the Pacific Ocean near another ship under sail.

"I can try."

He presses Jonas to sit at the drawing table. "Go to it boy. Illustrate it and we will see what Abraham—Master Ortels says."

Gulping short breaths, Jonas considers copying and modifying one of the sea creatures he has seen on other maps in the collection. One image decorates a map of the northern countries of Europe—the Scandinavian lands. His struggle to survive the surge that killed his family insinuates itself and guides his fingers as he draws the miniature beast. He finishes in less than a half hour; his hand trembles as he shows his sample to Gilles Coppens de Diest. While the publisher takes the drawing to Ortels for approval, Jonas arranges his gravers, mimicking how Frans Hogenberg sets them up, and awaits de Diest's return. He shivers unaccountably, as his mind summons the memory of his near drowning.

"Master Ortelius approves," de Diest proclaims, returning with the illustration. "But he says the face should be turned east, not westward."

Jonas observes immediately that Ortels is correct; the illustration would be the reverse of his drawing when printed, and the creature he drew would be more dynamic if the maw of the beast was profiled in the opposite direction.

He redraws his creature on thinner paper, reversing the head and spewing plumes that shoot from the fixtures. Again, he submits his work. He has several hours of work ahead. He melts a thin layer of beeswax over the copper to be etched.

He steadies his hand and uses a sharp scribing tool to begin outlines of his image. The menace of the open maw, the serpent's claws, and the thrashing flukes on its knotted tail—all scream to him that he must contain this beast. Its body is mostly on the surface of the water, but Jonas adds a tray-like plate on which the beast reclines. Then he draws a broad strap across the back of the beast where the thick tail begins. *This beast will not be able to dive below the surface.* Jonas feels feverish. *This beast will not terrorize children caught in a flood.*

His breathing is labored. A voice in his head is shrieking. *This beast would not kill his parents, or his sister!* He becomes less agitated. *This beast will be immobile, cinched down on a tortoise shell atop the ocean through the end of time.*

Hours later he restores the latitude and longitude lines to further incarcerate the sea-beast where the melt had removed them. Soaking with sweat, he tingles with this achievement as he cleans up the last of the burs.

Gilles Coppens de Diest, who had hovered like an expectant father, then busied himself elsewhere to allow the apprentice to complete his unexpected first official engraving job, claps Jonas on the back. Sofie, lingering nearby, also sees the emergency task as a heart-pounding triumph for Jonas. When he is done, she applies a cool damp cloth to his face and forehead. Jonas breathes easier and smiles for the first time that day enjoying her attention.

Masters Ortels and de Diest order the print run to commence as scheduled, late that afternoon and into the night. The colorists, initially overseen by Ortels himself, set to tinting the double-folio map of the world so it can be stitched into the first group of ink-dried signatures for the most favored subscribers of the first edition. The accompanying Latin text describing the Round World has been printed on the verso of each double sheet. The Ortelius *Theatre of the World* is officially issued the next day, 21 May 1570.

CHAPTER 18

San Francisco, Thursday Morning, April 12th 2016

Owen's first stop is a gallery on Geary Street where he exchanges the framed Mucha lithographs for a $750 check. Because parking is always at a premium in town he uses the Union Square Garage on Geary Street. Then he walks to the corner of Kearney and Sutter. He rides the elevator to the fourth floor of the old office building that houses the Fleming Auction Galleries, the bailiwick of Rodney Pinkham.

The Fleming Auction Galleries is also where an acquaintance, Matt Warburg, works. Patricia and Owen had met Matt and his girlfriend at an art installation in San Mateo, which he was filming for a YouTube submission.

Book auction cataloger is Warburg's day job, as he struggles for a foothold in the Bay Area's film industry.

Owen nods to the receptionist and walks into the viewing area for the lots going up for auction where the bearded Matt Warburg is engaged in conversation with a potential bidder. Bookshelves line one wall of the room with the lots in the order of their appearance in the catalog. The graphics are mounted on white 4×10 poster boards suspended from the ceiling to his left. The object of Owen's trip to San Francisco immediately catches his attention. The map is unceremoniously housed in a temporary sleeve, fronted with clear acetate. The stain that mars the plate makes him cluck with sadness. His gaze roves over the double-folio map of the world. This cartography specimen, on once-white rag paper, now darkened by the passing centuries, has deckled edges. The feathery fibers provide irregular edges at the four sides of the sheet as the paper dried in the manufacturing frame.

He knows that he is looking at the seventeenth page, the first map in the *Theatrum Orbis Terrarum*, a depiction of the world, part charted, part imagined by mapmakers, redrawn, and compiled in an informative volume of cartographic plates for the first time. A handwritten 3×5 card with sketchy information catches Owen's eye. It is tacked into the pressboard next to the print. The lettering reminds him of European handwriting. The double-folio leaf has been taken from a "broken" book, removed and consigned by a book breaker, Owen surmises. Individual plates, suitable for framing, fetch far more than the original book, especially if the book is degraded. The gutter or centerfold of this plate is darkened at the crease, which shows pinpricks where the folio had been sewn into a signature of leaves. The sheet is less than two feet wide and nearly 17 inches high.

The plate has been printed off center. The margins betray either the lack of care the printer took to perfectly align the print surface or that the engraver only approximated when etching the rectangular copper plate. No mat frames it, which only accentuates its irregularities. It is, however, handsomely hand-colored. But the pale brown-red stain that blemishes a quarter of the double folio page mars the green, red, and ochre hues that distinguish the continents from the oceans. The spill forms an irregular diagonal that begins over eastern China, Japan, and the Pacific Ocean, and continues across

Southeast Asia to the western shore of modern Madagascar. A sea monster that pulls Owen's attention is awash in this stain.

Owen focuses on the sea dragon, blowing geysers from two pipe-like protrusions in its head. The fanciful illustration, a combination whale, snake, and amphibian, occupies roughly an inch and a half section of the plate. The creature embellishes the Indian Ocean, the "Mar di Indi." Its tail twists with flukes in the air, claw-tipped front appendages, a comb of iguana-like spikes along its back, and lizard's jaws facing east to reveal its head in profile.

To Owen's eye, this decoration is oversize, and the island or plate that the beast sits on, defined by the engraver's slash marks, seems haphazard and busy. Owen pulls out a jeweler's loupe to take a closer look. This map makes him feel uneasy, even nauseous. His brow speckles with moisture. He wonders if he is coming down with something. But he looks again at the odd depiction of the sea monster in the Indian Ocean. Owen's heart seizes for a moment. The sea monster floats in the Indian Ocean of course, but the brown-cinnamon stain—irregular, some bits darker—surrounds the sea lizard. Soon he takes in the entire stain and his dead mother-in-law's deathbed ramblings roll about in his mind. *"I see the map of the world dripping with blood."*

Shaken, Owen collects himself, wipes his brow, and searches the room to see if Matt Warburg or the auction gallery owner is free.

CHAPTER 19

Boekprintere Scheldt, Antwerp, Late Morning, 22 May 1570

The day after the subscription is issued, Jonas knocks at Abraham Ortels' chamber on the second floor. Silence. He raps the beechwood door harder.

"Enter!" booms the voice of the cartographer.

Jonas steps into the room warily. The 43-year-old scholar inspires awe, his long face framed by a crisply cut beard, still blond, receding into his darker short-cut hair, thinning in a widow's peak. A pulsing vein in Ortels' temple

knots Jonas stomach. He scowls as he studies the large projection of the
world that his friend Gerardus Mercator has fashioned, which the *Typus
Orbis Terrarum* replicated for the book of maps. The chart hangs from the
rack with wooden pins. A proof sheet of the copper plate that Jonas had
hastily fixed covers part of the clutter on his oak desk. Ortels fixes his finger
on the sea beast, and peers at Jonas.

"What's your name, boy?" Ortels asks.

"Jonas Hoen," the apprentice says, trying to put more voice in his response
with each syllable. Ortels fixes his gaze on the boy. A smile warms his face
and the tension building in Jonas slips away.

"Your work is quite acceptable for such short notice and experience. Your
sea monster is an apt choice." The scholar waves a hand at the landmasses
inscribed *Sumatra* and *Iava maior* on the copper plate proof. "There is a big
lizard, called a dragon by some—in these islands." Ortels looks penetratingly
at him and Jonas becomes wary again—but is relieved when the cartographer
says, "I like what you did, and I may use this beast again on other mappings.
I have an imagined land called 'Utopia' in mind. But no one needs to know
this."

"Yes, sir," Jonas says, uncertain. He has no idea of what the scholar speaks.

"Young man, I like that you bound that ugly creature so it could not wander
everywhere across the ocean."

Not comforted by the compliment, he ekes out, "Thank you, sir."

"You made a choice informed by something deep inside, yes?"

Jonas hesitates, then realizes what the scholar says is true. "Yes, sir."

"Master de Diest says you were orphaned by the big tide five years ago. We
see so many of these floods because we are the low country. But look. What
do you see here?" Ortels points a long finger at the chaotic coastline of the
Netherlands, then west to the North Sea and provinces to the north. "You
see the Hoek of Holland? And now, you see the coastline of Anglia?" He
points to the southeast of the English island. Jonas imagines a powerful
hand wrenching England from the mainland. "Now look here," Ortels says,
his voice a whisper, as though confirming the sight for himself. He points
first at the proof copy of the map of the world and hovers his finger over

the bulging part of the New World's southern continent, an area called *Brasil* that the Portuguese claim. He waves his other hand over the intriguing space on the western edge of Africa where the rest of the American continent's southern hemisphere could readily fit. Jonas' eyes widen.

Ortels smiles as Jonas, with minor guidance, has made the discovery, too: *The world is not a constant. Forces are at work, shifting lands, changing shapes and sizes of the land that one has walked on.*

This is unheard of. Jonas presses his hand on the big desk to steady himself.

"Interesting to think about, yes?" Ortels booms, grinning broadly. "So much to discover. So many things happening while we sleep and dream and rest for the next day's labors. For example—" Ortels' tone turns sharp, putting Jonas on guard. "How did that coin get between an inked copper plate and a proof sheet and then the press roller passed over it the very night before we are to complete the press run?"

The cartographer's smile has turned from benign wonder at the nature of things to a corrosive anger building behind his eyes. "You wouldn't know anything about this, would you?"

"N—no, sir." Jonas stammers. "I only heard of this yesterday morning when Master Coppens de Diest—"

"How could this have occurred? Can you think back to the end of the workday the day before yesterday?"

"I know that a meeting of four—no, five—of the cartographers you acknowledge in your catalog of map authors—they met around the big press. A celebration—with tankards of ale and wine."

"Nearly ninety names are on that list. Can you tell me who these men were?"

"Sir, I don't know their names. Master Hogenberg is my trainer and warden. I never knew the originators of the maps, only Master Hogenberg's reductions—sometimes the Arsen brothers' work, but not the original cartographers."

Frustration creeps across Ortels' face. Then Jonas thinks he can help.

"Perhaps one of the other apprentices might—Joop Baldus might know. He says he knows many cartographers from when he worked at Master de Jode's—"

"De Jode?" Ortels repeats, then explodes: "Gerard de Jode!"

"Sir, I didn't mean to say that Joop has anything to do with this."

"What? No. Don't trouble yourself about—" Ortels cuts himself off. "Young man, please ask Master de Diest to join me."

Jonas withdraws tentatively. Ever since he had challenged the sneering Joop when he first arrived, the bully has looked at him with a threatening eye. Now, as he listens again to how he had said it, it sounds like he has accused Joop. He knocks again on Ortels' door and cranes his neck. "Sir?"

Ortels looks up, regards Jonas sternly.

"I hope you don't think Joop—that is—that Joop had anything—"

"Fetch Master de Diest, boy." The request is spoken with no warmth. Fearful that he has exasperated Ortels, and implicated the bully Baldus, he closes the door quietly. He stands for a long moment before searching for Gilles Coppens de Diest.

CHAPTER 20

San Francisco, April 12th 2016

Owen sees that Matt Warburg has broken free from collectors viewing the lots and has returned to his desk, piled with books he catalogs for future auctions between making himself available to preview visitors.

Owen still feels clammy and a little sickened. His dying mother-in-law's words rattle through his thoughts. He had long divorced himself from emotional attachment to pieces he sought for clients, but this is different.. Owen moves away from the map and feigns interest in other graphics, pausing briefly before a Frederic Remington lithograph. He walks toward Warburg, who might provide further information about the piece. The auction catalog estimate is $1500-$2000, low due to the severe staining he surmises. A computer-printed card on his desk announces, "Matt Warburg, Chief Cataloger." A pale red handprint adorns a corner of the card. Owen smiles at the wry humor—the red handprint is a Native American symbol for a brave who has died or has been wounded in action.

"Hi, Matt."

"Owen!" the thirty-year-old, bearded cataloger smiles. "I thought I saw you by the maps." He rises to shake hands across his desk. "How's Spencer Graphics?"

"Okay. How's the chief?"

"Okay for a day job," Matt replies. Owen recalls that Matt had directed an independent film that garnered decent reviews at the San Francisco Film Festival.

"How's show biz?"

Matt shrugs in disdain. "Surprised to see you. Anything I can show you?"

"The Ortelius. Can I look at it under a glass? And if you know something more about this particular piece...."

"Ah, the mystery map. Guy brings it in hoping for an outright sale, but the Old Man only takes it on consignment. It's kind of distressed; pretty bad stain."

The "Old Man" is Rodney Pinkham, who bought the auction business and its stock of books at a fire sale price when the last of the Flemings died ten years ago. It makes a marginal living for Pinkham and helps support four part-timers and a day-jobber like Matt at fifty cents above the minimum wage.

"Boss around?"

"Dental appointment." Owen fixes a mental image of Pinkham's incisors, which remind him of a rat's orthodonture.

Matt dons soft white cotton gloves and removes the map from its sleeve. He places it on a bare oak table under a fluorescent fixture.

"What's the stain? Wine?" Owen asks.

"I'm no expert, but I think it's more than fermented grape."

Owen brings out his jeweler's loupe. "May I?"

"Knock yourself out, Owen," Matt says. "I've got some rare first editions I'm going to discover over on that desk. Let me know when you're done."

Owen fits the loupe against his right eye. He leans to avoid casting a shadow and traces the edges of the stain. The blurred residue of whatever caused it creeps like capillaries toward Madagascar across the fiber page. He surreptitiously touches the stain and detects *or did he only imagine*—a difference in depth, like a scab might make.

His heartbeat thumps. *Was this why Maurice Bregmann called him? Blood…? Was Yad Vashem looking for an artifact that proved something about the Holocaust?* Then the flashing thought crosses his mind. *Patricia's mother!* Dared he even think that? *Was this stain dried blood spilled by Hetty's lifeline in the Netherlands?* He feels excited but unsure. *Could this be what Patricia's mother saw as a young girl?*

He focuses the loupe on the tiny hash marks that form the edge of the perch the sea beast sits on. He circles the table and is captured by what look like letters J-O-N-A-S. *That's odd. And there's more.* H-O-E-N. *Is that a name? Or are these a random burin strokes?* But these questions are tangential to what he needs to know today. He returns to Warburg's desk.

"Say, Matt? Can you tell me anything about the guy who consigned this?" The chief cataloger squints long and hard at Owen. "Don't worry," Owen assures, "I'm not going to make a private arrangement." Matt continues to stare. "Honest," Owen says, punctuating his remark with his right hand in the air, his left on the stack of books Matt is cataloging. "Old guy? Young guy, old woman? Young woman?"

Matt shrugs. "Guy about as old as Pinkie, maybe older. European accent. Pinkham's got his contact info. I can't help you."

"Hmmm. It doesn't look like a pro's consignment."

"Naw. I'd say it came right out of the book. He got it to us barely in time to get into this month's catalog."

"Do you know when Pinkham is due back?" Owen asks.

"Didn't say."

"I'd sure like to know the consigner's name."

Matt Warburg gives him a commiserating shrug.

"I'll try your boss later. Thanks Matt." Owen takes the elevator down and steps onto Kearney Street. He needs a park bench to sort out what to do next. He walks toward Portsmouth Square to join the pigeons and the homeless scratching for sustenance. But the barely audible words of Patricia's mother filter through his memory: *'I see blood on the book of maps the man so loved.'* Owen stops abruptly. *'I see the map of the world dripping with blood.'* "She said it!" Owen says aloud. An Asian woman holding a little girl by her hand stops and looks at him quizzically. He smiles in embarrassment and steps into a doorway to speed-dial Maurice Bregmann's UC Berkeley number.

CHAPTER 21

Boekprintere Scheldt, Late Morning, 22 May 1570

Around him, journeymen and printers' devils scurry, barely drawing breaths because the volume of work is staggering as they hasten to fill the orders for the first subscription. Jonas finds Coppens de Diest annoyed, examining a tinted title page on the drying bar against the west wall. He asks with impatience. "Yes?"

"Master Ortels requests to see you straightaway, sir."

The master printer mutters. "What now?" Jonas thinks better of speaking further, but de Diest says, "Jonas, I need you to take this to Andreas Grober. Look at this." He points at a slapdash job in the area of central Africa. He hands the poorly colored title page sheet to Jonas and tells him to take it to the warden of the limners. "One of his colorists has stinted on the Naples Yellow here and here." He points to the richer version on a rack that Ortels had colored as a standard to follow. "And Andreas' people must be more careful about losing precision." The master printer points at three areas on the tinted sheet of Africa where the colors exceed their borders and merge with vermilion to make a color that verges on muddy brown.

"Yes, sir."

"Oh—and we are running so behind, I need you to join the colorists for the next few days. That monk said you were also adept at illumination."

"But Master Grober will object. I am not a member of the Limners' Guild."

"Tell Andreas Grober to talk to me if he is troubled. And here," de Diest removes the sample colored by Ortels and hands it to Jonas. "Andreas and the rest must mix these colors, exactly."

Jonas has overheard that the hand-colored version of the *Theatrum* will cost sixteen guilders, three times the price of a black ink version, an amount equal to two months of a journeyman printer's yearly compensation. He understands now why the publisher is adamant that the limning meet a high standard. This first edition, printed entirely in Latin, is intended for those with university educations. Scholars, merchants, men in the shipping trades versed in Latin were targeted to read the thirty-five pages of commentaries written by Ortels that were typeset on the versos of the recto-printed maps.

Jonas arrives at the hall on the second floor where the limners work. The room overlooks the courtyard below and natural light shines in for the artists to apply their washes and tints. He relays his message to the guild warden, Andreas Grober, and gives him the offending samples and the Ortels-colored original. The steel-gray-haired supervising artist peers wearily through eyeglasses spattered with specks of color from the pots arrayed on his worktable.

"If he wasn't so cheap, the colors wouldn't run. Look what he buys," Grober mutters to no one in particular in gravel tones and points at the miniature vats of powdered pigment. "It does not dissolve properly and so more water is added and it weakens the color, then it applies too thinly and runs."

"Sir, I merely repeat his message. He is in a meeting with Master Ortels, or he would talk to you himself."

Grober waves an arm to dismiss Jonas.

"Sir. That is not all. He bids me work with the limners—to help for the next few days."

Heads rise from the other worktables.

"Your name young man?"

"Jonas Hoen."

"Hoen? Jonas Hoen? I never saw your name on the apprentice list approved by the Limners' Guild. Aren't you an apprentice engraver on this book? You are not yet qualified by the guild to limn."

"Master de Diest thinks I could be useful. You said yourself the pigments were difficult. Perhaps I could—"

"Shut up."

"—make the tints flow smoothly off the brush," Jonas continues in a quieter voice. "Mix them with a finer whisk, perhaps. I've had such training."

"I said shut up, boy," Grober warns.

"Master de Diest says that you should talk with him if there is a problem. In the meanwhile, how would you like to employ me?"

A darkening red colors Grober's face. He plops his brushes into a copper bowl of solvent, undoes his apron, glares at the young usurper, and stalks out of the room.

"Can I be of help to anyone," Jonas calls to the half dozen faces still looking his way. The limners return to the maps they are tinting. Their disapproval of his impertinence seems universal. But one colorist, barely twenty, with a shock of red hair and liquid blue eyes, gestures for Jonas to approach.

"Nicholaus Bockel," the young man says. "Second-year apprentice."

Jonas recognizes the carrot-topped young man who had arrived two weeks before when the coloring of the maps had begun in earnest. "Jonas Hoen," he says, taking the offered hand and shaking it once.

"Alcohol," Nicholaus says. "Use alcohol to break down the lumps in the pigment. The colors are by those shelves." He waves at the rack of vats that hold the powdered dyes. "The alcohol—you will need to find. Downstairs, jeroboams of alcohol are somewhere, but I'm not sure—"

"The papermaking hall!" Jonas exclaims.

"Quiet. You should not even be here," hisses a limner from his workbench.

"Petrus!" Nicholaus snaps. "Maybe he can make the work easier and better."

"I'll find the alcohol," Jonas says, eager that he might spend time in the naturally lighted studio. He heads for the door to go downstairs. But Andreas Grober blocks his way, arms folded.

"Where do you think you are going, boy? Master de Diest has given you to me. Slacking already?"

"I'm getting alcohol for the colors, to dissolve the lumps."

"How do you know about alcohol, boy?"

"Nicholaus Bockel—"

"Hah, another know-nothing who thinks he knows it all. Well, fetch it, and be quick about it," Grober mutters.

Grober reminds Jonas of Brother Uwe who was snappish until he came to know Jonas. He walks briskly through the main printing hall, where bookbinders and apprentices prepare the first few books to be bound. A room off the main hall accommodates worktables used to drill holes and sew the signatures of the double folio sheets with linen thread. Pots of glue and pasteboards for the covers and spines are laid out on the tables according to the tasks assigned. Several of the boards have already been covered in the prized white vellum, which will be further decorated according to the subscribers' wishes. Already-tinted maps and printed sheets have been collated and checked and rechecked for proper order. These pages are for the first ten books to be delivered to subscribers.

Across the room, Jonas glimpses Joop Baldus carrying three sets of the pages folded into signatures ready for sewing. Master Coppens de Diest accosts and talks animatedly to Joop. The master printer wrests the signature sheets from Joop and strides to the room where the signatures are to be drilled and sewn.

Jonas and Joop's eyes meet for an instant. No matter how nonchalant Jonas hopes to appear, he is certain that Joop thinks he has betrayed him. Jonas hurries through the rear passage to locate the alcohol for the limners when he overtakes Sofie. Laden with wooden deckles—she walks awkwardly toward the papermaking hall.

"Jonas," she cries brightly.

"Sofie, can you help me? The limners need alcohol."

"Yes, I can help you. But can you help me?"

"Oh, yes, certainly," Jonas replies.

"Good. Take these," she says, thrusting the five deckles into his arms. She holds tight to the frames, however, and Jonas, off balance, is pulled close to her. She sees no one in the passage, and thrusts her lips against his. He is shocked, but even more astonished by how soft and arousing her lips are.

She breaks off the kiss abruptly, leaving him with the deckles in his arms and confusion on his face.

"So-fie!" Jonas whispers still tasting her lips.

She pats her reddening cheek. "Now, I'll get you your alcohol. Put those in the wash bins." Dazed, but thrilled by Sofie's forward behavior, he follows slowly into the papermaking hall. This secular world is a far cry from the abbey.

The master papermaker looks up from his scouring barrel. "We have something special here, eh, lad?"

Jonas worries about what Master Du Brul means. *Has he seen us kissing?*

"This first edition," the beaming man continues. "Already over-subscribed. We will be busy with the second subscription right away. More paper. More printing. More revisions. More, more, more."

A second subscription means that this book had already been well received in Antwerp and beyond.

"The limners. They need alcohol to help with the pigments. May they use some from your stores?"

Sofie carries two jeroboam bottles plugged with cork stoppers.

"Ah, Sofie, how did you—But of course." Du Brul smiles. "Does he need you to help with those, or can you get to scrubbing the deckles?"

"Thank you very much, Miss Sofie," Jonas says taking hold of the large bottles. She does not release them immediately. He fears that she will repeat the theft of a kiss in front of Master Du Brul.

"Go on with you, then, *Mister* Jonas," she coos, releasing her hold.

Jonas grasps the necks of the bottles and walks through the passage, unable to lose his broad smile.

But Joop Baldus advances on him, flanked by three apprentices. The lout Ritsaert kicks Jonas' shin, tripping him. Jonas pitches forward but instinctively spins onto his back to keep from smashing the jeroboams before he hits the floor. Not a drop spills, but he skids across the floor, and his head bounces off the baseboard. His neck feels like a hot poker has struck it. He hurriedly sets the bottles on the floor and rises in a crouch, ready to fight Ritsaert.

Joop pushes the thick boy aside and hisses: "You lying pig. Why did you say I broke the copper plate? When everyone knows it was you, you miller's orphan."

"You're mistaken, Joop!" Jonas cries. "I never said you broke it. Only that you might know which of the cartographers stood around the press before the accident."

"You miller's weevil," Joop spits. "You made it sound like I did the damage. And you, you are the one who would get the chance to fix the plate. You made the 'accident' so you would get to make a show of it."

"That is not true," Jonas replies. "Shut your lying mouth!"

Jonas swings a cocked fist at the sneering Joop, but he is rushed and pinned by Ritsaert and another apprentice. They wrap his arms behind his back and Joop strikes Jonas' face with two smart slaps.

Gilles Coppens de Diest's voice rings out. "Stop this now! Release him, and if you strike again, Joop, I'll call the watch!"

Jonas' face stings from the smacks. Now the passage is filled with onlookers.

"Jonas!" Gilles Coppens de Diest shouts. "You will come to my chamber. Joop, I will deal with you later."

"The alcohol," Jonas says, torn between his seething anger and completing his task for Andreas Grober. Nicholaus Bockel steps forward.

"I will take charge of those."

Jonas sees Sofie momentarily and a wave of humiliation sweeps over him. The sting of Joop's palm smacking his face intensifies his disgrace. If only he had given a better account of himself against Joop's false accusation, especially in front of Sofie. Smirking Joop Baldus is the last face Jonas sees as he falls in behind de Diest. He lowers his head as the gawking apprentices part. "Back to work! Everybody," the exasperated publisher barks.

CHAPTER 22

UC Berkeley, April 12th 2016

Shortly after Owen calls Bregmann from Portsmouth Square in San Francisco, he shakes hands with the curator of the University's Judaica Collection.

"I'll make this as brief as possible," Owen begins. He describes not only what has observed at the preview, but his belief that his deceased mother-in-law was the rescued girl. "I think that this page from the Ortelius' atlas—" Owen shows the camera image of the stained map to the curator. "It's the one that a righteous gentile named Dijkstra, from Eindhoven, the Netherlands, died over, trying to protect a young Jewish girl named Hetty, who grew up to be my mother-in-law."

Maurice Bregmann takes off his gold-rimmed glasses and presses two fingers into the pink dents on the bridge of his nose and looks long at Owen. "Your personal connection to this…." His words hang in the air of the curator's office. "As I told you on the phone yesterday, Yad Vashem in Jerusalem has an interest." Bregmann explains. "'A place and a name' is close to the literal translation for Yad Vashem, from the *Book of Isaiah*. It is an institution of remembrance for those who lost their lives in the Holocaust. They have a hall of honor for gentiles who tried to save Jews from the Nazi killing machine."

"Righteous gentiles…."

"Yes, actually the Righteous Among Nations. A garden in their honor celebrates those who put their lives on the line to rescue Jews. I think your story is of great interest to my contact and more so if we had further corroboration about the stain on this map."

"I am trying to get hold of the consigner. Thanks for your help, Professor." They shake hands and Owen walks down the Bancroft Library stairs. He pulls out his phone on his way to the parking garage with intention of dialing the gallery to see if Pinkham has returned, when his cell rings.

"Owen Spencer," he answers brusquely, annoyed that he would be delayed in speaking with the gallery owner.

"Matt Warburg, Fleming Auction Galleries."

"Hey, Matt."

"You remember the three by five card tacked up by the Ortelius map?"

Owen feels a fluttering in his chest. "Ye-es?"

"Something's written on the back of it, might interest you."

"Go on."

"It's handwritten. Says: 'Property of Michael D-I-J-K-S-T-R-A.'"

"Michael Dijkstra." Owen says aloud, and his breathing quickens. *Was this someone related to the man who saved Patricia's mother? And more to the point, following his conversation with Bregmann, could he get further clarity regarding the stain?*

"You still there, Owen?" Matt asks. "There's a phone contact, nine-two-five…"

Owen takes measured breaths to calm the thumping in his chest. He copies the number onto the back of one of his cards. The 925 prefix is in the East Bay and he is already across the bridge.

"Now," Matt urges, "You *read* this, right? From the card posted at the preview, right?"

"Of course. I read the card and flipped it over and what did I see but his name and number," Owen agrees.

"And an address," Matt adds.

Owen cannot believe his luck. "Which is?" Owen repeats the number and street and finishes with "Walnut Creek."

"Matt, you've been really helpful. "

"Full service cataloger, that's me."

"I think there's a lunch on me for this. Talk to you soon."

Owen quick-dials Patricia, hoping she has switched on her phone following her last class. But her voicemail message comes on.

"Call me as soon as you get this, sweetheart. It's important." He speaks slowly, knowing that his questions would bear little context for Patricia. "Might the guy who married Gerdi be named Michael? 'Gerdi,' the woman who helped save your mother by moving her from Amsterdam to Eindhoven? Did Gerdi marry the Dijkstra son when he was repatriated from Germany? And was his name Michael? I'll explain later. It has to do with that map I came to San Francisco to preview."

Owen hears the tension rising in his own voice.

"I hope your day is going well, hon; my day has become quite exciting." He ends his message at his car in the university garage. After calming down. He dials the number Matt has given him. The phone rings four times and an elderly man's voice speaks with touches of guttural European in the clipped message. "Leave your message, please."

Owen introduces himself. He says that he is interested in the Ortelius map, that he would like to confirm details about of the piece, and that he is on his way to Walnut Creek. He notes the time and finishes by leaving his cell number. "I'd very much like to talk to you, Mr. Dijkstra."

He enters Dijkstra's Walnut Creek address into the car's navigation system and learns that he can be there in less than half an hour. The afternoon rush has begun, but traffic is moving at speed on Highway 24. His phone rings ten minutes after he emerges from the Caldecott Tunnel. Patricia's voice sounds impatient.

"Owen. What are you asking? I don't think I understand your message, and I've got a million details to tie up for the Mission field trip tomorrow. The bus driver, Jim—Ugh. Don't get me started."

"I'm sorry, sweetheart, I'm actually on the road now—so here it is in a nutshell. The woman who helped save your mother when she was a kid in Holland—her name was something like 'Gerdi,' right?"

"Gerdi." Patricia repeats, sounding distracted.

"Do you know if she married Old Dijkstra's son when he got back from Germany, and is his name 'Michael Dijkstra'?"

"That name…no. Mother was overwrought. I don't remember that name—when she spoke about hiding in the walls of that house and the shooting—My God, I dreamt about that last night!"

"I know," Owen said. "You woke me with words you were saying to her. And I remember, too, because I was with you, honey, in Santa Barbara. She asked you to never reveal that you were Jewish."

"I never knew I was, not definitively." Patricia's voice becomes a whisper, laced with barely controlled tears. "Mother was so frightened. It all came pouring out. She bottled up all that terror—only a kid, nine or ten."

"I know, sweetheart, and I'm sorry to…."

"She blamed herself for the Germans finding her family and the old man who saved her—killed, like she was at fault. And I carry it too! These nightmares just wring me out. And Gertie—that's right, someone named Gertie or Gertrude, arrived and saved her once again, hid her with another family. But I can't help with the 'Michael' name."

"Hmmm," Owen utters seeing a roadblock where he'd hoped there would be a convenient path.

"Doesn't sound like I've helped much," Patricia says.

"That's okay. I'm hoping to meet this fellow shortly in Walnut Creek. His name is Dijkstra and he consigned the print for auction."

"I remember mother saying something like 'Oyster,' something like that."

Oyster? Doikstra? Owen wonders. He hears a change in Patricia's tone—much more collected. "Should I leave a plate for you?"

"I'll catch dinner on the road and call when I start home. Love you." Owen ends the call as he turns onto Michael Dijkstra's street indicated by the car's satellite mapping system.

CHAPTER 23

Antwerp, Early Afternoon, 22 May 1570

"Joop Baldus claims *you* damaged the plate." Ortels stands behind his desk, drills down on Jonas with eyes like hardened steel.

Desperation sends the words spewing from Jonas' mouth. "That is not true, sir. Never would I do such a thing!"

"Did this Baldus boy or his cohorts do this?"

"I have no such knowledge, sir," Jonas says, agitation pitching his voice high. "My first knowing was yesterday morning when Master de Diest told me to heat the irons. I swear." His cheeks burn with fury and fear that he could be so dishonestly accused. He verges on panic and more words fail him.

Ortels sighs and looks past Jonas to Gilles Coppens de Diest.

"I believe him, too, Abraham. The boy has performed every task with energy and intelligence. This other one is a laggard and a bully. He's the son of a printer who has standing in the guild. His father is Coert Baldus, a journeyman in Gerard de Jode's print house."

"De Jode." Ortels sinks into his chair. "Gerard de Jode! Do you know, Gilles, that he and I joined the Guild of Saint Luke at the same—twenty-five years now."

Jonas backs away to lean inconspicuously against the wall.

"I shared with him my idea for the compilation of maps. A mistake. Now he is trying to move heaven and earth to publish his book of maps before ours." Ortels shakes his head and changes the subject. "Gilles, this is a long day for me. Can you spare this boy to help carry a load of books to the Kloosterstraat? If not, I will get a porter on the street."

"Of course. Jonas, help Master Ortels with anything he needs."

"Yes, sir," Jonas says, relieved, but still shaken by Joop's accusation.

"I'll tell Andreas Grober he'll have to do without you for the afternoon, and I'll have a word with the Baldus boy." Coppens de Diest leaves the chamber and Ortels rises to gather books and open a leather bag. Then he turns to Jonas, who feels the cartographer's flinty eyes soften.

"I apologize, young man."

"Thank you for believing me, sir."

Ortels puts a book back down onto his worktable with deliberation. He looks kindly at Jonas. "I did not mean to distress you so. How did you feel, being falsely accused?"

Jonas is taken aback to be asked such a personal question. "Helpless—and unjustly blamed," he replies.

"Yes. I apologize again. 'Unjustly blamed,' like an Inquisition." The cartographer continues packing books. "I, too, and my father before me." Ortels' voice drops as Jonas strains to hear. "The Spanish and their mission to make the entire world papist. We learned soon that prudent men develop paths to safety." Ortels chuckles, "Some even make maps." He begins tying the rawhide laces to the bag of navigational charts.

Ortels' comment on an escape route when Spain's Inquisition presses near makes Jonas' mind spring to his father's stinging rebuke about calling the priest's attention to his family.

"Can you manage this weight?"

Jonas hefts the bag of books over his good shoulder. A pinching ache in his neck reminds him of the fall he took saving the bottles of alcohol.

Ortels hoists his bag of charts over his shoulder. On the street, Ortels turns to Jonas. "This book of maps we are making—convenient, eh? Open a book and there is a new map when you turn the page. Great endeavors grow from the tiniest seed."

Jonas hopes to hear more, but Ortels says nothing. Curious, Jonas asks, "Can you explain that, sir?"

"Well—this is the first book that shows the whole known world. Where there is a need, there is solution. I have a friend, a merchant." Ortels lowers his voice and looks about. He grunts as he spies a cadre of recently arrived Spanish soldiers from Brussels up the street. Armed with truncheons and swords, they are part of the contingent commanded by the Duke of Alva, sent by King Philip to pacify the restive provinces. The Spaniards pass around the corner and Ortels resumes speaking, but in a quieter voice. Jonas strains to hear.

"With rebellions against the Spanish, we have dangers in the land. A merchant needs maps he can use for calculating freight. How best to transport merchandise to avoid the perils that boats or carts might face. The canny merchant estimates the cost of alternate routes depending on the reports of wars all over Europe and the Levant, not only in our lands."

Jonas skip-walks to keep up as they they cross a wide intersection near the public market. The Iron Duke's soldiers regard the burghers of Antwerp with boredom or outright disdain. They lean against walls of buildings, wrists resting on the hilts of sheathed swords while residents haggle over produce.

"Like these vendors," Ortels continues, nodding toward the farmers, their wives and children trying to interest passersby in vegetables and loaves of bread and cheese, "who need to navigate safely back to their farms and mills and go out again the next day. Merchants like my friend hate having to roll out great maps of all sizes. A few Italian mapmakers have already begun binding maps together to ease the tasks for their merchants and ships' captains."

As they turn down another street, Jonas and Ortels glimpse Antwerp's port on the Scheldt. Ships under sail glide across the busy waterway. The docks are active with trade. Ox-drawn carts stand at the ready along the quays, and cargo is stacked high. Sailors' and draymen's voices ring out above the cries of terns flying overhead. Here, too, Spanish troops keep a watchful eye on the foot traffic.

"So, my merchant friend's assistant passes a remark to me that it would be very useful to get all the maps on sheets that could be bound together. That was the seed. It has taken ten years to compile." Ortels directs Jonas' attention to an impressive building, recently erected. "See that great house?"

Jonas peers up at the four-story brick building with five arches at the end of a cobblestone courtyard.

"Christophe Plantin's printworks. Reductions and enlarging of the charts for the *Theatrum* were begun there. God willing, if it is propitious to issue more editions, we will make use of their greater resources in the future."

Jonas nods, understanding that Plantin is an important intimate of the cartographer. They walk on and then turn into the Kloosterstraat. Ortels stops before a handsome stone and wood lodging and turns to regard Jonas.

"Illustration and engraving. Your time with Master Hogenberg—this apprenticeship you serve is important work that is giving you your craft."

Ortels removes a key from a leather pouch bound around his waist. He opens the great door and turns again to Jonas. He appears distracted. "I have known Gerard de Jode for a quarter of a century. One shares one's ideas with one's friends. But sometimes—" Ortels breaks off. "It is important to know who are true friends and who just lie in wait."

He sees that Master Ortels feels deeply betrayed by his long-time acquaintance, now his competitor. Ortels takes the heavy bag of books from Jonas' shoulder and places it on the hallway floor. He reaches into his leather pouch and withdraws three double stuivers and hands them to Jonas. Then he extends his hand. "Thank you, young man, for your help, and for helping to make this book of maps."

Jonas flushes with embarrassment for the largesse. "Thank you—very much, sir," he manages to say before stepping back onto the street.

"Wait!" Ortels commands, struck with an idea. He turns on his heel and steps into a room off the hallway. Jonas returns to the anteroom. Paintings of landscapes and copper plate prints hang on the leather-covered walls. Jonas' eyes are drawn to a chaotic scene of burghers and soldiers. As details leap off the painted board, of livestock defecating and lunatics engaging in debauchery, he feels uneasy, but fascinated by the willingness of the artist to be so daring.

Unexpectedly, a door opens behind him and a matronly woman with grey hair wearing a rich grey brocade dress, is brought up short.

"Well, then, who are you, young man?" She inquires, sternly.

Jonas begins to introduce himself when Ortels returns, a leather sack in hand. "Ah, dear Anna. This young man is Jonas Hoen, a vital reason for us to have made our print deadline. Jonas, my boy, this is my sister, Madame Anna Ortels."

Jonas bows.

"Well then, welcome to our home," Anna Ortels says, kindly.

"He cannot stay long, however, as he is needed back at the printery but I wanted to give him these. He hands the bag to Jonas. The bag has heft to it. "You need tools of your own in your craft, young man. These have seen good use, so they are not pristine, but they will do for one starting out."

Ortels opens the pouch for Jonas to see a set of well-used burins, stipple gravers—copper plate engraving tools. Jonas can utter only, "Thank you, sir." But his heart jumps at the sight of the prism-shaped hardened steel shafts with wooden handles, his very own gravers.

"On your way, now. Master Coppens de Diest needs your skills."

Jonas backs onto the street in a daze, and bows once again to Ortels' sister

The de Vette Hen district is rich with book printers. Jonas walks past several publishing shops, making note of each. He comes upon the modest sign that signals the printing house of Gerard de Jode. He sees several printers through the leaded glass windows and wonders which might be Joop Baldus' father. He shakes his head and remembers the conversation Ortels shared with him, especially the shapes of the lands separated by water on the map of the world. Could it be that the land was shifting under his feet even as he walked the cobbles of the printing district?

He is on Vrijdagmarkt now, looking up at the Onze-Lieve-Vrouwekerk cathedral spire, the tallest in the city, a few streets away. He walks past the stalls of the Friday market and again finds himself before the imposing printworks, De Gulden Passer, owned by Christophe Plantin. Jonas has often seen the sign of the Golden Compass decorating title pages of volumes at Boekprintere Scheldt. He had been intrigued by the Latin motto on Plantin's dingbat decorating his company's title-pages: *Labora et Constantia*, "By Work and Constancy," somewhat similar to Saint Benedict's precept, "Work and Prayer."

But Plantin's company is secular, focused on interaction between people, challenging intellect and human relationship, not theology and God according to the Benedictines. He sweeps his eyes across the court to the dormer windows, and considers that Master Ortels and Plantin are friends. Loyal friends he believed, constant friends. Jonas' recalls Ortels' sense of betrayal when he wondered if de Jode had ordered the sabotage to interrupt the release of the edition. Ortels was saddened to think that de Jode had acted so falsely to him.

As he looks through the arches at the main entrance of De Gulden Passer, he imagines what it might be to work there. Plantin, revered for his type design and foundry, is an intimate of both Ortels and Gilles Coppens de Diest. He also knows that Plantin is engaged in a massive project of printing both testaments of the bible in five languages, a polyglot bible, all in only one volume. Idly, he fantasizes what it might be like to make engravings for such a book. Weren't his illustrations at the monastery on biblical themes? After the swirl of events that day, Jonas thinks of his future but is reminded of the newfound wealth in the palm of his hand and he ponders what might be his first new purchase.

He retraces his steps to the market where he had passed a flower seller and a vendor of baked sweets. *Would she like yellow flowers? Really sweet smelling ones like those?* He gives over one of his stuivers for a spray of fragrant yellow daffodils. With the change in grooten coins, he buys two apple cookies from a vendor of baked sweets. He sets off quickly to return to the Boekprintere Scheldt.

CHAPTER 24

Walnut Creek, California, Thursday Afternoon, April 12ᵗʰ 2016

The robotic voice of the navigation system announces that Owen has arrived at his waypoint, a gray duplex townhouse with peeling paint. He parks and is about to redial the number for Dijkstra, when he sees a slow-gaited, thin figure with a shoulder book bag and a cloth grocery tote approach. Owen rolls down the passenger window and calls, "Excuse me, sir. Are you Michael Dijkstra?"

The man looks down in alarm, which makes Owen hurry to say. "My name is Owen Spencer, and I'm a graphics dealer." Owen opens his door, and offers his card to the spindly white-haired man who towers over Owen by a half-foot. Dijkstra wears metal-rimmed glasses perched on a sharp beak of a nose above a trimmed gray beard. A yellow knit tie presses against his Adam's apple under a tan shirt collar. He takes Owen's card and peers at it, then Owen's face, then the card again, trying to fit face to name to his business. "Forgive me for intruding on you like this, but I was at the Fleming Auction Galleries earlier today looking at the preview lots and saw your Ortelius—"

"How did you come to know that was my consignment, young man?" Dijkstra asks testily."And my name is Dijkstra, he says sourly." To Owen's ear it sounds like "Doykstra," and he again hears Patricia saying "Oyster or something."

Owen fumbles for words. "Your card, describing the print, had your contact information on it, sir." He smiles his most innocent, winning smile. Before Dijkstra can say something else, Owen races on. "I am interested in the map, and hoped to get particulars regarding its provenance. It looks like a print from one of the early Dutch editions. My business is down the Peninsula and it's a long drive to San Francisco, so I'm trying to gather information as quickly as possible."

The nonagenarian grunts. "Since you're on my doorstep...."

"You're very generous, Mr. Dijkstra."

He looks sharply at Owen. "That card should not have been available to bidders. I was assured—"

"It's no one's fault, an accident, I'm sure. A bit about the plate's history?"

"Come up, then, if it important." Dijkstra, says haltingly.

Owen follows him up the stairs. One down-at-the-heel leather shoe keeps catching a fraying trouser cuff of his blue-grey suit, the knees baggy.

"I did call earlier, and left a message on your answering machine."

Indeed, as they step into the modest living room, they both hear the peep of the answering device. An odor of aging furniture hangs in the air.

"Excuse me," Dijkstra says as he drops his book-bag on a chair and walks into the kitchen with his groceries. The sounds of the refrigerator door opening and closing and the answering machine being turned on drift into the living room. Bits of Owen's message play back. He looks around the living room, sparsely furnished with a settee and stuffed chairs that suggest higher end twenty-five years ago. Rectangles on the living room walls reveal where paintings, prints, or other décor had hung. Owen concludes that his host has been selling off art to sustain his life. He's seen these signs before in the homes of elders struggling to survive on fixed pensions. Three flies circle lazily as the afternoon sun filters through dusty venetian blinds.

"Sit down, Mr. Spencer. Can I offer you tea or coffee?"

Owen follows Dijkstra's veined hand that points to a settee. On a table that backs it, lies the book that had recently housed the *Typus Orbis Terrarum* plate.

"That's it, isn't it," Owen says, trying to contain his excitement.

The old man nods gravely. "I hate to have to do it."

Owen returns his nod. "Do you have any more like that?"

"No, of course not. That book was in my family for generations."

Owen pauses, and then decides to ask: "Did your family live in Eindhoven?"

"Yes. How did you know that?" Dijkstra asks suspiciously.

"I will share that presently, sir." Owen presses on. "The stain on the plate, on the right side. Can you tell me how it came to be?"

Dijkstra's eyes narrow. "I was not living at home when that happened and so I cannot say." His neutral tone is turning surly.

"Forgive me for what might seem an impertinent question, but were you married to a woman named Gertie?"

"Who are you?" Dijkstra's voice rises, his thin throat wattles quiver. "Maybe I made a mistake inviting you up."

Owen fears his mission could unravel. He says with urgency, "I am married to the daughter of a woman—then a child—who Gertie saved in Amsterdam. It is sheer coincidence that the people I represent have an interest in this print."

"Gerdi! Not me. You mean my brother, Pim. Dead maybe ten years now. He was married to Gerdi. Married after the war—Wait!" Hardness rises in Michael Dijkstra's voice. "That girl—was she named Hetty? She cost my father his life."

"Sir, I don't mean to upset you. But can you say what stained that map?"

Tears puddle in Dijkstra's eyes. "The stain! The goddamned stain! His blood—my Papa's blood. Nederlandsche SS shot him—in his own house, for harboring a Jewish girl." Dijkstra's fists tighten with fury and then open in helpless supplication.

Confirmation. A weight lifts from Owen's shoulders. But the man's pitiable state tempers his relief. Owen speaks softly. "It is tragic, Mr. Dijkstra. But thank you for saying how the bloodstain came to be. He was a very brave man, your father." Owen's words tumble out: "Your father gave his life for a young girl to live. That is a blessing that grateful Jews call 'the righteous among the nations.'"

Michael Dijkstra has no interest in what Owen has to say. He sinks into an armchair and his eyes look down to the worn rug. Then he looks through Owen as he speaks. "We came home, Pim and me, from Krümmel, the war factories. No word from our father for two years. Gerdi tells us of how he—he...." Dijkstra becomes quiet for a moment, collects himself and then continues in a trancelike monotone. "I return to work in the light bulb factory, Philips, in Eindhoven. Pim and Gerdi marry and move first to Rotterdam where he helps rebuild, and then to Amsterdam where she has family. I get training in electronics, circuits, and more education with Philips.

In 1992, I come to California to help develop LED technology. I make bad investments in tech companies. When the markets rebound I invest in real estate. Another mistake. So now I have to sell off maps from this book. I tried to clean the plate with carbon tetrachloride. But I am afraid to do damage, so I stop."

"Mr. Dijkstra. The people I represent need a statement about the stain. Would you write a note about how your father gave his life? Also that you are the owner?"

Dijkstra's voice turns angry. "This book is one of the few things that survived the war. I'll write that I am the owner. But that is all. I give it to you and you go, yes?"

"Very kind. Yes, with such confirmation my client may have serious interest."

As Dijkstra prepares a sheet of paper from a lined pad, Owen asks, "Sir, would you mind if I photograph the cover and the title sheet of the book?"

"No objection," is the clipped, grudging reply.

Owen hovers his smartphone over the battered brown leather cover, and photographs the title page, an ornate classical depiction of the continents as characters in a theatrical setting. The coloring of this allegorical page, like the map coming up for auction, is meticulous. However, Herman Dijkstra's dried bloodstains cascade down the side of the book. Owen photographs the discoloration at the edges of the pages. Several bloodied sheets of paper stick out between the cover and the back-facing folio page along the bottom of the book. He is about to ask Dijkstra for a glimpse of the loose sheets, when the old man approaches.

"My father made notes about the bombing of Rotterdam, and…and what followed, when Pim and I were taken from our jobs at Philips and forced to Germany to work in their factories. There is something about the young girl he hid."

Owen catches his breath. Dijkstra lifts the bulk of the pages of plates and fishes out a sheaf of twenty pages or so, some still stuck at the edges by dried blood, written in a neat hand on both sides in Dutch, sometimes in pencil, otherwise in ink.

He taps the first page. "Here—My father starts when my mother is trapped in Rotterdam, 1940 in May. Her cousins. A birth she was helping the family with." Dijkstra's voice catches. "She was killed in the bombing. The city was flattened." The old man shakes his head in painful remembrance. "My father is never the same after that. None of us—Our house in Eindhoven was like a tomb. And then…"

Dijkstra walks back to the table, riffles through the pages, and smacks a page in the group of papers. "Here it is. In April 1942. The NSB comes for Pim and me, and we are put on a train—part of a labor battalion. He complains later, that the German payments for our work become erratic. Then, here, for two pages my father talks about the scared child Gerdi brings to him to keep safe. I can translate for you."

"'I think Hetty is feeling more at ease here. She is a bright little girl. It is a pity Marthe and I never had a daughter.'"

"I tell you, Mr. Spencer," Michael Dijkstra says, his voice constricting, "I am still angry that my father did not lift a finger to help his two sons. But he could provide a safe harbor for a complete stranger." Tears well in the Dutchman's eyes again. "I was barely seventeen when they came for us. The goddamn Black Police. My father only makes feeble objections." His voice rises as he speaks. "Fourteen when my mother is killed by the goddamned bombing. Then with my brother, three years older, we are forced to go to Krümmel to make shells for the people who killed our mother. We sleep underground, cold, and above us, the Allied bombers for weeks at a time. Our father is not taken for war work. He gets to stay home and take in a Jewish girl that he dies for and ruins the one thing that can keep an old man like me from living on the street. Do you know what that book of maps could be sold for, undamaged?"

Owen nods, "I do. Mr. Dijkstra, I hate to stir up these memories—"

Dijkstra rises. "When he bled over that book, he robbed me of the possession that allows me to pay my mortgage and taxes. The Germans, the Jews, the Black Police—a conspiracy for my father to bleed on the one item of value in our house!"

Frustration and bitterness are palpable. Owen speaks softly to calm this man and to restore focus to his own mission. Without thinking deeply he says, "You might wish to meet my wife. She is alive because your father took in my wife's mother, a child then, when over a hundred thousand Dutch Jews, including her mother, father, and little brothers, were gassed in the camps."

Dijkstra says nothing, but sinks into his chair and becomes lost in his father's writings again, until he interrupts an awkward silence. "Hmmm. I never saw this before. He says he is worried about Emma." The elderly man takes in Owen's puzzled look. "The housekeeper. He's not so sure he can trust her to keep the secret about the Jewish girl. This is on the last page…."

Dijkstra screws his face in a pinched frown. He lingers over the statement he is writing for Owen's client. Owen sees Dijkstra peering at him, as though he were trying to read through to a deeper truth that Owen might be concealing.

"Gerdi…" the old man begins. "The last time I see her is in Amsterdam in 1991, just before I come to Philips' campus in Sunnyvale, still a do-gooder, helping Palestinians with an entrée into the College of Arts, the Rijksmuseum—or whatever. She is what people call 'a bleeding heart.' She hates injustice. But I had my own upsets with her because she brought a ticking bomb into my father's study. That girl was the explosion that chewed him up."

Owen struggles to stay silent. This was Patricia's mother he so blamed, an innocent child, and one step ahead of a gas chamber. The Dutchman continues bitterly, "Gerdi. I have always resented her for that. Made bad times between Pim and me, too."

He scowls and returns to add another sentence to the statement. "You see, it was part of an atlas handed down in my family since the time of the Eighty Years War." Michael Dijkstra hands over the single sheet, signed and dated. Owen scans the letter, composed in a neat but tremulous hand. He is strangely touched when he reads the last line of the letter, "I apologize for the discoloration that my father's blood left."

"I am sorry for the tragedy in your life and your father's. And I'm sorry you need to break up this book, which is so understandably precious to you."

"This statement suffices, yes?" He says wearily.

"Thank you. My client is likely to want this plate based on what you say." Then Owen asks, "Can you tell me also, is the book broken any further? Have other plates been sold or on consignment? It looks undisturbed, otherwise."

"Fleming's has the only plate removed so far. The bigger houses—Christie's, Bonham, Sotheby's—not interested with the stain. Didn't think it would fetch enough to make it worth their commissions."

Owen forges on, "My client may have interest not only in the world map, but the book because of your father, especially if those sheets or copies of your father's commentary are included. This is a client of means, Mr. Dijkstra, extremely interested in recognizing the courage of those who saved Jews from the Nazis."

Dijkstra opens his mouth to speak and then shrugs and says nothing. Owen sees a ninety-something son beginning to reassess the story he believes about his father because a stranger has come into his house. Owen observes that the emotional overwhelm is having its way as he seeks to redefine some seventy years of his bitter mindset.

"Look here," says Dijkstra, wiping his eyes and fixing on a line of text in his father's memoir. "The Black Police told me that my boys would be sent to the Eastern Front if we did not comply."

Owen chooses his words carefully. "Your father may have provided for you in ways you could never have imagined. You have my card if you have any questions. I wish us both very good luck on Saturday."

Owen offers his hand. He feels Dijkstra's light tremor and frail grasp. The man's struggle shows in his eyes, which he quickly averts.

Owen takes several deep breaths to calm down in his car. He snaps a photo of Michael Dijkstra's statement, and then dials Bregmann's number at UC Berkeley.

"Maurice Bregmann," the curator answers.

"Dr. Bregmann—"

"Ah, Owen. Later tonight, I will place a call to Jerusalem. You know they are eleven hours ahead."

"Much appreciated. I have the owner's statement regarding his father's blood on the copper plate print. I'll send a photo of this and snaps of the Ortelius book. But perhaps even more important: the man who gave his life to save a little Jewish girl wrote commentary about taking her in."

"Really," Bregmann says, animation in his voice.

"And his son," Owen continues, "the current owner might part with the whole book, which has Herman Dijkstra's bloodstains on the edges of the plates from page seventeen onward. That book is otherwise completely intact and possibly for sale."

"Ah. I will pass this on and get back to you with anything I learn, and advise that you are prepared to act as the bidding agent. Will that be satisfactory?"

"Yes, absolutely," Owen replies.

"I will put you in contact or act as an intermediary, by their wishes."

"Dr. Bregmann, thank you. I have strong reason to believe that that little girl grew up to be my mother-in-law. It is too long to explain now, but we have been living in a nightmare limbo lately because of issues that bloodstained map brings up in our family."

Owen rings off. He will be caught in serious rush hour traffic if he tries to go directly. He calls home on the chance that Patricia has already arrived. When voicemail comes on, he confirms that he is leaving Walnut Creek and will get something to eat on the road, but that he has some extraordinary news to share.

CHAPTER 25

Antwerp, Late Afternoon 22 May 1570

Sofie scours her eleventh-in-a-row deckle with a brush bristled with the tough hairs of a boar. She sees Jonas rush through the doors of the papermaking hall with a fistful of yellow daffodils. Her sour face melts and then hardens.

"You get into too many fights," she chides.

"I don't start them," Jonas says defensively. "These are for you." Jonas presses the spray of sweet smelling blooms into her palm. With lightning fingers she grasps both the bouquet and Jonas' hand. He feels a pounding in his chest, the same rush as when she kissed him. "I would like to—to see you alone when Master Du Brul gives you a rest," Jonas stammers. She tries, but cannot suppress the smile that softens her face and makes her radiant in his eyes. That, and the odor of the flowers, is an intoxicant for Jonas.

"All right, then. You will tell me that you did not steal them, yes?"

"Yes." Jonas could drown in her dancing dark eyes.

"You again," the master papermaker says in mock anger. "Turning her head, plying her with posies, interrupting her work!"

A light step carries Jonas out the door through the corridor where Joop and his coterie had attacked him. He climbs the stairs to the colorists' studio, where immediately, dour Andreas Grober scolds him for being gone.

But Jonas only replies, "How would you like me to assist, Master Grober?"

"See Nicholaus and help him mix up batches of vermilion and cobalt blue."

Bockel waves enthusiastically, and Jonas strolls to the color-mixing table to join his new friend and young instructor in the arts of limning. He carefully lays the bag of gravers that Ortels had given him near the edge of the table and receives instructions from the second-year apprentice.

That evening, Jonas knocks on Sofie's door, where the girl apprentices are quartered. Sallow-skinned Janine, who shares Sofie's room, opens the door. Surprise splashes across her face followed by an adolescent lascivious grin.

"I suppose it is Sofie you have come to visit, and not me," she says snippily, and steps aside. The fragrance of daffodils envelops the doorway. The spray of yellow flowers cheers the room from a vase on the simple bureau. Sofie steps past Janine and takes Jonas by the arm into the hallway.

Jonas clears his throat. "I came by to ask—would you like to take a walk with me to the abbey where I lived? It is only a few leagues and we are all dismissed this Saturday for the Festival."

"Yes, but I wanted to go to the celebration."

"Oh," Jonas says, his enthusiasm slipping.

"I always go to see the clowns," Sofie says, her voice unsure, now. "That's right, you are not from here. Antwerp celebrates the hero, Brabo, for cutting off the arm of the giant Antigoon. He terrorized everyone in ancient times."

"Perhaps we could do both, the plaza for the parade, and then…a walk to the monastery." Jonas says brightly. "We could take bread and cheese."

Sofie looks up and down the corridor. "Yes," she whispers touching his face.

Jonas puts his palm to her cheek, warm to his touch.

"We shall, then," he says. "I will show you what Master Ortels gave me, and I want you to meet Brother Thomas and Maria de Vries. You will like them."

"Your flowers are like perfume at an apothecary's," she says.

"I'm glad you enjoy them."

A long silence follows. Jonas breathes deep, savoring both the daffodils outside her door and, especially, Sofie's lavender scent. Impulsively he kisses Sofie on her lips. She steps back and smiles brightly. But consternation wrinkles her brow.

"Many people, heretics, homeless, fill the roads. You think it will be safe?"

"It will be daylight. We will be safe," Jonas declares. Then he remembers and reaches into his waist pouch. "Oh, here! For you and Janine." He presses the two apple cookies he had bought at the market into Sofie's hands.

Through the remainder of the week, Jonas works with the colorists. He begins applying tints to the maps according to instructions from Nicholaus and Master Grober, who softens toward him with each passing day. Grober's forte is to delicately color title pages for the subscription books that call for color. Designed by Ortels and engraved by Frans Hogenberg, the title engraving is a series of symbolic images, which Hogenberg had reluctantly explained to Jonas.

"Think of it as a stage play," Hogenberg begins. "Have you ever seen a play?"

"No sir," Jonas replies.

"Well, then there's no point in explaining," Hogenberg says brusquely.

"Please?" Jonas asks earnestly.

"Very well." The engraver picks up an etching needle to use as a pointer. He begins chuckling. "Abraham may have wanted to be an actor. This is a very singular design for the title plate. Five actors. Five continents. Here is the stage house, what the Greeks called a '*proscenium.*' Across the top is Europa on her throne—haloed by grape vines; 'Europe' with the artifacts of the highest civilization, learning, Christian wisdom, the virtues that the rest of the world can only hope one day to attain."

Jonas follows Hogenberg's etching pick, gliding and pausing over the scepter in Europa's right hand, the crown of the queenly figure, the sovereign's orb in her left over a much larger orb with crucifix behind her left knee. To the right and left, two massive spheres, on vertical axes, depictions of the Earth.

"This is, after all, a geography crammed into this theater." Hogenberg laughs again at a secret joke that is not in Jonas' understanding.

"And here, before one column that supports the capitol on which Queen Europa reigns, is the actress 'Asia,' mysterious, a continent barely being opened and explored by the navigators and merchants from Spain, Portugal, the Italian provinces, and, of course, the Low Countries. She is less clothed you may notice, young man. She holds an incense burner issuing smoke of spices from the East."

Hogenberg makes a circular gesture around the title, etched in classic Roman letters on what, in a theater, would be the first scene to greet the viewer's eye:

THEA

TRUM

ORBIS

TERRA

RUM

"The name of this tragic, comic stage play is: 'Theater of the Round World.'"

"Across from Asia, Abraham places the actress 'Africa,' before the classic column, in her headdress of wild grasses, barely clothed—Africa, holding a branch of flowers. And below, at the lowest level of civilization, the newcomers, the New World, 'America, the north,' naked in her primitiveness; her scepter a spear. Arrows lie beneath her bare leg; she holds the severed head of a European explorer; untamed, uncivilized, dangerous to explore. And finally, 'America, the south,' barely formed, a head and breasts only, not yet emerged from the block of stone, volcanoes, insufficiently explored to accurately chart. She casts a shadow, still an enigma."

"Symbols." Jonas said.

"Yes. Personifications of the continents," Frans Hogenberg says, softening his tone. Hogenberg recognizes that his apprentice is not a dolt.

"This title page provides a challenge to the colorists," Jonas ventures.

"That's what I said to Abraham," Hogenberg smiles. Then his tone becomes more formal. "We're falling behind. Back to your work, and me to mine."

In the limners' studio, Jonas watches Andreas Grober create depth and detail with his paintbrushes on the bodies and clothing of the figures representing the continents. He sees how the master colorist marries his art with the engraver's work. Jonas strikes up a conversation with the brash apprentice who is hardly as meticulous as Grober. "Your abilities with color make you very important to this enterprise, Nicholaus." The red-haired limner cocks his head urging Jonas to go on.

"I mean I see how a delicate hand and craftsmanship makes what is engraved radiate light and color. It shows how limited black and white alone is. Perhaps one day we can make colored engravings that can change the world."

Nicholaus smiles, and disarms Jonas with his reply. "That would interest me, too. What do you think would change the world, Jonas?"

Jonas answers immediately, confiding in his new friend. "Imagine religious strife as a thing of the past and toleration as the law of the land."

"Like Willem van Oranje and the nobles of the northern provinces insist on?" Nicholaus Bockel's eyes twinkle with mischief.

Jonas shrugs coyly.

CHAPTER 26

Palo Alto, Evening, April 12ᵗʰ 2016

Patricia places the phone receiver in its cradle following conversations with three parents who will assist on the field trip the next day. She blows a sigh of relief, and checks off several items from her Mission Dolores to-do list. Then she sees the red light flashing on the answering machine. Owen's message says he has extraordinary news. *What could that mean? Something to do with the damned map?* In no hurry to call him, she is rapt by concern for a harrowing field trip the next day.

She fixes a meal of leftovers and drops into an overstuffed chair. She leafs through her dog-eared teaching notes for the California Missions unit when she hears the key in the front door lock. She sees Owen's face smiling broadly.

"I thought after your message you would be dragging in here."

"Oh, Patty, you look beautiful." Owen slides onto the arm of her chair and holds his wife close for a long time, tousling her hair.

"Maybe I should have slipped into something a little more…." She tilts her shoulder, provocatively, an empty invitation.

Owen's eyes twinkle. "I love it when you think dirty."

"Yes, you do," Patricia strokes Owen's face and chuckles.

"Something to drink? Did you eat yet?"

"How about a beer?" Owen falls on the sofa, and flips up the leg-rest.

"You're bubbling," Patricia says as she goes into the kitchen.

"The map I told you about? Your mother saw this actual map in the house she was taken to when she was a girl in Holland." Patricia returns, with two beers and an opener, her brow furrowed."

Is that why you left such incomprehensible messages earlier today?"

"Yes!" The lightness in Owen's tone contrasts with the constriction she feels.

"Okay, Owen Spencer. We've both been pretty busy the past couple of days and I'm not up to speed on your…. You previewed a map going on auction, right?"

"Not just any map. This map is connected to your mother. Her name is on some notes written by the man who died—"

"What am I missing here?" Her voice rises with annoyance.

"Your mother's story about the Dutchman who saved her in the Netherlands? The world map from that book, is up for auction. And Yad Vashem is interested."

Something is coming together that clutches her insides. When her mother revealed details of how she survived, it had been an anguished jumble. Now

Owen is charging into that dark time and pain again. She doesn't want to be dragged into those feelings. *Wasn't pulling together a field trip with her class stress enough?* The kernel of a colossal headache begins. *No, no, no!* A well of terror roils barely below the surface. She dares never give it a name. *If I were a good enough girl, mother wouldn't go into those dark moods... But Owen, dear, sweet, dumb Owen was going down that rabbit hole and he wants me to go with him.*

"This old guy I saw today, who consigned the map?" Owen continues. "Can you believe it? He's the son of the man who took Hetty in."

Patricia forces herself to smile and emits sounds of active listening, but a voice in her head is crying, *No, no, no.* She begins massaging her tightening jaw. She is hearing gunshots through the wall of a crawlspace. She blinks with each report.

"He has such anger about his father having lost his life to protect a little Jewish girl. I had a hell of a time trying to convince him that his father was really a very brave man, a hero. And I don't think I succeeded."

Patricia puts a hand to her brow to hide the glint of fear in her eyes, but he is wrapped up in his experience and presses on. "He found a document that his father had written, kind of a diary that he—what's wrong?" Before she can answer, Owen recalls a crucial detail and embarrassment contorts his face. "Oh, Jeez...." In an apologetic tone, he says: "There's an outside chance he will want to talk to you."

"What?" Her eyes blaze. "What's that all about?"

"I'm sorry, it just came out when I said something like 'I'd like you to meet my wife so you could see your father harboring the girl—'"

"Oh, Owen!"

"It was a 'blurt out,'" Owen pleads. "I meant it because, thanks to her survival, you were born and are in my life."

"That's still not all right without talking to me." Patricia's tone sounds like hot coals hissing.

"I see that, I see that. Forgive me. I had no right without checking in with you." With every phrase Patricia sees him sawing the teetering branch he stands on.

"You can't just take me for granted," Patricia insists in a flash of panic.

"It was wrong. I get it. I don't know how to make it right," he counters, "Except I can try to get him in the morning and tell him I misspoke."

The tension in her face goes on unabated. "Would he really call?" Patricia asks in a voice like an overwound spring.

"I doubt it," Owen reassures her. He tries lightening the moment. "But you might actually hit it off with him. He's quite well spoken, an engineer with Philips, immigrated to Silicon Valley in the nineties. Ran a research division in LED technology—you know, light bulbs that last forever? He did well, but he got nailed in the downturns and lost a bundle in the stock market. That's why he's trying to auction off the Ortelius map."

"You just have to take better care of me. Do you understand?"

"Yes, I wish I could take back what I said to him. But it is absolutely true that I am so grateful you are in my life," Owen says.

She sighs and slips, worn out, onto the couch beside him. They both fall silent.

To break her mood, she clinks her glass of beer against his and they sip. The significance of the brand is not lost on either of them. They had both developed a taste for the beer that bore the name of the Amstel River in Amsterdam on a trip that included the Netherlands early in their marriage. In addition to the exhibitions of Rembrandt, Van Gogh, Van Hals, Rubens, and other Dutch artists, Amsterdam presented the moving experience of a visit to the Anne Frank House. The exhibits and commentary had drained them. When Patricia tried to describe the visit to her mother fifteen years earlier, her face had become a mask of grief.

"Why her, not me?" The old woman asked. She said no more, but sank into a month-long depression that took on clarity to Patricia only after Hetty's deathbed utterances. Patricia's eyes begin tearing.

"Hey," Owen prods gently.

Patricia puts down her beer and lays her face against her husband's chest. Her voice fails her, and Owen presses her head against his breast as she sobs.

"She's showing up every night, isn't she?" Owen asks, softly.

"This feels worse than mourning. It's like *she* wont let go of me. I'm ready to say goodbye to her, but she doesn't want to leave *me*...." Patricia trails off.

He kisses her hair. "It sounds like you feel 'inhabited'—Is that how it is?"

"Yes," she whispers. "As if I was a ten year-old, but more like when *she* was a ten-year-old."

"Oh, my sweet Patricia."

She senses his attempt to stifle his impulse to fix things. It becomes a minefield when he tries to make things better for her. But she lets him to hold her.

Owen allows himself to look across their living room at the Matisse lithograph from the "Jazz" portfolio, the bold primary colors applied with abandon. He scans the other art on the walls in his line of sight: two lithographs from the 18th Century—plates from an issue of Punch, mildly grotesque caricatures, a poster commemorating a Pre-Raphaelite exhibition at the California Legion of Honor, San Francisco, four watercolors bought from a local artist who had struck their fancy.

Eclectic, he thinks, and then *Chaotic?* But, surprisingly, the décor does work together. *Or are we just used to it?* "Sweetheart?" Owen asks softly. "The stuff we have on the walls—do you really like it, or are we just habituated to it?"

"What are you asking?" An edge creeps into her voice. The lines around her eyes become pinched.

"I wonder if the wall isn't getting stale?"

"No," she says sharply. "Don't change anything, please. Leave it as it is."

Then she adds in a gentler voice: "It's comforting. No changes please, not now."

Owen nods.

"Except maybe the Legion of Honor poster." Patricia murmurs. "Maybe that could go. I always think of the Holocaust Memorial out there. The white sculpture—"

"George Segal," Owen says, identifying the sculptor who fashioned the emotionally devastating white painted bronze installation.

"The goddamn barbed wire."

Owen looks into Patricia's eyes and sees the unleashed demons again, the source of her nightmares. "Okay, the poster goes," he says quickly.

"I didn't need to hear that, Owen? Did you do that on purpose?"

"No, I'm just trying to—" He stops speaking and shrugs. Talking to Patricia feels like walking barefoot on shards of glass.

"I'm wrung out," she says, finality in her voice. She rises.

His mobile phone rings as Patricia carries the empties into the kitchen. An edge enters her voice as she says, "Let me know if it's going to be a long chat."

Miserable, Owen puts the phone to his ear.

Maurice Bregmann's voice rings with cheer. "Definitely interested, more in your man's written commentary—the pages that he wrote, that you said that were tucked into the atlas. If the only way to get that document is to bid to get the whole package, they will back you as their agent. What do you think?"

Owen pauses trying to separate himself from the charged talk he'd had with Patricia. But now he is emotionally invested in the map, the whole book, and the tragedy that had occurred in Eindhoven. This would mean more cajoling of the prickly old man. Patricia comes through the living room on the way to their bedroom. She does not mask the look of annoyance on her face.

"Tell them, Dr. Bregmann, that I will try very hard on their behalf. I will call Mr. Dijkstra tomorrow to see if he will photocopy his father's pages. We can discuss the other details afterward, if that's all right with you."

He hears Bregmann assent, and says "Goodnight. Thank you very much."

Owen ends the call and follows his wife into the bedroom resolving not to continue speaking about anything that could lead to more stress between them.

Within moments of Bregmann's phone call to his contact in Jerusalem, a man in Belgrade, Serbia, dials a cohort in Utrecht, Netherlands. The message is brief: "We have an intercept. Sending it on."

Shortly, the entire conversation between Dr. Maurice Bregmann and Dr. Chaim Rubikoff in Jerusalem arrives as a sound file, along with the images that Owen had snapped and passed on to Bregmann. They appear on Gerhardt Schroeder's computer screen.

Moments later, Schroeder forwards them to his associate, also in Utrecht. After an interchange of emails, the 76-year old Dirk Berghuis uses a search engine to find the website for Fleming Auction Galleries in San Francisco. He makes two more calls to numbers in Europe and jots a note to call a contact in the San Francisco Bay Area. The recipient of the call makes another call and speaks to a graphics dealer who says he is happy to act as the agent, as requested. He says he knows the Fleming auction house well and can preview the plate in question. He wants to know the top bid available to him. The agent is advised that he would be contacted and to stand by. Two hours later the dealer learns the top figure. He is also given the name of the man who consigned the map and a contact number. He is instructed to strike a deal or have have the item removed from auction and destroyed.

CHAPTER 27

Antwerp, Pentecost Morning, 28 May 1570

Jonas ties the sack of gravers Ortels has gifted him to his belt and tries to quiet his dancing innards. He and Sofie meet at the foot of the back stairs. She carries a basket with bread and cheese lunch for the walk to the abbey. But first, they will attend the day's Ommegang, the Pentecost processions, and the Brabo enactments. Apprentices, heady with laughter for their day off, part and pass around the two as they walk silently through the alley leading to the street. Jonas wonders if it is just shyness that stops Sofie from talking. He loves to hear her speak; and he is loath to say the first words, because he does not know what they might be or how they would sound.

"This is my first Brabo," he ventures.

"Hmmm." Sofie stops to appraise him as though he were a sheep in a pen on view at a livestock sale. "You are a country boy, Jonas. My father would not approve." Sofie marches off while he is rooted, at a loss to know what he is feeling.

"And I might not approve of him," blurts a voice coming from Jonas' mouth.

She turns slowly, a broad smile forming.

Jonas, still unsure where his nerve is coming from continues, "Why would your father not approve?"

"You're a country boy, an orphanage boy. A Catholic orphanage boy."

"He doesn't like orphans? Catholics? Country boys? Or all boys?"

Sofie tilts her head. Her smile stays mysterious. "You would make him very angry. But that is not a bad thing."

"Why angry?"

"You have nothing to offer. He says a bride's dowry should match the worth the boy brings. So perhaps, since you are penniless—you are penniless, aren't you?"

He is puzzled, and then screws his face into a picture of annoyance. "I am learning the engraver's trade," he snaps.

"I am only playing with you," Sofie says at his sour look. "Don't you know how to play with a girl?"

"No. I never knew any, just my sister and she was no fun."

Sofie pushes him on the chest and wanders ahead, behind families surging toward the Grote Markt to see the entertainments that wind through the streets.

Jonas hurries to catch up. "Why we are being crushed in this crowd?"

Sofie smiles and replies loudly to compete with the noise of the throng. "Well, I see you are an ambitious boy who wants to become worldly about our town of Antwerp. What draws most of us is not the religious parades, but a Roman soldier, a legend, Silvius Brabo, who gave the name *Brabant* to this region. He saved the burghers of Antwerp from the giant, Druon Antigoon, who charged a toll for boats to sail past or enter Antwerp. If the boat captain was unable to pay or refused, the giant would cut off his arm and throw it into the Scheldt. This was long ago, when the Romans were here. Brabo singlehandedly entered the castle on Matthewstraat and battled Antigoon, lopped off the giant's right arm, and flung it into the river."

"Did this really happen?" Jonas asks skeptically.

"Don't you believe in heroes?"

The drone of sack pipes, trilling of flutes, and rat-tat-tat of drums drowns out his "Yes, sometimes." Competing street fairs emit a din from the Grote Markt. Spanish soldiers oversee on the celebrants who mass in the square. Fear nags Jonas that things could turn violent at provocation by either the exuberant revelers or the nervous soldiery. Only a dolt would miss the point that the occupation army under the Duke of Alva is regarded as a second coming of the giant Antigoon.

Onlookers are engaged by colorful performances. But his concerns detract from the spectacle for Jonas. Dumbshows are enacted continuously. Clowns portray hapless sea captains losing their arms to an oversize Antigoon standing on a three-foot box in a long cloak, waving his bloody sword. A hundred feet away, a marionette stage presents the same story with the victims losing their arms after a swift slash from the Antigoon puppet's sword and replica arms flying into the air. The marionette depicting Brabo dances onto the stage and slices the sword arm of the giant. An apparatus jettisons the arm, red streamers issue from the disembodied limb as it sails forty feet into the air toward the river to the shouts of the audiences.

Several rowdy young men taunt Spanish soldiers who move toward the group of provocateurs. Jonas steers Sofie away from the potential mêlée.

"It will soon be warm, and we want to be on the Mechelen Road," Jonas says. Sofie lets herself be guided by his grip. She smiles as he takes charge and they settle into a brisk walk away from the crowds and toward the city gate.

"That was exciting. Thank you for suggesting we attend," Jonas enthuses. What a colorful tale."

"You seemed distracted."

"I have a worry about soldiers going out of control. Silly, perhaps."

Sofie puts a hand on his breast. "I don't find you silly."

He thrills to hear her speak with such respect. "Except when you *are* silly," she says, puncturing his bubble. "Why do you bring that sack of gravers?"

"To show to Brother Thomas. He's the one who insisted I come to town to learn the engraver's craft." He begins to chatter happily—"and to show you off. You will enjoy meeting the Brother and also Maria de Vries—she was so kind to me at the abbey." He feels his face reddening. Secretly, he wants to get Madame de Vries' approval. Sofie has to skip to keep up with Jonas' accelerated pace.

"We will be worn out if we race so quickly," Sofie objects.

"You set the pace, then."

They slow to an amble. Shortly after exiting the gate, they pass groups of beggars, people with blankness in their eyes, once reasonably well-to-do burghers, now reduced to the rags on their backs. Even if they renounce affiliation with Lutherans or Calvinists they are made poor by the harsh taxes and heresy proceedings against them. Spanish soldiers or Flemish constabulary have confiscated their goods, according to King Philip's

Inquisition. Neither Sofie nor Jonas is especially well dressed, and so they are not bothered by the ragtag groups with their starving dogs and pushcarts bearing their possessions.

Nevertheless, Sofie presses closer to Jonas as she grows uneasy. They proceed farther from the Antwerp precincts and the wayfarers become fewer. They notice encampments along the road. Some house displaced families; others are billets for soldiers recently moved into the area from Brussels.

Jonas and Sofie soon forget the misery around them and entertain each other with stories of her family and his time with the Brothers.

"My father has a temper. I'm glad I get to live elsewhere from my father's house for a year now. My older brothers and sisters envy that I learn a trade and must be away from home. Do you have...?"

"Dead. The floods. All of us, except me," Jonas shakes his head, holds out his arms and shrugs. "My father was angry a lot, too."

Sofie takes his outstretched hand and squeezes it for a moment. They walk in silence on the rutted road, trying to stay on the smoothest track, stealing sidelong glimpses of each other.

"You will like Maria," he says earnestly. "She is the only woman at the abbey, like a mother to everybody, even the oldest Brothers." Jonas relates how she rubbed his injured left shoulder with herbs after his rescue. "She would insist I eat her barleycorn soup and fresh-baked bread when I was too heartsick to have an appetite. She is not my mother, of course, but her heart is unstinting in her love."

Jonas and Sofie walk on, holding hands for periods of time.

The soldier is a veteran of two campaigns in the New World, conquests of the Maya of Mérida, and the Itza in the Petén Basin of Central America. Sent back to Spain for insubordination and "failure to carry out orders with Christian restraint," he had leapt at the chance to join the regiments being raised by the Duke of Alva to pacify the Dutch Lowlands. For two days he watches potential prey along the road. This afternoon, he licks the sweat on his lips and watches the young couple walking the footpath alongside the road laughing and tentatively touching hands. The boy looks puny to him. He smiles when he hears the girl's high-pitched giggle. He watches the girl skipping now, tugging at the boy's hand, as he shadows the couple from behind a stand of trees budding with new growth. He hears the girl giggle again, watches her break away and skip-run to a dense thicket. He sees that the boy does not follow and knows that she is off to relieve herself. He circles to spy where she is squats, calculating how he would take her. Her skirt is hiked above her knees.

"*Muy fácil*," he thinks, and savors his expected conquest. He unties the flap of his codpiece, unbuckles his scabbard and sword soundlessly, lays them on the ground, and takes off his helmet to be less encumbered. However, in his haste, he clinks the steel headpiece against his breastplate armor.

CHAPTER 28

Walnut Creek, Evening, April 12th 2016

On Thursday night, Michael Dijkstra fixes himself a meal of chicken strips, fried potatoes and three leaves of steamed kale. He sits down to eat, and, with unexpected trepidation, reads his father's hand-written pages now painstakingly separated from each other where the blood had bound the sheets. A sheaf of photocopies of his father's words is stacked to the side. Fear of going back in time gives him pause, and he allows himself to be distracted because some of the photocopied pages are clearer, with greater contrast between the handwriting and the bright-white paper he had requested from the copy service down the street.

He helps himself to a cognac from a rarely poured bottle. Michael recalls an American engineer in his group using the phrase "Dutch courage," as he tells himself he is celebrating what might be real interest in his consigned map. But he knows that he is really trying to steady his emotions, which have wrenched him this way and that since the afternoon when the print dealer had stirred long dormant feelings. He fingers the card Owen has left—*Spencer Graphics, Fine Prints.*

Who was this young pup who stirred such grief, anger, dredging up the past?

These feelings mix with a desire to discover how his father had been betrayed. He leafs through the photocopied pages to gain perspective on his father's life from the time he and his brother were sent into forced labor in Germany. This time, he closely reads his father's entries and fixes the date of Hetty's arrival:

12 February 1943. I put the little girl in Michael's room. I told her 'don't touch his things. Sleep in his bed, but that is all.' I think I scared her. I am angry with Gerdi that she involves me like this.

Michael feels comforted that his father had given her rules, and is cheered that Pim's fiancée had been in disfavor. He reads on to learn that his father spent several months afraid of being found out. The *Nationaal-Socialistische Beweging—Black Police, indeed—are everywhere in town,* Herman Dijkstra complains on 5 April 1943. *I could not pass over the canal to get to the factory— goddamned checkpoints.*

He sips his cognac and begins fiddling with a pencil, scratching equations on a pad. Was it his advanced education in physics? Surely it was what made him a successful semiconductor engineer. His symbols and numbers had nothing to do with the words his father had written, but he is being drawn into a place he does not want to go, a vortex of uncontrollable sadness. He becomes calmer as he moves away from the feelings his father's words provoke. He applies theorems about convergence and unity. If he deals in algorithms that keep his psyche far from his emotional core, he becomes calm. The part of his brain to do with emotions annoys, even scares him. It is an area of experience over which he has no control. Years before, sudden sadness, then fits of rage had rocketed his mind, and so he tries to stay distanced from that part of himself. One outlet was research, the study of global optimization algorithms that might help his company produce better products. The words *unary* and *convergence* nag him. He doodles with several equations. *If I could bring things together, I could achieve unity, a unary state.*

Then he puts his pencil down and returns to his father's notes. *I am angry with Gerdi that she involves me like this.* Michael's thoughts jump to the time Pim introduced Gerdi to his family. She is a vivacious university student with blonde hair and a smile that turns radiant when she is completely at ease. Pim brought Gerdi down from Amsterdam in the Spring 1939, to meet his parents and brother.

"I almost lost the dribble when I first saw Gerdi in the stands," Pim bubbles.

"He is driving downfield with only one Ajax defender," Gerdi jumps in. "Pim goes this way, and then that way, and the poor defender trips over his own feet to give Pim a clear shot. And he wins the game with less than thirty seconds to go. He was terrible. He tricked the Ajax defender."

"Yes, terrible." Pim laughs. "Me, a reserve striker with the winning goal."

Within moments, however, after introductions to his parents, Gerdi turned the talk to politics and the danger that Hitler poses. She keeps bringing up *Kristalnacht* in Germany the previous November and the worsening persecutions. His father asks, "Are you Jewish, Gerdi?"

"No, but don't you see the immorality?"

Mother changes the subject, Michael recalls, to the sports awards Pim has won in secondary school.

"She speaks her mind," Father says, after Pim and Gerdi go out for a walk.

"Yes," Mother agrees, in a tone that suggests both pride in the young woman's gumption and concern for Pim's wellbeing all in one sound. "Michael, please help me set the table," she says, ending further discussion of Gerdi's qualities. Michael recalls his mother's hand touching his face. He was her favorite. The teenaged Michael knew that his father had been taken with the outspoken girl.

He was a pushover, Michael recalls. *Of course he could not say 'no' to her when she knocks on the door with the little girl in tow.*

Repeatedly, over the years, Pim and Gerdi call and send notes to Michael asking him to visit, to put aside the ill will that never seemed to abate once his older brother and Gerdi picked up their lives after repatriation. Michael wondered if they knew explicitly why he had become so estranged. He sips the cognac and travels in his mind to a hateful weekend in Amsterdam, a rare and last visit with them in 1991.

He agrees to see them because his technical visa had come through for his relocation to Philips' Silicon Valley. Assured of many years in the States, he takes the train from Eindhoven and arrives that afternoon. He taxies to the restaurant-tavern that Pim and Gerdi own on Bloedstraat in the Central District. The place is busy through the dinner hour and beyond. It attracts many tourists and locals. Either Pim or Gerdi come by to join Michael periodically to share dinner and dessert, but each has to tend to business until ten o'clock that night. Pim has kept his younger brother's schnapps glass filled through most of the evening. After-hours, the couple says goodnight to the waitstaff and last customers, collapsing in chairs at Michael's table. They reminisce about working for Philips where Pim had operated machinery that fabricated glass globes for specialized theatrical lamps. Michael had only recently begun to work as a maintenance assistant when both boys were unexpectedly shipped off to a munitions site at Krümmel as "volunteer" labor.

Pim empties a pitcher of wheat beer into each of their glasses and casually remarks: "I don't really know why you stayed on in that town." Michael seethes inwardly. *You, you betrayed our dead parents.*

"Eindhoven, at least, makes stuff." Michael says defensively. "What do you have here? Tourists, and dope smokers and—and hookers from the Eastern Bloc?"

"He's messing with you, Michael," Gerdi says. "Don't get so huffy."

Michael remembers his sister-in-law, still vivacious even fifty-some years after first meeting her, lively and bright-eyed. He raps on the dining room table when he thinks of Gerdi's words. *Huffy? Was I huffy? Goddamned bleeding heart.*

"Don't be so bitter, Micaha," Pim wheedles, also in his cups. "It's too long ago to still be bitter."

"Your goddamned do-good wife killed our Papa! When she drops that poison Jew-girl in our house it was Papa's death warrant."

"Hold your tongue, damn you!" Pim yells.

"Oh, Michael, I'm sorry you feel—" Gerdi begins.

"You killed him with your kindness for someone you did not even know." Michael hurls his words at Gerdi.

"You make me ashamed, you coward," Pim roars, rising so quickly he topples his chair. "Gerdi took so many chances to save us all. You may not speak about her in that way. Get out of here. You pick up your bags from the apartment and you find a hotel tonight. I do not want you in my house."

Old Michael clenches his eyes in stinging recollection. So many years earlier he walked into the cold Amsterdam night, furious with his brother and Gerdi. He had picked up his overnight bag wordlessly and spent the night in a hostel before boarding a train back to Eindhoven the next morning.

Michael sees his chicken dinner getting cold. As he thinks back to their last fight, his mouth tastes like he had chewed a bitter root. A nausea creeps up his gullet tasting of cognac as he realizes how he had nurtured that bitterness. He thinks of the loss of his youth, the loss of his father, the loss of his mother. The bitterness has kept him going. *It was converging now.* He had moved up the engineering ranks at Philips, because of his focus on work. He was choking on the burning gases that erupted from his insides. He had never taken an interest in a woman—that might lead to a commitment or deep relationship. He was committed only to his work in physics and patents he could earn for his company. A fit of coughing turns into vomit that he cannot stifle. He totters to the bathroom and regurgitates what he had eaten of his meal. *My technical papers were published in the journals, but my heart froze. My life died in the 'forties with the loss of Mama and the humiliation of forced labor in Krümmel.* He is on his hands and knees on the bathroom floor.

Sadness, worse than he could ever remember, presses hands around his throat. Tears well and finally stream from his eyes. *Lost, lost. All those years lost.* He weeps until exhaustion stops his heaving body. He washes and dries his face and returns to the dining room table. He pushes his cloth napkin against his eyes. He is pulled inexorably back. Behind the patterned napkin, behind his closed eyes, he is back in the 'forties. He is posing a question from his cramped bunk in Krümmel to his father in Eindhoven. *Why did you take her in?*

"But that is crazy," Michael says aloud in his fading duplex in Walnut Creek. "I did not even know he had taken in the girl."

Then Gerdi, as he remembers her from the 'nineties, begins speaking: "*Let him answer,*" she urges. "*Let your father answer.*"

Michael concentrates, trying to quietly listen for his father's voice. When he only hears the faint rumble of the BART system a street away, he knows he is not going to learn anything from his father this way.

He opens his eyes. They fall on the sheets of scrawled text. He reads closely every word his father had written from the time of Marthe's death in the Rotterdam bombing to the very last entry.

CHAPTER 29

The Wood, Mid-Day, Mechelen Road, 28 May 1570

Sofie hears the Spaniard's helmet strike his breastplate. Before she can turn her head, however, he pulls her backward. The powerful hand, stinking of tobacco and sweat, presses her mouth closed. She tries to hold her footing but cannot. He drags her deep into the thicket. She screams "Jonas," but the only sound that escapes her nose is a muffled "Mmmmphh." Her wild eyes see nothing but the mottled sky through the branches overhead. She summons all her strength to scream for help, but the hand stifles her cry. His unforgiving breastplate digs into her back. She kicks, thrashes, slams the ground with her heels, but is no match for him.

Jonas hears indistinct sounds and calls out uncertainly, advancing toward the narrow track between the trees. "Sofie?"

The next moments pass very quickly, but agonizingly slowly for Sofie. She tries desperately to lock her knees and pry the smothering hand from her mouth. If only she could—but the brute spins her onto the ground. She bounces free enough of her attacker's hand to shriek "Jonas!"

Now he is atop her—his grinding mouth, foul breath, then he flips her over, hand still clamped across her jaw, the ground pushed into her forehead, his hardness clumsily pressing between her legs. She feels him tear at her, pull her skirt above her waist. One hand continues to clamp her mouth shut, the other shreds the underskirt trapped at her ankles. She can see only a light being extinguished, an end to all the light in her life. Somehow she manages again to shout Jonas' name.

With a fury fueled by her cry, the soldier forces his sex into her. *He will kill me, tear me apart*, her brain screams. She bites his finger; he thrusts harder; she shrieks with the tearing pain.

Shock pounds Jonas' heart to see the soldier atop her. He discards thoughts about how to stop this six-foot beast. *Slam the bag of engraving tools over the brute's head? Like a gnat biting an ox.* He fumbles through the bag of tools and withdraws the longest graver by its grip. The familiar handle shoots resolve through him. Both fists grasping the handle of the graver, he reaches high and plunges the hardened steel through the straggled hair, into the sweating neck, through skin, sinew, and muscle. He feels the crunch of bone. He ratchets and twists his weapon violently, using the breastplate armor as a fulcrum to lever the tool. The graver severs the soldier's spinal column and cuts the carotid artery. The attacker, first paralyzed and brain dead, rapidly bleeds out onto Jonas' doublet.

Sofie pushes with all her strength and cries from a place deep inside. Jonas pulls the lifeless soldier off her and twists him onto his back, his bloody mouth open. Jonas crushes his heel onto the soldier's still-swollen sex, then kneels and pulls the shaking Sofie against his chest. He tugs her raised skirts back over her ankles. Sofie heaves with a moment of relief, shakes in his grasp, and clutches his blood-soaked doublet. She clamps her eyes in an attempt to shut out what has befallen her.

"It will be—it will be—" Jonas says once, twice. *What will it be*, he wonders. The atrocity Sofie has just endured? The dead solder at their feet? *What will be? But we need to get moving.* "We must leave here quickly and quietly," he pants.

He realizes he is still holding the burin, the steel shaft bloody. He swipes the dripping tool twice across the dead man's hose, retrieves his leather bag and drops the burin into it. He brings Sofie to her feet. Pale, shocked, she totters precariously. Jonas grasps her waist and supports her shaky steps. Sofie gives herself completely to his direction. He begins guiding her to a farm he knows is nearby. Her breath is short; she walks dazedly, emitting pitiful cries. Jonas knows they court danger only if seen on the road.

Less than a league from the monastery, he fears that she lacks the strength to continue. They come to a pasture, and he pulls her toward a cowshed that backs onto the wood. As though awakened to reality, she turns and shrieks, "Jonas—Oh, Dear Jesus—You *killed* him!"

She collapses in a faint. He carries her the last two hundred yards into the shed. Two milk cows from the pasture follow them in as Jonas lies her on a pile of straw. He sees a bucket near the door, shoos the cows out, and scoops some water from a trough outside the shed. He wets the sleeve of his shirt and dabs at her face. The coolness brings her around immediately.

"Jonas—Oh, Jonas. What will we do?"

Sofie touches her bruised jaw. "Oh, God," she cries. Her fevered wail splits the air of the dusty barn, and she turns away, cowering.

He sees the brown stream of dried blood staining her leg. Overwhelmed and wracked by tears, she again twists away from Jonas. He tries to hold her close, but she pushes him away. He stifles his impulse to hold her again and beseeches, "Please, I mean you no harm. I just want to hold you."

They cling together. Then she pushes him from her yet again. He brushes her teardrops with his fingers.

"They will come after you," she whispers.

"Do you want me to leave you?"

"No!"

"Then you must come with me."

"Yes!" She looks into his eyes and squeezes against his breast.

The bellowing moos of the dairy cows rend the air. A moment later, a grizzled farmer with gapped front teeth pushes past the brown cow, waves his wooden-tined pitchfork, and shouts "Get out of here, you beggars! No beggars here! This is a Catholic farmstead, you heretic scum!"

They spring up clutching each other. Jonas' bag of gravers lies at the feet of the furious farmer. The farmer does not hold his gaze. He is looking aghast at the spray of mercenary's blood on his doublet.

"We are going straightaway," he assures him. But as he tries to pick up his bag, the farmer swipes at Jonas.

"I'm getting my—"

Again, the angry farmer thrusts the sharp-tined fork. Any one of the pointed barbs could cut a mortal wound.

Jonas grasps the shaft of the hayfork and pulls, pitching the old man forward onto the mound of hay where Sofie had lain.

"Help! Murderers!" the farmer shouts, cringing.

Jonas throws down the pitchfork in disgust, picks up his sack of gravers, and leads Sofie quickly into the wood.

"They have murdered me. Beggars...heretics...." The old man's cries fade as they put distance between themselves and the cowshed.

"Oh, Jonas," she wails.

"We must get to a safe place—the monastery," he says breathlessly, pushing the brush aside for her to pass. "Don't you think?"

Sofie does not answer. They walk on, Jonas nearly dragging her by her wrist.

The silence deafens Jonas. He stops so abruptly that she stumbles into him.

"I can't be seen like this. It would be more than I could bear. And Jonas, no place is safe—that brute—a soldier—" Sofie's voice drops. "You killed him. Thank God. But this farmer thinks you wanted to murder him, too."

"I shall go to the regiment commander and—"

"No!" Sofie whispers in terror. "They won't see your side—or mine."

"Only ten minutes—Brother Thomas will help. Maria—she will help."

Arm around her, Jonas quickens the pace, and they cross onto the fields of the monastery grange. She seems to take strength from the certainty Jonas projects.

"My father must never know. He would whip me. Promise me you will never let him know."

"Never," Jonas agrees.

Shortly, thatched roofs of the stone and wattle buildings come into view. About to push open a gate to the side courtyard of the monastery, Sofie breathes a sharp intake of air—a sound that stops him in his tracks.

"My cap," she whispers in terror. "My cap must have fallen when he—when he…."

She stops speaking and both know that the lost cap is a map to the door of the printing house: sewn on the inside of the cap is "Boekprintere Scheldt." All the girls working in the paper fabricating rooms wear these caps.

"I will find the cap and return. But first…." He leads Sofie to the kitchen building.

"Maria?" Jonas calls.

Maria de Vries bustles into the doorway. As she recognizes Jonas, she breaks into a broad smile beneath a Flemish hood.

"Bless us all," she exclaims. "Look at you! And who is this?" But uncertainly stops her enthusiasm when she sees the blood on his doublet and the distress on their faces.

"Sofie Van Alsing," she says, curtseying respectfully despite her pain.

"Aha," Maria nods apprehensively.

"We need your help," Jonas says.

"Come in, then," she says quietly.

Sofie collapses on a long bench and wraps her arms around her breast. "It was awful." Within moments she blurts the story of the mercenary's rape, never mentioning Jonas' actions, except to say that he had helped her escape.

The woman holds her and rocks her in her arms. "We can help you, my dear. Of course, I can help you for now. Jonas, leave us for a while. Just add some peat to the fire under the kettle."

"I will be back within the hour," he says. "Sofie, I will find your cap."

Jonas touches her cheek. Her eyes tell him she knows she is in safe hands.

"Thank you, Maria."

"Go along now. Wait! Take off that doublet."

For the first time he notices the spatter of blood. Maria points to a pale yellow leather vest hanging behind the door.

"Wear Willem's jerkin. He won't be coming back. He went off and joined the Oranjists," she says, and rolls her eyes. The soft leather jerkin fits Jonas surprisingly well. "Go safely. Speak with the Brothers, too," Maria says, shooing him outside.

He looks past Maria at the miserable Sofie, and forces a reassuring smile. He drinks deeply at the well in the courtyard and sets off at a run.

CHAPTER 30

Walnut Creek 8:00 p.m., April 12ᵗʰ 2016

Leaning on the dining room table, Michael Dijkstra begins reading anew. Earlier, his eyes had flown past the tiny cursive letters and the subject of the first entry. Herman Dijkstra had begun his account in a constricted hand.

"Try to be brave," says a voice in Michael's aching head. "That means go through your fears, not around them." So he reads from the beginning.

> *16 May 1940*
>
> *The news came today. Marthe is gone. The bombing. I have to tell the boys. Why did she have to go Rotterdam? She insisted she had to help. It was family.*
>
> *When I told the boys, Pim was broken up. Tears like a winter rain. Michael looked like a statue, annoyed with his older brother for crying. He kept to himself all morning. No tears, but sullen, angry. He was very still. I think he could be a dangerous boy when he spills over. But he holds it in. I feel worse for Michael than Pim because at least Pim does not hold down what he feels. Poor Michael.*
>
> *5 June*
>
> *We buried Marthe. I comforted Pim as best I could. Gerdi came down to be with us. She makes a good support for Pim and is with him now downstairs. I tried to rub Michael's shoulder, but he shook me off. He is in such deep pain and I don't know how to comfort him.*
>
> *—Listen to me—My dear wife is dead. Who will comfort me?*
>
> *Before I went to bed I knocked on Michael's door. No answer. I looked in and saw him on the floor with his head in his hands. Around him were pictures of broken houses. He drew broken houses like they were bombed. Against my better judgment, I put my hand on his head. He pushed it away.*

Michael lets his fingers touch the back of his head where he had felt his father's hand in 1940. With his right hand he touches his father's words: "He pushed it away."

He presses one finger to the text and the other hand to his white mane trying to recall the moment of his father's touch. He pushes his father's hand away in his memory, but grasps for it now in the gloom of his living room. He closes his eyes. The chill begins in his feet. He is standing at his workbench in the Krümmel factory.

His thin seventeen-year-old body shivers on a numbing, damp November day in 1942. His fingers are beyond cold in the concrete cavern where, for nearly four years, he and his brother will fabricate ammunition for the German war effort. Their section is assigned to pour liquid TNT, manufactured in other buildings scattered over the eight-hundred-acre complex, into shell casings.

When they first arrive by truck, Michael is surprised to see that their workplace is one of several massive concrete buildings with roofs covered by half a meter of soil, growing grasses, shrubs, and dwarf trees.

"Look how clever they are," Pim says to Michael. "They camouflage the buildings so that from the air they look like more forest near the Elbe River."

Michael nods petulantly, still unbelieving that life as he had known it in Eindhoven, has ended. They wear thick work clothes and are assigned for a week to a building with huge vats to mix ingredients of nitroglycerine. When paperwork shows that they had technical backgrounds thanks to their Philips experience, they are moved to a shell-filling building, a noisy, clamorous sound tunnel of clanging metal casings on metal-topped worktables. Thousands of rounds of anti-aircraft, tank, and mortar shells roll out of the Krümmel factory at all hours bound for gun batteries in Africa, France, Belgium, Italy and Germany. As green recruits they are given simple tasks. Michael's first job is to stencil markings on the brass cartridge shell casings. He follows strict instructions to keep the print in a straight line and use the color of paint according to specifications. When Michael discusses particulars about their jobs with Pim, his elder brother changes the subject to: "Do you notice where they keep the cutting tools? Michael, do you see that in the far cabinet they keep the tools they sharpen near the grinding stone, and the hammers in the cabinet to the left?"

As the months wear on, the brothers move up the line to more complex jobs. They clear the machined threads of burs with knurled files and steel brushes, mix compounds of powdered iron impregnated by paraffin wax into bands that circle armor-piercing high explosive projectiles that detonate on impact. By their sixth month, they fabricate parts of the fuzes that ignite the high explosive shells. Michael finds fascinating the design by which the multiple components become a lethal explosive. His interest is in the mechanics, physics, and chemistry of the ammunition. Early on, the workdays race by with his brain thus occupied.

The overhead factory lights throw eerie shadows at all hours of the day across the chilly cement aisles, the workbenches, and the tumult of workers. When their rotation includes working on flak shells, Michael notices Pim taking more of an interest. His brother is fascinated by the spring-wound 30-second timed fuze used in anti-aircraft flak. He engages his younger brother more in conversation on how the fuzes work. "They can set the timer in the field, Rudi says," Michael reports. "So, with a screw driver you can delay the charge for ten or twenty seconds."

Michael glances at his brother, Pim, once a strongly built athlete with ruddy face. Now he is gaunt and pale after six months of mind-dulling, repetitive work. But his brother's eyes glint with mischief.

"Hey, Rudi," Pim calls out. Michael looks up as Pim coughs at the end of his call. Steaming breath blows from his mouth and his voice bounces off the whitewashed concrete walls. But the sound is lost amidst a gabble of other forced laborers—Ukrainian, Italian, Greek, Belgian, Danish, barked instructions in German, and the clink of brass cartridge housings. Slave laborers from the Ukraine, wearing blue OST patches denoting they came from the Slavic "East," push handcarts laden with cases of shells on noisy steel wheels across the concrete floor. At the far end of the sound-reverberating hall, a stamping machine hammers incessantly. They are nine hours into their 12-hour workday.

"Rudi!"

Michael sees the slight ex-Wehrmacht soldier look up from his workbench three meters down the line, his face attentive to Pim. The German has taken a liking to the two Dutch brothers because they can understand him, unlike the laborers from other occupied countries.

Michael has difficulty warming to Rudi Müller at first. Here was the enemy, the murderer of his mother, and thief of his homeland, who had wrenched him from his secure future with the Philips Metal Filament Lamp Factory. But Michael soon appreciates the good-natured little German who had soldiered against the Bolsheviks on the Eastern front. Michael sees that he bears no ill will toward the brothers and shares tips on how to get along with the guards, and get soap, toiletries, buttered bread and a full bowl of soup.

"Rudi!" Pim shouts a third time.

The smiling ex-private pivots his crippled foot. Michael knows from Pim's voice that his elder brother will be having fun at Rudi's expense. He doesn't like that Pim makes Rudi the butt of his jokes. He sometimes catches himself wishing that Rudi had been his older brother.

Two months earlier, Michael had said, "I'm sorry, I'm sorry," when Rudi told Michael that two toes were ripped from his right foot when he stepped on a landmine near Stalingrad in the summer of 1942. When he told Michael that he was separated from the army but then required to work in the war effort, Michael had said, "I'm sorry you got wounded, Rudi."

"It's not so bad, kid," Rudi replied. "My wife and Willi—he's eleven months now—they're nearby in Geesthacht. Better than me getting shot at by the goddamned Red Army."

Michael learns that Rudi's family lives outside the barbed-wire perimeter that surrounds the crazy-quilt complex of 800 factory buildings that manufacture TNT and cordite paste. Rudi gets some nights off to spend with his wife in town. He would sometimes share food with Michael and Pim from the ration his family receives as German nationals. When Rudi returns from a day at home, Michael notices his mood is lighter, as though he had been renewed. Michael sniffs to appreciate the recently bathed ex-private. He notices his work clothes even seem cleaner and cared for. "Is little Willi talking yet?" Michael asks.

"Ja, he sounds like you, speaks very bad German. But he will be walking soon. Ilsa is dreading the day."

"Rudi," Pim shouts above the din, again.

Rudi Müller drops his spanner wrench with a clang on the steel worktable and limps over to the two Dutch brothers who assemble fuzes on a rack of .88mm shells. Each, like the other members of their work gang, wears heavy gray twill work uniforms and close-clipped hair.

"What do you want, Edam?" Rudi asks, smiling, clearly grateful to take even a short walk to the Dutchman's bench from his assigned workplace to hear better.

"You have an in with the bosses, huh, Rudi? I want two weeks away from this bone-chilling work for Michael and me. Can you arrange that?" Pim asks.

"Ja, I'll tell them you and your brother are the best workers and you should go on holiday. We'll somehow get along while you are in the tropics, ja?"

The ex-private chuckles mirthlessly and stumbles back to his workbench.

"What's the slowdown back there? Stay at your own workstation," bellows another wounded soldier, still enlisted, in uniform and wearing a sidearm. "Rudi, if you slow down I'll put you on report. It'll be on active duty again. No malingering!"

Rudi shrugs, slaps the crotch of his elbow in a rude gesture, and turns to Pim and Michael. "Okay, you Holland cheeses, no more interruptions," Rudi yells, imitating the corporal. He lowers his voice to say: "Herr Field-Marshall Corporal Putz says so."

Pim winks at Michael and turns to go back to his job. Michael does not smile back at Pim. *Someday your smart mouth will get us both killed.* He spends the next hour ruminating on how his brother, always quick to speak with an impulsive wit, could say anything first and apologize later. Whenever he sees the armed corporal walk past, Michael wonders if there would be a chance to even apologize. He also grows more and more annoyed at how Pim baits Rudi.

Michael's link to anything that smacks of normal is now bound up with the little German. He sees similarities between Rudi and his own father when his father had been in a good mood. He sees Rudi as a loving father to little Willi who he never fails to ask after. And he thinks kindly of Ilsa, who has to share in the decision to divide their rations with the "two Dutch kids" as he hears Rudi speak of them. Michael soon regards Rudi like he was a cousin.

CHAPTER 31

The Woods, near Mechelen Road, Afternoon, 28 May 1570

Jonas runs, driven to find Sofie's cap before the Spaniards do. He skirts a wide path past the farmer's cowshed to the copse of trees near the attack. Stealthily, Jonas creeps on hands and knees through the spring grasses and spies the soldier's helmet. Beneath it, the long sword is burrowed in its scabbard.

"No one has been here," he exhales to himself in relief. Buzzing flies lead him to the soldier's corpse, bloody mouth agape. No feeling of remorse comes over him, only thankfulness, that it is the rapist's body that lies dead, and not Sofie's or his.

He sees, not her cap, but remnants of her underskirt on the ground near the body. He warily gets to his feet, strains to hear human voices, the clang of Spanish steel, the mercenary's comrades jabbering words he does not understand. When the sounds continue to be only birds, wind rustling through the branches, and the hum of horseflies, he snatches up the destroyed linen undergarment and continues toward where he believes her cap might have fallen. Signs of her thrashing, divots of earth where her heels had dug in, reignite his wish that he could have acted sooner. He sees the cap at the very point the rogue must have first grabbed her. He thrusts it with her soiled undergarment beneath his jerkin.

He turns to retrace his steps, but stops abruptly and thinks about the wound at the back of the soldier's neck. Guided by impulse, he decides to divert suspicion that the mercenary had been ambushed and killed from behind in a cowardly manner. Jonas quickly retrieves the heavy sword from its scabbard and places the tip in the mercenary's gaping maw. He calculates the angle at which the graver had entered the neck. With both hands, he presses the hilt handles downward. He hopes that the authorities will deduce that a blow though the throat had killed the soldier. The leering horror mask rekindles his anger. He does not know how it would appear when he confesses to Brother Thomas, but, at the moment, the sword, swaying from his effort, protrudes from the villain's mouth, the perfect adornment for this rapist's final repose. He places the helmet over the soldier's privates, to further confuse whoever finds the corpse. He adds one last refinement. He raises both arms of the dead soldier and intertwines the fingers around the hilt so that the first viewing of the body might suggest that he took his own life.

He strains again to listen for the dead soldier's comrades. Then he remembers the small basket of bread and cheese that Sofie had left with him before she went into the wood. He spots the small wicker hamper and snatches it up. He wonders what further clues he might have left in his haste. With a prayer that he now has it all, Jonas steals back through the woods.

The sun is high in the mid-afternoon sky. When he comes through the field this time, he sees the familiar forms of three of the black-clad Brothers and several of the orphans. Jonas easily identifies Brother Thomas, with his coppery hair, pulling a hoe along a furrow newly planted. Old Brother Theo and young Brother Aristide assist. They have their backs to Jonas. Quickly, he steals past their line of sight and races to the courtyard. He taps on the kitchen door.

Maria opens the door a crack. The look of concern on his face causes her to smile and wordlessly touch his cheek. "Fifteen minutes more, Jonas," she says softly. He nods and withdraws Sofie's cap and linen from his jerkin. Maria snatches the cap from Jonas' hand with a smile. She points to a wooden bin alongside the exterior wall, and indicates that Jonas should dispose of the shredded undergarment.

"She has a fresh one," Maria whispers. "Come back a little later, yes?"

Jonas backs into the courtyard. He lets himself through the courtyard gate and walks to the field where the monks and the orphans have completed their work.

"Brother Thomas!" Jonas calls.

The monk turns and recognizes his young ward immediately. He beams at the boy he had helped rescue. The other monks wave in greeting.

"How fares our young Jonas?" Brother Theo inquires. The old monk, worn in body but strong in spirit, greets the young man with affection.

"I try to be—to be the best apprentice at the printing trades, Brother Theo," Jonas shouts to assure the monk can hear. "The ink is blacker than your robes. Look, he says, displaying his fingernails. "Nothing to be done."

"Soap, young man." Brother Theo replies, hearing only bits of Jonas' comments. "But I must make water." The monk hastens for the monastery outbuilding as fast as his aged legs can manage. Brother Aristide, a Walloon who speaks no Dutch, waves, collects the straggling boys, and follows Brother Theo.

"Frère Aristede! Merci," Brother Thomas calls, tossing the young monk his hoe. While the two other monks head toward the abbey, Thomas says, "Welcome, Jonas. We have missed you,"

"Brother Thomas. Please." Jonas interrupts. "Hear my confession."

"What?" the monk asks in confusion. "You have sinned? Come to the chapel." He turns to lead the way.

"You must hear it now," he blurts. "I have—I have killed a Spanish soldier."

"Oh, *Jesu*," mutters Brother Thomas, quickly crossing himself. He raises his eyes to heaven, whispering "Forgive me Father, for speaking the Lord's name thus." He looks down at Jonas. "Did you say what I think I heard?"

"Yes. It is true."

"Do you seek sanctuary?"

"No, not sanctuary. I only need to confess this act to one who might understand."

"Did you do this in anger?"

"Yes. He was—he was—attacking—raping a girl. An innocent girl."

Brother Thomas' eyes blink uncontrollably. "Are you in danger, Jonas?"

"I don't think so. Maria tends to the girl."

"Maria! This girl is here?"

"We were walking here—when he attacked—And I have come, not for solace, but to say—I had to do it. I pray I need never do anything the like again."

The Brother looks skyward in silent prayer. At length, he speaks. "You do not wish to make an act of contrition?"

"I believe that even you might have taken this action, Brother Thomas."

The Brother crosses himself again and squeezes his eyes shut, deep in prayer. Finally, he asks, "What do you want of me, Jonas?"

"Only to acknowledge—you have heard my confession."

"I have."

"Then I thank you."

"We will not speak of this again."

"Good." Jonas exhales. "Come meet Sofie. I wanted you to see her, especially."

Brother Thomas puts an arm around Jonas' shoulder, and they walk a path through the late spring grass toward the abbey courtyard. The monk stops, unexpectedly. "In a moment," he says, turning away. Thomas drops to his knees. Jonas hears his mentor mouthing words in Latin, beginning a confession prayer, as though the monk were the one who needed to confess.

Jonas turns and pats his mentor's shoulder softly, wishing he had the power to exonerate *him* from guilt. Brother Thomas pinches his eyes in annoyance and then understands. Jonas *is* guiltless in his own mind. Brother Thomas has no reason to do anything but accept his young student's sense of right and wrong.

"Well, then," the monk forces himself to sound casual, "I expect Maria can help this young woman. Shall we find out?"

"I hope Sofie can greet you—she is a chaste girl—works in the papermaking rooms." Jonas holds his breath as he opens the door to the kitchen and enters warily.

"Maria? Sofie?"

He hears the two women speaking softly. Sofie is far from her usual self, but Maria has helped her clean up, and she is wearing her linen cap. Her cheeks have regained color.

"Do you feel well enough to meet my dear teacher?"

Sofie darts a look at Maria, who nods encouragingly. Sofie gives her hand to Jonas who squeezes it to reassure her. She tries to cover the pain as she rises from the bench. He leads her outside where Brother Thomas tries to appear nonchalant, frowning at an area of the kitchen roof where the thatch seems thin.

"May I present you to my guide when I was here. Brother Thomas."

"Look at that," the Brother says. "Some of us are falling down on the tasks to keep rains from drowning poor Maria."

"You always say it will keep," Maria chides.

"Yes, well, I am mistaken. This is fitting work for Brother Aristide. We will discuss these repairs forthwith. In the meanwhile, young Miss, welcome to our abbey. I hope Maria has been of service." Jonas detects a nervousness he has never seen in the monk. Brother Thomas is shy and at a loss for words in front of the young girl. Still shaken, Sofie smiles faintly and nods deferentially. But Jonas can see that an idea is forming in Brother Thomas' mind. "Maria, I think we need to lay in some thatch for the repairs, which means a trip to town. Jonas, would you and the young miss like a ride back to Antwerp? If we leave directly I can return before nightfall."

CHAPTER 32

Road to Antwerp, Late Afternoon, 28 May 1570

Brother Thomas urges the donkey over the rutted road. Jonas, seated next to him, tries to calmly describe an apprentice's typical day at the Boekprintere Scheldt. He turns often to look at Sofie who wedges herself into a corner behind Jonas. She tries to work out a position to minimize the jostling on blankets that Maria has assembled on the floor of the cart.,

Not far on the road to Antwerp, Jonas abruptly stops speaking. He sees a unit of Spanish soldiers ahead, some afoot, others on horseback. Farm carts, dray animals, and wayfarers are stopped where the soldiers question them. They are closing on the thicket where Sofie was attacked. Sofie grips Jonas' hand from behind. Brother Thomas slows the donkey and soon they are at a standstill.

"This is not good," the monk mutters.

"Much worse," Jonas whispers as he sees the farmer who had threatened them with his pitchfork among the soldiers. "Is there no other way we can go?" Jonas asks. "That farmer, he saw us not far from where I—"

"Quiet," the monk snaps.

A moment passes.

"Stay here," says Brother Thomas, alighting from the cart. He makes his way to the head of the line.

"Maybe he won't recognize us," Sofie says, tucking all of her hair under her cap. "I have my cap now and you wear a different top, nothing like your doublet."

Jonas does not answer. Soldiers are leading the farmer down the road toward a line of travelers coming from Antwerp. Jonas holds his breath as the Spaniard who seems to be in charge orders Brother Thomas back to his cart. The monk gesticulates toward the spires of the city in the distance. Brother Thomas begins shouting in Spanish, when a higher-ranking officer rides up, a grandee in black doublet, burnished breastplate, boots, jet-black mustaches, and a feathered, broad-brimmed hat. Brother Thomas holds forth in commanding tones and the Spanish noble appears to be assenting. The grim-faced monk strides back to the cart.

"Say nothing," Brother Thomas hisses.

He leads the donkey forward. The cart proceeds, half on the road, half in the ditch beside it, past scowling farmers waiting impatiently at their carts.

When a Spanish cavalryman rides out to provide escort, Brother Thomas mounts the cart and presses the donkey to follow. As they roll by the checkpoint, they pick up the pace past the line of foot traffic and wagons recently departed from Antwerp. Sofie ducks low as they pass the farmer, who is making a show of deciding whether or not a couple of young wayfarers on the road are the guilty parties. As the line of traffic thins, Brother Thomas speaks in a low, urgent voice.

"If anyone questions you, we are granted passage because you are required to give testimony. You are ordered by the Procurator for the Inquisition in Antwerp to appear at the heresy trial of two kinsmen of the House of Oranje. And I am delivering you. This is only if we are stopped and questioned." Brother Thomas looks meaningfully at them, as though to say, "Do you understand?"

Jonas nods, and turns back to view the soldiers at the edge of the wood haranguing travelers on the road and the old farmer, now looking toward the receding cart. He wonders nervously at the inventive excuse of his former mentor.

"They say the soldier was mutilated," Brother Thomas, says. "They think it was the work of a witch."

Jonas holds his tongue.

"Tell me about your work, Jonas."

He finds it difficult to speak.

"Your work—" the monk urges, quietly.

"This bag of gravers," Jonas begins in an unsteady voice, "A gift from Master Ortels...." He retells the story of the cartographer's generosity. All the while, Sofie squeezes his hand. They finally come to the north gate where two other roads converge. As they enter the city, the escort on horseback stays with them. A look of alarm crosses Brother Thomas' face.

"We had better seem to be going to the law courts," the monk whispers. "When we get there, begin to get down from the cart. Let us see how far we have to go before our friend completes his mission."

They continue to follow their escort past the cathedral, Onze-Lieve-Vrouwekerk, past the city square, with a few Brabo festival revelers staggering about the Grote Markt. They pass the recently completed Antwerp city hall and the guild houses. Finally, the cart winds through the narrow streets of the *Oude Werf,* where the massive stone fortress, *Het Steen,* with its turrets and ramparts, obliterates the view of the river. Here are the law courts and the prison, where the Procurator charges and prosecutes anyone brought before the Inquisition.

"Oh, Jonas," Sofie cries in a whispered voice. Her hand is shaking even as it clutches at him. Several Spanish soldiers hold positions near the gate.

"If the escort merely hands you off…" the monk mutters to Jonas, thinking to fashion a tale to keep his young charges from being conducted by the guards.

Brother Thomas maneuvers the cart to tie the donkey at a tethering post outside the main gate. The mounted escort waves, "Adios, Dom Tomás." He spins his horse and heads back toward the gate that leads to the Mechelen Road without a word to his countrymen.

Brother Thomas waves after the escort, relief evident. Then he looks hard into Jonas' eyes.

"I will pray for you, Jonas and I hope you will pray for *my* soul."

"I will do my best," Jonas replies. Brother Thomas makes a show of looking at the donkey's hoof. Then they set off again. Brother Thomas puts a hand on Jonas' shoulder. They ride in silence over the cobbles. Jonas is not sure who is comforted more by the monk's gesture. Ten minutes later, he helps Sofie off the cart at the alley that leads to the rear of the Boekprintere Scheldt.

"Be safe," Brother Thomas calls. "I need to load some thatch quayside. I will take a roundabout track to avoid those brigands."

He smiles reassuringly in Sofie's direction. Then he flicks the reins. The cart clatters again over the cobbles toward the Scheldt quays.

"Come to my room, I cannot bear to be alone." Sofie whispers. "Janine is with her family tonight."

Sofie clings to Jonas' arm and winces with every step. They slowly steal up the back stairs to the third floor and into Sofie's room. He stands by the door uncertainly as she climbs painfully onto her bed.

"I should let you rest," he says, turning to leave.

"Yes…" As he pulls the door open, she says "No. Not yet." She leans awkwardly against the bedstead. "You saved me today," she whispers.

"If only I had come sooner," he chides.

She reaches her hand to him. In a tiny voice, she says, "Please, don't go yet."

"What can I do for you?

"Go. Go away."

Jonas' face contorts in confusion.

"I don't mean that. Be a pillow for me. I want to know that a man can be a gentle holder for me. Do you understand?"

Jonas nods, uncertain, as she struggles with the rawness of what befell her. "I would never hurt you," he says.

"Just hold me with gentleness, please."

Jonas gingerly slides onto the bed and forms his body into a bolster for her to lie against. He feels her warm body through her clothes and smells her hair. With each intake of breath, he feels more easy, despite the horrors of the day.

Sofie presses her head on his breast. "You saved my life," she raises the intensity of her whisper. "He hated me. He would have killed me when he finished. I know it."

Jonas cups his fingers on her cheek, puffy from the Spaniard's mauling. "I would kill for you to be safe, Sofie. I will do anything to keep you safe." She closes her eyes. They fall asleep wrapped in each other's arms.

Pale light filters through the north-facing window and stirs Jonas awake. He breathes in Sofie's odor and a tingle of love darts through his body. Then he feels ashamed. *For wasn't it the same with that brute.* "I am not like him," he thinks, putting an end to his self-recrimination.

She seems to have slept peacefully, pressed against his chest. Memories of the previous day flood in, but he dismisses them, ending with a silent prayer. "Please keep Brother Thomas safe in this life and whatever might come after."

He sees the now purple bruise where Sofie's attacker had forced her mouth shut. He touches her cheek tenderly, but she awakens with a start and winces from the soreness in her loins. Jonas bites his lip to feel pain also. The image of the rapacious soldier stings him with fury. Sofie, enfolded in his embrace, calms him and he tamps down his anger for the Duke of Alva's mercenaries in the occupation force. But the embers of his rage glow deep within.

CHAPTER 33

Apprentice Quarters, Boekprintere Scheldt, Morning, Antwerp, 29 May 1570

"Turn away," Sofie says, stepping stiffly to her standing closet. The morning sun suffuses the dormer room with a thin light.

"I'll leave so you can dress."

"No, don't. But turn away." He tries to look only at the walls and through the dormer window.

"I am not looking," Jonas says rubbing his shoulders, tight from the cramped position he held while Sofie slept. He focuses on a tern circling over the river.

Sofie cries out as she struggles to undo the laces to her kirtle. He turns and then averts his eyes.

"Please help me, Jonas," she says, in resignation. "But look away, too."

Jonas gingerly assists her with her garments. He is angered anew to see the bruises on her body, fingernail gouges on her thighs, reddened and purple welts on her torso and breasts.

"Jesu," he utters sadly. Sofie snatches the bedcover to hide her nakedness.

"You should go home to your father's house, have care for your—your... what he did to you," he says.

"No," she snaps. "It would be worse. Here, only you know. My father would throw me out. It is only soreness, now. I will heal. Maria said I will heal and it will only take time, a little time."

"But Master Du Brul will wonder why your face betrays pain. Janine will ask."

"It was the fall, I am certain, climbing over the fence," Sofie insists. He shakes his head in confusion. "The fall," she repeats. "You dared me to climb over the fence." She stares at him like he is a dolt.

"Ah," agrees Jonas, feeling dense. "The fall. I told you it was dangerous," He says, trying on the lie.

"No, it was your fault because you dared me to climb over."

"Oh. Yes. It was stupid of me."

"I'm all right now," she says, pushing him toward the door. Jonas hears an attempt to suppress a tear. "Where are you today, the colorists? The printing hall?"

"I don't know. I will ask Master de Diest. Will I see you below, then, later?"

"You had better, or I'll start climbing something again to find you."

Smiling at her wit, Jonas moves in to touch her on the tip of her nose, but she recoils. He is poised between pity and rejection but realizes he cannot begin to know the trauma she endured. He touches his breast, a gesture of atonement, picks up his sack of gravers and leaves. He follows the corridor toward the boys' dormer rooms.

Ahead, Ritsaert Mesman steps into the hallway holding a weighty chamber pot. Jonas finds himself between the enormous boy with his pot and the staircase where Ritsaert is headed to empty two days' worth of human waste.

"Jesu," he curses under his breath and turns away to let him pass.

"You look like the cat that ate the canary," Ritsaert says as he feigns dumping his load on Jonas, and sloshes past.

"From the smell of your mess, you must have eaten the whole flock and the birdcage, too," Jonas rejoins.

In his room, he lays the engraving tools across his bed. He inspects the burin he used to kill the Spaniard and is relieved to find no sign of blood. He changes into his other pair of breeches and fresh hose. He rather likes Booten's leather jerkin and wears it downstairs to find Gilles Coppens de Diest for his assignment that day. While on the second floor, he pokes his head into the limners' studio. Nicholaus is at his worktable, the only one there.

"Where were you for Brabo's Fest?" Nicholaus asks. "Oh. You look like you didn't get much sleep. I knocked on your door before I came down. Busy night, Jonas?" His smirk is off-putting.

"What does that matter to you?" Jonas snaps.

"Nothing, of course. I was too smart for my own good, as Master Grober is fond of saying. So. Are you here today to help us?"

"I'm not sure. I need to ask Master de Diest."

"Ah, before I forget, the print master's son, Mark Anthony, stopped by." Nicholaus arches an eyebrow. Jonas notes the redhead's gesture of suspicion.

"Perhaps I'll see you later," Jonas says. He steps back into the hallway, dismisses Bockel's quizzical look, and knocks at Mark Anthony's chamber.

"Good." Mark Anthony Coppens lowers his voice. "Shut the door." His brow is pinched as though he were deciding whether or not to speak. Finally, he does. "Jonas—if I gave you something to read, do you think you could illustrate it?"

"I think so, yes," Jonas replies immediately.

"Even if it urges taking up arms against Philip and the Duke of Alva?"

Jonas blinks, under the weightiness of his question. "Ah. I would like to make up my mind about that after I read the text."

"Why is that?" Mark Anthony asks, testily.

"If I am to put myself in danger, I would like to have a good reason."

"How old are you?"

"Nearly seventeen."

"You speak like a boy much older. Sit down. Tell me what you think."

Mark Anthony passes Jonas a hand-written diatribe. He scans the first line silently. *Our taxes buy the best chains for our masters to enslave us.* His eyes widen at the seditious tirade, the possession of which would be grounds for immediate imprisonment, or worse. But he carries on, stirred by the passionate prose.

> *The Duke of Alva has pinioned the provincial estates to levy a tax of the hundredth penny on all property. These grinding taxes pay the soldiery that every day clutters our streets and roads and interferes with our affairs. These mercenaries prop up the Spanish king in the Netherlands, enforce the hated Inquisition, and render us subservient to Philip's despotic rule.*

Jonas fights being swept up by the rhetoric and the urge to shout, "Yes!"

> *All hope for tolerating religious belief other than the dictates of Rome, is dashed by the iron rule of the Spanish occupiers.*
>
> *Refuse to pay the blood tax that keeps us in chains.*

"This is so dangerous," he whispers. "You write very stirring words, Mark Anthony. Why do you need an illustration when this writing is so clear?"

"We are fortunate," Mark Anthony says, "to have so many able to read. But also many who cannot. One picture can inform them with more meaning than the most passionate words." He pauses. "Will you do it?"

Jonas has already seen an image in his mind's eye to complement the incendiary text. But he continues to fight the urge to immediately say, "Yes, yes, yes." Brother Thomas' voice speaks in Jonas' head. "When you commit, commit with all your heart, but be sure." Nothing could satisfy him more than to take up the fight against the occupiers after what that rapist had done to Sofie. But it is concern for Sofie's that holds him back from agreeing. *What if he were found out? He would not be able to fulfill his promise to her, to keep her safe. Taken away, punished for sedition? Even linked to the murder in the woods and killed?*

Mark Anthony takes off his spectacles, rubs the lenses against the sleeve of his linen shirt. "Jonas, I promise—I would never let anyone know who engraved such a plate. You would have complete anonymity in this. But I believe—I know—you already have a picture in your mind to illustrate this call to act."

Jonas' face gives him away. He cannot hide the tiniest smile creasing his lips.

"I'm right. I can see that you have an idea. I only ask you to make a drawing and then engrave it. This is very important to the burghers, not only of Antwerp, the Brabant and Flanders, but also the provinces to the north. And they will never know that it is you who made the image."

He imagines using the gravers Ortels has given him. He throws caution to the wind and nods.

"I can tell you also that there is a small stipend for your work," Mark Anthony adds, shaking Jonas' hand.

"I will give you a sketch later this afternoon, if I am allowed the time," he says. "Octavo sheet?"

"Yes. The back leaf of a four-page pamphlet." Mark Anthony pens a note and hands it to Jonas. "Take this to my father."

While he walks down the stairs to find the proprietor of Boekprintere Scheldt, Jonas is designing an image in his head. By the time he reaches the ground floor he decides that the primary figure will be a blacksmith forging links in a chain that stretches to a point of infinity. The chain binds the people of the Netherlands in leg and neck irons marching like slaves, while other citizens drop their levied taxes in a coin box and walk into an area to be fitted with a part of the chain. Spanish cavalry in full armor watch in triumph. He has thought in symbols, much as Frans Hogenberg and Abraham Ortels had in executing the title page, decorations, and cartouches of the book of maps.

Jonas finds Gilles Coppens de Diest to learn where he is assigned that day and gives Mark Anthony's message to the master printer, who taps the note and nods appraisingly at Jonas. "I'm told my son has a special project for you. Take the rest of today to give him what he wants."

The newly commissioned illustrator can barely keep from smiling. At his worktable, he cuts a folio sheet into eight leaves. He makes three sketches before he is satisfied. When Sofie limps into the engravers' alcove, Jonas looks up and beams. His face, crinkled with joy is infectious, and she returns the smile. Then she leans in, inches from his smile, and whispers, "I think I love you." His spirits soar ever higher.

She sees his drawing and narrows her eyes to take in the graphic detail.

"What's all this?" she asks. He can hear the tinge of fear.

Voice lowered, he says, "To illustrate a pamphlet that Mark Anthony Coppens has written."

"But that—that looks dangerous." Sofie whispers back. "What are you doing?"

"Shhhh. I have to show these to him. I think this one is best." His drawing shows the blacksmith at the center of the sheet forging chain links. The road continues past the anvil and tongs, and newly chained people join a file of walkers who disappear in the distance on the left side of the sheet under the eyes of Spanish cavalry above the road. Her look betrays her fear.

"Don't worry. Mark Anthony assures that my name will be protected."

Sofie sees Ritsaert Mesman waddling toward them. She snatches the two rejected drawings and holds them flat against her kirtle so they are not visible.

"Hah, love letters?" Ritsaert asks through a spray of spittle. "And your face! Does he beat you, already?"

"This is none of your business," she snaps, touching her blemished cheek.

As the rebuffed apprentice recedes into the main printing hall, Jonas chuckles. Before he can speak, however, she hisses at him. "Do you not see how you must be more careful? Dangers are everywhere, especially Ritsaert and Joop. They would denounce you in the blink of a gnat's eye."

He nods soberly.

"I have only just found you," a tremolo of fear sounds in her voice. "You must not be carted off to prison for illustrating Willem van Oranje's revolt."

"I will take pains to stay safe. I promise," he tries to reassure her, but the hard look never leaves Sofie's face, despite his cocksure grin.

"I love you even when you scowl like a fishwife," he whispers, taking the two sheets of rejected images from her grasp. He taps her on her nose with his forefinger and strides to the stairs that lead to the second floor.

"I don't like it when you do that," she snaps.

Jonas hears the sharpness in her complaint, but he dismisses it with a shrug.

CHAPTER 34

Krümmel Munitions Factory, Germany, Summer 1943

In late July, Michael and the others hear bombers overhead for the first time. They learn from Rudi that British and American planes have firebombed Hamburg, 35 kilometers away. While nervous concern tugs at Michael's insides, the news brings a smile to Pim's lips. Thereafter, the Allied bombers becomes a nerve-wracking drone that reignites Michael's memories of his mother, killed in the Rotterdam *blitzkrieg*. He thinks of how those bombers might sound to Ilsa, alone with Willi, while her husband has to bunk in the Krümmel dormitory most nights.

After their shift, moments before the dormitory lights are doused, Michael voices his concern. "We're in the worst place possible if we receive a direct hit."

His brother puts his hands on Michael's shoulders. "Michael, be brave. You must walk through your fears and be brave."

Michael nods, but has no faith that he can do such a thing if the factory became a bombardier's target.

In September 1943, the work at the Krümmel plants increases exponentially. Michael is surprised when he sees that the German guards have begun abusing the Italian laborers. Subtle at first, but then more and more evident, they are looking for any excuse to malign the Italians. He seeks out Rudi to discover what is going on.

"Cowards. That fucking *Makkaroni*, Mussolini," Rudi complains.

"What. What?" Pim asks, with sudden interest.

"Last month, the *Makkaronifressers* surrender. Now we alone have to supply our troops who fight the Allies in Italy. They've cut down my days with my family." He glowers at two Italians sullenly working under the gaze of one of the guards.

As production steps up, Michael and Pim notice that the previously rigorous quality-control checks are becoming more slipshod. One afternoon, Pim furtively twists his wrench only a quarter turn on fuzes instead of the required half-turn.

"Pim, that's not to spec," Michael whispers, fearing the spot checkers.

Pim glares at him and says nothing. He also does not correct the mistake before the high explosive projectile is passed on to the next worker on the production line, a Belgian, who adds the detonating charge to the base.

Michael watches, aghast, as Pim over-tightens the wrench, crushing a few threads. He wonders what Pim's changes would do to the finished ammunition. On some shells, Michael also sees his brother add a dollop of heavy grease to promote fouling after the completed rounds are loaded into their steel shipping containers.

That night, bundled in his straw mattress against the cold and damp, through fearful eyes, he watches Rudi go into the latrine. Nearby, the two Italians and a Greek are still awake but they only speak and understood their own languages. He forces himself to ask Pim in a whisper, "Why do you not follow specs on every one?"

His older brother holds his gaze in the dim light. "Do you want a straightforward answer, Micaha? Or can you figure that one out on your own?"

Michael, now three inches taller than his older brother, feels stupid. He absorbs the rebuke the way younger brothers do, feigning annoyance but letting in a self-loathing that he is not as bright as his elder sibling.

"You will get us killed!" Michael shoots back in a panicky hiss.

Through the murky light of the dormitory, he sees his brother smile.

"Or I could help shorten this war so we can go back home."

Michael perspires with fear and helplessness. What Pim says next shakes Michael even more. "Little brother, I see you losing hope."

"I'm not," Michael snaps. "Not—which is why I don't like you doing idiotic stuff like..." Michael mouths the word, "sabotage."

"The stink you guys make in that latrine," Rudi jibes as he comes back into the dormitory holding his nose. "When we win this goddamned war, all of you will be in your own barracks and latrines so none of us will have to smell your shit."

Michael shrinks into the shadows. This banter and fear for the course his brother has set make his bowels clutch. Predictably, his brother needles the German.

"So hurry up and win the war, Rudi," Pim drawls in exaggerated Dutch imitation of Rudi's Low German. "So we don't have to hear you complain every day like your shit doesn't stink."

Michael rolls out of his bunk and hastens to the latrine, as Pim, like a dog gnawing on a bone, continues his assault loudly.

"By the way, Rudi, why are your bombers dropping bombs so close to us?"

"They're not our bombers. They're the goddamned British and Americans."

Michael finds a privy in the foul smelling latrine as the lights are extinguished. He hears Pim's closing rejoinder.

"Oh. So win the war. So they stop trying to kill us."

"Hey, Holland cheese, time to shut it," Rudi shoots back, ceding the darkened field to Pim.

Hugging himself on the cold toilet, Michael stifles an impulse to cry. His mind races with an avalanche of incoherent thought. *Pim doesn't understand me. He never did, never will. Oh, Mother. I feel crazy most of the time. I go to sleep thinking you will awaken me from this awful dream. Goddamned factory. The Ukrainian prisoners—like living skeletons. If Pim's sabotage is discovered, we can blame it on them. Only yesterday when the Ivan with the hand-truck slips and those rounds make a racket on the concrete, I think, "How can it be made to look like they are the ones who damage the fuzes Pim is trying to make into duds?" I want to get out of this place. I want this war to be done so I can go home. I don't sleep. Mama, I dream of you holding me when I hurt myself on the ice. You wiped my tears and hugged me and made me feel warm.*

A tear dribbles from his eye.

Dead. I feel like I died with you in Rotterdam. My best friend here is the cripple. He's not so quick with his words like Pim, but that's maybe why I like him. And he shares his bread with us. Oh, Mama, I miss you so.

Michael rocks in his own arms. Finally, he pulls himself together and picks his way back to his bunk in the inky darkness. He sleeps fitfully under the thin blanket and returns again and again to the imagined time of how soothing his mother's arms felt when he fell on the ice the winter he was six years old.

The next day Michael waits until the overseers have passed his station to try over-tightening his own wrench. He pushes the spanner, but backs off immediately as he feels the threads seize. The "wrongness" of damaging the intricately engineered fuze stops him. *I can't do it.*

In a curious way, he also feels he would be betraying the wounded private whom he has befriended. Most of all, he wants someone, *anyone*, the Germans, the Allies, to win the war quickly so the awful bombings would stop and he could go back to work for Philips in Eindhoven.

CHAPTER 35

Palo Alto, 9:30 p.m., April 12ᵗʰ 2016

The late night call from Maurice Bregmann infuriates Patricia. Her annoyance is evident as Owen follows her into the bedroom. She brusquely stuffs her class notes in her briefcase, quickly disrobes and disappears into the bathroom. Owen hates late night arguments. These are the ones that fester because they rarely reach resolution. He looks around their bedroom. They had made a joint decision to leave the walls bare, to make this room a place of refuge from his print business, from her classroom, painted in pastel warm colors, from peach to pale violet, depending on the hour of the day and the lighting in the room. This night, the unresolved argument in the living room renders this room's bare walls cold and inhospitable. He slowly removes his clothes and listens to sounds of running water, electric toothbrush, and water glass clinking on the tiled sink. It signals that Patricia is very far away. When she comes out of the bathroom in her nightgown, she barely acknowledges him. She picks up her book and slips under the covers, a dull frown on her face. Owen, still in his underwear begins walking to the bathroom.

"Maybe, if we had had kids—" Patricia murmurs, but stops abruptly. Owen cocks his head. "Go on," he urges. She isn't looking at him, but is lost in some other time. She is shaking her head. "Chlamydia," she utters. "That… that Canadian kid on Ayers Rock. Chlamydia."

Owen forces himself to say nothing. Years ago, before they were married she had talked about an idyllic affair when she was barely twenty on an Outward Bound adventure to Australia. They had done a quick recounting of the "meaningful" moments of love they had had before they knew each other. The Ayers Rock sunsets—or were they sunrises—with the boy that Patricia is recalling was one of those indelible events. *And here, more than two decades later, Patricia calls up the past, saying they were childless because of complications due to chlamydia?*

"Maybe we'd have a whole different way with each other." Patricia's voice is far away, drained of its usual presence. Owen's heart sinks as she goes on.

"We've been together over twenty years, and now is about the time when we would have become empty-nesters if we'd become parents."

Owen draws on a robe and sits in the easy chair near the dresser. Maybe, they could come to a resolution tonight. "*What* about the way *we have* with each other, Patricia?"

Her voice continues to sound dull, but she regards him with fierceness. "You are so tough to talk to when your head is all wrapped up in a deal. You could have told that Berkeley professor to call you during business hours!" Owen feels his jaw tighten. "You know what I mean. There's a tension. I always seem to disappear when you are all wrapped up." Owen tries to stay calm. He has heard words like this before—he "*always* disappears." He wants to blurt out, "That's crazy, I'm always here for you." But he keeps his mouth shut and tries to listen.

"You never really hear me," she continues, intensity creeping into her tone, putting Owen on high alert. The glimmer of the little boy holding the horseshoe looking out from distrustful eyes flashes in his mind. He tries to push the hurt from what she has said to a place where he can stay separate from her growing anger. "It's just like how I grew up," she goes on. "Not being heard, never really. My mother, high-strung, and my father so protective of her—I just got lost along the way. And here it's happening again." Patricia is fighting tears. "Like it has over the years."

Owen has stopped breathing regularly and he feels stiffness in his hands. When Patricia uses words like "again and again" and "always" or "never" he feels unjustly accused. But if he responds angrily, they will be at loggerheads for weeks. *She's trying to tell me something. Listen and get out of the way.*

Patricia warms to her fears, like a razor stropping to a keen edge. "I get so involved in my work and you're bound up in yours and we're like ships in the night crisscrossing each other. Before you know it, our lives will be done and we won't have known real intimacy, something beyond our honeymoon period. That's not intimacy. If we keep trying to get back to that—I just don't know.... Like we missed the boat."

Owen feels he is being dragged under, but this time it is his life together with Patricia going down. Patricia is rolling now. "It's all boat imagery, isn't it? Because I think I'm drowning in a hopeless cause. You won't hear me."

"About what, Patricia. Not hear you about what? Tell me, please," Owen says despite a rising numbness, hoping she would get concrete.

"You are always in such a self-protective mode." *Always, again.* "You say stuff to try and make me happy but you don't hear me." This grinding away at how Owen perceives what she has to say starts a white noise in his ears. His face flushes, and his jaws press together to the point of aching.

"I keep saying it louder and you seem to hear me even less. It's like I'm not there. You rarely ask for anything from me. Am I so fragile to you?"

"Yes," Owen says, quaking within. He envisions a complete collapse, a free-fall that knots his stomach. "You go to tears so quickly. Your nightmares, your mother—I hear you and I try to shake you awake. Then you slough them off instead of telling me. You rarely share those terrors with me." He barely masks his exasperation. Patricia kneads the paperback.

"Because I can't trust you to hang in there with me." Her face quivers with fury. She presses her forehead with tight fingers. Owen's eyes are wide. "When you do hang in, your trust—it drops off as soon as you are in the hunt for some goddamned client—for some object for their collection."

He feels gut-punched at her charge. *And there is that blasted horseshoe kid again, unjustly perceived. Furious.* But Owen lets in another thought. *Was that so? Have I betrayed her trust? Become inattentive because my business means more to me?*

"Oh, Owen, I don't mean to disparage your work. That's what it may sound like. But what I mean is, I disappear when you go into that focus for a client. Just foghorns in a dark ocean."

Owen's voice deepens in anger. "Patricia, please. That's drama. It's not true. I am here for you, but you lock yourself away like your mother told you to." Patricia's eyes flash, but Owen continues. "You have more armor, more ways of locking me out than I know how to find my way in."

"You give up!" She counters. "You wouldn't do that if you had a client who wanted you to go the extra mile."

Owen cuffs the chair arm loudly with his fist and his voice pitches higher. "That's completely untrue." Both sounds scare him. His desperation hides in his words. "Patricia, you can't mean that. If you do, I've acted horribly.

And I don't believe I have. I love you so much. I can't begin to tell you how much I love you."

"But you don't hear me," Patricia snaps, again. Owen rises, furious.

Patricia persists, the soft-covered novel twisted in her hands. "This is not about love. My parents loved me, but did they hear me?. They discounted me—like I couldn't possibly know how dreadful the world really was. They had an awful time, and they made sure I would be protected—everything proscribed for me." Owen loses track of her point, and he becomes bound up his hurt. The little boy with the toy horseshoe backs away in fear and loathing.

Patricia rolls on, her voice more shrill. "I could never have my own opinion because it would get me into trouble. If I really ever wanted something I was dissuaded. 'Oh you don't want to stand out.' 'That's too, garish.' 'What would some complete stranger say?' 'No sweetheart, that's not right for you.'"

"I don't do that. I know I don't," Owen tries to sound reasonable.

"You never bother to hear me deeply enough to know." Patricia's voice sounds strangled.

Never. Again. Owen takes a deep breath. His face reddens, and he fears cataclysms that he knows nothing about. "I promise," he says slowly. "I promise that I will hear you." Patricia is shaking her head. "You don't believe me."

Patricia's voice takes on a weary tone. "I don't think you really understand. Maybe you do in your head—why we can't clean up the messes, finish stuff, instead of going to our separate rooms, our diversions. I've got classes to prepare for. You've got some goddamned recalcitrant client, or some dealer who is being an asshole. It's always something and we let each other slide." The emotional moment he had with the old man in Walnut Creek that afternoon surfaces.

"A few hours ago, I made the awful—unforgivable mistake of telling this guy that he could call you. I did that because I was so absolutely grateful that your mother survived back in Holland so you could eventually be born and come into my life." His voice breaks, unexpectedly. But he presses on. "What I'm trying to say is that you are so important to me that I do stupid things that confirm how absolutely devoted I am to you." Owen struggles to get the words past the lump in his throat. "I want to hear you. I wish I could open up every pore to receive all messages good or bad that you have for me." Owen is weeping now. Patricia holds her head. His tears seem only to deepen her depression.

The phone on her bedside table rings. It rings four times and the answering machine comes on in the kitchen. Owen and Patricia hear: "Patricia, this is Sherry McNeil. I'm sorry to call so late, but my kid has come down with something and I need to beg off teacher's aide duty for tomorrow's field trip." Patricia picks up the phone, and steps into her responsible teacher role."Hi, Sherry. I completely understand, let's see how we can…"

Owen exhales loudly and goes into the bathroom. A moment later, he opens the door with such vehemence that Patricia snaps her head up in fear. "You might have said you'd call her back," he glares, acid dripping from his words. Her sharp look says that she would not cut short her conversation with Sherry McNeil.

CHAPTER 36

Boekprintere Scheldt Apprentice Quarters, Evening, 29 May 1570

After Sofie's evening meal, she retires to her room, uneasy with Jonas' slapdash dismissal of her concerns. Her annoyance has been building for hours. She endures Janine's simpering about how unfair Master Du Brul has been that day.

"Thin!" Janine whines. "He calls fourteen sheets I made by myself 'too thin.'" She mimics Du Brul's booming voice. "'Janine, these do not pass. Too thin for the press. The type will shred this paper.'"

"You be careful not to get on his bad side," Sofie warns, wincing from pain, as she swings her legs onto the bed.

"He doesn't even listen to me," Janine natters.

Sofie pounds her pillow and tries to get comfortable. "You know nothing of people not listening to you. Stop your prattle."

Janine pouts in silence. Sofie's thoughts fly to the attack—the tobacco stench, the calloused hand gagging her until Jonas stops him. She relives the smothering hand over her mouth and fumes inwardly. *He pins me on the ground like some insect and shuts down my cries.* She hears again the sound of her silent shriek in her head. Her face contorts. *I hate being silent! I won't be silent, ever again!* In a leap of consciousness, Sofie ruminates on Jonas treating her like a child. *And now Jonas does not take me seriously!*

She springs from her bed in a fury, oblivious to her aches, and leaves Janine open-mouthed, slams the door behind her. She hobble-runs through the corridor. She raps on Jonas' door and flings it open.

Jonas jumps up in confusion. "What's the matter?"

For a moment she is disoriented then sees his work in the glow of a single candle on his table. "Look," she whispers in a white heat, points at his illustration of a sword snapping chain links. "So easy for someone to burst in and catch you making drawings that could get you killed. Jonas, you must listen to me."

"Sofie! Please, do not be so fearful."

"Not fearful? For Jesus' sake, don't put yourself in such danger." Her voice rises. "I couldn't bear it if you were taken away for such—such…what is this—pictures of insurrection? People are tortured, burned for less. We barely escaped with our lives on the Mechelen Road, and you enlist in a rebellion like this?"

"Sofie, lower your voice," he pleads. "Joop or Ritsaert—"

Her words jet out like the hiss of steam escaping a kettle. "I won't be silenced again. What's the difference between that beast who tore me open and you, if you clamp a hand over my mouth? I must speak and you must hear me!"

"I beg you, Sofie," he pleads. "Speak softly. I promise I will listen. I will hear you. But you must hear and understand me, too. If I am unable to fight even in my small way, against the Iron Duke and the Inquisition, then you silence me, too. I cannot live in fear always. If I hide from the truth, I am a coward. I may be fearful, but I'm not a coward." He speaks resolutely. She realizes, sadly, as he makes his case, that he is fully committed to his beliefs.

She takes a deep breath and tries once more, in measured tones. "Don't you see how you put us both in danger? You must work in secret or you will be found out. And, even in secret, look!" She points at the illustration Jonas has been sketching, then steps over to the unbarred door, opens and shuts it.

"What if Joop or Ritsaert sees these drawings? Spies are everywhere, ready to betray. Joop, especially, aches for a way to get back at you.

"I must take care. You make that very clear. And of course, you are right."

He takes the chair he had sat on and presses it at an angle against the doorknob. He pulls and the door stays closed.

"I did not take pains enough to sketch in safety. Tomorrow I will ask Mark Anthony if I can work in his chamber."

Her face crinkles in a pained and sour look. Jonas gently cups Sofie's face.

"I let my great wish to be useful in these events overtake my sense of safety. Willem van Oranje—"

"No, no, no, Jonas! Please do not even speak about his cause." She takes his hands and clutches them.

"Sofie, the House of Oranje—Prince Willem's rebellion is the only hope. I am not a reckless boy. I took no joy in killing that brute. I had to throw him off your back any way I could. I want to throw the Spaniards off *our* backs. And my weapons are my gravers and my drawing tools." He grasps the collar of his yellow leather jerkin. "This vest was Willem Booten's—He's run off from the monastery to join Willem of Oranje's armies. I don't have his foolhardiness, or willingness to die. But I believe the Duke of Alva and his garrisons must be driven from our lands, and I know how I can help even if it is only a small way." He reaches out to her. "I don't want you to be always angry with me because I did not abandon what I must do."

She pulls her hands back. "Then you must promise me that you will be *so* careful—as careful as you are when you finish Master Hogenberg's copper plates. Tell me you will take care not to be caught illustrating pamphlets for Mark Anthony. If you want to be his best friend, you must be mine first, and honor our bond."

"Yes." Jonas puts out his hand. His eyes beg her to take it. Sofie fights back her tears. She is not convinced. But she extends her hand so that it folds into his. She tugs, and he tugs harder. She finds herself enfolded and pressed in his hug. But she feels far from playful.

Jonas sees her continued unease. "I do want you to feel safe," he says in full sincerity. She exhales and allows herself to lean into him. For the moment, this is her entirely safe existence enfolded by the boy she has feelings for. It is not the outcome she expected when she stormed into his room, but something deep within has shifted. She is warmed—even buoyed by Jonas' resolve. She feels he is someone she can push against.

"Would you like me to walk you back to your room?"

She shakes her head "no."

"Good. There is no rush then. But I want to do one thing. I want to draw you. May I?"

"Like this? Beaten and bruised?"

"No, no marks on you, only your beauty; it radiates like sunshine for me. Let me try, please."

"Very well, then. Draw me like you would like to see me."

Jonas lights two more candles. He leads her to recline on his narrow bed. In the flicker of light, he picks up a board and a sheet of paper and sits at the foot of the bed. He takes up his graphite stick. She releases her self-consciousness as she watches him sketch her.

He speaks as he draws. His voice undoes her knitted brow. "You are like one of the classical women Master Ortels drew and Master Hogenberg engraved for the title page. You are like the woman who is America, the Northern New World. But instead of holding the severed head of an explorer, you hold my heart."

She flushes and cranes her neck to peer at the drawing as it takes shape. She watches his pencil fly over the paper, seeming to revel in her black ringlets, capturing her eyes in a way that catches both her wonder and amazement at the boy who is drawing her face and form. He shakes his head, rubbing out and trying again to get the folds to look like the draped fabric of her chemise.

She shivers, and he looks up from his drawing.

"Are you chilled?"

"A little."

"You will have to pose for me again."

"Can I stay here with you tonight?"

Jonas is unsure how to respond. He stammers, "Do—do you—?"

"Just to hold me, that's all. I am too—too—" At a loss for further words, she concludes. "Too angry with Janine."

Jonas removes his shoes, blows out the candles, and again becomes a mold for her, each fully clothed. They pull the blanket up. The singed tallow tickles their noses. Starlight through the dormer window plays on the knuckles of his right hand. As their breathing synchronizes, she contemplates a lifetime of allowing this young man to be a bolster for her.

CHAPTER 37

Walnut Creek, Late Night, April 12th 2016

His eyes stinging with exhaustion, Michael Dijkstra stretches his stiffening body at the dinner table. The memory of his one attempt to damage a piece of ammunition makes him snort. "Coward!"

He looks at the wall clock approaching 10:00 p.m. The sound of a car driving down his street and the muted hum of trucks passing on the elevated freeway remind him of his surroundings. He looks again at his father's scrawl on his memory pages. He has barely read past the text reminding him that his father had tried to comfort him when he learned of his mother's death. His eyes travel back to his father's query. *Who will comfort me?*

Michael pours another finger of cognac into his empty glass. The Hennessy bottle had been a Christmas gift from his team at Philips 20 years ago. He lingers on the pleasing memory of his fellow engineers showing their appreciation for his leadership. The team had won a company quality award for the year and the engineers were honored by name at the annual Christmas party. He sips again and sees a card taped to the bottle. "Merry Christmas, the team appreciates being so well LED." He flips the card to sees the Christmas message in Dutch, *Vrolijk Kerstfeest*. The Korean engineer, the kid named Kim…something…had asked him to spell out the greeting in Dutch two weeks earlier.

Emaciated Michael is fixated on the globules of fat floating in the stew made special for Christmas, 1943. The workers are treated to an extra ration of some kind of meat in a stew of a few root vegetables. The sour taste is somehow sweetened that meal. "*Vrolijk Kerstfeest en een Gelukkig Nieuwjaar!*" Pim says, raising his spoon and tapping Michael's tin cup.

Michael wonders how his brother can still be so lighthearted. He smiles to hear the holiday greeting and replies, "*Fijne feestdagen.*"

"And Happy Holidays to you, too," Rudi says, laying a grease-stained brown paper bag on the table. The bag is tied at the neck with red yarn. "From Willi and Ilsa." He has brought the brothers bones of a chicken his wife cooked. The brothers both nod their thanks. Michael and Pim suck on the marrow for several days following.

Michael is anxious in a way he hasn't been before, impatient with his brother's mocking of Rudi. Alone with Pim on the Day of Epiphany, he says, "Stop picking on Müller." He watches Pim widen his eyes at what passes for "brazen" in his younger brother. Might no rejoinder from the older brother mean he was being taken seriously? Was he finally getting respect from Pim, who picks at his teeth with the sharp tip of a broken chicken bone.

Michael turns nineteen in the brutally cold January of 1944. He finds himself anticipating a letter from their father, which would have birthday greetings. Months have passed with no letter. Late April, however, Rudi drops an envelope on Pim's iron cot, addressed to Pim only. Michael sees that it is postmarked Amsterdam, not Eindhoven. They are eating a meal of thin rutabaga soup. Rudi has given the brothers two chunks of black bread from his family's ration to augment their scant portions. Pim absently thanks the ex-Wehrmacht soldier. The postmark confuses him. Their father's letters always arrive postmarked from their home city. Michael sees the look on Pim's face turn from curiosity to a grim mask.

"Gerdi says Papa is dead." Pim reports tonelessly. "She does not say how."

Michael puts his hands over his ears.

"It happened last month." Pim says.

Michael snatches the letter and reads the first lines. When mail had come before, Gerdi's letters always included their father's bland accounts of daily life, a veneer of optimism over the reality of food and fuel shortages, and a general desperation under the heel of the NSB and the occupying Germans. Michael always dismissed Gerdi's notes as sappy love letters.

But Pim reads them as code for the Allies' progress. Just before ending her notes, Gerdi's declares her love for Pim, "*Ik hou van je.*" She precedes her message of love with cryptic three-word statements—"*olie zwengel omváren*"—oil pumphandle circumnavigate—"*omlopen zee oker*"—go around the yellow ocean. The meaning, however, is clear to Pim—OZO—*Oranje zal overwinnen.* "The house van Oranje shall triumph." The monarchy of the Netherlands, Queen Wilhelmina's government-in-exile in Canada since the German invasion, is descended from the House van Oranje.

"Look what she says here." Pim would beam. "'I love you like tulips pushing up through rich black earth. I can't wait to go to the cinema when the war is over.'"

Michael is unimpressed. "Michael," Pim insists, "She's using these phrases to say that the Allies are having success in Africa, and that the Americans are starting to win. You know how Gerdi and I love the American pictures."

With the surrender of Mussolini's Italy, her message had been "a plate of spaghetti was dropped and what a mess, but Georg has a mop." *Georg* is her code for the U.S. or Washington. "Uncle Tommy has been an angel and he sends his love"— meant that the British were conducting bombing runs.

But no joy is evident in Pim's tone that November day. Holding the sheets of paper in numb fingers, Michael reads Gerdi's words in this letter. *"I have sad news—your father was found dead. I am so sad for you and Michael. He was a wonderful man and I know this will come as a shock, but we believe he died bravely."*

The words ring like a deafening bell in Michael's ears. *A heart attack? A stroke? What could kill so suddenly? How could she know he 'died bravely'?*

"The fool," Michael growls aloud. He is still furious with his father for letting his mother travel to Rotterdam the week it was bombed. He knows it is illogical, but he cannot contain his seething. When the NSB demanded the two sons for a labor battalion and his father was powerless to stop the forced deportation, his anger intensified. He thinks that the complex scheme for money to be paid to the elder Dijkstra is the reason their father's defense against their deportation had been so feeble. Pim scoffs at Michael's suspicions. And now, Gerdi writes, that their father is dead.

Michael slips into a deep depression in the months following. He reaches his nadir when, unexpectedly, Rudi Müller is called back into the shooting war in the summer of 1944. He is ordered to active duty after the Allied invasion of Normandy.

"They can't do that to—to—*you*," Michael says, indignant. He almost said *me.*

Rudi smiles in irony and tries to stand tall despite his mangled foot.

"But you did your duty. You can barely…." Michael stops himself. He presses his palm into Rudi's shoulder blade, in part to hold himself up if his knees gave way. "It's not fair," Michael trails off.

Rudi puts out his hand and Michael squeezes harder than he intends, fighting tears. Michael turns away, but sees Pim take Rudi's hand, press his other on top of it, "Be safe, Rudi."

The little private shrugs and turns back to Michael. "You want to know something long-face? I wish you were more like your brother." The stinging words follow. "If I live, I'm going to remember him. He has spirit. He's the one who makes me laugh."

Rudi limps out of the factory, shoulders dropped, knowing his days in the relative safety of the underground fortifications have come to an end.

Despite the barbed goodbye, Michael has no idea how badly he will miss the German, forced to work like them, except that the same sadness that had descended with his mother's death now envelops him.

He loses interest in the brilliance of the design of the munitions as one day bleeds into the next. The other workers, the ghostlike Ukrainians, the despairing Italians with sunken eyes deepen his desolate mood. He nods at the shuffling Slav who loads his cart with his completed projectiles to transfer up the line. He is met with glassy-eyed indifference.

A few weeks later one of the Belgians begins eating the caked amatol propellant a few stations up the line from Michael. He falls over in a stupor and the plant guards pull him off the factory floor. Michael never sees him again.

One day, Michael raises his eyes from his work and looks across the table at another Belgian, or was he a Dane? In his mind he is in conversation with the silent worker hunched over the brass components. *We never look each other in the eye. "We are humiliated by our bad luck." Some might say this is good luck. "At least we get better food than the deportees from the Eastern countries. The OSTs—"* Then he only hears his inner voice. *Best if no one sees me. Never be caught watching someone else. Must not stand out. We survive because people do not see us.*

The months that follow Rudi's departure in August 1944 are especially grim as frequent bombing missions by the Allies fly across northern Germany. That fall, the targets are Bremen, Munster, Duisburg, and, repeatedly, Hamburg, just 35 kilometers up the Elbe River. Michael know from conversations with Rudi that the Düneberg munitions site is only six kilometers away. As the war enters 1945, and Michael turns twenty, the overhead rumble of bombers and the tremors of exploding bombs in the district intensify at all hours. Air raid sirens pitch Michael's anxiety higher, though the bombings are still some distances away.

"It won't be long now, Micaha," Pim whispers. "Soon, you will be back at Philips, or wherever you want to be." Michael regards his brother, once a stocky, muscled footballer, good enough for the company's football team, Philips Sport Vereniging, as they contended in their division in 1938 and 1939. These days, the PSV Eindhoven reserve striker is not in his red home uniform or his blue visiting colors, but the gray twill work clothes that drape sack-like on his shrinking form. Michael judges Pim is now barely 50 kilos, muscles flaccid over his nutrition-famished frame. Michael is more wraithlike, in his leaner, longer body.

"Look at me," Pim demands, so his brother regards his eyes. "This will all be over soon. We must hang like bats until we can take wing."

CHAPTER 38

Antwerp, 20 June 1570

Three weeks after Jonas illustrates the first pamphlet commissioned by Mark Anthony Coppens decrying the hundredth penny tax, 200 copies circulate across the Brabant and Flemish provinces. Mark Anthony gives him a proof copy and a broad smile. Jonas hides the incendiary pamphlet with other sketches he has begun to work on deep in a drawer in his room.

In the privacy of his tiny quarters, with a chair wedged against the door, he examines his image of the blacksmith and casts a critical eye on his engraving skill. He has not yet mastered the use of negative space, the un-inked portions of the engraved plate, to create the illusion of folds, for example, in the fabric of the blacksmith's billowing sleeves.

He wishes he had someone like Master Hogenberg to instruct him, or even scoff at his efforts. If the opportunity presented itself, Frans Hogenberg would eventually point out how Jonas might improve his technique. In the meantime, he calculates how he might etch the copper differently to create the illusion of foreground on the flat sheet of paper.

Boekprintere Scheldt, with its full complement of printers and apprentices, hums in preparation for the second edition of the *Theatrum*. Ortels and de Diest have ordered a press run of 275 copies this time.

"Savor this, young Jonas," Pieter Du Brul, the master papermaker holds forth. "It is not every boy who is apprenticed to as successful an enterprise as this."

Du Brul sloshes a deckle into his vat, rolls the white liquid as though he were making crepes. His practiced eye watches the thin, whitened water run back into the tub, leaving the screen coated with a double-folio-sized layer of fibers that will dry into a leaf of paper to become a page in the book. He passes the deckle to Janine, who shuffles in a surly daze to stack the frame flat on a drying table against the rear wall of the building.

Jonas smiles at the infectious grin of the cheerful master, whose hands are cracked and reddened from the ravages of his trade. Smile lines etch Du Brul's fifty-year-old face. Jonas knows that the man to whom he was mistakenly apprenticed when he first arrived has a fondness for him. He has seen the sly smile beneath the man's bushy eyebrows as Jonas' puppy-love attraction to Sofie Van Alsing has blossomed over the past half-year. In the absence of Sofie's father, Du Brul is *in loco parentis* for her. Jonas senses that Du Brul feels responsible for her wellbeing and, thus far, approves the budding match.

"The *Theatrum Orbis* sells well," Du Brul says. "But know that early success makes you hungry and expectant of more—and life is not always so generous."

The master papermaker claps Jonas on his back and returns to his vats and deckles. Jonas walks through the corridor toward the main printing hall. He hears the clack of typesetters resetting moveable type into the formes, the thump of the inker's fists tamping down daubers of sheep's fleece wrapped in rag to apply black ink onto the type forme, the grunt of a muscle-bound printer turning the massive wheel of his press to roll the heavy cylinder over the paper rack. He hears the crackle of newly inked proof sheets pulled off the platens, the clap of trenchers laden with wetted double folio sheets slamming the tabletop. These sights and sounds with the omnipresent odor of ink are what Jonas sees, hears, and smells every day now. Like the first edition, this is printed in Latin, but even more books are scheduled for full coloring. He takes a moment to breathe in the hubbub of a successful enterprise before he returns to his workbench to do maintenance on the collection of copper plates.

The same fifty-three map plates will be used, but typographical errors on the text pages need correction, bits of text some clarification, and more biographical notes added to the *Catalogus Auctorum*. In the weeks following publication of the first run, Jonas learns that Ortels and a few of the scholars and librarians who purchased the initial offering have found several errors in the printed text. Gilles Coppens de Diest decides to make his son, Mark Anthony, the primary proofreader for Boekprintere Scheldt, to assure that typographical errors are minimized.

The newly appointed chief proofreader, looking grim behind his glasses, steps into the engraving alcove. Jonas is using lavender oil to clear dried residue ink from one of the plates that he had incompletely cleaned after the first edition press run. Jonas looks up and sees immediately that something is amiss.

"Upstairs, please?" Mark Anthony asks in a tone that removes the question. His gaze falls two inches above Jonas' eyes.

Jonas follows his rigid back to the second floor. "Good fortune on your advancement, Mark Anthony," he says, trying to lighten the moment.

"Close the door," Mark Anthony says in a constricted voice. He clears his throat; his eyes dart everywhere but at Jonas. Despite the warm day, a cold dread creeps up Jonas' spine.

"I'll come straight to it. You must leave Boekprintere Scheldt, immediately."

"What?"

"The Iron Duke's soldiery may come any day, arrest you, and shut down the entire shop."

"I don't understand—" An icicle of dread catches in his throat. He sees panic in the eyes behind Mark Anthony's spectacles.

"They know the pamphlet was printed here. They know the engraver of the blacksmith image works here. If we don't want the building to be razed to the ground, we have to tell them who engraved the plate."

"But you told me—" Jonas begins.

"Jonas! You don't understand—a run of nearly three hundred new books is scheduled—"

Jonas' mind burns through the words his supposed friend says and Mark Anthony stops speaking. Instead of issuing an explanation, he concludes, "I am sorry. These words cannot console you, of course, but you can no longer work here."

"You would betray me?" Jonas asks in a low register that smolders. He sees that every word is thunder in Mark Anthony's ears.

"Master Ortels wants to see you." Mark Anthony's tone softens. "He understands you did this at our request. He can help."

Jonas feels misled and lied to. Hadn't Mark Anthony assured his anonymity in this very room, only three weeks ago?

"I will find my own way." He turns on his heel, intent on collecting his things from his room and does not think beyond the pain of the moment.

"Jonas," Mark Anthony calls earnestly. "You *must* see Master Ortels. He has a way out. You must understand that this was not foreseen, but we were warned in time to help you."

Jonas only half listens as Sofie's words ring in his ears, "Spies everywhere, ready to betray," and then he thinks of her deepest fears.

"Very well, I will see him, but I want to know who alerted—Was it Joop Baldus or Ritsaert?"

Mark Anthony lowers his voice. "One of the limners."

What! Had he made a slip of the tongue to Nicholaus, the apprentice he had befriended? "Bockel?"

Mark Anthony nods. "Bockel's elder brother assists the district Procurator. He is a tool of the Inquisition. After the limners' warden, Master Grober, objected to his apprenticeship, Bockel's brother sent a note to my father— advising that Master Ortels' undertaking would not be unnecessarily scrutinized if certain objections were waived. We thought it had to do with Nicholaus' advancing in the Guild, but now we know that he is here expressly to spy."

Jonas groans. "If that is so, Mark Anthony, I may have said something to Nicholaus that I should have kept to myself. Oh, that snake."

"Yes, we must tread carefully. Ever so carefully in these times." Mark Anthony puts an arm on his shoulder. "What did you talk about?"

"I spoke my heart about religious toleration. Then he asked, 'Like Willem of the House of Oranje and the rebellious nobles?' And I didn't say no."

"Anything else?" Mark Anthony asks. "Anything about the pamphlet?"

Jonas searches his memory. "No. In fact this was before you and I spoke. And it was only that one time, but he wore a kind of crooked smile. Oh, the snake!"

"Please. Hasten to Master Ortels' house. He works there today, and he can help you. Do not bother with your things from your room. I will have them carted to Master Ortels' for you."

"First, I must see—" He stops as Mark Anthony raises his hand.

"Master Du Brul will take Sofie Van Alsing to the Ortels house on Kloosterstraat. You can discuss plans when you get there."

Pulse racing, Jonas feels a mixture of upset, that everyone knows so much about his private affairs, and gratitude that Mark Anthony, de Diest, Ortels, and even Master Du Brul were organizing to take care of his future, whatever it might be.

Finally, he says, "Thank you, Mark Anthony."

"Jonas," Mark Anthony captures him with penetrating eyes, an expression so different from how their meeting had begun. "These are early days in a struggle that will not be easy to win. We must survive to fight stronger another day. Until we see each other again, then," Mark Anthony takes Jonas' hand and pumps it robustly. Jonas presses back and turns to go.

"Wait! You will be going abroad. I have something for you."

He turns, confused. Mark Anthony selects a narrow book at the case behind his desk. "These phrases may help you when you debark in England. And this to carry it," the chief-proofreader adds, passing him an empty brown leather pouch.

"England?" he asks.

"Master Ortels may want you to deliver copies of the *Theatrum* to friends."

Fighting bewilderment, Jonas works the buckles and affixes the carrying case at his right hip. He adds the book of English phrases and forces a smile, to be so well outfitted.

Mark Anthony presses his shoulder and nudges him to the door. Instead of going directly downstairs, Jonas walks to the archway that leads to the limners' studio. He sees Bockel bent over the map he tints.

Andreas Grober catches Jonas' eye and subtly nods, his brow knotted. Jonas smiles thinly and backs away without being seen by Bockel. He hastens down the stairs and exits through the alley to remain unseen from the second-floor windows of the limners' studio. He follows the path he had taken with Ortels to his residence in Kloosterstraat. Body memories of a child trying to hide from his sister overtake him, and then panic, as roiling waters tear him helpless from his mother's grasp.

CHAPTER 39

Ortels House, Kloosterstraat, Antwerp, Noon, 20 June 1570

"English. You will have to learn English."

Jonas frowns and has the briefest realization that his face could be read too easily. He adopts a neutral look as he sits dwarfed in an overlarge, richly upholstered settee. Dazed by the rapidity of events, he listens attentively to Anna Ortels, the master cartographer's sister. Dressed in gray velvet, she commands her second-floor sitting room as mistress of the house that Abraham also calls home.

"But our sister will help," she adds. "You will enjoy Elizabeth's family." She nods to Abraham, also seated across from Jonas.

"You will find the English tolerant of us," Ortels assures. "Our sister Elizabeth will be very welcoming," he says, rising and offering his hand to his sister. "Anna, he will need to leave soon. Let us retire so he can have some time with Miss Van Alsing." Jonas rises and nods gratefully, but the pain of his departure turns his smile into a wan mask.

Anna shakes Jonas' hand formally and whispers, "You will be safe in London." She takes her leave through the carved double doors, as Master Du Brul enters guiding Sofie whose lips tremble. Sofie curtseys before Anna and comes to an abrupt stop when she sees Jonas.

Ortels nods to the master papermaker. "Ah, you have a few minutes with the young miss. Come, Master Du Brul, let me show you some papers they manufacture in Paris and Lisbon." Ortels ushers Du Brul to the doorway.

"England?" Sofie's eyes glisten. Her fingers dance uncontrollably, dabbing at moist eyelids.

"Not so far, but a world away for me, too. 'For safety's sake', Master Ortels says." He sees how difficult it is for Sofie. He kisses her salt tears and soothes her cheeks with fingers still smelling of oil from his last task as an engraver's apprentice.

"Will you write to me?" Sofie asks.

"Yes, but you must be sure to keep my letters and all things you hold dear away from Nicholaus Bockel. He is the rat in the barley crib. Joop Baldus, Ritsaert Mermen and that lot may be stupid curs, but sweet-talking Nicholaus is the spy."

Sofie frowns. "I thought he was your friend. Oh, Jonas…." she trails off. A deep furrow creases her brow.

"Sofie?"

"I thought he was your friend," she says again. She chews her lip.

"Have you spoken to Nicholaus about me? Or us?"

"He asked about where we walked on the day you…that brute in the wood…."

Fear grips Jonas. Sofie's face turns pale.

"And what did you say to him?"

"The Mechelen Road…." she says, trying to grasp the details from her memory. "Only that we saw a commotion of soldiers asking if anyone knew anything about the murder of one of them."

"And that is all?" Jonas asks, hoping that was an end to it.

"A farmer saw the guilty ones. Nicholaus says they found the killers, a brother and sister from Mechelen, dispossessed in a heresy trial the week before. Spanish soldiers put them on the street, so they took revenge. That's what Nicholaus said. He said the farmer pointed them out."

"Oh!" Jonas grunts in anguish. "He—he accused some innocent...? Oh Jesu!" Jonas folds himself into a chair in grief for the guiltless strangers.

"It disturbs me, too, Jonas, but—" She kisses him on his forehead, shaking her head helplessly.

He needs to change the tone of their parting, which has become unbearable. "So, you see how Nicholaus knows all," he says. "Dangerous to confide in him."

"Yes."

"If he asks, tell him I have gone to learn bird engraving in Bruges. Master Hogenberg says an artist, a skillful teacher, a Master Gheeraerts, resides there."

Sofie's lips quiver.

"Shh," Jonas urges, rising and holding her by her shoulders.

"I don't want to lose you." Sofie's words waver, and she bites her lip to not weep.

Through the lump in his throat, Jonas utters, "I am being *saved* for you, not lost." He tries to lighten his voice. "Would you like me to send letters to you at your father's house or to Master Du Brul?"

"Master Du Brul," she replies immediately.

They both look up as Abraham Ortels and Du Brul step through the doors.

"I hope you have said your goodbyes," Ortels says.

Sofie curtseys. "Yes, thank...you..., sir." Through her tears, she draws a deep breath that climbs a ladder of short, shuddering steps.

Jonas clears his throat, tight with sadness. "We are grateful, Master Ortels."

"Time will pass quickly, and you will be very busy, I think. Your skills will be vastly elevated when you return." Ortels nods to Sofie's warden. "Master Du Brul?"

The master papermaker touches Sofie's shoulder. She puts on a brave face, and locks Jonas in long vise-like embrace. She steps back, presses her lips together, and precedes Du Brul out the French doors.

"She's a brave girl, Jonas."

"Yes, sir," Jonas manages. He tamps down his terror of losing her forever.

"Six months to a year, that's all. Make ready. Antonius will take you to the quay. You will be boarding a small merchantman, the *Tortelduif*, mastered by Captain Vandeven—he is expecting you. These are letters to my sister, Elizabeth, and her husband, Jacobus Cole. They live in Lyme Street at the Sign of the Cock. When you arrive at London, take the parcels I have had packed to their house. I sent them letters last week. We have known of this burrower Bockel since Andreas Grober ferreted him out. Oh, yes. Here is also a letter of introduction to Marcus Gheeraerts. Our sister Elizabeth will help you meet him."

Jonas puts the collection of letters in his newly acquired leather pouch.

"Sir," Jonas remembers in alarm. "I told Sofie to tell Nicholaus I would be apprenticing with Master Gheeraerts." His face betrays the fear that he has drawn a map for the spy to follow.

"And where is Master Gheeraerts?" Ortels asks, mischievously.

"In Bruges."

"Ah. Old news. Two years now, since Marcus and his son made a similar trip to the one you take today. The Duke of Alva was close on his heels, and now Marcus is resident in London, not Bruges. But if the spy with the limners' thinks you fled to Bruges, why disabuse him? Oh, yes. Captain Vandeven says you may assist the crew on this trip across. He is short of able bodies."

Ortels proffers his hand and Jonas tries to gauge and match the firmness of the grip. Then the cartographer passes him three gold escudos. Before Jonas can protest, the smiling Ortels, able to project a major increase in his finances due to the spreading fame of his book of maps, raises a hand to silence his protégé.

"This will get you established. We shall stay in communication. Give your letters to Elizabeth. And you will hear from me through her. In the meanwhile, tell everyone you meet about our *Theatre of the World*." Ortels puts a hand on Jonas' shoulder and pushes him in the direction of the double doors.

Jonas follows Ortels' servant, Antonius, to the side entrance. He breathes deeply and tries to quiet his mind as it swims with a rush of too many thoughts and emotions. He tries to stifle his sorrow at being separated from Sofie. Outside, a dapple-faced horse is hitched to a two-wheeled trap. The back of the rig is piled high with cases. Jonas calms himself when he sees that his personal items and treasured bag of burins is packed in a leather bag that he can sling over his shoulder. These items are his only material connection to Antwerp as he embarks on an utterly foreign experience. He strains to remain calm: he will board a merchantman for an ocean trip to a country he has only heard of and seen in a book of maps he has had a small part in helping to produce. But the closer the trap draws him to the river, the more Jonas' calmness gives way to terror. England lies across the North Sea; he fears the power of the ocean, a maker of orphans.

CHAPTER 40

Walnut Creek, near Midnight, April 12ᵗʰ 2016

Like bats ready to take wing. Michael paraphrases his brother and takes a sip of the diminishing Hennessy at the dining room table. He shudders recalling the day of the bombing. The cognac burns going down.

7 April 1945. A drone of bombers overhead in daylight shatters his belief that their facility would not be a target. *It can't be happening here!*

Michael's heart hammers in his throat. Sirens screech, the guards scramble, and workers throw themselves under their workbenches or press against the whitewashed walls. Seemingly endless tonnage of Allied bombs falls on the Krümmel and nearby Düneberg plants. Their building shakes from the concussion as a dynamite magazine explodes a hundred fifty meters from their factory. The light fixtures swing crazily from their chains. Idiotically, Michael tries to control a rack of 20-pound projectiles from toppling from his tabletop.

"Where is Pim?" he asks fearfully. He looks about but cannot see his brother anywhere near his workstation. The overhead girders groan with stress; the insane waggle of the swinging lamps throws bizarre shadows across the factory interior.

"To the shelters!" The guards shout, herding most of the workers to corridors behind the six-foot reinforced concrete blast walls. Through the high windows, Michael can see black smoke of exploding chemicals, nitroglycerine, and gunpowder. Inexplicably, Michael is confused by the familiar scent of his mother's nail polish wafting through the factory, only to realize it is burning cordite. He scans frantically for Pim, who clangs steel cabinet doors in the maintenance section. He watches in disbelief as his brother pulls a tinsnips from a closet, then searches the factory for Michael who still grasps the stack of uncharged projectiles at his workbench.

Pim is scrambling toward him when a blast at the other end of the factory floor sends him spilling onto the concrete aisle. Some of the piping that routes liquid dynamite into their factory runs along the concrete girders. One of the pipes bursts, and the propellant oozes onto the floor.

"Pim," Michael calls, finally letting the stack of projectiles clatter in the aisle. "Let's get to the shelter."

"No," Pim says. "Brother bat, we fly out of this cave."

Michael can barely take in what his brother means. Pim pushes him toward one of the wide double doors that now hangs off its hinges. They wedge themselves through the narrow opening to the dust and smoke outside. Numb with terror, Michael trusts that his elder brother knows what he is doing. Outside, the air is alive with incendiary odors. Raging fires throw up three huge plumes of smoke from exploding chemicals and collapsing hillocks of turf-covered concrete. At Pim's shove and point, they run between a nitro glycol factory and an acid storage tank toward an objective that Pim has in mind. A deafening cluster of bombs explodes and bodies of Ukrainian workers are tossed like matchsticks in their path from an unfortified shed.

Michael's knees buckle and he clutches at the ground wishing for a hole to sink into. When he opens his eyes again he sees his brother running toward one of the workers who shrieks and struggles on the ground ahead. A fireball of burning gases bears down on the man. Pim races and pulls the man by his collar. He drags the fallen OST worker out of the path of the flames and then manages to lift him onto his back by wrapping his arms over his shoulders. When the oily smoke clears Michael sees that both legs of the man have been blown off at the knees. He is leaving a trail of blood in the dusty track and Pim's pants legs.

The screams of mangled workers caught in the blast are a nightmare in daylight. A river of smoking nitric acid pours from the damaged tank. Michael springs up and races, closing to a distance of ten meters behind his brother.

He shouts, "It's no use. He'll bleed to death!"

But Pim pays no heed. Only when the Ukrainian's groans stop, does Pim check the breathing of the man he has been carrying. Michael sees disgust contort his brother's face. He has seen that look of angry hopelessness once before when he had missed kicking a goal after stealing the ball from a defender. He leaves the corpse on the ground near a factory entrance, and scours the terrain for his next move. Moments later, several bombs miss their targets but set off ear-splitting roars as part of the forest throws up tree limbs and shattered trunks like confetti. Michael's ears ring, blotting out all other sound. He is beyond terror now, convinced he is deaf. Finally, Michael comes abreast of his brother. Pim taps Michael on the shoulder and points. They scramble to the barbed wire where Pim cuts the steel strands with his stolen tinsnips. Together, Pim and Michael make for the trees away from the last bombing pattern. Pim winks at Michael who is breathless with fear. "Are you all right?" Pim asks wordlessly with his head cocked and a thumb up.

Michael nods, fighting for breath as waves of dry, acrid heat from the exploding factories suck the oxygen. Then an enormous gunpowder magazine explosion from a dynamite factory at the Düneberg plant rocks the earth beneath their feet and sends a tremendous fireball into the sky. Michael and Pim see smoke and a geyser of earth and concrete flying up and raining back down in the distance. Collapsed on the ground where he has fallen, Pim twitches his head in the direction of one of the fire-watch bunkers, a narrow silo made of foot wide concrete. These have been abandoned in the heavy bombardment. The brothers run toward the nearest one, but when another explosion sends them both flying headlong into the turf, Pim's head hits the trunk of a sapling and he crumples in a senseless heap.

Michael stops thinking and functions on instinct. They are still much too close to the Allied targets. He gets to his feet and pulls his dazed brother upright. Together, they stumble farther into the forest, but cramping of their malnourished bodies slows their progress. The pains in Michael's thighs are excruciating. Michael and Pim pitch forward five or six meters then collapse on the forest duff, breathing heavily, desperate for water. The concussion of close secondary explosions behind them convinces Michael that they need to press on. He brings Pim to his feet again, throws his brother's arm over his shoulder and together they stagger deeper into the woods. Through the gauzy sense of hearing beginning to return, Michael discerns the rush of a stream that feeds the Elbe River. He guides Pim down an embankment toward the water. The nearly comical "bloop-bloop-bloop" sound of water running peacefully through a narrow channel makes Michael exultant. They revive their cramping bodies by drinking their fill. Pim soaks one of his sleeves in the stream to hold against his bruised forehead.

"Are you alright, Pim?" Michael asks, desperation in his question.

"Yes, Micaha," Pim replies, and forces a smile. Michael knows that his brother recognizes that he is his best hope. "We'll rest here for awhile," Pim says. The sureness gives heart to Michael and he happily cedes the leadership role to him. They spend a half hour in the well-hidden gully.

Another explosion from the Krümmel compound reminds them of their perilous position. His brother taps Michael's arm and they make steady progress along the stream, stopping only to ease further bouts of leg cramps. Following close, Michael sees the dead Ukrainian's blood on the back of his brother's pant leg. He watches the stain slapped by the underbrush, bits of green sticking to the gore. He thinks of Pim's relentless drive to save the living. Finally, they collapse a distance from the complex of high explosive plants, some now smoking ruins. Evening is falling and soon the only light is from the fires that periodically ignite flammable propellants. Their greatest fear now is running into armed guards.

Pim nudges Michael's arm. They creep to where a concrete bunker had been built to protect the factories. Camouflaged by a roof with sod plantings and netting entwined with ivy vines, the blockhouse appears to be abandoned. Pim pulls out the tinsnips to use as a weapon, enters; moments later Michael see his hand wave him in. They see, in glimmers of light through the gun ports, that the bunker had been a machine gun nest. Nothing remains, except some empty ammunition cases, a half-eaten box of salted crackers, and the odor of feces and stale urine in one corner.

After two weeks of diminishing rations, the stale crackers are like a full course meal. They sit, leaning against the wall farthest from the fouled corner.

"Some people have no manners," Pim says wearily.

Michael says nothing. He prays inwardly that this will all turn out.

"Michael, you saved my life, back there," says Pim.

"Yes," Michael fills an awkward silence. Then he adds, "I only want you safe so we both get out of here."

"Thank you, Michael. I do want to get home."

"You have a plan?"

"Only this. Let's find our way home. We'll start tomorrow morning."

They wait out the nighttime hours in the bunker. The smells of burning munitions from the two gunpowder plants filter through the forest and linger in their temporary shelter. They press themselves against the walls and try to sleep.

CHAPTER 41

Scheldt River Docks, Antwerp, 20 June 1570

When Antonius and Jonas arrive quayside, thick-bearded Captain Vandeven puts Jonas to work unloading the trap. The captain regards the unforeseen passenger with a scowl of disdain. Jonas tries to mask his nervousness, but his hands feel like he has thumbs for every finger. He has never been on a seagoing vessel. Jonas gingerly carries six crates holding copies of the *Theatrum* below decks of the merchantman with the name *Tortelduif* carved into its nameplate. More experienced hands than his lash down everything while he fumbles with the lines and protocols easily handled by men and boys familiar with sailing ships. He is embarrassed, as though he should know how to handle himself, even though logic dictates otherwise. But logic had flown from his experience three hours earlier when Mark Anthony Coppens told him he must flee. Jonas thinks for a moment of Brother Thomas, the one living man who knows him best. Would he ever see his mentor again?

"Release the forward bollard!" Vandeven hollers, pulling Jonas from his reverie. Jonas sees a deckhand toss the slack jute rope connecting the fore of the craft to the quay. He holds his breath as the separation between boat and land begins. Nudged by the helmsman and the current, the sixty-five-foot *Tortelduif* slowly dips and rises into the breeze. "Release the aft line," comes the call. A hand on the quay tosses the heavy line onto the deck and hops aboard after pushing off a piling. The masts groan with canvas sails billowing as they catch the breeze. The merchantman is guided into the deep channel by commands that are a new language to Jonas. "Staysails up," bellows the captain, and two sets of arms strain to raise more canvas and capture more wind. "You, there, boy, lend your back and help them sweat that line taut." Jonas looks confused. "Pick up the rope, greenhorn," a sailor translates, gruffly, kicking the end of the line toward him. Jonas grasps the tail of line and heaves with the other two deckhands to raise the wind-whipped canvas into a more efficient contour to catch the wind. The muscular first deckhand in their row ties off the sheet on a deck cleat and then winds the excess line into a neat coil.

They are in the middle of the river now, the boat nosing to the southwest. Jonas shifts his weight to keep his balance and sees that they are slowly passing the forbidding Steen, the massive turrets of the Antwerp fort with guns looming at ports high above their heads. The mass of stone is also the prison where, Jonas fears, two falsely accused burghers of Mechelen, charged with the murder of the rapist soldier, await their fate. Despite the brisk breeze about his ears that sparks a moment of exhilaration, Jonas sinks into a doldrums of despair and self-loathing. The prison's weathered limestone oppresses him as the boat passes slowly. He fights back tears for his having created the dark future for the innocent brother and sister.

He is wrenched from his sadness when the cry "Hard alee" issues from the captain and a boom swings within inches of his head, making him duck quickly. The merchantman catches the rush of wind and picks up speed toward the open seas off the west coast of the Lowlands.

The captain catches Jonas' attention. "Keep your eyes up, your head down, and your hands ready to grab onto something attached to the boat at every moment, young man."

He sees a longboat rowed from a Spanish galleon at anchor in the middle of the channel. Soldiers guard a group of Flemish nobles in black, seated on the center planks of the longboat. They are being hauled through a sally port into the stone prison. A venomous anger spreads through Jonas as he clutches the starboard rail of the merchantman. He peers aft of his boat that is headed for freedom, as the Spanish military tie up at the Steen to throw Lowlanders into captivity.

The Captain's voice shakes him from his fury. "Get below, now. Find the galley and help the cook prepare the evening meal."

Jonas looks up at the sails, pregnant with the afternoon wind; the whistling breeze flies between the masts and spars and slapping lines. He feels the exhilaration of a first-time sailor carried forward by the wind. He squints at the late afternoon sun appearing to the west above a bank of clouds and fog that they will pass under in the coming hours. Less than four hours has elapsed since he was called into Mark Anthony Coppens' chamber at Boekprintere Scheldt and his entire world had been turned upside down.

He learns from the cook that, by morning, they will be off the province of Zeeland and quayside in Vlissingen, the port of Middleburg, before setting across the North Sea to England. "The ale tastes like piss there. That's where you debark. But we pick up cargo in London and then on to Bremen, then back down to Amsterdam and Rotterdam, before we enter the Scheldt and tie back up in Antwerp."

Jonas is only beginning to gain his sea legs, shifting his weight to anticipate the rolling of the vessel across the tidal waters. Numbly, he cuts potatoes for the galley cook. Queasy, he knows he will not partake of the ship's meal. Below decks, he hears the water rushing by as the craft cuts downriver through the light swell. In dim light cast by a gimbaled lantern, he climbs into a hammock. The creak of the woven hemp, tied between two beams, plays a tune with the timbers that hold the fore mast aloft. The irregular lapping water splashes as the boat plows northwest toward the open seas. Jonas hears the abbreviated chatter of the two deckhands above him as the boat navigates toward the mouth of the river.

Eventually, he hears only his thoughts. *On the run from the Inquisition. Will I ever see Sofie again? As adrift as when the flood turned me into an orphan.* He salves his fears with thoughts of the adventure to come in England. He concocts images of the unknown master engraver helping him to improve his hand. His thoughts bring him back to that morning and Master Du Brul's bushy eyebrows twitching as he says, "Early success makes you hungry and expectant of more—and life is not always so generous." The weight of the day finally presses his body to sleep.

CHAPTER 42

Outskirts of Krümmel, East of the Elbe River, 8 April 1945

The whine of aircraft snaps Michael's eyes open in the predawn hour. The sounds come from the west to strike German targets east of the Elbe. His body aches from the unaccustomed stress of running for their lives. His right knee in particular feels swollen and stiff. Pim is already standing at the entrance of the bunker. Michael clambers to his feet and holds the wall unsteadily. He has no idea when he injured his knee. Then he thinks of the legless Ukrainian Pim tried to save and he shakes off the ache in his own limb.

"We need to cross the river and go west, Michael."

"How?"

Pim shrugs. "We cross that river when we get to it," he smiles.

Michael scowls, as usual, duped by his older brother.

"We head north toward Geesthacht; maybe we'll find a skiff." Pim says.

In the faint light of pre-dawn, Sunday, 8 April 1945, they set off, Pim in the lead. Smoke from the bombing continues to linger and provide some cover for them. As dawn is breaking in the east, as though pre-ordained, they see a rowboat, listing, but bobbing in the river tied to a stake on the bank. With hand signals only, Pim urges Michael to follow him. They creep into the boat without incident, but find no oars. Pim points at a dilapidated shed and together they make for it. The door has a hasp and lock, but the hinges are rusted and easily pried from their rusted screws. The oars are immediately apparent. Pim picks up a rusting crowbar and a long screwdriver before they leave the shed.

They find a rhythm and paddle the 300 meters across the placid Elbe to the farm country on the west side of the river. Pim pushes the empty boat out into the light current and they watch it float north toward Hamburg. They see a farmstead and, avoiding the farmhouse, they creep along a hedge to the barn. Across the river to the east, wisps of dark smoke continue to curl into the morning sky. They hear clucking at the back of the barn. That morning, they dine on raw eggs. Then they hide in the hayloft. They hear a farmwife chastising her hens for poor production.

Through the evening, they cross several fields and spend another set of daylight hours in a farm shed. Their nutrition comes from beets and carrots growing in rows pried up with their stolen tools, near the shed, and once again, eggs. They have not eaten so well in two years.

They hear artillery fire the next day. Under Pim's direction, with little talk, they move west only at night. After five days they see straggler units of Soviet-battered Wehrmacht hurrying west, hoping to surrender to the advancing Allied tank corps. Pim tells Michael, "We will be home soon." They raise their arms and turn themselves in to the British and Canadian troops overrunning the German positions west of the Elbe River. "Nederlanders—Dwangarbeiders!" They cry. "We are Dutch, under forced labor!" Germany surrenders on 8 May 1945. Then comes the interminable time in DP camps administered by the Allied military.

Michael looks at the clock in his Walnut Creek home and sees it is after twelve. He feels leaden. Defeated. He has buried those years beneath layers of such deep pain that he never dares to retrieve his memories. He can barely believe it has been seventy years to relive his time at the munitions plant. He thinks again of Rudi, and chokes back a sob. He wonders if the lame German had survived. Flashes of the ghastly bombing and escape make him swish the last of the cognac in the bottom of his glass and swallow it. He has drunk the bottle dry but he doesn't feel drunk, only heartsick. He groans involuntarily as he rises and shambles uncertainly into his bedroom. Michael closes his eyes to avoid thoughts of his confrontational day with the auction gallery manager on Friday. He stops before the chest of drawers and roots through his socks and underwear to a yellowing manila envelope. He withdraws several snapshots and looked closely at one that had been taken not long after repatriation. The print has turned a dull brown, but he can still see his brother and himself in the fall of 1945, and between them the girl, Gerdi Ten Broeck, a day or two before she and Pim were married. Both still have the gaunt look of young men who had survived starvation. Pim is smiling broadly. Gerdi is vivacious. His face looks haunted.

In the mirror above the chest of drawers, he sees himself rocking like seaweed. He tries focusing on the decrepit face that bobs back at him. His liver spots seem magnified, and the alcohol has flushed his face with beet-red blotches. He tries to open his eyes wide but is repelled by the bloodshot whites, and the accusing pupils dilating in the pale light. His white hair looks stringy. He could pass for a bum on Skid Row. He puffs a dismissive "Phuh!" at the specter in the mirror. Fumbling clumsily, Michael replaces the photograph, steadies himself, turns, and collapses onto his bed.

CHAPTER 43

Vlissingen Dock, Scheldt Estuary, Zeeland Province, Early Morning, 21 June 1570

A Christian, as God is my witness, the voice cries. *Eduardo Orellano*—another voice insists like a hissing bladder, a sack pipe drone of Death incarnate: *You are a liar. You are a Christ-killer who has never renounced your Jew ways. You shall die for your heresy. Take him to the pyre!*

Jonas wakens disoriented, clammy in the predawn dark. He peers through the murk; his eyes stretch wide open. After a moment he decides that the sounds of the screams of Eduardo Orellano are, actually, merely the scraping of cargo on the deck boards above. The wretched man in his dream had no escape from the Inquisition in Seville, whereas Jonas is under the protection of a now-wealthy master cartographer. He would shortly set foot in England, known to him as Britannia, described as Anglia, Scotia, and Hibernia on the verso of the sixth map in the *Theatrum Orbis Terrarum*. He spins out of his hammock and onto the deck.

He climbs the ladder to the hatch and sees that they have tied up at the Vlissingen dock near Middleburg to discharge cargo and pick up more. The crew clatters about him as they untie crates and carry them to a gangplank and off the vessel. He shakes his head to waken from his nightmarish sleep and steps onto the deck. The sea breeze off the open ocean is bracing, and he is fully awake now. By the glimmering rays of the sun in the east, he sees the rolling swales of Zeeland, barely above sea level. He can make out at water's edge, an ominous prison citadel similar to the Steen in Antwerp. Two English merchantman vessels also offload goods. Jonas joins the cook, helping to carry an enormous case down the steep gangplank to the dock on the high tide. In the distance rise the shadowy walls and gates of Middleburg.

"Say goodbye to the Holy Roman Empire, young man," says the deckhand. "We set sail for Queen Elizabeth's island at first light." Once they hit open ocean, Jonas tries to peruse the phrasebook Mark Anthony had gifted to him. But descriptions of how to order food quickly turn his stomach.

For two of the sickest two days of his young life, Jonas races from the windward side of the vessel to leeward to retch whatever remains in his stomach into the North Sea. He tries to find a horizon in the overcast skies everyone says is the antidote to his queasiness, but his stomach does not obey the oft-quoted advice. On the third day, as they sail into the calmer Thames estuary, Jonas can make out passersby at work in fields, cutting rushes for thatch, oxen drawing carts laden with produce, cows grazing on the bluffs overlooking the river, skiffs with men fishing, and strollers along the banks. The elevations are higher on this island than on the land two hundred and fifty miles to the east from which he has departed. The afternoon is overcast, but a steady breeze brings their craft steadily toward London. River traffic becomes dense with fishing boats hauling their day's catches to market and with all manner of vessels crisscrossing the Thames, their hulls laden with goods, people, and livestock.

He sees smoke billowing from chimneys and more and more densely populated streets on the north shore, their buildings made of half-timber framing and white-painted wattle and daub, red-brick, with roofs of thatch and slate. Looming ahead, west of the Tower of London, the London Bridge spans the river to connect the north shore City of London and Southwark. He has never seen the like, and he wonders why the many legs of the bridge do not wash away in a surging tide.

"We'll make for the Billingsgate docks," Captain Vandeven announces.

"Ah, that's good," says the cook. "That means we'll lay over one night in town. The wenches here give you no guff if you've got the fare. You can wet your sausage with the sweetest of doxies." The cook winks at Jonas. When he realizes what the cook means, he cannot control the blush lighting up his pale and drawn face like a strawberry. He feels very young in the company of these old salts, and, yet, they have no problem including him in their rough talk.

A flotilla of watercraft passes their slowing vessel, and English accents cry "Westward Ho," as they continue sailing and rowing toward the London Bridge.

Jonas grasps the phrasebook. He will need an elementary command of English at the least in order to hire someone to cart the copies of the books of maps with which Ortels had entrusted him to the home of Jacobus Cole in Lyme Street.

"Hoen," the Captain calls. "You see carters for hire over there. Pay them two shillings and not a copper more." Jonas receives the two coins from the captain.

"These two shillings are worth one guilder. Each of them is worth twelve pence. With twenty-four of these shillings you've got an English sovereign."

"Yes, sir," Jonas nods, hoping he can retain the quick monetary tutorial.

"Two shillings is more than a fair price to take you and your goods to the house in Lyme Street. Tell the Coels' that Captain and Mrs. Vandeven convey our best wishes. Off you go, then, and good fortune, young man."

The babble of the unfamiliar language ties a knot in Jonas' stomach. Rowdy stevedores manhandle cargo onto the docks. A middle-aged man dressed in fine breeches and a rich black tunic is giving a porter a tongue-lashing. Both the language and the reason for the lambasting are complete mysteries to Jonas. He looks up the lane, where pushcarts with fish heaped high roll up the grade and smoke-darkened stone, brick, and timber buildings rise more haphazardly than they do in Antwerp. The familiar breastplates and helmets of Spanish occupying forces are absent here. He sees several carters, leaning on their drays, eyeing him.

He crosses the quay and walks up to the least ferocious-looking of the drivers. He holds up one coin to the grizzled driver. "Lyme Straat. Zign of Cock."

"Lyme Street is all uphill, Flemmie," complains the leather-faced porter, speaking loudly in the expectation that Jonas does not understand him and showing three fingers. "Three shillings."

"One shilling, six-pence," Jonas says, surprised at how easily he understands the London dialect.

"Three shillings."

"Two," he counters, and backs away, casting his gaze on another carter.

"Two, then," the carter says quickly through damaged teeth. He leads his horse and two-wheeled dray to the stack of crated volumes of the *Theatrum Orbis* and the leather bag with all of Jonas' worldly goods. One of the wheels is more oval than round, and the effect is that of a stagger rather than a roll, as though it was an old boat riding the swells or a clubfoot drunk making his way from a tavern.

As the dray thumps up Bride Street, the carter says, "A *Fleming*, eh?"

Jonas smiles, hoping he is not expected to reply. The street name changes to Mary Hill, and he sees limestone blockhouses, stables, chandleries, drapers, a bakery, brewers, and other shops on either side of the hilly street. People are dressed less neatly in these streets than in Antwerp. He notices a quality of grayness to the light, and the denizens, like the carter with rotted teeth, look unkempt.

"You said the Sign of the Cock? Lots of Flemings—Strangers—come and go, on the run from the Spanish tyrant."

Jonas grunts, unsure what he is talking about. The horse-drawn dray crosses Thames Street, and the nag defecates balls of shit that bounce on the cobbles. Jonas holds his breath and inhales again only on Rodd Lane one block away. Alehouses and stables border the cobbled street, and the clattering becomes routine sound. Meanwhile, the odd experience of rising and dipping as the cart rolls up the grade makes him feel as queasy as he had been for those two and a half days riding the waves. The street is longer than any of the previous streets and, at the end of it, the driver urges his horse to the left, traveling one more block, this time along Fenchurch Street. At the intersection of Philpot, Fenchurch, Lombard, and Lyme streets, the carter heads northward. Alehouses and meeting rooms line both sides of the narrow street where Lyme and Fenchurch meet. Jonas sees traders in heated conversation on the street and in courtyards, reminding him of the Antwerp trading halls near the Scheldt River.

He spies the bright red, yellow, and white rooster on a sign suspended from the façade of his destination, a huge, comfortable-looking house of four floors. A jettied overhang on the fourth level extends over the street.

"We have arrived, young Dutchman," the carter says, holding his hand out.

Jonas drops the two coins into the man's palm and steps down from the cart. He goes round the back and begins off-loading the wooden crates. The carter carries two of the crates to the front gate and sets them on the cobbles. Jonas brings up the remaining four and adds them to the stack.

"Danks-you," Jonas says in unpracticed English.

"And good luck to you, Flemmie." The carter flashes a rueful smile, walks his horse in a half circle and climbs onto his cart for the journey back to Billingsgate. Jonas practices a smile before the massive oak door dominated by a large brass rooster that serves as a doorknocker.

CHAPTER 44

London. Sign of the Cock, Lyme Street, Late Afternoon, 23 June 1570

Jonas raps the brass knocker three times. After half a minute, a doughy-faced, buxom woman of forty, ginger hair pressed under a cap and bosoms jiggling above her bodice, opens the door. Her broad smile reveals a set of snaggleteeth.

"Been expectin' you. You're for the Missus Cole, ain't that right?"

Jonas barely understands anything except "Cole."

"Jacobus Cole, pliss," he says stiffly, trying to cover his nervousness.

"Wait 'ere." The stout woman walks with effort to the staircase and disappears onto the next landing. Jonas lugs the cases of books into the entry hall of the four-story house, each floor the domicile of a different well-to-do family. Dark-stained wainscoting lines the walls to eye level. Once-white clay wattle walls rise to the timbered ceiling and burnt tallow stains show behind the wooden wall sconces. A woven rush runner covers the wide-planked floor.

A handsome woman dressed in stylish blue silks flutters down the stairs, followed by four children including a boy and a girl near Jonas' age. The concierge's wife follows, huffing, and smiling her broad grin of disastrously aligned teeth. Jonas has a fleeting moment of wishing to sketch her mouth.

The woman in blue silks, whose eyes looked strikingly like her brother Abraham's, is grasping Jonas by his shoulders, beaming broadly and speaking in Dutch—her rosewater scent is dizzying.

"Elizabeth Coels—'Cole' here in England. And you are Jonas Hoen. *Welkomst.* Such a journey you must have had," she bubbles on. "Are you exhausted? We will have a bath ready for you in minutes. These are my children; introductions later, and you met Margery who let you in. You will meet everyone, except Jacob—'James,' he is called here; my husband is in Constantinople on business."

"Master Ortels said to bring you these." Jonas points to the crates. "The books of maps." He touches the two crates marked with an X. "The six books in these cases have been illuminated. The others he gives to you to color."

Mrs. Cole grasps Jonas' hands and he is shocked and embarrassed to see how ink-stained they still are, enfolded in her soft white fingers. But she pays the stains no mind. "Oh, young man, I cannot wait to see this work. He is so proud of the undertaking, ten years in the planning. And now it is completed with another edition being readied. He also says you are a very brave young man."

He blushes at her compliment and wonders why "brave." She continues to hold his hands in hers as she gives orders. "Children, upstairs! Hot water for Jonas' bath. Margery, please have your husband bring these cases to our apartments." She begins leading Jonas up the stairs, still grasping one hand. Her touch is endearing, and Jonas has to surrender to being led by her firm grip. "Tell me, how is Abraham? Is my brother looking well? He said he was feeling fatigued last month. Is he getting enough sleep? Anna? My sister?" Her questions tumble rapidly.

Jonas has a curious sensation of coming home, as when he saw the thatched roofs of the abbey, and felt the enveloping hug of Maria de Vries.

"He is well; especially now that the first printing is such a success. He looks rested and contented," Jonas reports as they climb the stairs to the third floor.

"I am so relieved," Elizabeth Cole says, finally releasing Jonas' hand with a squeeze as they push open the door to the residence. The house is arrayed with comfortable furnishings, rich tapestries in reds and blues from Flanders, and several paintings of the Dutch countryside. One might even have been by the same artist whose works hung in the Ortels anteroom in Kloosterstraat. He reads "Pieter Bruegel" on an image depicting one of the seven deadly sins. The narrow sideboard near the apartment door displays several brass candlesticks. A thick Turkish rug covers much of the dark-stained oak floors in the hallway. A green silk-covered settee and several matching velvet upholstered wall chairs are set against a chair rail. James Cole is a quite successful silk merchant. Jonas can scarcely take in his good fortune. He is overcome by weakness, exhaustion, and exhilaration. Having barely eaten for two days, even the effort of climbing stairs cramps his limbs.

"A hot bath and you will feel good," Elizabeth beams, ushering Jonas to a chamber where her children are pouring pots of boiling water into a bathtub.

"I have letters for you," Jonas says, remembering the three wax-sealed papers in his leather pouch. "This one is an introduction to Master Gheeraerts."

"Thank you, Jonas," she says, smiling and taking the letters. She taps the script penned by Ortels as though he were in the room and it was his cheek she was touching. "You are a guest in this house, and we welcome you. I can see you left Antwerp hurriedly, and so here are clothes provided by Mr. Cole's eldest son, Thomas, until you can furnish new ones for yourself." A pair of gray breeches, a white linen doublet, and a black tailored jerkin is laid out on a chair. Clean black hose hangs from the chair arms. "Quiet," Elizabeth Cole says as Jonas tries to protest the gift. "Your room is the third door on the left outside this door," she continues. "If you go right, at the end of the hall you will find the kitchen, and you can eat anything you want there." She takes a deep breath, and smiles. In a softer voice, she says, "Both Abraham and I have known what it is to need and find a safe harbor. Jonas, I am so happy you are safe." She resumes her formal tone as mistress of the house. "We will be serving at the six o'clock hour and we will have guests who are eager to meet you. Get in before the water gets cold. You can put your travel clothes in the wicker hamper. No one will disturb you. Oh, yes, there is a hard-bristled brush for the ink beneath your fingernails."

Mrs. Cole turns abruptly, flipping through the three letters, and leaves, her blue silk gown catching the afternoon light through the leaded, diamond-shaped windowpanes. Jonas turns around in the room and wonders if he would ever be able to capture in an engraving the light as it had bounced off her gown. He feels lightheaded. Within moments he soaks in the hot water of the bathtub, soaping and burnishing his fingertips with the brush. His body uncoils days of tension and he closes his eyes to luxuriate in the care he receives. He hasn't bathed in hot water since his time at the monastery. He lets his head slip under and allows himself to float weightless. Then he lathers his hair with the soap, rinses off and lets the warm water surround his whole body again. His mind wanders. Sofie's face floats by; she wears the brave and fearful look she had given him as she and Master Du Brul withdrew from the Ortels' drawing room. He resolves to write her as soon as he has his bearings.

When he opens his eyes, he is startled to see Margery, kettle steaming in her hand, standing at the foot of the tub.

"Fancy a bit of the hot?" Margery asks, her crooked incisors catching the light, enjoying the view of Jonas through the soapy water. He does not understand a word and forces a smile as he slips a hand across his midsection. "Thank-you, no…" he begins, but she pours a long lazy stream of the boiling water into the tub. "Oh, you will like this, my boy," she declares.

Scalding droplets of water shoot up from the bathwater and spatter his face and chest. She empties the last of the kettle and is gone as quickly as she had appeared, carrying off the wicker hamper with his soiled clothes. He immediately appreciates the addition of the hot water. His mind leaps to an image of Sofie in his arms and pressed against his chest; he is kissing her black ringlets.

CHAPTER 45

Walnut Creek, 1:00 a.m., April 13ᵗʰ 2016

Michael's cognac-fueled head lolls on the pillow. In the cinema of Michael's mind, his tumultuous homecoming in 1945 flickers like a faded print of a movie in which he has played a bit part.

Pim and Michael shift nervously in a canvas lean-to at the edge of the transit camp. After a month in the limbo of an abandoned Wehrmacht barracks near Duisburg, the brothers await their fate. Allied army officers, two American, a Canadian, and a British sit at tables commandeered from the bombed out town hall. Anti-Nazi Resistance fighters in civilian garb from France, Denmark, Poland, Belgium, and the Netherlands sit smoking on a pew dragged in from the town's destroyed church. Outside, a ragtag line of men and women stand in line with similar "displaced" status as Michael and Pim, awaiting questioning, hoping for permission to return home or, in some cases, as far away from their homeland as possible. Dust and odor of charred timbers hang in the air. Michael's right leg shudders nervously as they wait to learn if their papers will be stamped, assuring passage back home.

Pim is explaining to the American intelligence officer in broken English, "Here against our wills, forced to work, or our father would have his rations cut."

Michael interjects nervously, in Dutch. "Sir, they said they would confiscate his holdings." He is terrified that the impassive American will disbelieve them.

"Yes," the Dutch Resistance fighter corroborates in accented English. "These guys are from Eindhoven. The Fifth Nederlandsche Standaard headquartered there. They used those threats to fill the labor battalions, besides saying these kids would be conscripted into the German army to fight the Soviets if they didn't agree."

The lieutenant asks his Dutch Resistance aide, "You're sure? They sound German to me."

Michael understands enough to interrupt in a voice tinged with angry desperation. "Our mother is killed in Rotterdam by their Luftwaffe. Do you think we would work willingly?"

"Lieutenant," the Resistance man says, "These guys are clean."

The officer looks up again at the scruffily garbed pair, and then nods to the MP at the table. Michael hears the thump of the stamp from pad to paper and releases his breath as the officer inks his initials. The MP at the table passes the papers to Pim and Michael.

"Thank you," Michael says to the Resistance fighter, a rawboned man of thirty with deeply etched lines in his exhausted face. Pim addresses him too. "I need to send a letter to my fiancé, also in the underground, part of the Anonymous Company in Amsterdam."

The Resistance man smiles and taps his armband with the initials NV inscribed. "That's my unit. Sure, write your letter. I'll post it for you. Her name?"

"Gerdi Ten Broeck."

The Resistance man smiles even more broadly and shakes Pim's hand. "Aart De Jong, Arnhem. Tell her I say hello. And congratulations."

The American officer growls, "We don't have all day, gentlemen." But he is smiling, too.

Michael and Pim have passed their inspection. "Aart, can you please help me telephone Gerdi?" Pim asks, as they file out of the tent.

"I'll see what I can do," de Jong waves.

Three days later they leave the transit camp for their homeland. A week's growth of stubble roughens their faces. Their clothes are sweat-stained and threadbare, like many others they see on the train, on the roads and in the streets. Their railroad car carries them across the border into the Netherlands in mid-June, 1945, after three-and-a-half years of forced labor.

Michael's heart sinks as the train slows on the outskirts of Eindhoven at midday. Their city looks much like the war–ravaged towns they have passed through and much worse for the bombing. As they pull into the station, Pim says, "Gerdi will arrive at six o'clock. Let's wait, then go to the house."

Anxiety gnaws at Michael. "That's five hours. I want to see if we still have a ceiling above our heads."

"We can get some food and—" Pim begins, pressing his wish to see Gerdi before searching out their home on Keizergracht.

"No! Let's see if our house is even standing," Michael says with vehemence.

Pim raises a calming hand and nods. "Very well, Micaha. Maybe we could clean up," he says, putting an end to the dispute.

They detrain and are immediately silenced by the destruction. Bombs and artillery have leveled several venerable hotels and cafes across from the train station plaza. Michael trades grim looks with Pim and they begin on foot toward their street that borders the Keizergracht canal. Michael walks in numbed silence through the sunshine, but a hazy pallor hangs over their city. On the route they merely grunt when they see familiar, but burnt buildings, crumbled churches, homes destroyed by both the Germans and the Allies during Operation Market Garden. A man shouts, "Filthy collaborator!" Pim and Michael watch another man pulled from a house into the street. Angry neighbors and Resistance members are beating him. The violence moves up the street, vigilantes dragging him to some version of justice.

The brothers don't comment. Their homecoming mood has turned grim.

CHAPTER 46

Sign of the Cock, Lyme Street, London, Early Evening, 23 June 1570

After he dries and dresses in the unexpectedly well-fitting clothing of James Cole's son, Jonas tidies up and finds the room Elizabeth Cole has said he is to occupy. He can scarcely believe his good fortune. The bedroom is much bigger than the dormer he had occupied in Antwerp. It is furnished with a table, chair, chamber pot, washbasin and water pitcher on a wooden stand, wall mirror, fireplace, a writing table, a comfortably padded wing chair, a chest of drawers, and a walnut bedstead. His leather bag is slung across the chair.

The windows overlook vegetable gardens behind the houses. He sees an enclosure with a huge pink sow and counts ten piglets at her teats. The light through the windows is ample and refreshing. He even spies some of the Thames well west of London Bridge, where the river bends sharply south. To his right, he sees the long, low building he will discover is named

Pewterers' Hall. Smoke curls from the chimney pots of the manufactory fires.

He touches the wool and feather-filled mattress and is seduced to fall face up onto the bed. He lies there; arms and legs spread wide, the back of his head cradled by a down pillow. Sleep engulfs him until a knocking at his door wrenches him from his slumber.

"Everybody is here. Everybody is here," a child's piping voice cries at the door. Small knuckles rap an insistent tattoo on the oak panels of the door, and Jonas swings his legs over the side. "Dinner is waiting," the voice squeals excitedly. Jonas cannot tell if it is one of the young boys or the young girls making these announcements. "Mama says it's time!"

"I'm coming, I'm coming," Jonas calls. He hears the voice fading then and footsteps sounding down the hallway. "He's coming, he's coming...."

Jonas splashes water on his face and shakes himself awake. He stands before the mirror and damps down his hair. He finds his brush in the leather bag to neaten his appearance. Drawing a deep breath, he opens his bedroom door and walks to the right, where a babble of voices comes from the drawing room. He hears laughter, a mix of Dutch and English conversation, and the clink of pewter tankards. He enters to see a dozen or more laughing guests turn as one to see the new arrival.

"Here he is, everybody," Elizabeth Cole announces, now dressed in a rich orange silk brocaded gown. "The latest burr in the King of Spain's saddle."

Laughter greets her remark.

"Everybody, this is Jonas Hoen, recently of Antwerp."

He is shocked to hear applause and cheers from these complete strangers. He picks out a number of the younger people as children of James Cole. Guests, aged twenties to fifties, raise tankards and glass goblets to Jonas' health. A serving maid hands Jonas a tankard of Rhenish wine. He sips, and blinks as it burns his throat.

A middle-aged man, wearing a short spade beard, similar to Master Ortels', proffers his hand. "Young man, I am happy to meet you. I am Marcus Gheeraerts, and Abraham says I am to make a full-fledged engraver of you."

Jonas grasps his new teacher's hand and pumps it once. "I am so honored to meet you, Master Gheeraerts. Masters Hogenberg and Ortels sing your praises."

"Not off-key I hope," laughs Gheeraerts, clinking tankards. They drink a draught.

"Come meet my little one. Marcus!" the master engraver calls. A seven-year-old breaks off speaking with another little boy, and comes over shyly. "This is my son, Marcus. Marcus, this is Jonas. You will be seeing much of each other in the coming days."

The boy waves shyly, and Jonas returns the wave. The wine loosens him, and he smiles. Mrs. Cole, holding the hand of the boy young Marcus had been talking with, says, "Jonas, this is my little boy, James. "He is fascinated by the *Theatrum Orbis Terrarum.*"

She turns to her son. "Jonas helped Uncle Abraham make this big book." She points to one of the open limned books, which has captured the attention of several of the guests at one end of a long table at the center of the room.

"Maybe, one day, Jonas will describe how the maps were made that went into this beautiful book," Elizabeth says to her son.

"I will be happy to show each of you," Jonas says, addressing James and Marcus. He is delighted to be speaking in Dutch and being fully understood by the children of the expatriates of the Low Countries.

Young James begins speaking, and Jonas recognizes his little voice as the one that woke him from his nap. "Mama says you're a hero, a hero in the fight for freedom for the United Provinces. Did you kill many Spaniards?"

Jonas is taken aback. But he shocks himself by replying to James, "No. Only one so far."

Marcus Gheeraerts, the Elder, laughs heartily. Elizabeth joins in, and the two boys giggle because their parents are so amused. Jonas' face burns with embarrassment.

Gheeraerts, picks up the explanation. "He draws pictures and makes copper plates that terrify the King of Spain. That is why the big bad Duke of Alva is so angry. Jonas tweaks the tail of the devil. He kills the Spaniard with his art. Boys, this is a man after my own heart."

Gheeraerts pummels Jonas' back.

"After our meal, you can tell us about the Ortels triumph and how life is in our land," Elizabeth says. She claps her hands and the book of maps is moved to a side table. Two cooks and their servants bring plates of food from the kitchen to the table. Jonas sits to the right of Elizabeth Cole.

She introduces Jonas to the assembled well-wishers. Soon, his head is swimming with the names and faces of strangers. They, like Jonas, are all safe from the reach of the Spanish.

"To Willem," a voice toasts. "Willem the Silent," a chorus of Dutch voices echoes.

People who can speak freely with no fear of reprisal surround Jonas. He ponders how he might bring Sofie across the water to this haven for Dutch and Flemish who have nothing to fear from the Spaniards.

The dinner continues, and Jonas accepts goblets of wine. Admirers of the *Theatrum* ply him with questions about how such an undertaking had been completed. One guest is especially interested in how Ortels has managed to get so many cartographers to allow their works to be reproduced. "You would have to ask Master Ortelius," Jonas answers honestly. "I was a mere apprentice brought in by Master de Diest."

"And how is it that you have come to England?"

"Why, to deliver copies of the book to Madame Elizabeth at Master Ortelius' request. I believe she is commissioned to illuminate several."

The questioner, a smiling man in his late twenties, with dark short-clipped hair, wears his beard sharply trimmed. He clinks goblets with Jonas, leans in, and, in a conspiratorial voice, asks: "Did I hear that you killed a Spaniard?"

Jonas' smile freezes. Alarms sound in his ears like church bells ringing out news of a break in a dike. He wishes he had not drunk so liberally.

"A joke. My only weapon is a pencil. And I am merely learning my craft."

"Pity," the man says. "The Saracens have a name for people who know how to work in stealth and take the lives of their enemies." Jonas' head needs to be clear for this conversation. He tries to slow his mind, so he can take in what is happening.

"Why would you tell me such a thing? I am merely an apprentice engraver trying to learn my craft to advance in the guild. I know nothing of taking the lives of anyone." *Spies are everywhere.* Jonas hears Sofie's voice warning. "Tell me your name, again, sir," he says.

"Jan Du Forché, Brussels," the man says smoothly and proffers his hand.

"Jonas Hoen, Antwerp," he replies, shaking the man's hand. Du Forché's grasp feels weak, but, oddly, it lingers after Jonas has released his own grip. Jonas fights to keep the wine, which he has rarely drunk before, from affecting him. The more he tries, the more light-headed he becomes.

"Pardon me," Jonas, says, rising. His legs feel rubbery, and he uses the backs of chairs to help guide him toward the doorway to the hall.

He quickens his steps to make his way downstairs. He needs to find the outdoor privy. He stays on his feet, using the wide bannister to keep his balance and, on the ground level, makes for the door at the rear of the building. In the pallid moonlight, he sees the two-stall privy over a stone cesspit in the bottom of the garden. His head swims, and he gulps in fresh air before stepping into the cramped, stinking cubicle.

I must be more careful about what I say. Du Forché makes him nervous. He reexamines his earlier thoughts about his safe haven, and recognizes that, in a time of upheaval, where continents could separate and move across the sea, safety is only relative. When he feels clear-headed enough, he leaves the privy and steps into the cool night. He would have a word with Mrs. Cole the next day to ask about Du Forché. He dares not drink any more spirits this night.

As he ascends the stairs to the third floor, he moves aside on landings to allow guests and families coming down to pass easily. "Goodnight, young man," an elderly gentleman calls. He returns the nicety. The evening is coming to a close, and, when he enters the hallway on the third floor, he observes Mrs. Cole kissing a middle-aged woman on both cheeks. As she walks past on the arm of her escort, she touches Jonas' face the way a maiden aunt might bid goodnight to a nephew.

Elizabeth Cole beams as she stops at the door to the dining hall. Even after three hours of hostessing, she is vibrant and radiates warmth. "To bed now, children. James, I'll be in to kiss you goodnight, shortly." She pushes her little boy who yawns all the way to his door.

"Sit down." She invites Jonas back into the drawing room, which servants clear, mopping spills, sweeping a broken stoneware plate into a pile of shards.

Jonas takes the chair she points to, a tall padded armchair that has been occupied by Marcus Gheeraerts most of the evening.

"Are you feeling well, Jonas?"

"Much better, yes."

"Have some light ale with me, if you are not too exhausted."

"Ale would be fine, Mrs. Cole."

"I will ask Millie to serve us. I need to tuck James in, and will join you shortly. Meanwhile, please select which book Abraham wants me to use as a guide to color for my commission, if you know."

Elizabeth Cole sweeps into the kitchen; moments later, Jonas hears her walking down the hall toward the little boy's room. Jonas peeks into three of the books of maps until he finds the one with the title page colored by Ortels that had been used as a sample for the limners. He opens the double folio to the title and positions it on the end of the dining table. He remembers again Frans Hogenberg's impromptu lecture on Ortels' use of symbols in the presentation of the continents as a theatre piece portrayed by classical female figures. He looks about him, in a strange room, in a strange city, in a strange country, and wonders, "Am I in a stage play too, invented by Master Ortels?"

CHAPTER 47

Eindhoven, Netherlands, Noon, 15 June 1945

Michael despairs when he sees that the waterways of the town and the streets laden with rubble. He fights off shock and sadness at a stretch of the garbage-strewn canal where he had sailed a toy boat. The scattered bricks and burnt timbers, the remains of a greengrocer's, remind him of where and his mother and he had shopped. Shattered memory transfixes him. He wonders if the shopkeeper with the bulbous wart pushing through his scraggly mustache had been in the building when it was bombed. The family had lived above the shop.

Pim elbows Michael's arm and smiles, pointing to a scrawl of anti-NSB graffiti on the side of a strafe-scarred warehouse. Hadn't Michael heard Pim say he would like to paint a sign of the NSB hanging from a gallows back in 1941? Next to the profane NSB slogan Michael sees "OZO" emblazoned, *Oranje zal overwinnen*—"the House van Oranje will triumph." Pim pulls Michael close, trying to get him to buck up. Michael nods, and together they continue to walk toward their street. A group of armed resistance fighters on patrol orders them to halt and show their documents. Each suppress his frustration when fellow Dutchmen, who had gone underground to resist, detain them. "Just getting home," Pim says evenly. He and Michael hand their stamped papers to the armband-wearing members of the Resistance.

"Where were you sent?" A hard-faced man asks Michael.

"A factory near Hamburg. They made mess kits." Michael answers flatly, as Pim had instructed.

"We spit in every one," Pim adds, with a wink.

The inquiring resistance fighter never changes expression.

"Where are you going?"

"Home, we hope—if it is still standing. On Keizergracht."

The man hands the papers back. "Good luck," he says in a tone that chills.

When they get to their row of houses they see two dwellings, front facades collapsed, spilling bricks and broken glass onto the street. Michael trembles with anxiety, shocked to see the wall of their neighbor's bedroom on the second floor, a view he had no right to see, in his mind. He is relieved when they find their house intact, but boarded up, closed by the NSB with an order still posted on the front door announcing that entry is forbidden. Pim and Michael go round back. After a brief discussion, they break into the kitchen.

The house smells musty and both Michael and Pim sense something very wrong. Two handsome serving plates of hand-painted Delfts from the mid-18th century are missing from a glass fronted display closet in the kitchen.

"The bastards!" Michael swears.

They walk through the rooms and see that several items of value, paintings from two centuries before, some furniture, and the Ortelius atlas are gone. Every loss is like a bludgeon to Michael and he seethes. Upstairs in their parents' bedroom they search in an armoire for their mother's jewels, passed down through the generations. The green velvet bag is missing. "Mama's jewels, too!" Michael's hands shake. The house hadn't been looted indiscriminately, their first fear, but prized possessions had been selectively removed.

"How do we find out who stole Mother's...?" Michael demands impatiently. He is between tears and menace, barely able to control his voice.

"Get into something clean," Pim says.

Michael hears a tone of resolve from his brother. Pim is already working something out.

Michael roots through his drawers and finds a clean shirt, underwear and a pair of pants that doesn't look too bad on his skinny frame. He sees that Pim has found ill fitting, but clean gray trousers, his blue "away game" football jersey, and a tweed jacket he last wore for his brother's graduation.

He hears Pim turn on the tap.

"Water still flows. Rusty, though. I found father's razor," Pim calls.

Michael cinches a belt for his too-wide trousers and takes the safety razor that Pim offers. Michael feels the weight of the brass and thinks of his father, imagining the last day he used it. He presses the blade against his cheek and decides not to shave his pale stubble. He replaces the razor in the felt-lined rusting case that had belonged to his father. Michael remembers the faint odor of lavender the metal case emitted. He has no idea why he cannot bring himself to use the razor.

His brother, relatively clean-shaven, looks better in his oversize pants and shirt. The familiar clothing, left in the drawers when they learned they were allowed only one bag each for the truck ride to the station and then on to Krümmel in 1942, raises Michael's spirits.

"We'll start with the De Groots. Let's learn what they know." Pim says, bringing Michael back to the present.

They walk down the street to a house only marginally damaged. Pim rings the doorbell. An old man squints and then recognizes the grown-up neighbor kids.

"You're alive, boys. Praised be. Were you in hiding?" Old Mr. De Groot's voice is thin and he looks malnourished.

Pim quickly explains how they finally came home, omitting everything except that they survived and escaped the bombed factory. He does not mention that the product was ammunition. "And your family, Mr. De Groot?"

They listen to a litany of fury-laced tales, as their neighbor describes the desperation they endured, starvation and fuel shortages, especially when the Allies bombed, then pushed through the southern Netherlands on their way to the German border. "The NSB were the worst. Traitors, every one."

Michael interjects, impatiently. "Mr. De Groot, can you tell us anything about our father? He died last year."

The old man looks at Michael, then Pim. "I only saw them carry out his body. The Black Police."

Michael is confused, his heart was pumping nervously.

"Why the police?" Pim asks.

"I don't know very much. Perhaps the housekeeper could help you."

"Some things are missing—" Michael begins.

"The housekeeper. She might know. Her husband was in the Nederlandsche SS. Maybe he would know if he has not yet been picked up." De Groot shakes his head. Michael sees that he is lost in his own tragedies.

"*Emma* something, wasn't it," Pim asks when they were on the street again.

"I never liked her," Michael replies. "I don't know why father hired her."

"To keep house after mother—house, house—Berghuis! *Emma Berghuis.*" Pim says, triumphantly.

They knock on more doors on the street and make inquiry with neighbors who give condolences about their father's death, but can offer no further details. From one, they learn that Emma Berghuis still lives in the Gestel district. "Something funny about that one," Mrs. Dressler adds. "At least that's what Mrs. De Groot was saying. She saw her skulking around even after the NSB put a lock on the door."

Pim asks, "Your son managed to hide?"

"No," Mrs. Dressler says, tearing up and pulling wisps of graying hair from behind her ear. "They told us Jef was killed in a mine cave-in in the Saar."

"No!" Michael blurts. "Jef is dead?"

"Yes," Mrs. Dressler says, weeping. "You boys went through school together, Michael. I'm sorry he bloodied your nose that time."

"I'm sorry," Pim says, as they take their leave.

Michael feels lost and weak-kneed. "Jef is dead."

"Yes," Pim says quietly. "I remember you used to play with him."

Michael stares vacantly up the street to the debris-cluttered canal where he and Jef once sailed their boats.

"Michael, let's take stock," Pim says resolutely. "The housekeeper, Emma, sounds like we need to find her."

In the kitchen of their house, Pim rummages through a drawer of scraps of metal, screws, nails, and hand tools. Michael, meanwhile, returns to the sideboard where their parents' prized atlas had lain. He envisions the book opened to some map, the hand-painted tints making the countries radiant, mysterious, and always a source of wonder when he was growing up. The bare lectern is dusty, the sideboard spattered with stains, another gloomy reminder of the present.

"Michael," Pim calls, shutting the kitchen drawer with a clatter. "The shed key! We have three hours before Gerdi arrives. Let's find the housekeeper."

Their father had hidden the boys' bicycles under tarps in the shed adjoining the house. The bikes had flat tires but were otherwise usable. Pim finds a note on his Ariel Grande. "Welcome home, Pim!" His father's handwriting. Michael sees the same note on his Gazelle. "Welcome home, Michael!"

"He thought of everything," Pim says. "I do miss him."

Michael is ambivalent about his father and does not share Pim's high regard.

They pump air into the tires.

CHAPTER 48

Cole Apartments, Lyme Street, London, Late Evening, 23 June 1570

Rattling spoons and crockery announce Millie, the fifteen-year-old scullery girl with stringy ginger hair escaping from under her cap. She carries a tray of cups and a pot of ale smelling like rosemary. The slight girl sets the contents of the tray on the table, curtseys nervously, and returns through the kitchen doorway, stealing a sidelong glance at Jonas.

"Ever beholden to the ancients for his inspiration," Mrs. Cole says, reentering and looking over Jonas' shoulder. "His colors, the detail. Look, even the fingers of the woman who is America in the New World are bloodied as she holds the severed head."

She pours ale into each of the cups and passes one to him.

"Nothing so good is easily rendered," Jonas says.

He turns back to view the precision of Ortels' master copy, then the detail of Frans Hogenberg's etching of the title page. He is lost for the moment in the burin work Hogenberg had used to create depth, dimensionality, even a tactile sensuality—so much detail, that most owners of the *Theatrum* would fly past because the heart of the undertaking is in the fifty-three plates showing regions and countries of the world.

"And your contribution, besides all of the hours in service to Master Hogenberg?"

He shrugs.

"Go on," she insists.

Jonas turns the pages to the first map plate, the *Typus Orbis Terrarum*. He points to the sea monster in the South Indian Ocean.

"Aha. This is a worthy engraving for a first time, and, as Abraham says, 'under urgent and unexpected circumstances,'" Madame Cole comments. Then she narrows her eyes. "The limner was not so meticulous, I see, as he was with the title page." She points at the job the colorist did on the world map. *Was it Nicholaus Bockel who performed the task so inexpertly?*

"I shall take more pains, Jonas, especially around your sea monster," she says, smiling her winning grin. "More good news," she continues. "You begin at nine o'clock tomorrow morning with Master Gheeraerts. It is an easy walk to his rooms in Abchurch Lane."

Jonas' heart leaps with excitement.

"And I will give you an errand. In that lane, Mistress Wells is the best baker in London. You will have all of the Cole children in your debt if you bring some sampling of her cakes when you return tomorrow evening. My James is particularly partial to the sweet oatcakes."

He laughs, and nods to assure her he would satisfy young Master James.

"And now, we each have our labors set out for us. I shall transform my sitting room to my limning studio, and you will receive instruction from dear Marcus."

As she rises, Jonas follows. She looks again at the map and touches a fingernail on the inscription that runs across the base of the world map.

"Cicero, eh? Can you help me translate? I never mastered Latin as well as my brother."

Jonas reads the inscription on the ornate strapping and translates it into Dutch syntax. "What human doings are important to he who views all eternity and knows the huge scope of the universe?"

"Abraham was never satisfied with small thinking. Maybe that's why he sent you here."

His face burns with embarrassment.

"Off to bed with you, and me to mine. Goodnight, Jonas."

"Mrs. Cole," Jonas begins, recalling something important. "Jan Du Forché—"

"Ach," Elizabeth Cole interrupts, wrinkling her nose. "A rotten apple, rotten to the core, not invited. If you ever share a table with him again, think of supping with the devil; use a long spoon." Elizabeth nods seriously to drive the point home.

She walks down the hall lighted by candle sconces past her bedsitting room to the master bedroom. Jonas closes the book. He walks to the hall entranceway as Millie comes through the arch with her tray. Jonas steps to his right to let her pass as she steps to her left. They do this dance three times, and Jonas laughs. She frowns in consternation. Her chin reveals a large dimple that makes Jonas consider how he could capture such a feature on a copper plate. Finally, Millie steps back through the doorway deferentially, and he proceeds to his room. At his door, he looks back and sees her staring after him, pressing the tray tightly to her indiscernible bosom. She drops her eyes and disappears into the dining room.

Jonas steps into his room, lit only by a faint moonlight through the leaded panes. Could he gather his thoughts to write a letter to Sofie? Writing a letter might be the only way he could gather them. He pulls up the candle pressed into the well of the pewter holder on his table and steps into the hall to set the wick to the flame from a wall sconce outside his door.

A squeak of surprise flies off the lips of Millie, poised to snuff the sconce.

He recovers from his surprise and smiles. He touches the tip of his beeswax candle to the sconce taper. Millie blushes and curtseys, and, with her eyes alone, asks permission to do her chore. He nods and smiles, hoping she will crack a smile to make her dimple appear. She obliges with the briefest of grins and curtseys again as Jonas steps back into his room.

> *Dearest Sofie,*
>
> *Where shall I begin? First, how much I miss you. All through my trip on the ocean, I was sick as a cur and yearned for you to hold a cool wet napkin to my head. I am a dreadful sailor. Thank heavens the boat docked earlier today, and I was on solid ground once more. I have met Master Ortels' sister and her family and even Master Gheeraerts, with whom I begin tutelage tomorrow. I am overcome by sleep, which wants to take me in its grasp forever. Because I cannot keep my eyes open, I will put down the quill and write more tomorrow.*
>
> *I love you so much, and already can scarcely wait to hold your body next to mine, to touch your beautiful face, look into your beautiful eyes, and kiss your dimple.*

"What dimple?" he asks aloud.

His cheeks sting with shame in the solitude of his room. He snatches up another sheet of paper and copies the letter verbatim, except that, when he comes to the word "dimple," he writes instead "*sweet lips.*"

He sets the new letter aside and tears the offending sheet into tiny pieces, then tosses them into the hearth of the fireplace. He sifts through his collection of illustrations and finds his unfinished sketch of Sofie. He had not captured her at all, he concludes. He puts his drawings away and hopes his apprenticeship with the engraver from Bruges will improve his art.

He blows out the beeswax candle. The odor of honey surrounds his table. Within moments of slipping under the blanket, he is fast asleep.

CHAPTER 49

Lyme Street, London, Morning, 24 June 1570

A pounding downpour startles Jonas awake as it spatters the windows. He dresses hurriedly and gathers pencils, gravers, and several sheets of paper, since he does not know what his tutor will expect. He selects samples from his meager trove of illustrations to show Marcus Gheeraerts a baseline of his skills.

He returns to writing his letter to Sofie, relating the previous evening's gathering, but his heart is not in it. Dutifully, however, he folds, seals, and addresses the letter in care of Master Du Brul at the Boekprintere Scheldt. The clock in the corridor strikes seven. Moments later, the galloping feet of the Cole boys clatter down the hall as they go off to school. Jonas walks toward the dining room and sees one of the male servants carrying a copy of the *Theatrum Orbis Terrarum* into the bed-sitting room where Elizabeth Cole arranges her work area. She arrays pots of pigment and adds droplets of water to dilute the colors to match the master copy. Daylight, such as it is this overcast morning, filters in from the east-facing windows.

"Ah, good morning, Jonas. Get some food in the kitchen and then we can visit here. Ask the cook—his name is Francis—for some bread and ale."

Jonas continues into the kitchen, where a sleepy-eyed cook stirs porridge of sweet smelling barley meal. A scullery maid lays out bowls before the two Cole girls. The girls titter a "good morning" and return to their conversation.

The cook looks up, and smiles. "Bread with ale, yes, Francis?" Jonas asks, trying to say the words as he had heard Elizabeth Cole speak them.

"Good choice, lad, we're well provisioned 'ere," the cook replies, and pushes a tub of butter toward Jonas. As he slices a wedge of brown bread, he seems to be appraising the newcomer. Jonas understands not one word, but matches the cook's broad grin. He eats and drinks ale that tastes of ginger. He nods his thanks and returns to Mrs. Cole's room, where she sets out her brushes for the morning's work.

"You slept well, I hope?"

"Yes, thank you, Mrs. Cole. I know you will be busy today, so I will not want to take up much of your time."

Elizabeth smiles. "Who taught you such good manners?"

"My mother made us aware of how to present ourselves. And later, I was six years with the Benedictines near Antwerp. They are strict." Elizabeth Cole smiles sympathetically for the loss of his mother and the time he spent in the care of the monks. Embarrassed, he looks away and realizes he has some business to transact.

"I have money for you. Master Ortels provided three gold escudos that I would like to give to you cover some of the expenses of housing me."

Jonas retrieves the coins from his pouch and places them on the table. Elizabeth pushes two escudos back to Jonas and takes one.

"One will do for now. I can convert it to more useful coin for you here." She walks into her bedroom. Jonas observes the neat array of her brushes and paints and concludes that the Ortels family has a firm grasp on how to be successful. Elizabeth emerges with a clinking leather pouch. She scatters a handful of English coins on the table and counts out shillings and a few pence. "For you to use as you wish. Take only a part of it as you walk in the town, and keep the rest safely in your room. Discuss with Marcus what he needs, and pay what he asks. I have asked Thomas, our eldest, to help with your English. It will be not so difficult."

"Thanks you," Jonas says, trying the English words. But he switches back to Dutch. "Can you tell me how I go to Master Gheeraerts? To where he lives?"

"Ah," Elizabeth says. "When you step out the front door, turn right and right again on Lombard Street. Continue to Abchurch Lane where you will turn left. Across the street from Saint Mary's Church, you will find his rooms— ten minutes, or fifteen if you dawdle. If you come to Candlewick Street you have gone too far."

"Oh, yes." Jonas remembers, putting the coins in his leather pouch. "I have a letter to post to Antwerp." Jonas proffers his letter.

"This Sofie is someone special?"

He blushes.

"Lucky girl. Good, I will take care of this. Oh! Take the brown cloak—rack by the stairs. This weather is changeable. Is there anything else you need, Jonas?"

"You are very kind," he says, rising.

"Convey to Marcus my fond regard for Susannah and his little one. And don't forget Mistress Wells. Her baking shop is up the lane from Marcus' rooms. And, Jonas," she adds. "Come home in daylight. Where Lombard crosses into Fenchurch, thieves, cutthroats stay at Culver Alley—unsafe after dark. Be careful."

Jonas collects his things and pulls the cloak about his shoulders. As he descends to the second story landing he comes upon Margery huffing with a heavy hamper of laundry on her hip and speaking words he does not understand.

"Rain," she clarifies in Dutch. "No sun, wet clothes." Her voice becomes louder as she tries to make herself clear in words foreign to her. He barely understands her attempt, but looks over his shoulder and smiles broadly, an expression that will serve as his *lingua franca* until he masters a few English phrases.

As he steps into the street, a river of muck washes downhill over the cobblestones. The street exudes a musty, drenched odor. However, the rain tapers off as he begins his walk. At the corner of Lyme and Fenchurch, Jonas is surprised to hear familiar Flemish phrases and Dutch words coming from a noisy alehouse. The men who frequent these tables are traders who replicate the bourse in Antwerp where merchants and bankers do their business over tankards of ale and wine. He half expects to see one or two of the guests who were at Elizabeth Cole's fête, but he recognizes no one. Still, he takes comfort to hear his native language spoken in this town. He notices native Londoners scowl as they walk past this Flemish corner. If he keeps his mouth shut, he might pass for a local.

He rounds the corner and takes in the sights of the wider street. As he passes an alley leading into the even broader street named Lombard he can smell the degradation of derelict men. *This must be where the cutthroats are.* He hurries along now and grasps his bag of gravers tightly. He passes Ironmongers'

Hall and continues west to Gracechurch Street. He looks toward to the entrance of London Bridge at the bottom of the hill and pauses to take it in. The street is very spacious, and all manner of animal and human-drawn conveyances roll along the broad avenue. A nearby church begins tolling the half-hour, so he hastens westward and crosses Saint Clements, and then Saint Nicholas, before finally reaching Abchurch Lane. Jonas exults that he is about to arrive at Gheeraerts' rooms, the third timbered house toward the river. The odor from a bakery he nears heralds that he is close to his destination. On impulse, he steps in and sees a table topped with cakes and small breads.

"Oatcakes?" Jonas asks, hoping to be understood, when the young woman looks up. "Fruit or spiced?" She asks.

Jonas frowns, at sea with the language. He guesses and holds up six fingers. Another customer enters behind him. The shop girl picks three fruit and three plain oatcakes, looking into Jonas' eyes, seeking confirmation.

"Thruppence." Luckily, for Jonas, the young woman holds up three fingers.

Jonas quickly holds up six fingers again, then points at the oatcakes.

"Sixpence," the woman says, adding another six cakes.

Jonas pays and fills the pocket he has found in the cloak with the dozen cakes.

"Thanks-you, Mis-tress-es Wells," he says in fractured English.

The young woman smiles at his attempt. "Just Sally," she says, flashing him a smile from beneath her cap.

"Jonas," he responds, and smiles back.

"Ahem," the woman behind him clears her throat.

Jonas touches the brim of his cap and turns to walk onto the street.

The woman's glare as she turns gives Jonas the proper impression—he is not welcome. However, moments later, it means nothing to him. The sun peeks through the clouds. Jonas has a pocketful of cakes, and he stands before the door to the house of the master engraver who will launch him on an arc to properly learn his new craft. He knocks, and the door opens immediately. Marcus Gheeraerts, dressed in street clothes, steps outside.

"We have a commission!" the older man exclaims. "We must be at the river for some important work. The Royal Barge," he says, in a half whisper.

"What?"

"Queen Elizabeth's barge. Gilt work."

"Marcus," a woman's voice calls.

Gheeraerts turns back into his doorway and kisses a delicately featured Flemish woman with red-blonde hair and blue eyes. A faint blush of pink colors her fair skin. "If you would like, I will kiss John for you," Gheeraerts says to the young woman. She giggles and playfully slaps the older man on his chest.

"Ah. Where are my manners? Jonas…Hoen, is that right?" Jonas nods. "This is the glorious Susannah de Critz, born in Antwerp. My dear, Jonas has sailed from the city of your birth, the Spanish dogs snapping at his heels." Jonas smiles dumbly as the woman cocks her head in greeting.

"Off we go."

Jonas hastens to keep up with Gheeraerts. They walk briskly down the hill toward the Thames, as though the barge were about to set sail.

"Not what you expected on your first day, eh? But we must strike when the iron is hot. The lady you just met has made good on getting me some work for the Crown. Her cousin, John de Critz, has crept into the inner sanctum of the Royal Serjeant-Painter. Not a bad painter, John. There will be plenty of time for instruction with the gravers another day. Today, we refurbish the Queen's Barge."

Jonas stifles his disappointment by reaching into his cloak pocket and pulling out two cakes. He taps the arm of the older artist with the royal commission. Gheeraerts accepts an oatcake. "Ah, you found Mistress Wells' shop." They walk on toward the river in silence. The odor of rotting fish hangs in the air. Gheeraerts guides Jonas onto Three Cranes Wharf, where the weathered wooden barge is tied up and a gang of workmen converges.

"You have learned the first rule in the arts, today, Jonas. 'Turn nothing down.' It may lead to something better. It may lead to nothing. But you eat another day." Gheeraerts pops the remainder of his oatcake into his mouth and points to the man they must see.

CHAPTER 50

Eindhoven, Netherlands, Afternoon, 15 June 1945

The brothers walk their bikes to the street in front of their house. Pim nods to Michael and they set off. "Berghuis," Michael says, and they pedal through the streets of Eindhoven into the Gestel district. They ask several passersby if anyone knows Emma Berghuis. Finally, a girl skipping rope says, "The next street, the one with the blue door."

Outside, Michael grows nervous, embarrassed to be intruding. He finds he does not want to confront the woman who had, in superficial ways, replaced his mother in the house. Does she know something about how his father had died? Was she trying to defend against robbers? Or did she have something to do with taking his mother's jewelry?

Pim raps on the blue door. "Mrs. Berghuis. Please open up."

Michael feels jumpy. *What did she know?* He fears he would not be able to control himself.

Pim knocks harder. The door swings open with vehemence. Michael sees a pale-faced man with crooked eyes he vaguely recognizes. The man demands, "What do you want?" Even the arrogant tone sounds familiar to Michael.

"Oh, Jesus God," a woman swears in shock.

Michael sees Emma Berghuis clenching a gray shawl around her shoulders, behind the man who had flung the door open. She is still the puffy-faced woman with eyes set too closely together and a twitching jaw, but today her eyes dart, first at Pim, then Michael.

Michael can sniff the fear emanating from the cottage.

"Mrs. Berghuis, tell us about the goods taken from my father's house," Pim says forcefully.

"They, they, they—" Emma Berghuis stammers.

"Where are they?" Michael's voice becomes an unexpected screech.

"Quiet, please," pleads the man, changing his tone. "Come in." He limps quickly, gestures them in to shut the door behind them against neighbors hearing their raised voices. His sweater had been hastily buttoned and mismatched, creating a disheveled and lopsided man, bent awkwardly to one side as he favors an injured leg.

Michael searches his memory. Something about the man nags at him.

"Please be calm and we can discuss how you might, we might—" The bent man is speaking rapidly, wheedling, when Michael's bolt of recognition strikes.

"You. I know you," Michael's voice intensifies, remembering he and his brother carrying their suitcases to the station under this very man's gaze. "Pim. He was Black Police. SS!"

"No!" Emma shouts.

Michael focuses on Emma Berghuis, clutching her shawl like armor. "Where are the paintings and the book of maps? Did you steal my mother's jewelry?"

"No, no…I swear, Michael," Emma whines. "I…we did not steal your mother's jewelry. We hold it for safety for when you come home. Your father was killed. There would be no way it would not be stolen. So my husband, this is Diederik, and I, we brought it here for safety. So it would not be looted."

"We can bring it to your house," the ex-NSB man sings in a tone tinged with fear. He glances nervously at a bulky wooden chiffonier in a corner of the room behind an armchair.

Michael steps toward the closet. He can barely control his rage.

"No! I will bring it out for you," Diederik cries, limping to intercept Michael.

"Wait!" Pim demands, stopping Diederik in his tracks. "Now I have it," Pim says. "I know you from *before*. You used to work for my father in the linen factory."

Words come from Diederik's mouth, but his eyes blink like terrified prey. He tries to put the armchair between himself and Pim. "Yes, I was very sad when he was killed. He was a fair—a very fair, manager."

"He sacked you for—what was it?" Pim drills deeper. "Stealing?"

"Diederik!" Emma Berghuis cries out.

"A-a mistake. I was never charged." Diederik's voice wavers weakly. He changes his tack. "Young sirs, we are so happy you have come home. Please, take your father's belongings."

He pushes the great armchair aside. It scrapes the floor. He unlatches the freestanding closet and tries to keep the doors closed while he moves the coats and dresses off to one side. Pim flings the doors open. Diederik lunges toward the cavernous chiffonier, which is brimming with goods. Michael pushes him toward his sister.

"Don't do that! He can barely walk," Emma cries.

In the half-light, the brothers see a tangle of articles that could stock a pawn shop, ceremonial swords, and two small paintings removed from their father's study leaned against the inside wall. The book of maps, the edges stained a deep red-brown, lay on the floor. On the upper shelf, Michael recognizes this mother's purple velvet jewelry pouch.

"Look at all this," Michael points to the cache of goods and pulls the familiar ones onto the armchair. He shoots a look of contempt for the looters with each item.

"For safe-keeping," Diederik insists.

Michael waves at several other jewelry boxes, an assortment of rugs and wall hangings in the closet. A gold menorah and silver candlesticks also are seen in the back of the tall wardrobe. "Are you a secret Jew, Diederik?" Michael asks, knowing these too are stolen goods.

Diederik's face twitches with ill-concealed loathing for the two returnees.

Michael fluffs two of the sleek, richly ornamented silk dresses and says, "Nice clothing Emma. Did you grow out of these?"

"Please, take them if you like them," Emma cries shrilly.

"But they don't belong to me," Michael says evenly. "Nor do these old swords. Look at this loot, Pim, and look at that, the bird plates!" Michael points at the wooden cabinet next to Emma with two familiar Delfts serving plates.

"Isn't it odd that you would have plates that look exactly like our mother's?" Michael asks.

In a constricted voice, Diederik says, "You get out now with your goods."

Pim steps within a foot of Emma's brother and regards his smoothly shaven face. "The last time I saw you, you wore the Nederlandsche SS black uniform with the lighting bolts. You and your traitor friends ordered my brother and me onto the labor transports like dogs. Do you remember that day in 1942?"

Michael glimpses where Pim is heading and his heart quickens. He feels the surge of adrenalin pushing his vengeance.

"Times were different. We had no control. Just the orders of the *standaard*."

"Show me your uniform," Pim demands.

"All gone," Emma interjects. "Burned."

"And you not in it when it was burned? Pity." Pim spits the word, mocking.

"Yes, destroyed in a fire," Diederik says, blinking furiously. Then he tries his saccharine voice. "Please. Take—take your parents' things and *anything* else you want and leave. Please."

"So. Mr. SS. Tell us about how my father died?" Pim says quietly.

Michael, on impulse, reaches into the closet and withdraws a ceremonial sword from its scabbard. He stares steely-eyed at Emma's brother.

"No," Emma shouts. "Please, we have a little boy!"

"Surely the Eindhoven Standaard of the Nederlandsche SS examined events around my father's death in March 1944." Pim pursues. "What did they turn up?"

Diederik's eyes flash with abject terror and he takes a step back.

"I know nothing!"

"He knows nothing," Emma Berghuis repeats, her voice pleading.

"But you do, Emma, don't you? You were working in the house when—"

"No! I was out by then. Already gone for the day, here when he was shot."

"Shot? How shot? Shot by who?" Michael bellows.

Diederik continues his retreat behind the dining table.

"Who shot our father, Diederik?" Pim asks, fury rising and fists clenching.

"Not me, not me! Rost! It was Henk Rost. I swear. Our group was sent to pick up the Jew girl."

"What? What girl?" Michael demands his brow knitted by confusion.

"Where is Rost?" Pim's voice rises.

"Dead!"

"The girl? What girl?" Michael asks again, baffled.

"The Jewish girl," Emma snaps. "Your father hid her."

Diederik jumps in quickly, "We—We never found the girl. Your father started shooting. He shot me in my knee. It was Henk who shot your father. He shot Henk too. Henk died after a week in hospital. I was wounded. We were under orders."

Pim shoves the dining room table aside and wraps his hands around both the sweater and Diederik's shirtfront. He pulls the terrified Diederik to him. Three inches from his face, Pim growls, "You saw our father die? You saw him shot down?"

Michael can make no sense of the jumble of revelations except that this man was one of the police who shot his father.

"Yes. But I was hit in the knee," Diederik whines. "I tried to run up the stairs to search for the girl but I was losing blood and could barely walk. I helped Henk to the car. I only know Mr. Dijkstra fell on the big book of maps." He points at the looted book. "I did not know he was dead!" The words tumble from Diederik's mouth. "I needed to get both Henk and me medical help. When the rest of my group came back, they only found his body. Not even his pistol, and no girl. They found some of her clothes in a room upstairs, but no sign of her."

"No reward was ever collected. We are innocent," Emma bawls.

The Berghuises cringe as their secret is revealed.

"How did your *standaard* know to round up a Jewish girl?" Pim demands.

Diederik's eyes flutter. "I don't know. We took orders."

Pim pushes Diederik against the wall. His flailing arm upsets a hanging shelf and sends the contents, glass and porcelain crashing to the floor.

Emma Berghuis screams, "Stop beating my man, he cannot defend himself. He can barely walk."

Pim glares at Emma who cowers against a doorjamb. "I don't suppose you would know, eh, Emma?"

"Just Jews," she says in chaotic candor. "It was awful that your father dies because a Jew-girl was dumped on him. You ask your girlfriend," she says, defiantly.

"What? What, does that mean?" Michael demands.

"Like Cleopatra's adder, she brings the Jew-kid."

Pim's eyes meet Michael's. Before Michael can formulate a question, Emma cries. "Her fault! His sweetheart, Michael! Please. I was kind to you."

"What does she mean about Gerdi?" Michael asks coldly.

"I don't know," says Pim, holding Michael's gaze and ratcheting his hold on Diederik's shirtfront.

"It was her fault, no one else's." Emma says, a smile curling her lips.

Michael sees she is trying to drive a wedge between the two brothers. Pim breaks off looking at his brother, pushes Diederik to arm's length and takes in the former housekeeper.

"Don't hurt him anymore," Emma pleads, "That Jew-girl. You have no idea how we suffered."

"I know how I'd like to see you suffer," Pim says in a low growl.

"Make some sense, damn it," Michael explodes at Emma. "What are you talking about?"

"A bounty on Jews who were hidden, yes?" Pim prompts.

"Yes," Emma admits.

"Our father was killed because you wanted to collect? How much!"

"Seven guilders and a half," she says in a croaking voice.

"Quiet," hisses Diederik wearing a mask of fear. Pim again tightens his grip of Diederik's shirtfront and twists until it tears at one armpit.

"Oh, look, I've torn your shirt. Surely you have a jacket to cover that up."

"Stop hurting him!" Emma wails. "He's a poor cripple."

"Yes. Dress him up proper. His uniform? Michael, find this man's SS costume."

"Burnt, burnt! I told you," Emma cries.

"I think this tin soldier has hidden it. Michael, go find it," Pim orders.

Michael throws the sword down and goes through the door into one of the back rooms and Emma chases after him crying, "No, no. You cannot."

Michael hears Pim in the front room accusing—"We were sent to Germany because you wanted revenge on my father, yes?"

"No, no. I never." Diederik protests in the front room.

Michael throws open a closet and paws through the clothing, all the while Emma shouting, "You may not! You must not. You have no right."

And in the front room, Pim harangues, "Something about a uniform, eh, Diederik? Where's your boots and thunderbolts now, eh, Diederik? You're sure your pistol wasn't the one that killed my father? How are you so sure?"

"It was Henk! Henk! Not me. I was bleeding thanks to your fucking father! My fucking kneecap keeps me in pain all the time because of your fucking father."

"Where's your uniform." Pim bellows.

"Here! Here it is." Michael calls in the back room when he sees the telltale thunderbolts on the jacket hanging in the deepest recess of the closet. The cap and leather belt are stuffed into the boots on the closet floor. "He's a liar." Michael shouts.

Michael enters with Diederik's black jacket and hat. "Not so burnt."

Emma Berghuis moans. Pim twists the shirt and sweater again and buttons spray onto the floor. Pim yanks his white singlet, soaking in Diederik's sweat, and swings him like a rag doll.

"Time to dress up for the parade, you filth," Pim says.

"No! No!" Diederik sobs as Michael unleashes his fury by pressing the brimmed black SS visor cap on Diederik's head. Pim twists him around so his arms shoot up and out. Michael pushes a sleeve over Diederik's arm. Pim spins him around to jam the other arm through its sleeve. He spins him again as Michael holds his arms up and Pim buttons the uniform jacket.

"Let's give him some fresh air." Pim says.

"You must not do that!" Emma Berghuis wails.

Michael flings open the front door and Emma, beside herself with grief, shrieks, "No, no, you cannot...."

Doors on the street open and neighbors see the hated Black Police uniform. Pim shouts, "Here is one of the traitors, got up in his SS finery." He pushes Diederik into the arms of the crowd of a dozen angry men and women forming around him.

Michael and Pim glare at Emma Berghuis, crying in the street, "Leave him him alone. He only took orders!"

Pim and Michael return to her cottage. They collect their family belongings, and mount their bikes and pedal, holding handlebars with one hand. Michael presses the two plates that his mother had treasured into his waistband. The screams and protestations of Diederik and Emma fade behind them as they bike toward the Keizergracht. A block later, Michael demands, "What does she mean, 'Talk to Gerdi about the Jewish girl?'"

"I don't know, Michael. She will be here on the afternoon train."

Michael begins talking to himself. "This is so crazy. Why would Father take in…? Did Gerdi make Father take her in?"

"Michael, shut up for Christ's sake," Pim insists. "When Gerdi gets here we'll hear what she has to say."

CHAPTER 51

London, Three Cranes Wharf, Thames River, 26 June 1570

After three days of sanding weathered paint on the Royal Barge, chipping dry rot out of deck boards, and mixing gold leaf gilt paint, Jonas fears that he will never get instruction from Marcus Gheeraerts.

One of the unexpected benefits of this job, however, is speaking Dutch with Lowlanders who have immigrated to England to avoid persecution. One of these, Anent Willemzoom, the son of an Anabaptist, had barely escaped with his life. The pock-faced eighteen-year-old engages Jonas in conversation as they sand flaking paint from the barge oars for hours, preparing them for new decoration applied by the more senior members of the Queen's serjeant-painter crew.

"Have you ever seen a decapitation?" Anent asks.

"No," Jonas answers, uncertainly. He is not keen to hear one described, yet is fascinated by the older boy's experience. The boy describes a harrowing event in which a trio of Spanish cavalry had run down a priest accused of heresy. "The priest begins running across an ice-covered lake, and they follow him, but the horses soon break the crusted surface, pitching the horsemen through the ice and into the freezing water. They manage to save themselves and their horses, but they hunt down the priest and trap him in the village graveyard. They are roaring with anger, drenched and freezing.

The Father is on his knees, begging for mercy from the biggest Spaniard leaning over him with his sword—whack—his head is completely severed in the snow. Blood everywhere."

Jonas blinks and tries to blot out the memory of blood spurting from the soldier he had dispatched with his meager graver.

"I see it all from behind a tree. We have already lost everything from confiscations. My family is destitute. But none of us had our heads chopped off." Anent invite Jonas to share *his* tale of woe, but he remains silent, having learned his lesson of too loose a tongue.

"I'm glad you got to safety," is all he says to Anent. The telling of the story, however, is seared into his mind.

Finally, on his fourth day assisting the Queen's serjeant-painter crew, Jonas feels a tap on his back from Gheeraerts. "We're done for now."

Jonas grins as he looks up from his tedious task of scraping drips of color and touching up railings on the port side of the Royal Barge.

"Three shillings and tuppence for your labors. Very good wages," Gheeraerts adds, plopping several coins into Jonas' sweaty palm.

"Susannah's cousin, John de Critz, says we may get more work from the Office of the Revels in a fortnight. In the meanwhile, let us tip a pint of ale and talk about what you came to do."

"Master Gheeraerts, I am eager to learn how to prepare a plate for engraving, to learn how to pressure, to select the right burin, to care for the gravers, to—"

"Whoa. You have exhausted me already and we have not even begun. First, some refreshment. After, perhaps we can talk Susannah into making a pudding if she's at home. I will show you my workroom, and we can begin."

They walk to the foot of Botolph Street and enter a tavern frequented by Lowlanders. "Tell me about yourself," the engraver says over a tankard of sweet ale. Jonas gives a brief history of his seventeen years, emphasizing his time illuminating religious texts with the Benedictines, and the past half-year at the Boekprintere Scheldt. "While I saw the results of Master Hogenberg's skill, I did not serve an apprenticeship in the full sense," Jonas says, hoping it does not sound like a complaint. "There was never enough time."

"Yes, well, good to be busy on such a project. But there is never enough time to make it perfect, and, yet, precisely enough time to do the best you can. But you have not come to England merely to learn from me. I think I was an afterthought. I believe that Abraham needed to keep you out of trouble with the Spanish."

Jonas holds tightly to his tankard. *One false word.* "No, sir, hardly an afterthought. Master Hogenberg has spoken of your skill in engraving birds and animals. And Master Ortels told me that you are a cartographer of great renown for your bird's eye view of Bruges."

"Yes, a bird on the wing, that's me. I am not a believer in the Pope's doctrine, as you know. I barely missed being snapped in the beak of the Duke of Alva. I packed up my son and boarded the first boat to London. Abraham helped, and Jacobus Coels. My wife is Catholic. She stayed safely in Bruges. I made an engraving inspired by the Calvinists breaking the icons in the churches. An allegory, but they accused me of heresy, mayhap for the image of the bloated monk who—slightly—resembles Pope Pius. I made the error of annotating the events depicted. Finally, I didn't want my son to see my head at the end of a pike, and I have no Spanish overseers here."

Jonas is reassured enough to admit: "I, too, am hunted, in Antwerp. With far less skill, I dared to illustrate a pamphlet criticizing the hundredth penny blood tax."

Gheeraerts smiles broadly. "You see how dangerous is the illustrator's burin? Are you certain you want to get better? You will be tempted to engrave more heretical images and they will chase you to the end of time."

Jonas detects the satire in Gheeraerts' tone, and he breaks into a full-faced grin. He clacks his tankard against his new mentor's tankard.

"Now that I have chipped paint on Brittanie's Royal Barge, what need I fear?"

Gheeraerts claps Jonas on the back and they both laugh. But Jonas cuts his light-heartedness short., when a figure rises across the room with a pot of ale. Jan Du Forché smiles at him. The "bad apple," as Elizabeth Cole called him, tips his tankard in salute, and Jonas nods, but shuts out the close-clipped bearded young man by engaging Gheeraerts with a *non sequitur.*

"Is Susannah good with young Marcus?"

"She's good with me. And the boy knows to keep us both happy. Why ask?"

Jonas sees, through panicked eyes, Du Forché staring at him. "I don't know why I asked that. I guess I can't believe we are finally getting started."

"Very well, let's begin," says Gheeraerts, rising. "We will leave directly, but I must pay the tavern keeper what I have owed for a fortnight. I can now," he says clinking coins.

Jonas avoids looking in Du Forché's direction, but, to his horror, the young man has come astride of him. "Aha, we meet again, and so soon," says Du Forché in Dutch. "How is it to work for the excommunicated Queen?"

Jonas shrugs. "I don't know what you mean?"

"These days you put lip paint and powder on the Queen's Barge, but it is still a pigboat." The Fleming smiles as he toys with Jonas. "Perhaps you haven't heard that Pope Pius has declared Elizabeth a heretic and favorer of heretics. Her adherents have incurred the sentence of excommunication, cut off from the unity of the body of Christ. Heed me, Jonas Hoen, if you wish to save your soul, you will confide what you learn to me. Trust that I will tell the Inquisition, when you return to Antwerp, that you have acted honorably."

Du Forché's eye darts toward Gheeraerts shaking hands with the tavern keeper. Jonas follows his gaze and when he turns back, Du Forché has already walked onto the street.

Gheeraerts pats Jonas on the shoulder and they exit from the tavern toward the engraver's apartments on Abchurch Lane. The annoying burr under Jonas' saddle is the intruding young man who keeps trying to make a connection with him. Finally, he asks, "Sir, do you have dealings with Jan du Forché?"

Gheeraerts stops abruptly in the street. "I do not!"

"Please sir, I did not mean to offend. But—in the tavern back there—" stammers Jonas.

"Yes, that mongrel turns up everywhere. Never engage him in discourse. He is one of those seven-stuivers spies, ready to sell out his countrymen, always looking for a secret to tattle to the Duke of Alva. The Spaniards have their spies and agents everywhere."

The scowl never leaves Gheeraerts' face until he pushes open the door to his apartments. Susannah de Critz welcomes them, eyes dancing. Jonas can see by the beaming attention she pays Gheeraerts that she is very much in love despite being twenty years younger. The thought flashes through his mind that he would like to sketch Marcus Gheeraerts and Susannah de Critz.

Jonas is immediately included in gossip Susannah relates that she had heard from the Mistress of the Robes. "Jacob Coels will sell many, many bolts of silk to the Royal House," Susannah says, lowering her voice as if the walls could hear. "I had it from Lady Stafford herself, Mistress of the Queen's Garments."

Gheeraerts laughs. "Good times for the Ortels'. Elizabeth gets a commission to limn the engravings in six books and Abraham is off on another edition. Good times."

Jonas barely listens to the chatty young woman's news and Gheeraerts' share of it. He is drinking in his surroundings. The rooms are not as elegantly appointed as the Lyme Street home of the Coles', but are, nevertheless, comfortable, and evidence of the seven-year-old son, Marcus the younger, is everywhere in the spacious main room. A wooden rocking horse stands ready, and a squadron of toy soldiers lies scattered in one corner of the room. A child's drawings of boats lie in a heap nearby. But, what captures Jonas' attention is the huge map of Bruges tacked to the wall, drawn from the perspective of a winged creature hovering hundreds of feet in the air.

"Ten plates to make that map," Gheeraerts says. "No chance for error, or the canals would flood the streets." He laughs at his oft-told joke. "Susannah, I need to show Jonas what a mess a studio can become unless he is careful."

A moment later Gheeraerts' son, Marcus, taps on the front door, and Jonas recognizes the boy from the gathering at the Coles' apartments. The boy is far more interested in Susannah's offer of a sweet than in conversation with either Jonas or his father.

"Come," Gheeraerts says. "Step into my workroom." He points at a passage that leads to the artist's studio. They emerge in a cramped, cluttered room, notable for every inch of wall space taken with paper engravings from Marcus Gheeraerts' edition of *Aesop's Fables*. Jonas gasps, caught by the fine detail, the telling realism of the birds and animals that illustrate moral tales by the fabled Aesop. He recognizes that he is in the company of an extraordinary craftsman. He examines an image of a lion entangled in a hunter's net, being freed by a mouse gnawing the rope of the net.

"Such life in this!" Jonas exclaims.

"What we strive for." Gheeraerts says, recognizing that this could be a teaching moment for his young charge. "God is the artist, and we merely try to imitate Him. Our little scratches and scrapes are a pale imitation, however, so we always must try harder, so God can have a sense, even a sensation, of Himself."

Jonas stares at the artist. He has heard Brother Thomas and the other monks speaking homilies from the traditional catechism, but the Bruges engraver's words make an impression on him as no invocation of God in scripture had ever done.

"Jonas, help me clean up, and we will begin in earnest tomorrow."

For the rest of the afternoon, they neaten and arrange the workbench and sequester copper plates on racks. When they are done with the tidying, the oak tabletop holds only the artist's whetstone, a set of gravers laid out on a board, and a cloth-covered disk—a sand-filled pad with a two-inch diameter. Jonas has seen Frans Hogenberg using such pads as he moved the copper plate, rather than the burin, to make certain circular cuts. Pads with wider diameters occupy the shelves that also hold additional whetstones, and a leather strop.

"Bring your burins tomorrow. Also bring a drawing you want to transfer."

Jonas walks home, elated. Permutations of Gheeraerts' statement about God making artists so He "can have a sense, even a sensation, of Himself" reverberate as he finds his way back to the Sign of the Cock in Lyme Street. If he learns nothing about engraving, he has already heard an important touchstone regarding the craft he chooses to make his vocation.

When he arrives at the Cole apartments, he finds the door to Elizabeth's workroom closed, so he turns toward his room. The door opens behind him, and Elizabeth calls, "Hello, Jonas. I thought I heard your tread. She studies his face. "You look in better spirits.

"Yes, Marcus Gheeraerts and I are free to begin. The Queen's Barge is finally prettified."

"Join me for a light dinner? I need a change from bluing the oceans that surround Europe on three sides."

"Yes, I understand the tedium of suggesting vast oceans with tick marks from the tip of a scribe. That made me hungry, too, not to mention an aching wrist."

"I'll get us something from the kitchen, then." While she is gone, Jonas notices a pamphlet in Dutch on Elizabeth's worktable, *Collected Commentaries from Willem van Oranje*. Jonas is absorbed by the text as Elizabeth returns with cakes and ale.

"May I read this?" he asks.

"Ah—not too dry for a young man like yourself? Yes, you may. Of course, you will not remove it from the house."

"I will return it directly."

Jonas describes what it is like to refurbish the Queen's Barge, but also how he can barely wait to get started in earnest with his tutor. Later, before he retires, Jonas devours Willem van Oranje's commentaries, especially these words:

> *It seems to me neither right nor worthy of a Christian to cause this land to be swarming with troops and inundated with blood for the sake of differences with the doctrine of Calvin and the Confession of Augsburg.*

Jonas lights a candle, closes his eyes to reimagine his vision when he read "troops inundated with blood" over Reformation doctrine. His mind's eye sees an army of Spanish mercenaries run havoc in his village before the flood had washed it away. In the floodwaters' place, a raging horde of soldiers lays waste to farm folk.

He begins. He uses a pencil, becomes unsatisfied by the point, and scrapes it on a stone by the hearth to sharpen the tip. He scratches the act of murder—a Spanish mercenary slices through a baby with a short sword. He sketches a begging old man on his knees as a soldier drives his lance into the supplicating burgher. Another tears the kirtle off a woman, whose children clutch at her skirts as she tries to hide her nakedness. He draws the leer on the Spaniard's face like it is the mien of a madman. The indelible image of the man Jonas had plunged his burin into guides his hand, directs his hate. No objectivity here, only the brutality of the occupation by the Duke of Alva's army and fury for the wanton rape and slaughter of the Lowlanders. He has them now, horrific images that, one day, he will hold up to a mirror and etch into a flat plate of copper. As the candle gutters, he is covered with perspiration. He finds himself sobbing unexpectedly, uncontrollably.

CHAPTER 52

Eindhoven, Late Afternoon, 15 June 1945

The brothers rehang the looted paintings and silently clean the house, unlived in for half a year. Despite retrieving their property, a pall hangs over the brothers in the house in which they grew up. Michael replaces jewelry bag in his parents' armoire. He comes downstairs as Pim positions the Ortelius atlas on the sideboard. Pim looks closely at the darkened stains on the sideboard and kneels to pick up scattered papers. Similar dried brown patches speckle the wide-planked floor.

"Is this from father's blood?" Michael asks. Pim nods. Michael tugs on the half-open drawer. "He kept his Belgian pistol here."

Michael tries to reconstruct events based on Diederik's rant. "He shot Emma's husband," he says in wonder that his father could do such an act.

A smile plays at Pim's mouth. "I hope it hurt like the fires of hell."

"Why did Emma say what she did about a Jewish girl?" Michael asks again.

Pim only shrugs. "Tomorrow let's try to find out more about this Henk Rost. I remember a 'Rost' used to work for Philips."

Shortly before six, the sun still shone in the west and the two brothers pedal to the Stationsplein to meet the train carrying Gerdi. At six-twenty she emerges from a third-class coach carrying a straw bag laden with wine, bread, sausages, and eggs. She runs to Pim, her fair hair tied in a thick purple ribbon flying behind her. They hug and kiss on the station platform, interminably, in Michael's eyes. Eventually, she breaks away and embraces Michael with the same enthusiasm. Michael involuntarily stiffens and Gerdi releases her hold.

"I am so glad to see you back home. Oh, how I have missed you, Pim," she says. Pim looses a torrent of tears in a way Michael has never seen before.

"Me too, me too," is all he can say and both of them are sniffling, laughing, and crying unashamedly. Their reunion is so emotional that Michael does not immediately ask about the troubling issue Emma Berghuis has raised. He has to admit to himself that she and Pim make a handsome couple. She has not lost her trait to be quick to smile, and her sincere demeanor disarms, revealing her open, intelligent, and pretty face. She wears a nondescript jacket over a violet cotton dress that flares in the breeze as she sits sidesaddle while Pim pedals them home. Michael follows on his bicycle.

They eat a light meal from Gerdi's bag and share a bottle of wine. Gerdi relates what she knows about the killing of Herman Dijkstra; pieced together mostly from what Hetty van Aalt could tell her. "But the poor girl hates to talk about it."

"I have to ask," Michael says nervously. "Why did you bring this girl here? She was a complete stranger to our father, yes?"

"Yes, Michael. He never knew her before."

"You convinced him, then?" Michael is bent on assigning blame.

"Michael," Pim says sternly, reading his brother's intent.

Michael struggles to keep an open mind.

"It was your father's choice," Gerdi interjects. "He was surprised when I showed up that night with the little girl. But he understood entirely what he was so willing to do. He missed you two so. That was part of why he agreed. I dared not let you know in letters, and your father knew he must not reveal this in letters he sent you. It all turned out terribly, of course, for your father, I'm saddened to say. Your father was a courageous and gracious man."

Michael hears a ringing in his ears that bars hearing Gerdi's explanation. So much makes no sense to him ever since his mother was killed five years earlier, he cannot accept yet another poor choice that has now cost him both his parents.

Michael begs off when Gerdi invites him to join Pim and her at a gathering of Dutch resistance fighters who are celebrating that night. Michael pushes back his chair with no words and walks out of the kitchen.

"Think about it," Gerdi is saying to Michael's back with as much compassion as she can manage. "He chose to not turn in the little girl when they came for her. He saved her. He chose to save her."

Only a snippet of what she says enters Michael's consciousness. Michael restores the Ortelius *Theatrum* to its low stand on the sideboard in the living room as it was displayed in his memory. He hears Pim in the kitchen describing what they had found at Emma Berghuis' cottage. His brother is filling in the circumstances of his father's killing from what he had learned from Diederik. Gerdi says that it matches what Hetty had told her. "She especially remembers the partial run up the stairs as her hiding place was just beneath them."

"That was Diederik—" Pim says, "with his kneecap shot."

Michael loses track of their conversation. He notices that the last pages of the atlas are adhered to the edge of the back cover where his father's blood had pooled before drying.

He does not know until nearly seventy years later, when he unpacks the book in California, that the blood had sealed like a sarcophagus, housing Herman Dijkstra's unread commentary. By then, he has no interest in his father's words as he has cast him in the role of a fool, misled and taken in by his sister-in-law.

CHAPTER 53

Walnut Creek, Morning, April 13ᵗʰ 2016

On Friday, at barely 7:00 a.m., head and neck throbbing, Michael Dijkstra answers a phone call from a man with a rasping voice who says he has an interest in an antiquarian map of the world, published in the Ortelius atlas.

"Good," Michael says through the foul taste in his mouth, and he wonders how all of these people know that he is the consigner of the map. "How did you get this number?"

"The map is a well-known specimen," the caller says, evasively.

"Can you answer my question?"

"Oh, in the business, the auction gallery will provide that information for the safety of transactions, and provenance," Michael screws up his face in disbelief. He knows dissembling when he hears it.

"What is your name?"

"Horst Harmon. My business is Harmon Prints and Collectibles, San Francisco. I understand there is an entire atlas available."

"Mr. Harmon—" Michael stops mid-sentence. He does not know what to say next. The day before, a stranger named Spencer had come into his house and put him through an emotional wringer, and now some other party appears to be worming his way into his life.

"Mr. Harmon," Dijkstra begins again, "the Ortelius map is at auction on Saturday. I signed an agreement with them. I wish you luck in acquiring it. Goodbye."

He hangs up. He wants desperately to call the auction house and give them a piece of his mind for giving out his number, but no one would be in the office until nine o'clock.

When Michael is awakened that Friday morning by the phone call from the print dealer named Harmon, his conversation with the intrusive dealer is only one portion of what is going through his mind. The other is the question, "Where was it Gerdi went, when she left Amsterdam and found assisted living quarters, some years ago?" He resolves to find the card —or had he followed through on his original impulse to toss it in the trash?

But something the first dealer had said sticks in Michael's mind. He walks uncertainly to his dining room table, still littered with last night's dishes, the pages of his father's notes, and…"Ahhh, here it is."

He picks up Owen's business card and calls the number.

Owen's phone rings while he is shaving, still hurt and angry over his and Patricia's inability to come to resolution of their deep divisions the night before. Scowling, he sees the number has a 510 area code. With shaving cream on half his face he hears, "Hello? Mr. Spencer?" The European-tinged voice asks in an early morning voice. "Michael Dijkstra, here."

"Mr. Dijkstra," Owen repeats, trying to get his bearings. "Good to hear from you, because I—"

"Mr. Spencer," Dijkstra interrupts, nervously. "Yesterday you said—among many other things—that you would like me to talk to your wife because— well, I don't recall exactly why. But she is the daughter, yes?"

Owen looks in the mirror at his half-shaved face and frowns. He again hears Patricia's irritation when he'd told her that Dijkstra might want to speak with her.

"Mr. Dijkstra, yes, she is Hetty Baron's daughter. 'Baron' was her married name. Her family name was van Aalt, I believe, but my wife would certainly know."

"May I speak with her?"

"My wife teaches today, and she has already left for school. But more importantly, I was going to call you and apologize because I had no business offering a conversation with her without speaking with her first. I'm afraid I overstepped good sense when I suggested that.

"Ahh," the old man says, disappointment easily discerned by Owen.

"Well, wait a moment." Owen says, making a snap decision. "I can call her and ask that she call you. If she flat out refuses, I'll call you."

"Yes, of course. I would appreciate if she could, you see, because I have been doing a lot of thinking, and I—I also want to apologize to you for some of the things I said yesterday. I…I don't expect you would understand."

"Mr. Dijkstra, there's no need to apologize. I do understand how bringing all this up is upsetting."

"Thank you and I know it may be an imposition, but I would very much appreciate your wife speaking with me."

"I will try getting her and see if she can manage a call to you. But I know she has a field trip today with her class, so I cannot assure you a quick response."

"Hmm…" Dijkstra grunts. "The people you represent, they are a Jewish Holocaust—" What would you call it? Archive? Museum?"

"Yes. Full disclosure, Mr. Dijkstra. They are Yad Vashem in Jerusalem. Do you know them?"

"No. I never…. No."

"They are the largest documentation center in the world of everything to do with the fate of Jews in the Holocaust, including a recognition of those non-Jews who reached out to save even one Jew."

"Then they honor Gerdi Dijkstra, my sister-in-law? Her family name was Ten Broeck."

Owen hears a plaintive tone in the old man's question. "I can try to find out for you, Mr. Dijkstra," Owen says quietly.

"Hmm. I hope they honor Gerdi."

"While I have you on the phone—" Owen starts to say.

But Michael Dijkstra rings off before Owen can complete his message about his new clients' interest in the whole atlas and, especially, his father, Herman Dijkstra's memories of the Nazi occupation.

Owen looks at his half-shaven face in the bathroom mirror and wonders what had transpired for the old man that he would try to follow up on speaking with Patricia. He hastily completes shaving and calls Patricia's cellphone.

Her car is not equipped with onboard hands-free telephone service and so her cell rings and goes to voicemail. Owen leaves a message for her ending with: "And yes, I know you are slammed with the field trip to the Mission today, but please call me as soon as possible."

CHAPTER 54

East Palo Alto, April 13th 2016

From the moment Patricia enters the school parking lot she coordinates parents and the driver of the school bus for the field trip. She turns in parental consent forms at the front office and marshals the kids and her parent-aides onto the bus. At 8:40, sitting amongst 35 chattering children and the five parents along for the expedition, she allows herself a breath of relief as the bus pulls onto the freeway headed north. Twenty minutes later she remembers her ringing phone on University Avenue and sees that she has a message from Owen. She plugs a finger in one ear and speed-dials his number.

"Me," she says. "Where are you?" She wonders if she sounds as harried as she feels.

"Oh, boy," Owen says. "Highway 92, on the bridge. Berkeley today."

"Right."

"So remember last night when I told you Mr. Dijkstra might want to speak to you?"

"Oh, Owen. Not seriously, please." She cannot keep the irritation from her voice. But she listens as Owen soldiers on.

"Yes, he called this morning and I explained that you had a field trip, but if you could, would you give him a call?"

Patricia says nothing. She knows that all Owen can hear is the babble of children on the bus.

"Patty?"

"I heard you. What's the number and what's his name, again?"

"I'm really sorry to burden you with this," Owen says before he reads off Dijkstra's number and spells his name. "It seems to be very important to him, Patricia."

The apology in his tone is evident. "I understand. But think of something really nice to show me how sorry you are to drag me into this, Owen, dear."

"My pleasure," he replies breezily.

She smiles despite her displeasure, and whispers an exasperated, "Bye."

"Jamie, stop teasing Imelda," she orders and watches the boy's face cloud over. Then she wonders if she isn't kicking the cat out of spite for Owen.

"Take a deep breath," she advises herself and dials Michael Dijkstra's phone number. But she is switched to his voicemail.

Walnut Creek, April 13th 2016

Shortly after 9:00 a.m., Dijkstra places a call to Fleming's and asks for Rodney Pinkham.

"This is he," Pinkham snaps. "I'm quite involved with Saturday's auction so I hope you will be brief."

"This is Michael Dijkstra. I consigned the Ortelius map."

"Oh, yes. I believe there has been some interest in that piece."

"That's good," Dijkstra says, "but why are these people talking to me? Harmon this morning and yesterday Spencer?"

"Who? Who?"

"Mr. Pinkham, I expected some discretion. That's what you promised when I signed our agreement."

"Mr. Dike—sir, I assure you that your identity has been kept confidential."

"Then where did these dealers get my name?" Dijkstra demands. "And how to contact me? This Harmon said it was auction gallery policy to provide such information—"

"Not so, Mr. Dike—sir. Let me get to the bottom of this. I promise I will find how this information slipped out. I will get back to you, and I apologize if this actually came from any of my staff. Let me get back to you."

"Very well," Michael says.

"Goodbye," Pinkham says in a studied lightness.

During his call Michael noticed an incoming call that went to voicemail. He is heartened by the message.

"Hello, this is Patricia Spencer, Mr. Dijkstra." A din of juvenile voices accompanies the woman's voice. "I'm on a field trip with my class today, but my husband says that it is important that I speak to you. Sorry I missed you." A silence follows and Michael thinks she has completed her message. But it continues. "Call me if you really do need to speak to me today. I'm sure you don't like playing phone tag any more than I do."

"Aha." Michael is debating how to proceed. He glimpses his father's words at the bottom of the page. *I am afraid for Hetty.* His answering machine displays Patricia's number beginning with a 650 area code.

Shortly after 9:20 a.m., the school bus is passing Candlestick Point, when Patricia's ringtone sounds. The kids have quieted down considerably. "This is Patricia."

"Ah. Aha. Mrs. Spencer. Forgive my intrusion but your husband said it would be all right to speak with you. My name is Michael Dijkstra."

"Yes," Patricia says, a bit surprised by the warmth in her own tone. The elderly man's Dutch-accented English is oddly reassuring that he wasn't some crank. But a long silence follows. She hears his labored breathing, and she wonders if the man is unwell. "Mr. Dijkstra? Are you all right?"

"I'm sorry to be emotional." She hears him fight for his voice. "Perhaps this is not a good time for you. I really—I maybe need a few minutes to sit with you somewhere and say what I want to. My father... you see...."

"Mr. Dijkstra," Patricia says softly. She decides that if he understands that her primary attention would be on her class they could meet as long as it was a public place. Her parent-aides can keep the class in hand if she met briefly with this man. "Owen says you live in Walnut Creek. I will be in San Francisco today with my class. But for about half an hour around one o'clock near Mission Dolores, my kids will be eating their lunches. I will be supervising them, of course, but we could have a short conversation as long as you understand you may not get my full attention."

"That's very generous, and I will not intrude on your duty."

Do you know Dolores Park at 18th Street across from the high school? There are benches near the south end by the playground."

She hears life come into Michael's voice. "You're so kind. I can take BART easily to 16th Street and walk over."

Patricia offers: "I'm wearing a lime green suit, and if the weather stays like it is now, I won't be too rumpled." On days when she had the students on outings she always wears an easy to spot outfit for her kids if they needed to pick her out in a crowd. This time, the bright shade of green, not her favorite color, but practical as a beacon, could come in handy.

"You are so kind, Mrs. Spencer." Michael repeats. "Thank you. I will see you at one o'clock and we have phones if something comes up. I will wear a brown suit."

Patricia makes a note to talk to her parent-aides to be sure the kids are supervised while she has the impromptu meet-up with the old man.

In Walnut Creek, Michael sees that another message has been recorded on his machine while he was in conversation with Mrs. Spencer. The tone is cold and clipped. "This is Rodney Pinkham, Fleming Galleries. I'm sorry I missed you, but I wanted to tell you that the person responsible for your contact information being made available has been fired. Please accept our apologies and assurances that it will not happen again."

CHAPTER 55

San Francisco, Mission Dolores Courtyard, April 13th 2016

At 12:45 p.m. Patricia sits Mario Kinsella down on a bench overlooking the graveyard adjacent to the old adobe Mission. The rest of her class, separated into groups of seven monitored by Grace Richardson and the other four parent-aides, listen dutifully to a docent who tours them around the paths among the gravestones and replica of an Ohlone tule reed hut. Outside the walls, the hum of the city reminds Patricia that she is sitting in a place of history preserved in Franciscan amber.

"So what's so great about a bunch of old dead people," the boy demands with a snarky whine. "Look. Some of those gravestones are even broken. It's creepy here. Whyd'ja take us to such a creepy place, Mrs. Spencer?"

Patricia finds herself smiling.

"Mario. Here is a piece of history of our state. Not even the quake in 1906 could destroy it. See that big church next door? Burned to the ground and had to be rebuilt. But this old adobe made it through. These graves hold some of the original people, the Ohlone and the Miwok, who had to build this mission for Father Serra."

"They're all dead. What's so great about that?"

"I don't know the answer to that, Mario, but when we have the test on this unit, I would like to see that you were actually on this field trip and saw a few things about how the California you're growing up in came to be."

Mario stares sullenly at his classmates, some walking like zombies among the gravestones.

"Go back to Mrs. Richardson and no more shouting. Do you understand?"

Once again, the kid has reduced her to pulling rank. After an unintelligible mumble, the boy slow-walks across the concrete path and follows his class into the gift shop where the docent is finishing her presentation.

What was so compelling about dead people? Patricia asks herself. *I seem to be in their grasp.* A memory surfaces of her mother bundled in winter clothes and she in a snowsuit. Her mother is snapping with impatience over Patricia having lost a glove in the snow on a family outing at Big Bear that Thanksgiving weekend. "You could catch cold and die by such carelessness," her mother had said in exasperation. Only her father's comforting squeeze of his six-year old little girl's cold hand kept her mother's doomsday pronouncement from making her feel like an abject failure. "If you coddle her she will never learn to take care of her things," her mother reprimands. "Hetty, don't blow this up into something so big," her father insists.

That is all Patricia remembers, except that her fingers ached with the cold. From her bench, Patricia looks at the façade of the Mission, the statuary and gravestones in the cemetery. She reflects on a pallor of misery that lingers in the walls and artifacts. This building, the forced conversions, and the enslavement of the Native Americans were undisputed facts.

She follows the straggling students into the gift shop and squeezes Grace Richardson's arm.

"Thanks for sending Mario to speak with me," she tells Grace.

"You've got him every day. He's a little tough guy."

Patricia smiles, briefly, checks in with the other parent-aides, then thanks the docent, and announces: "Okay, kids, we're going to walk up to Dolores Park now, and get our lunches from the bus. We will walk in two rows and you know who your partners are and your section leaders. There are bathrooms in the park. Boys will follow Mr. Alvarez to the boys' bathroom if you need one. And Mrs. Richardson will take you to the girls'. Remember, we are walking on public streets, so you can have quiet conversations. No shouting, or running, and keep in line. How about a big goodbye to Mission Dolores and remember the Spanish word for 'Goodbye?'"

A cacophony of pre-adolescent voices cries, "Goodbye—Adios, Mission Dolores! Adios!" Patricia leads the class onto the street and an orderly march of fourth-graders heads south, in check by the five assisting parents. The kids carry on lively conversations about everything but their experience on the Mission grounds.

Patricia drops out of the lead and speaks with Raymond Alvarez, the one male parent-aide. "Keep a special eye on Mario, please. Bring him to me if you need to. I'm going to bring up the rear."

"Not to worry," Alvarez assures her.

"The bus driver says he will be parked on 20th Street across from the playground." Patricia scans her phone for messages and sees none. Just before one o'clock, she fears it was a poor idea to squeeze in even a brief meeting with Michael Dijkstra while she chaperoned her class.

The roar of two motorcycles jars her moments after she follows her kids across 17th Street. She feels her body clench and veer toward the steel fencing of the high school and almost knocks over Imelda Ramos, who is lagging behind. Patricia hurries Imelda to catch up with her group. The tension in her body ebbs only after the loud mufflers dissipate over a second rise on the hilly street going south. The line of kids crosses busy 18th Street with the light, and Patricia breathes a relieved sigh because that is the last cross-street. She sees the comforting sight of the yellow school bus inthe distance, with Jim, the driver, leaning against it. The kids pick up the pace as their late lunches beckon. She walks more quickly, too, and glances to her right across the rolling green swales interrupted by pods of palms and shade trees. This park had been a burial ground before all the bodies were exhumed and moved to a town south of The City.

"Dolores Park," she muses. "Perfectly sad name." After walking steadily toward the playground, she slows when she sees a very old, gray-haired man in a brown suit seated on a bench. Most of her class has already passed him. She smoothes her skirt and quickens her pace. The old man rises stiffly to greet her and offers a shallow bow. The man has recognized the lime green suit. He carries a worn manila envelope.

A wave of apprehension rolls over Patricia as he forces a smile.

CHAPTER 56

London, 18 July 1570

As his weeks in London pass into months, Jonas finds himself deeply missing Sofie. He eagerly reads her letters and learns that Master Du Brul will no longer be the prime source of paper for the succeeding editions; a Lisbon papermaker will be supplying most of the double folio sheets. As a consequence, Janine has been let go and Sofie's job is more of wetting the imported paper in preparation for engraving and printing the next edition. Du Brul will continue to fabricate paper for other books printed by Gilles Coppens de Diest at the Boekprintere Scheldt. She writes:

"I am so alone now, and think of you every night in my lonely room. Do you still care for me as much as I do you? I miss you every day."

Jonas fills his letters trying to share that his days are now an exciting mix of learning how to sharpen and use his tools, that his world is new every day and he is progressing in learning English. He reports that Elizabeth Cole and her children now speak English with him, and little James is fascinated by bugs. Susannah and young Marcus Gheeraerts also drill English phrases into his speech. Only the elder Marcus continues to converse in Dutch.

Jonas learns how to hone his gravers on a whetstone. "I can't believe Abraham gave you this old set of burins and did not instruct you on how to keep them sharp and useful," Gheeraerts complains.

Jonas counts the strokes on the whetstone so that the cutting edges of his gravers are exactly symmetrical. He imitates Gheeraerts' steps needed to restore a forty-five degree angle to the face of his primary cutting burin. He learns to roll the graver to widen the cut and maximize ink retention for the transfer to paper. He uses the cloth-covered pad to perfect the technique of turning the plate to achieve a curve under the graver, while his palm holds a steady pressure on it. Soon he is practicing sweeping curves and short, acute curlicues. What had been magic at the hands of the skilled Frans Hogenberg becomes a craft that he can master with practice. He learns quickly and feels gratitude for Gheeraerts' tutelage.

The master gives him paper proof sheets of engravings to practice both the sketching and crosshatching that coaxes the viewer's eye to see foreground and depth on the paper's surface. Gheeraerts is at once patient and a taskmaster.

"No, no. You can't gouge like that. You build your engraving bit by bit. Use your pressure. Use the scraper to cut the bur away immediately. You are too impatient!" Gheeraerts' enthusiasm makes his voice go up and Jonas has to learn that his instructor is not angry with him, but impassioned.

"You think you can merely—zip-zip, incise this image into the copper? No. It has taken ages for this copper to form in the ground. Respect this metal; it is soft for you to work it. It is not going anywhere. Use your hands lovingly, like it is a woman's body you are touching. Bring the art out of the copper. Like bringing the blood up. Like touching a woman's parts. Slowly. You make the art want to leave the metal, to come to your touch. Let the plate rise to your burin. Apply the pressure like a lover."

Jonas' face flushes to hear his tutor describe the process. It reminds him of how he had felt with Sofie. He realizes he is grinning.

"Don't be such a schoolboy," Gheeraerts chides.

But Jonas learns a new lesson. If he infuses his work with the same passion that he has for Sofie, he can be in love with what he is creating. *Is this what "God having a sense, even a sensation, of Himself"* really means? He keeps his question unasked of his tutor, but asks it of himself several times in a day.

Afternoons, when Susannah has business at the Royal Court, Jonas accompanies Gheeraerts to the tavern where they talk about the flatness of their homeland. "If this damned island did its job properly, we would not have the floods across our lowlands," Gheeraerts grouses.

"Master Ortels thinks the British Isles slipped out to sea," Jonas ventures.

"Perhaps they foresaw the future, eh? Philip's vengeance against the Dutch and the Iron Duke of Alva," he says venomously. "If I were an island, I'd try to escape the Spanish boot, too. Abraham should stick to printing maps, not inventing crazy ideas," the older engraver scoffs. "I do want to return to Bruges. I miss it."

Gheeraerts has been away the better part of three years. Jonas wonders how long he needs to stay abroad himself. He abruptly stops and grips the table edge as Jan Du Forché and a companion, wearing Spanish livery, enter the public house.

"Killed any of the king's pike men lately, Young Mister Hoen?"

Jonas screws his face into a sour scowl to meet Du Forché's false smile.

"Juan Carlos, this is my young friend from Antwerp," Du Forché says in English. "Don Fernando Àlvarez de Toledo takes an interest in this young man, I believe. Yes, the Duke of Alva, himself."

Juan Carlos raises his dark eyebrows in what Jonas takes to be a mocking respect. "Ah, you will be a guest on the Duke of Alva's gibbet soon?" The jibe is delivered in English laced with a Catalan accent.

Jonas asks Gheeraerts in Dutch, who is looking grave, "Do you smell something odd?" Jonas makes a show of inspecting his boots, and wrinkles his nose. "I thought I stepped in something, but mayhap the something just came walking in."

Jonas peers into Juan Carlos' black eyes, which reply with pure hatred.

"Jan, do you smell it, too?" Jonas mocks. "Or are you used to that smell?"

"I would be very careful," Jan Du Forché hisses, and nudges Juan Carlos toward a table across the room.

"They seem to let anyone walk the streets in this country," Jonas says, rising.

Du Forché restrains Juan Carlos and glares back at him. Gheeraerts pushes Jonas toward the street. Jonas makes a show of waving his hand in front of him to clear the air and precedes Gheeraerts onto Saint Botolph Lane.

"Jonas," Gheeraerts pauses to weigh his words, "I'm spending a great deal of time trying to make you a craftsman worthy of guild membership. My efforts will go for naught if you are found floating in the Thames because of your rapier wit. It happens all the time in this city."

He hears no mirth in Gheeraerts' warning. "I understand, sir," Jonas says. But he falls silent and ponders if he overstepped himself with Du Forché and the Catalan. He sees how he is prey to his anger, which manifests in sarcasm. "I apologize, Master Gheeraerts." He walks on in silence toward Fenchurch Street where they go their separate ways. Jonas waves to Gheeraerts. "Tomorrow morning same time?"

"Ah, no. Come later. Susannah has arranged a meeting with her cousin, John—more to do for the Tudor Court. It will give us a good afternoon session. Do up some sketches for transfer to a prepared plate. I should be back by noon."

"Until tomorrow," Jonas calls as the sun gives way to shadows between the buildings. He stops at a stable on his way to sketch a horse tethered to a post. He leans against the wall of a draper's shop across the street and draws the horse standing dumbly. Then a street dog trots nearby and begins barking at the horse. The horse becomes agitated, kicking and rearing on its short reins wrapped in three turns on the post. Jonas captures the dynamic scene, first the rearing horse, its huge eye, and tossing mane, while the dog bares its teeth and leaps at the flashing front hooves. The horse whinnies loudly and the barking becomes louder. Then the stableman comes out with a whip and shouts. "Christ, damn that mangy cur!" He cracks the whip and the dog is nipped on the back by the sharp leather. The dog runs up the lane whimpering, ears flat, tail between its legs. Jonas' images fill three sheets. He plans to work on this subject later that night. His sketches merely capture the arc of the action. The details—the swirl of the mane, the crazed eye of the horse, the toss of the forelock, the angle of the hooves, the dog with its pinned ears—he will add these details and transfer them to the copper plate tomorrow.

Another scene plays in his mind, as he makes his way to Lyme Street—the story his countryman told of the harried priest, beheaded in the graveyard of his church. In his room at the Coles' apartments, he draws a picture of the terrified priest a moment before the sword beheads him. Jonas is shocked to see that he has drawn the face of Jan Forché on the hapless priest grasping a headstone, and the face of the man named Juan Carlos on the body of the Spanish executioner.

By candlelight in the wee hours, he reviews and, in his mind, steps into the images he has sketched on the street in greater detail. He sees himself as the whipped dog racing up the street after he taunts the horse. He imagines his own teeth bared and nipping at the fetlocks of the horse. He wants to strike the head off Jan Du Forché with a blow from the weapon of his Spanish co-conspirator.

He is surprised to hear a light tap on his door. He notes that his candlelight creeps under the door into the hallway announcing his awakened state. He opens the door and is stunned to see the scullery maid shivering in her nightdress. Her lips are trying to say words, but they are quivering. She quickly comes in and shuts the door behind her. "I was very scared," she whispers. "May I sleep with you?"

"What—What scared you?" Jonas asks, flustered.

"A rat. I can't sleep there tonight. Let me sleep with you. I'll be very good."

Before Jonas can think, she is under the covers, wriggling out of her shift. Jonas stands dumbly. Then he finds his voice. "You can't do that, no. You must leave."

"I can't, I can't. I'm too scared," she implores. She reminds Jonas of a noisy actor overplaying his part in the Brabo festivities. Even with Jonas' scant expertise in English, he can discern that she is making that up, or has been coached. A crooked attempt at a lascivious smile creases her lips. Naked, she rises from the bed and, feigning shivering, she pulls him against her.

"I'm so scared, hold me close."

"Millie, you can't—" he begins, but standing on her tiptoes she presses her lips on his and grasps her hand around his sex. Her movements are jerky, her hands claw-like, her laughter crass. "Stop this," he demands, and pushes her at arms length. He picks up and holds out her shift and opens the door. She backs into the hallway.

Jonas puzzles over her behavior and his revulsion, then gives up, utterly confused. Ten minutes later, he blows out the candle and falls asleep, his weariness brought on more by the day than by what he has just experienced in a stupor of exhaustion.

When Jonas awakes the next morning he can barely recall the confusing encounter he has had with the cunning little maid. He washes himself with tallow soap and the chilly water from the porcelain pitcher. Despite knowing he didn't encourage the girl in the least, feels beset by guilt for even having let her into his room. He begins a letter to Sofie before he dresses, saying how much he misses her and cannot wait to press her body against his, and his lips on hers.

An urgent rapping on his door interrupts his letter to Sofie.

CHAPTER 57

Dolores Park, San Francisco, Afternoon, April 13th 2016

"Mrs. Spencer?" Michael Dijkstra asks, in a sonorous, accented voice. He attempts to smile, but his look appears pained on his ancient face, ruddy and pale at the same time, his neck lined like dinosaur kale. His suit and shoes are worn-looking. He holds a manila envelope. Patricia chides herself on being focused on his clothing.

"Yes. Mr. Dijkstra?"

"You are very kind to meet with me, Mrs. Spencer. Please sit."

She tries to suppress the flutter in her voice, a nervousness she blows out of proportion, sparked by a memory of her frail mother's breathless recounting of her survival as a terrified young girl. But she calms down enough to be charmed by Dijkstra's accent. She smiles. "Mr. Dijkstra, I'll need to keep an eye on my class. If you don't mind, let's move closer to where the kids are going to eat lunch. They'll be supervised by several parents, but you know...."

"Of course," Michael agrees and follows her to the bench of her choice with a direct view of the kids and the school bus.

Patricia senses that the old man is studying her—trying to recognize her. She cocks her head as she sits and realizes that she, too, is studying him between glimpses at the kids returning from the bus to have their lunches on an arc of benches along a running path. Satisfied the kids are all right, she makes full eye contact with him. They each seem to attempt to read each other through the present into another time. She smiles with the insight.

"I know this is an unusual request and I am intruding on your privacy and your busy life during work, but I have felt—feel…compelled, really…to meet you."

As Dijkstra pauses, Patricia sees him battle for his next words. "You see, my father—I'm not sure that you know any of this. But in the time of the German occupation, my father took in a girl, who, your husband told me yesterday, was your mother. I never met her because I was in Germany—a forced labor battalion before…before…."

"That must have been awful," Patricia says, moved by his struggle to speak and then by such a concept of a labor battalion. She imagines a lightning image of Ohlone Indians setting adobe bricks under the muzzles of Spanish muskets. Dijkstra grasps the back of the bench. He looks away. Patricia, at first confused, decides that he is overcome by the unfamiliarity of expressing what he had felt. She breaks eye contact to survey her class again. Millie Jenkins is laughing too raucously in conversation with Imelda Ramos. "Excuse me a moment." She stands, about to walk over when her parent-aide takes charge. *Oh, good. Grace Richardson is on top of it.*

She turns back to Dijkstra who is looking into the mid-distance.

He speaks: "It *was* awful. You are very kind to say that. It was a terrible time for me. And I can only imagine, now, that it was even more terrible for your mother who was only a young girl."

"Yes, the wound went very deep for her; she kept it a secret from me," Patricia acknowledges, uncomfortable and saddened. She sits down and watches the old man's face contort with his pain and then listens to him trying to gain his voice. "I was not sure of what I would say to you, but it must be this. Why I asked to meet you is that I want to apologize for years of ill will I had for your mother even though I never met her. My father was shot and killed to keep her from being discovered."

Patricia hears the effort and anguish in his words. "I am so sorry you lost him," she says with sincerity. "I think my mother—" Patricia loses her voice to a rush of sadness as she recalls the dying woman saying he was killed because of her. After clearing her throat, Patricia adds in full voice: "I am grateful for the safe refuge he provided my mother. Truth be known, I understand feeling helpless and wanting to blame someone, even a little girl, for having someone ripped from your life so violently."

A flash of what it had been for her mother to be separated from her father's grasp in Amsterdam informs her last words. She blinks, shaken, but she also sees that Dijkstra can barely take in what he is hearing. "Mr. Dijkstra, correct me if I'm wrong, but I think that no one has ever given you understanding about the thoughts you had about the stranger who moved in."

"She slept in my bed, you see, while I was forced to work for the Nazis. The bastards—forgive me—who killed—first my mother with their bombs in Rotterdam—and then my father. No. No one ever said it was all right that I feel so much anger for that girl."

He clears his throat several times. Finally, he can only proffer his hand, which Patricia grasps softly. She feels the bony fingers, tremulous.

He squeezes her grip. "Your mother raised a wonderful daughter. I am glad she survived and grew up, your mother, so you could be. Mr. Spencer is very lucky."

"I'll let him know you said so," she says, lightening the mood, and completing the handshake.

Mario Kinsella and two other boys come running by. "Hey, Mrs. S, when do we get this circus on the road. Jim says he's 'just waiting for the word.'"

"Mario. Boys!" Patricia calls. "Come over here."

The two others move immediately and Mario brings up the rear. "James and Colin, and Mario hanging back there, this is Mr. Dijkstra."

"Hello," the old man nods, unsure of how to address them.

"Mr. Dijkstra helped invent a light bulb that lasts for years and years. So he is a very important man, and you just got to meet him."

"What kind of name is 'Doik-stra'?" Mario asks, skeptically.

"Dutch. What kind of name is Mario?"

"I dunno," Mario answers.

"Well maybe we can figure it out on the bus ride back," Patricia says, and the boys know they are dismissed.

Michael pushes down on the bench and rises slowly. He realizes he is holding the manila envelope. "Oh, I must not forget, I have this," he says.

Patricia gets up and takes the offering.

"I found this behind the bedstead in my room, the room your mother slept in. It was tucked in a children's book, which I'm afraid I did not keep. But this—For some reason I kept this. It belonged to your mother."

She opens the manila envelope and unfolds a very old engraving, creased like a triptych. The image showed three panels: the first is of a large dog snapping at a rearing horse, where the horse's eye is immediately compelling as it bulges with fear; the second pane shows a stableman whipping the dog; and the third shows the dog running away in pain, *its* eye now registering enormous fear. The print unsettles Patricia. She is unsure if it is because of the violence of the image or because she is holding a print that her mother treasured when she was a child. The initials JH show in the corner of the third pane.

"Thank you," she says in a subdued voice. "This is quite a picture."

"Yes, I thought so, too."

Patricia extends her hand. He takes it, shakes it formally, and steps back on the path. On impulse, Patricia hugs the old man. He is a head taller than she. His body tenses and then relaxes. He hugs back briefly and then they part.

"Thank you for seeing me," he says.

She folds the engraving back into the manila envelope and begins walking toward her class, now being marshaled by her parent-aides toward the waiting bus. She turns back to wave at Dijkstra.

He raises his hand in what could be construed as a return wave. Patricia is surprised to see Mario Kinsella wave back, uncertainly. She turns to see

Michael Dijkstra's face smile for the first time. He begins walking toward downtown.

On the ride back to her school in East Palo Alto, Patricia tries to process her meeting with the old man but she can get little further than the stranger's apology for his life-long attitude toward her mother, an innocent ten-year-old. Patricia can't quite get hold of the thought, but she knows she carries a sense of being victimized, too, the way daughters take on the anxieties, prejudices, and anger of a mother who could never be good enough. Hetty could never be good enough because she survived while her family was killed. Patricia goes deep into thought for a moment trying to "be" her mother, Hetty as a little girl. As she construes it, all of that was her fault. These ideas helped her mother make sense of the brutal world. Patricia thinks again of Dijkstra's apology for heaping one more fault at Hetty's feet, the death of his father. Then she opens the manila folder to take in the mysterious engraving. It was not pleasant to look at. Her thoughts drift to her mother's deathbed. She hears the rasping voice fighting through the morphine haze. *"The horse knew. The dog knew."* What? *Abject terror? Insurmountable fear?* She would show the engraving to Owen. Perhaps he would know who JH was.

As the bus rolls south, passing the town of San Bruno, she pushes into one of her periodic stand-ups to see how the kids are doing. She is surprised to see Mario Kinsella without a characteristic smart aleck look on his face. He gives the impression of being deep in thought. She smiles and sits, savoring the boy's introspection.

Owen shakes hands with Dr. Bregmann in his office on the UC campus as the professor says, "If you sign this fax, you have an agreement with the Yad Vashem Remembrance Authority to act as their agent for the purchase at auction of this map. Here's the English translation from the Hebrew." Bregmann pushes a paper across the desk.

"I had a phone conversation with Mr. Dijkstra this morning," Owen says. "He asked if a woman named 'Gerdi Ten Bruk' was acknowledged. From what I learned, she was the person who rescued Hetty and took her to Eindhoven for safety. And while I'm at it, Hetty's maiden name was van

Aalt. A-a-l-t. Her family was from Haarlem, near Amsterdam. I'm not sure how 'Bruk' is spelled."

"I'll email Chaim with those questions and add that information for the girl."

Owen reads the translation of the document and is pleased he is also authorized to negotiate with Dijkstra for the complete book of maps. Following inspection of a copy of Herman Dijkstra's written comments, Yad Vashem also considers Owen their representative in such negotiations, if they have interest in the documents.

"Looks kosher," Owen laughs and he signs the agreement.

CHAPTER 58

San Francisco, Afternoon, April 13th 2016

Leaving Dolores Park, Michael Dijkstra opts not to turn right toward the BART station. His meeting with Patricia Spencer buoys him to walk several more blocks to Market Street to take a streetcar rather than go underground. He feels a spring in his gait for initiating the unusual meeting. His attitude has elevated since he has made the gesture of apologizing to the daughter of the woman who had slept in safety in his room for nearly two years during the terrible times.

As the trolley clacks down Market Street, the sight of the feisty little boy, Mario, reminds him of his brash brother at twelve. "Micaha" was Pim's mocking name for his younger brother. "Micaha," what kind of name was *that*?

"My name is Michael," the nine year-old protests. "Mama, Pim is making fun of my name."

"Stop it, Pim," Marthe Dijkstra says offhandedly, as she walks in front of the two boys toward the market square in Eindhoven. "Michael is a beautiful name. You have my father's name. Pim, stop picking on your little brother."

"I wasn't," Pim insists, while pinching Michael's neck. "Was I, Michael?"

"N—no," Michael squeals.

"Then stop whining," Pim says, cuffing Michael's head lightly.

Michael runs ahead to press his head against his mother's hip as they stride down the street.

Yes, this Mario kid, like my brother when he was that age. What a misery when you're the younger brother.

As the streetcar stops and picks up passengers, Michael drifts to a remembrance of a family outing in a meadow near town. His father is kicking a soccer ball and calling to Michael to dribble it, alternating legs to control it.

"That's right Michael, you can do it, too, like Pim."

But he is nothing like the athlete his brother is. Michael remembers tripping over his own feet trying to dribble the ball before their picnic, and pitching sideways into a mud puddle.

Michael's mother brusquely wipes the soiled nine-year old. He tries to pull away, humiliated to see his father and Pim sharing a laugh.

"Next time, *you* clean him up, if you insist on playing rough," Michael recalls his angry mother saying to the sniggering Herman Dijkstra, who waves her off and winks at Pim.

"Do good at what you do good at," Herman Dijkstra says to Michael. No meanness was in in his tone, but Michael thinks he hears the disappointment behind his father's comment.

"Here, Pim," Herman says flipping the ball to his elder son. Try and get past me." Michael watches as Pim dribbles to beat the defender, his father. The laughter rings and rings across the meadow.

"Help me shell peas, Michael," his mother says, tapping a place close to her on the picnic blanket. While he sits with his mother shelling peas, his laughing father catches his eye. His father waves at him, encourages him to come to the meadow to join his brother in their game. Michael looks down at his collection of peas and peapods and continued to shell.

His drift into memories of his family brings up the consignment of the map. As the streetcar nears Kearney and Market Streets, Michael makes an abrupt and energized decision. He must see the consigned map one more time.

CHAPTER 59

London, 19 July 1570

The urgent knock on his door spurs Jonas to hurriedly pull on his nightshirt and remove the chair barring the door to admit Elizabeth Cole, Francis the cook, and Millie the maid. The cook carries a meat cleaver. Millie holds her shift like it was evidence.

"Jonas," Elizabeth Cole says. "Millie and Francis have made claims that you—" The mistress of the household searches for her words when the cook cuts in, "Millie 'ere says you made 'er with child last night."

The puffy-eyed girl looks terrified. Jonas stares at the cook, who has blood in his eye, and at Elizabeth Cole, whose stern gaze makes it clear he is in deep trouble.

"She said a rat was in her room, but I did not let her stay," Jonas pleads in Dutch. He keeps a wary eye on Francis' cleaver.

"Did she share your bed?"

"Yes. For a moment—that is, she—"

"What were you thinking?" Elizabeth Cole demands.

"I didn't, wasn't—thinking," replies Jonas, his eyes searching the floor for a knothole in the wood to disappear into. "She wouldn't leave."

"And what about Sofie," she says, with accusing eyes.

"I was just writing her. This girl took her clothes off and jumped into bed. I ordered her out and dropped her...her nightdress outside."

Elizabeth Cole turns to the scraggly haired scullery. In English she asks. "Millie? Did you push yourself onto this boy?"

"No!" She cries venomously pointing a shaking finger at Jonas. "Got me with a baby last night 'e did! As soon as I knocked, 'e pulls me in and makes a baby in me."

"No," Jonas objects. "I asked her to leave. She keeps talking about a baby," he says in English. In Dutch, he asks Elizabeth Cole, "Is she trying to make out that I am a father of her baby? I never touched her. And," he says indignantly, "I grew up on a farm. What livestock or person knows it's pregnant the next morning?"

Elizabeth Cole turns to Francis. "How long have you known Millie has had a muffin in the oven?"

Francis scowls. "The first I 'eard, this morning." He eyes Millie who is shaking.

"Look at me, Francis." Mrs. Cole demands.

The cook is incapable of looking the mistress of the house in the eye.

"Millie. Who is the father?"

The maid shrugs, a picture of misery, tears running down her face.

Mrs. Cole turns once again to Francis. "Did you put her up to this?"

"No!" Francis cries, hiding the cleaver behind his back.

Elizabeth turns her full wrath on Millie. "You wanton. You trollop. You belong in Southwark with the rest of those stew girls. If you ever bother this boy again I will throw you out and you can find your way on the other side of the river. Francis! If you cannot control your help, I will find a new cook and scullery. Jonas, see me when you are dressed."

She turns on her heel and leaves the room. Francis cuffs Millie on the ear, and stalks out. Millie, in tears, follows, never looking back at Jonas.

He closes the door and stands rooted before he takes a full breath. A jumble of questions confounds him. *Would Elizabeth throw him out for stupidly letting her in? Was Millie really pregnant? Were they trying to make a quick husband of Jonas with this simpleton's ruse?* He is furious that the cook brandished a meat cleaver. He returns to his letter and writes. "There is treachery everywhere. I'd rather face it all with you, my dear sweet Sofie."

He dresses and sheepishly taps on Elizabeth Cole's workroom door.

"Come in," she says in English, an edge to her tone.

Jonas awkwardly shifts his weight while his hostess regards him with steely eyes from her worktable where she snaps the bristles of brushes against a rag. In that moment he would have gladly been set afire.

"I—" begins Jonas.

"Quiet, and listen closely," Elizabeth orders. "There is a line that one never crosses with servants in this house. Do you understand?"

"Yes," he replies, stiffly.

Elizabeth drops the brushes on the tray with finality. "Good. I understand the game that little ninny was playing. I don't know if it was her stupidity, or if Francis put her up to it. Either way, it is beneath you to have encouraged her in any way."

Jonas stifles his impulse to object, shutting his eyes. His face burns.

"We have children in this household," she continues. "Lewdness is not countenanced. And what about Sofie?" she asks, accusingly.

"I only want to make Sofie happy." Jonas answers immediately.

"Hardly. How would this make her happy? I don't know what you have been up to outside of this house—but—" She points to a ladder-back chair. "Sit down."

"Nothing, I swear," he says, tears welling. "That is—" he begins, sitting, miserable with embarrassment. "I have no experience."

Elizabeth's face breaks from its stern mask to momentary surprise, and then back to a pinched-browed questioning look.

"The Benedictines brought me up. I have held Sofie close, but we never—" He searches for words. "I hope someday to make Sofie feel good with me." His chair creaks with each move. "She deserves a tender husband and I want to become him."

Her look softens to a curious consideration of Jonas. "You love Sofie?"

"Oh, yes. I did not let Millie in last light because I love Sofie less."

"Do you mean you want to be…ah—competent when you—with Sofie?"

"Yes Exactly." *Was it possible that Elizabeth understood?*

"Hmmm," Elizabeth mumbles, distractedly. "You are an unusual boy."

"I apologize for my behavior and the trouble I have made."

"We'll find our way through it," she says, putting an end to the subject.

"I know not what to say to Millie and Francis," he frets.

"You can say 'thank you' when they serve you, if you are pleased. Those two are lucky to get work in a respectable house."

Jonas nods gratefully and rises from the squeaky ladder-back chair.

Elizabeth nods once, but puts up a hand. "You really love your Sofie, yes?"

"Yes, you have no idea…."

"And you would like to be a gentle lover, yes?"

"Very much," he says, feeling his face redden.

"Perhaps a tutor can turn up like Old Marcus for those arts, too."

Jonas blinks at what must be her joke. Then he sees the map she has begun to limn. It is the tenth map, France, called *Gallia* in the Latin cartouche. Elizabeth has tinted the pale background wash and begun dabbing the red brown to highlight the innumerable tiny French towns represented by two or three church towers and the outline of buildings, each grouping drawn individually by the tireless engraver.

"It's harder to color once the book has been bound, yes?" Jonas asks.

"That's why I am only up to the town of Charenton. It takes a day to dry before I can go on to the next engraving. But I also have started the second and third volumes of the six. Imagine, barely a month since you arrived and only ten maps and the title page illuminated. Are you off early today?"

"Not until noon, when Master Gheeraerts comes back from court. Oh, Susannah says Mr. Cole will have orders for silks from the queen."

Elizabeth smiles. "Susannah is a treasure. Everybody knows everybody's business." She touches her nose, reminding him to keep his own counsel.

"Yes, intrigue everywhere," he replies, thinking of Du Forché and Millie.

In the hallway, he considers bypassing breakfast and returning to work on the drawings he had made the previous night. He conceives of his copper plate as a three-part story—the dog attacking the rearing horse, the stableman's whip striking the dog, and dog racing up the lane. This morning, he feels an affinity for the dog. With several hours before he is due at Gheeraerts' studio, he walks into the kitchen.

"Would the young sir like a sweet ale? Some bread and butter?" Francis asks. "Today we have a salted kipper, too." Millie smiles and curtseys as though nothing had happened between them.

He takes his meal in his room, adding details to his illustration. He transfers his trio of horse-dog illustrations to thin paper, so he can trace directly onto a wax-covered copper plate. He struggles to restrain his tendency to apply too many strokes. He imagines Gheeraerts saying, "Not so busy here."

After checking the hour on the hallway clock, he begins another illustration in his room, a single image, one that has haunted him since Anent Willemzoom's story. He draws the decapitation of the priest over a gravestone by a Spanish horseman. In vain, he tries to shed dark thoughts of his homeland, overrun with mercenaries and spies like Nicholaus Bockel and Jan Du Forché.

Another figure calls to him to be included, a tangled-haired waif with a chin dimple pointing accusingly at the cavalryman beheading the priest. His head aches as the richness of subject matter whirls within.

CHAPTER 60

Fleming Book Auction Galleries, Kearney Street, San Francisco, April 13ᵗʰ 2016

Michael gets out of the elevator on the fourth floor and walks down the hall with a jumble of feelings, paramount that he get another glimpse of the page once smeared with his father's ebbing life. *This woman, Mrs. Spencer, has unleashed such an impossible, unthinkable change in how I hold my father, now. Both of them, the print dealer husband—getting me to view events so differently.*

Michael abruptly stops his rumination when he sees the sign on the auction gallery doors. Private Viewing Only Today, By Appointment.

He pushes on the door and steps into the reception area where a dark-haired co-ed looks at a clipboard and nods expectantly at Michael for his name.

"I'm a consigner," he says and gives her his name, which doesn't match any on her list. Her perplexed look spurs Michael to say, "I'm here to take a last look at the Ortelius map to be auctioned tomorrow."

"Oh, that's on the left wall," she says and returns to her previous task. From her gesture, Michael feels invited into the gallery to view the auction lots. He walks into the large room with books and cataloged prints on view. Seven or eight others, private collectors and booksellers, he assumes, check catalog entries against the displayed lots. He sees the map tacked up on a whiteboard in its forlorn acetate sleeve. No one is near and so he goes up to it to it and reaches toward the ragged stain line on the map when he notices the index card he had given to the auction manager the previous month tacked alongside. He tears the card off the whiteboard and spins around to try and find the man who's phone message said there was no way his private information would be available to others. The card with his name, address and phone number has several pinpricks. In his agitated state he feels dizzy and nearly collapses, upsetting the display panel to keep his balance. The bearded young man at a desk stacked with books, races to his assistance.

"Are you alright, sir?" he asks with a hand under Michael's elbow."

"Why was this card…?"

The auction manager emerges from his office. "What going on, Matt? Pinkham asks.

"He lost his balance, Matt Warburg replies."

"Let's get you a chair," Mr. Ah—"

"Dijkstra, which it says on this card, tacked out here next to the map for everyone to see," Michael says with rancor.

"You must have a seat, sir. Come into my office." Michael's raised card seems to spur the solicitous tone in the auctioneer's voice.

"Matt, water, please." Warburg hastens to the service room behind the door and arrives with a plastic bottle of water a moment later. Pinkham indicates that he should help guide Dijkstra to his office.

Together, the auction house owner and Warburg ease Michael into one of the client chairs.

Matt opens the bottle and hands the cool water to Dijkstra, who takes a sip.

"That's very kind, thank you." Then he turns to the auction house owner. "Mr. Pinkham. You assured me that there would be discretion taken with my identity. And here I am, contacted by two print dealers who—it makes me wonder if I even should let a sale proceed.

"We have a contract, Mr. Dikes…uh! You cannot pull that print for private sale after the catalog is printed. Our contract very clearly—"

"I want you to understand that you had no right to disclose my name and phone number."

"I understand completely, and, as I told you, we have—we are taking steps to remedy the situation. And you must understand that the upfront costs of auctioning your map, of advertising, promoting, researching, cataloging, and printing the catalog does not come free."

"So how do two people who have no right to my personal information still have that information?"

"Mr. Dike—sir!"

"I simply ask that you acknowledge that the damage is already done. How do you propose to make that right? I don't think you can make it right and so I will consider—"

"Wait just one minute," Pinkham says quietly and dangerously.

Michael feels Pinkham's eyes drill into his like they were carbide tipped bits. "Before you walked out the door with that plate, you would owe us over a thousand dollars. The effort already done in your behalf is easily calculated, and there isn't a courtroom in the land that wouldn't back us up. Then think of the court costs. The contract states that while you have the right of withdrawal, you are responsible for the effort we've already put in."

"You don't understand," the old Dutchman says. "This map—This map is stained with my father's blood. I thought I could part with it easily, but I discover—"

"Sir," Pinkham interrupts. "I am sorry for your personal loss. And I know that many items have sentimental value to consigners."

Michael sees that the young man, Matt, wears a look of horror listening to his boss' tone as he continues to berate Michael. "I remember when you brought it in for consignment, I asked you what you thought made the stain. You said you didn't know. You said you *didn't* know, sir. And now you change your story. That's really not quite ethical, sir. Now you change your story once again. This is highly unfair, bordering on fraudulent, and no court in the state will think otherwise."

Michael springs up with suddenness, shaking with fury. "I thought my heart was frozen unto death, but you are a calculating machine with no sense of what's right or fair."

He does not wait for Pinkham's retort. He throws open the office door, totters toward the exit, puts the half empty plastic water bottle on Cheryl Vasquez's desk, and departs.

Michael is breathing heavily. He presses the elevator button and waits, but he can not get the jagged line running diagonally down the right side of the world map out of his mind. He thinks of the baggy-eyed auctioneer and feels steamrolled by the old shark. The elevator is arriving at the fourth floor and he stands uncertain. Technically, that map is still his property. Why should he keep it in the auction? The financial hit would be severe, and he is near the end of his available funds. The property tax on his town house is already in arrears.

The elevator doors open and a man emerges with a leather case for prints slung over his shoulder. He wears a tan sports jacket and dark green trousers. He nods briefly to Michael who wavers in indecision. The odor of citrus cologne fills his nostrils.

"Excuse me," the man says in a high, raspy voice, and he proceeds down the corridor to the double doors that open on Fleming's Auction Galleries. The voice nags with familiarity. The elevator door closes. Michael turns as his decision is made. "Be brave, walk through your fears," Pim's voice in his head says. He strides toward the double doors to reclaim his property, come what may.

But when he arrives at the doors they are locked. He jiggles the handle and knocks with his knuckles. Michael slaps the door with his palm. He realizes he has missed his chance. *Why didn't I simply take down the map from its display on the way out? And why was that man just admitted?*

He breaks into a sweat, knows he has just been swindled. He backs away from the auction house doors and shuffles back to the elevator. The residual citrus cologne in the lift makes him feel lightheaded again. He longs to be on the street, the brisk afternoon breeze on his face pushed by the incoming San Francisco fog. He walks to the BART station on Market Street oblivious to the rush hour foot and auto traffic.

CHAPTER 61

Palo Alto, Thursday Afternoon, April 13th 2016

While Patricia is engaged in her field trip to San Francisco, following his meeting with Bregmann on the UC Campus, Owen stops at print galleries in Berkeley and Oakland, then crosses the bridge to San Francisco and visits several galleries in Dogpatch, named for one of the oldest parts of the city bordering the bay on the east shore. Recently opened galleries there keep him in touch with rising artists and printmakers. He keeps abreast of upcoming trends to advise clients of material that suits their collecting tastes. He returns to his office in Palo Alto shortly after 3:00 p.m. and listens to his messages on his office landline. One call piques his interest.

"Hello, Mr. Spencer. This is Sandra Bergen, with Peter Phelan's office? I wanted to apologize—oh, jeez—you must excuse me—I need to get off."

The perfunctory click of her ending the call leaves Owen puzzled. Yesterday, she was officious and clearly under the watchful eye of her boss, Phelan, a technology hedge fund operator. Today, it sounded like he walked in on her apology and she swiftly hung up. "Drama everywhere," Owen muses. His mobile phone rings.

"Just leaving now," Patricia says, distraction in her voice. I won't have any energy for cooking—plenty of stuff in the fridge, I think. See you soon."

The awkward phone conversation with Sandra Bergen, one of Phelan's executive assistants, on Wednesday had become irritating. The client insisted that the plate was contemporary to the time of Gutenberg's life; meanwhile, the clothing depicted was of a century later in an engraved portrait offered by a Berlin print dealer. Owens tamps down residual anger for Phelan's disdain of Owen's expertise. In the time he has before Patricia arrives home, Owen selects the print seller's Contact page, and emails him requesting provenance and his guess as to the variant state.

When Patricia comes in, frazzled from the field trip and the draining experience of meeting Michael Dijkstra, she and Owen eat leftovers. "How was your trip to Mission Dolores?" he asks, with interest. He watches her brow cloud over. "Except for Mario Kinsella—" she begins, and then stops. "Actually, Mario was no problem at all after he met your guy, this Mr. Dijkstra." A tiny smile creases her chin.

"How'd that go?" Owen asks with a hint of trepidation.

"Not half as bad as I feared. I rather liked him. I could see how he could charm you into having him call me. He apologized for thinking so poorly of my mother when she was a kid. He was really quite touching."

Owen breathes a barely concealed sigh of relief.

"He even gave me this." Patricia passes the manila envelope with the engraving across the table. Owen is surprised to see the centuries-old paper folded like a triptych. His eyes open wide with surprise and admiration when he sees the gripping images of a horse, the stableman, and a dog. "Who is JH?" he asks.

"Who *is* JH," she asks. "I'm only a schoolteacher. This is your bailiwick, bud."

"Did the old guy give you some background?"

"He said my mother left it behind at his house in the Netherlands. He found it after the war, tucked in a children's book. He says it was...was my mother's book."

"Wow," he exclaims softly. "Your mom...."

But Patricia puts up a hand to stop the conversation in its tracks.

"Well, I'll try and find something on this engraver, JH." Owen squints, assessing the work. "Hmm. Raw, but powerful. From a copper plate. I wonder how Hetty came to have it."

"I'm exhausted, Owen," Patricia says, taking off her lime-colored jacket. "Straight to bed with me. You have a big day tomorrow, don't you? The auction?"

Owen, still looking at the brash lines of the engraving, grunts in assent. He is distracted by the initials. He has seen these strokes somewhere before. The sea monster on the plate he viewed at the Fleming Gallery floats into his mind.

"Good night," he calls toward Patricia's back as she enters the bedroom.

He snaps a smartphone photo of the initials on the triptych and returns to his garage office where he brings up the gallery's online catalog for the auction on his laptop. He turns to the color image of the Lot 156 map and enlarges the section showing the plate the sea monster is bound to. He spins the computer screen around and compares the J and H lettering he saw through his loupe at the gallery. His jaw drops and he sits back in wonderment.

On a whim, he keys in commands to open a Library of Congress presentation of the Ortelius book, enlarges the map of the world image from the first edition of 1570 and zeroes in on the sea monster in the Mar di Indi. No name or initials appear in the hash marks of the first printing. He does a search on the name Jonas Hoen and turns up nothing. "The mystery only deepens," he muses.

CHAPTER 62

London, 2 August 1570

Jonas watches the bur of copper curl up and over his burin. He scrapes the waste thread of copper into a tiny pile of shavings. His concentration is as keen as his cutting tool and he revels in getting the knack of varying pressure with each stroke on the copper. He tries his new illustration on a practice plate—the decapitation in the graveyard. Gheeraerts barely hides his distaste for the image, inks and polishes the face of the copper, then places the burnished plate face down on a sheet of moistened paper. Using a hand press with an iron platen attached to a deeply threaded screw, he winds the pressure plate onto the paper and holds it there for ten seconds. Then he unwinds the screw and peels the paper from the plate. All of the successes and failures of Jonas' technique are revealed.

"Good curvature," Gheeraerts notes. "Imprecise lines here and here, and the pressure of the crosshatching too heavy here. See how the ink makes a dark blot? The crosshatching is the most important detail for the viewer to interpret." Gheeraerts nods to drive the point home regarding the technique Jonas should practice. Then he ventures his comment on Jonas' subject. "Dark. Very dark."

And so it goes for Jonas; sharpening the face of his gravers, maintaining a pitch of forty-five degrees, developing an inner sense of how much pressure is used to incise the copper surface and vary the thickness of a line by increasing and decreasing the pressure he exerts with his palm.

While Jonas improves his technique on a corner of Gheeraerts' workbench, the old engraver is preparing his collection of *Aesop's Fables* plates for a new edition, this time with the text in French. Jonas watches the care that Marcus takes to crisp an etched line. The practiced engraver's critical eye compares the proofed engravings covering the walls of his studio to the plates. His preparation consists of removing tiny burs and fixing imperfections in the original copper.

"To not lose your skills, you must practice every day, Jonas."

Gheeraerts speaks offhandedly, focused more on the scribing tool he is using to smooth a roughened crevice. Jonas looks up from his practice plate and sees that the plate Gheeraerts is refurbishing tells the tale of the Tortoise and the Hare.

"You mean, to win the race, I must keep plodding, eh?"

"I mean that exactly, boy." Gheeraerts laughs. "For the next few days, we will be at Whitehall Palace. John de Critz has work for us. When the Queen is away, we mice get to play, prinking out the royal rooms with gilt and color."

"How do I practice, then?"

"You take your gravers and several practice plates home, and you burn your midnight tapers. Dress well tomorrow or they won't let us in."

The next day, Jonas meets Gheeraerts at his studio and the two of them walk along the Strand into the City of Westminster where the imposing Palace of Whitehall, with its dozens of state rooms, stretch behind the royal park down to the Thames. They climb the wooden stairs of Whitehall and are admitted through a commoners' entrance on the east side of the royal residence. "Aha, Jonas Hoen," de Critz says, in welcome. "Susannah says that you ably assist Marcus." John de Critz carries rolled up plans under his arm. He is one of a number of exiled expatriates from Antwerp, only a few years older than Jonas. But he has full command of English as his family had escaped from the Habsburg persecutions of Flemish Protestants early in his life. He cultivates a neat brown beard to appear older. "Today we begin redecorating a suite of rooms," he says, ushering Gheeraerts and Jonas down the elegantly appointed corridors. Jonas has never seen such luxury. He ogles the wall hangings, the pilaster ceilings, and the stiffly posed portraits that line the corridor.

Hammers striking chisels ring behind a closed door. De Critz opens it to a suite of rooms and invites them in. The rooms are bare, smelling of sawdust and oil stain. Several wood joiners nail wainscoting along two sides of the room.

"We will be painting the panels above the wainscoting," De Critz says. He leads Jonas and Gheeraerts to an inner room, already fitted with the wooden wall décor. The frames above will receive the paintings on wood that De Critz has designed in the paper rolls under his arm. He displays his illustrations on a worktable in the center of the room. The images, generic scenes of country life, are to run the perimeter of the room where doors allow. In all, eighteen eye-level panels will portray idyllic farm life, shadowed by great manor houses in the distance. On a dropcloth, numerous unpainted boards fifteen inches wide lay stacked by their lengths. Six boards are three feet in length, and Jonas observes the six spaces they will occupy. Gheeraerts and De Critz will execute illustrations on these boards milled from a horse chestnut tree. "These surfaces need to be prepared with base coats of deep blue." De Critz points to a tub of the midnight blue pigment, stirring sticks, and wide paint brushes.

"Marcus, come with me. Jonas, we will be back in two hours. Two coats should be ample."

Jonas ties on an apron and goes to work immediately. He begins by stirring the base coat pigment. He lays out the boards end to end in several rows and paints his way across all eighteen sections. The once pale brown wood glistens, coated by a deep blue. He is hunched over the last panel, completing strokes to eliminate defects, thin spots, and irregular brushstrokes, when a woman's voice cuts through the swishing sound of the bristles laying on the base coat.

"Blue, eh?"

Jonas looks up and sees a vision in lace, pink silks, ribbons, and a bodice pushing bosoms demanding an audience. He rises, flustered and blinking.

"You're the Flemish boy Susannah said would be here today. Come with me."

Bewildered, Jonas stares. The woman is in her thirties, with flashing eyes, a dark mole on her cheek, and a flouncing walk that takes his breath away.

"Madam—" he begins.

"Come, come. That has to dry, so walk with me. Leave your apron here."

Jonas returns his apron to the center table and follows the woman through two doors leading from the rooms under construction to a passage.

"How old are you, and what is your name?"

"Seventeen and Jonas Hoen," he replies in accented English he hopes doesn't sound too butchered.

The woman turns to him and stops walking. Her smile is so infectious, that Jonas smiles back immediately. Her deep brown eyes devour him and his face reddens with the rush.

"Oh, you will be fun," she says and they continue down the passage, Jonas a half-step behind.

"You can call me Joan, when no one is in earshot, otherwise, Mistress or Baroness. And no more 'Madam,' please."

The woman pushes on a wall. Jonas finds himself unexpectedly in a richly furnished and tapestried bedroom. He shakes his head, which is now swimming with the odors of her boudoir, her perfumes and powders.

"I am informed that you want to learn the arts of being a good lover. First you will wash your hands. This is how we begin. Later we will study Italian. You know the poet Aretino?"

Jonas shakes his head.

"His sonnets are illustrated. You will enjoy learning Italian. I do." Her eyes flash and Jonas is captured by this beautiful woman, easily fifteen years his senior.

CHAPTER 63

Whitehall, London, Early August, 1570

Jonas, cheeks flushed, delirious with new knowledge, and requested to knock on the Mistress Joan's door the next afternoon, walks back to the wing where the suite is being furbished. Gheeraerts and de Critz are deep in discussion at the worktable in the center of the room. They nod to him and continue to discourse on the coloring of the ornate ceiling molding. Jonas retrieves his apron and begins to apply the second coat of midnight blue. The harsh chemicals of the paint are rude odors compared to the emoluments and perfumes that transported Jonas a short time earlier.

For fourteen days, Gheeraerts and Jonas return to the project. De Critz roughs in the rolling hills and forests, peasants in the fields and nobles on horseback. Gheeraerts sketches pastures with cows and sheep, deer at the edges of forests, dogs in a hunt, newly caught fish hanging from a fisherman's pole, birds in trees, mice scurrying at the base of barns, horses in paddocks or pulling drays. Jonas puts finishing paint strokes on the herds and flocks, adding enough detail to let the viewer's eyes grasp a scene at a distance of eight feet.

"This work is to make the room look pleasing, not attract much attention to each scene," de Critz explains.

At roughly two o'clock each day, Jonas excuses himself, and returns forty-five minutes later to continue his assistance as the artistic embellishment of the room proceeds. No one says a word. Jonas knows the two artists are completely aware. Only Susannah de Critz's eyes twinkle knowingly when next she sees Jonas.

Late in their third encounter, Jonas discovers that odors beyond the lip paint, and fragrant perfumes and powders of his instructress bring even more aphrodisiac to his performance. Sweat, salt, stink from secret places spur his desire. His senses warm to the tang, saliva, viscous emanations, and buttery bean. He thrills to touch responsive flesh and hear coos, murmurs, pants, yips, and moans. And the cool-down—nips, bites, pinches, endearments— take on a new eroticism.

At their fifth meeting, Mistress Joan Casterleigh passes Jonas a book she calls Aretino's *"The Sixteen Postures."* The poses cause Jonas' mouth to fall agape. Joan laughs at his shocked expression. As his jaw drops, his blood rises. "Oh, I'm glad you like these. I like—that one especially, today," she points. "Shall we try it?"

The sensuous-mouthed baroness stretches languorously, replicating the woman in the woodcut engraving. Jonas looks at the muscles bulging on the mythological male subject, massive sex at the ready, and is confronted by competing thoughts: the lasciviousness of the illustration and overriding analytical wonder at how the artist achieved the light and shadow mix to create such an erotic scene. Mistress Joan claps her hands sharply, reminding Jonas of Brother Cornelius at the abbey regaining his wandering attention when the catechism had become uninteresting. Jonas snaps to, realizing he is in the completely wrong frame of mind.

He gives his full attention to the voluptuous woman on her bed, who urges *"Bene, bene,"* in her English accent. He pushes his own 17-year-old body into an imitation of the ancient hero. *"Multo buono, benissimo,"* she coos. Jonas adds to his fantasy by imagining he is the Roman Brabo enjoying the charms of a voluptuous Antwerp maiden after dispatching the giant Antigoon's right arm into the Scheldt River. Mistress Joan and nature conspire to create another memorable lesson.

"May I sketch you," he asks, at their tenth meeting. The Baroness basks in a flush of a lesson well taught, auburn hair streaming onto the folds of the comforter.

"What. Now? Like this?" She asks, giggling.

"No, no," Jonas stammers. "I mean at an appropriate time, in proper dress."

"You embarrass so easily," she sighs. "It is time to return to your work. Until tomorrow." That ends the discussion. She says nothing more about being sketched.

Gheeraerts and de Critz have finished the scenes on the chestnut panels. and Jonas must fit each one into its frame built above the wainscoting. When he is done, he and Gheeraerts admire their work and Jonas receives his portion of the fee.

"I've already received recompense, far beyond my contribution."

"I'll warrant, you have, lad" Gheeraerts says, pounding Jonas on the shoulder.

Jonas winces. When struck just right, his shoulder explodes with pain as when he slammed into the tree. "Yes, I learned some Italian," he says, smiling through his momentary pang.

CHAPTER 64

Walnut Creek, Saturday, April 14th 2016

On Saturday morning Michael makes a light breakfast, all he can manage on his jittery stomach. Today his map will be auctioned. He turns off the flame under the pan that hisses with his scrambled egg. He is wracking his brain. Of course this is auction day. He knows that. But he has to do something today that he thought of last night. *What is it?* He folds his long frame into a dining room chair and nibbles at his egg. His brain wants him to run from learning what he has to do. Finally, he stops eating, shuts his eyes and tries to retrace his steps that might lead him to the thought he had not so very long ago. He opens his eyes and sees the short stack of pages written by his father during the war, notes that have set off a wrenching tour through his own life from the time his mother's life was snuffed out under bombed building debris to a glimpse of his father's life while he harbored a Jewish girl. More to the point, the notes have created a reprise of how he and Pim had survived and recovered the art and jewels stolen by the Berghuises. The empty cognac bottle with the Christmas greeting in Dutch, penned by the Korean—*Kim Sook was his name...*

His mind keeps jumping to the mess he made trying to retrieve the map from the auction the day before—his deviousness in saying he wanted the map withdrawn because his identity had been compromised. That was nonsense. He wanted the map back because it was what his father had collapsed on as he died—a tangible reminder of the loss of his papa, *and* his mother, whose family had handed down the *Theatrum Orbis Terrarum*. He again experiences the impotence he had felt as he walked out and then tried to return to the auction rooms, only to be locked out. He thinks how Pim would take the bull by the horns. "Ach!" Michael remembers. He has caught the moment. "The snapshot," he says aloud.

The chair scrapes the floor as he pushes himself back from the table and returns to the chest of drawers in his bedroom. Surely the rest of what he has to do will come by finding the photo taken in 1945 of him, Pim, and Gerdi.

His shaking fingers open the manila envelope and he again looks at the yellowed photo. *It was Gerdi.* He has to speak to Gerdi. She had moved from Amsterdam only three or four years ago, and had sent a card to the Sunnyvale campus of Philips. The card had arrived in his home mailbox, forwarded in an envelope by the human resources department. *The card, the card.* He hopes he has not thrown it away. "Oh, my foolish actions," he says aloud. "Come, come, and show yourself." He reaches into the back of the drawer, under his passport and checkbooks. He finds it—a printed card with her signature.

Dear Family and Friends,

I have changed residence to....

He read an address and a phone of an assisted living residence in the town of Soest.

Michael looks in the mirror and sees his face smiling back at him. He is pleasantly shocked to see his eyes dancing with light. He hastens to his desk and picks up the phone. Nine hours difference, he recalls. *Good, it is still daytime.* He dials the international prefix and the number. His chest flutters, and he has the fearful thought that he could die before he speaks with Gerdi. Worse, was *she* still alive?

"Halloo," a strong woman's voice says in Dutch.

Michael's lips move but words are not coming out. Finally, he blurts. "Gerdi?"

"No, this is Aleida. Who's this?"

"Michael Dijkstra," he says, terrified that this woman would know who he is and would slam down the phone. Michael listens nervously as a heated discussion takes place between Aleida and someone else.

"Michael?" A thin voice asks. "Is this Michael?"

"Gerdi? Is that you?"

"Yes. It's me here. Hard to recognize your voice, it has been so long."

"Who is Aleida?"

"My eldest daughter. Michael? Are you all right?"

"Yes, yes," he says, his throat constricted. "I'm sorry, I am really so happy to hear your voice, but I am also so sad I had to wait this long."

The voice across the world only grunts in understanding.

"I wish to apologize. I am…" He coughs to break a chokehold of emotion. "I am sorry. These words sound so empty when I think of how deeply I have dug a hole to bury myself in. I acted so poorly to you, and Pim, too, especially badly to Pim. I had no right. And I don't think I could ever atone."

"You don't get off so easily, Michael." Bitterness surrounds her words. "You have no idea at all about how awful Pim felt losing you like that. You dropped from the face of the earth and declared your only living brother dead to you. That was not fair. You may have had anger for me, but it was not fair to close down with your brother. It weighed on him."

Michael hears Aleida saying somewhere in the room, "Mother you must not tax your heart so."

"I'm fine. He has to hear," Gerdi says loudly for Michael to get every word.

"Yes. I—I made a complete mess of it." Michael searches for what to say next and lights upon his meeting in Dolores Park. "But I thought you might be interested. I have met the daughter of the woman—the little girl—you and father saved."

"What?"

"Right. Her name is Patricia, Hetty van Aalt's daughter. Hetty was the girl."

"Hah. Hetty is well?"

"No—no. She died in the last year, I think. I never met her, but I did meet her daughter. This story is long, complicated, but it is about the big book of maps that father had in his study. The one Pim and I recovered that day we came home."

"Terrible times," Gerdi says.

Michael hears Aleida, in the background. "Mother, is this upsetting you?"

"No, sweetheart. This is your uncle. The long lost uncle. Michael, where are you calling from?"

"California. I came here after that awful time in Amsterdam at your restaurant. I have been here ever since. More than thirty—" Michael is so choked up he cannot speak. He sniffs loudly, and blurts, "I'm so sorry, Gerdi, for holding such anger. You were very brave and I was cowardly. And father, very brave."

"Michael, I always knew you were deeply troubled by your mother's death, and I wished I could have comforted you back then. But you were not ready."

"I know that now. I am being comforted by you being willing to even talk to me after I hurt you and Pim so badly."

"If you weren't halfway around the world I would hug you," Gerdi says.

Her words become the sluice that opens and breaks the dam. "Aaaahhhh!" He cries. Michael thinks that his heart has burst with such a pain that he fears he is having a coronary seizure. He cries uncontrollably and loudly into the phone. All the while, Gerdi's voice speaks soothing words in his earpiece.

"Good. Have a good long cry. It cleanses the bitterness. It dispels the gall and turns your heart whole again. My poor Michael, I am so happy you called. You make me want to cry with you. I am so full of joy that you chose to speak with me. Can we visit? Is there any chance you can come to Soest and see me in my old lady home?"

Michael is pressing a tissue to his eyes and heaving great gulps of air.

"You have such a good heart, Gerdi. You—you always did. Pim was very lucky. I hope you had a full life with him."

"From the very beginning to his dying day, Michael. He loved me. And he loved you, too. He was always sad about you two falling out. He never understood it, but I think I did. He was wonderful, and straightforward. You were a still water that ran deep. I think you always felt so acutely that when pain tore at your heart you had to build a wall around it to keep from being torn apart."

"Oh, Gerdi," Michael utters. "How did you become so wise? You were wise when you were twenty. I am looking at the photo that was snapped a day before you were married in Eindhoven. You and Pim look deliriously happy. I look like death."

"Is there a chance you could visit, Michael? You never even met your nieces and nephew. Aleida and Michelle—Pim named her 'Michelle'—and your nephew—His name is Herman. He is a civil engineer. Aleida runs a school in Haarlem and Michelle is partners in a coffee shop near our old restaurant."

"'Pim named her, Michelle,'" Michael repeats. "And a nephew? Herman? Oh, Gerdi, I have been such a stranger to all of you." He squeezes his eyelids together in self-chastisement. "What a fool," he says under his breath.

"Did you ever marry?"

"No," Michael replies, a trifle forlorn.

"Then you must visit and meet your family. Will you?"

"I will try, Gerdi."

"Promise?"

"I promise. My sweet sister-in-law, I promise." He feels his face flush.

"Hmm. It's nice to hear. Aleida is tapping her watch. You will call again soon? Oh, Michael you have brightened my day so. Goodbye, Michael."

Michael puts the receiver down and basks in the moment of reconciliation.

"Michelle," he muses. *I hope she is nothing like me.* An incomplete thought begins. "What if...?" Michael thinks, as he looks across the room at the battered leather book that has survived four centuries of upheavals, thefts, and wars.

CHAPTER 65

Westminster, Whitehall Palace Gardens, 28 August 1570

Nearly a month after their commission to paint decorative wall panels, Jonas and Gheeraerts are back at Whitehall on another project, but the baroness does not reappear to continue her instruction. While repainting an outdoor balustrade, Jonas hears voices through a tall hedge. Two of the court's nobles have taken a turn around the gardens and seated themselves on a bench behind a tall topiary hedge. Jonas hears, but does not see them. Their conversation, however, captures him.

"But Baron Burghley," the younger voice says, "the Dutch Sea Beggars raid indiscriminately."

"True, but just now, they attack more Spanish and French shipping than our friends," the more senior of the two rejoins. "I say, let their fleet have its sway at Dover so long as they don't overstep English toes."

"Well...perhaps there will come a time when this William of Orange will be grateful," says the younger man.

"It's good to keep King Philip nervous about his rebellious provinces in all events," the older voice says. "No need for a state of war to keep them from trying to conquer us, either by enthroning the Catholic pretender, or by main force. Let these Dutch keep them uneasy. Was it not the Spanish king who pressed for Elizabeth's excommunication? Anything that sizzles the feet of the Duke of Toledo or King Philip is good for us. Let the Dutch privateers be our presence on the seas for now."

Jonas remains frozen, but his thoughts burn with what he has heard.

"Besides, Francis," the older man continues. "Do you know how many stout oaks it takes to build even one ship of the line? Twenty-five. Can you imagine? We would denude the entire Thames Valley to Oxfordshire to properly build our fleet. The treasury has more pressing needs. Let the Dutch Beggars be our navy for now."

Jonas hears the aged man cough noisily and struggle to regain his legs. "The smell of fresh paint is too heavy here, Francis. Let us move on."

"Yes, William," the younger voice says.

They pass out of hearing. Jonas weighs what he has heard. He considers what Du Forché might do with such overheard words. Then he drifts back to his lessons in love and he wishes to be back home in Antwerp, with Sofie in his arms.

Later that afternoon, on the walk back with Gheeraerts, Jonas asks, "Do you know who Baron Burghley is?"

"No, but Susannah might. She exhausts me with her court gossip. You can pick up some practice plates from my studio and ask her yourself." There, he greets Susannah and asks her what she knows about Baron Burghley.

She pinions him with her eyes. "Why do you want to know?"

"Only curious." Jonas makes his comment sound off-hand. "He complained about the paint odor near the garden from the section of staircase I was painting."

"Oho, Jonas. You wrinkled the nose of William Cecil. He advises the Queen on matters of State. Old Burghley is her most trusted counsel."

A chill travels down Jonas' neck. What he has overheard gains even more in value. "Oh, I hope he wasn't too upset. Well. Say hello to young Marcus. Good day."

On his walk home, carrying three copper plates under his arm, Jonas ruminates about hearing intelligence uttered by the highest authority in England next to the Queen. The conversation he has eavesdropped is about the *Vater Guezen*, the Sea Beggars, Dutch nobles and their desperado crews who raid shipping as a poke in the eye to the Duke of Alva in his mission to subjugate the Low Countries. Jonas has overheard expatriate conversations in the alehouses that focus on the exploits of these privateers. Many of these ships' captains are Huguenots and Calvinists, declared heretics. Their enemies are the Catholics and the Spanish royal house, enforcers for the Holy Roman Empire. One burning subject in the Flemish-speaking taverns is that Willem van Oranje has given letters of marque to eighteen of the ships in the ragtag fleet. They are chartered as warships fighting under the banner of William the Silent, licensed as privateers against enemy shipping.

The idea comes slowly and then in a rush—that he must illustrate an image showing England granting safe havens for this fleet. Dare he? To draw such an illustration might be dangerous, but to engrave a plate for a broadside and circulate it? *This idea courts disaster.* But his thoughts are like small dogs biting a shoe. He even plays with the word "broadside" and the double meaning of a ship's cannons firing simultaneously from one side of the vessel and a sheet printed and posted on the side of a building or a kiosk. Jonas becomes so lost in the pros and cons that he does not notice that he passes Lyme Street and continues from Lombard into Fenchurch Street. A band of toughs gathers at the mouth of Culver Alley.

A gruff, grizzled man, stinking of sack, thrusts his face in front of Jonas. "Give me a penny, boy." Spittle gathers at the edges of his lips. He smells of offal. "What do you carry, boy?" His face bears a scar that closes an eye. He wears a long sheath at his belt; the leather-bound handle menacing. Jonas presses his bag of gravers in his pocket and tightly grips the foot-square copper plates he carries under his arm.

Jonas is aware of other men closing in on him. "Let me pass," he demands.

Laughter from the foul smelling gang makes his heart pound, and his brow beads with sweat. "Give over your coin, Flemmy-boy."

Gripped by fear, he is forced into the narrow close. He smells the stale piss that marks their territory. Instinctively, he raises his right arm with the copper plates clenched in his fingers and slashes the air. He feels an edge strike the stubbled face of one of the assailants and sees a line of blood on his cheek.

"Auahgh! This young'un cut me," the voice squeals from a bleeding mouth.

"Let me pass!" Jonas shouts. He grasps his practice plates with both hands and spins. Four men, stinking of spirits, foremost, the one now wielding the leather-handled knife, lurch backward. He hears what sounds like mad dogs growling. Jonas realizes he must whirl crazily and so he cuts figure eights in the air, and works his way toward the main road again, backing toward Fenchurch Street. The cut man whimpers and curses. "Kill him for this, Charley."

"You lot, leave off!" a commanding voice orders. "Or I'll perforate you."

The hiss of a two and a half foot rapier cuts the air and Jonas' assailants beat their retreat deep into Culver Alley.

"Are you in one piece, young fellow?"

By the accent he is being addressed by someone of the upper class, an English noble. "I thank you for your aid, sir. They came upon me in a rush and I would have been cut, beaten or worse."

"You strangers from—where, Holland? The Brabant? What is your accent?"

"Dutch, recently from Antwerp. Jonas Hoen, with many thanks," he bows. "May I buy you a refreshment for your brave service?" Jonas asks. The words emerge from his mouth without thought. Ordinarily, he would keep his counsel, especially with the English whose tongue still baffles him. "My speech is still very poor. I hope I do not offend."

A smile forms on the brash swordsman, a well-turned out member of the peerage, perhaps thirty. "Not at all, young man. Be more careful where you walk."

The stranger passes on and Jonas realizes his error in crossing into Fenchurch Street. He gives Culver Alley a wide berth and hastens to his lodgings. His pounding thoughts bounce between the horrific encounter he has just had and the nub of an idea of engraving a broadside extolling the Dutch privateers.

CHAPTER 66

London, Late Afternoon, 28 August 1570

Jonas' face flushes, reliving his assault at the hands of the Culver Alley cutthroats and the fortuitous appearance of the young swordsman. A coach is drawing away from the entrance to the Coles' home. When Jonas enters the main door of the apartments, he is greeted by squealing children in the hallway. From the babble he discerns that the father of the family has returned after a triumphant sailing from Constantinople where he has concluded arrangements for multiple shipments of silk to London. In the hallway, the waft of incense from the East, new to Jonas, transforms the usual odors of the wood-walled room into an exotic, mysterious venue. Elizabeth Cole beckons Jonas from the drawing room doorway and makes introductions while the older Cole children chirp and scatter, having received their presents. Jonas shifts the copper plates he has brought from Gheeraerts' studio from his right to left hand and shakes the hand of the seated Jacobus Coels, who everyone in England calls James Cole. The merchant, in his early fifties, rests in a thickly upholstered armchair near the fireplace of the drawing room. He is a pale-cheeked businessman with short graying hair and a fashionable spade beard, a linen ruff topping his black velvet doublet. Jonas sees that Elizabeth Ortels and he make a handsome match. Beneath his smiling bearing, however, he looks exhausted from his travels. Despite Coels' outward fatigue, Jonas sees where little James Cole, the seven-year old, gets his keen eye and intelligent mind. "Look, James," the boy's father says, unpacking several glass-framed display cases from packages scattered at his feet.

"Flutterbys!" Little James exclaims.

"Indeed, lad, from Turkey, for your collection."

"Mama," the boy cries, showing the framed specimens to his mother. "Look Jonas. Look what Papa brought for me from Turkey."

Jonas' eyes widens at the mounted specimens pinioned forever behind glass.

"May I sketch these, James?"

"Yes, but only after I've looked and looked at them. See those markings?"

Jonas nods at the son of the beaming silk merchant. "Very pretty, and a challenge for me to get right. Let me know when I may sketch your new treasures."

"Francis, Francis looka' the flutterbys," James calls running into the kitchen to show off his new acquisitions.

A new glow has come over Elizabeth as she pours wine into her husband's goblet and touches his cheek and ear tenderly. It is evident that she is delighted with her husband's return from his trip abroad.

"Three more boats loaded to the gunwales with fabric from Persia, China, and the Holy Lands," the elder James effuses. "They arrive next week. And yes, the royal house has an order for two hundred forty bolts; China silk, and three or four miles of white sarcenet." He smiles to have business from the well-heeled royal circle.

"The ladies-in-waiting will be very busy in the coming year," Elizabeth gossips. "So Susannah de Critz thinks, at any rate, and she is well placed."

"Master Hoen," James Cole sighs. "Forgive me, as I must retire following my crossing."

"My pleasure to meet you," Jonas says, backing out of the sitting room. "And I'm deeply indebted to your kindness in lodging me."

Cole waves off Jonas' thanks and turns to his wife. Wordlessly, she takes his hand. Jonas bows and walks into the hallway. He stops abruptly when he sees the blood on the fingers of his left hand. A startled cry escapes his lips and his knees jerk in confusion. Blood is smeared on the corners of the practice copper plates where he had clipped the jaw of one of his assailants in Culver Alley. Should he return to the drawing room and apologize? He quickly examines his right hand which he had shaken with James Cole and sees no blood. Relieved, he retires to his room and looks in the mirror to see the state of his body following his narrow escape. Happily, he has no marks on him or his garb. He exhales a deep sigh that he hadn't embarrassed himself before his host or Elizabeth.

Jonas rinses his hands and face in the washbasin's cool water and sees it cloud up with soap and the remnants of the ruffian's blood. He remembers the satisfying slice across his assailant's ugly jaw.

Moments later, he sits down at his table and sketches his ideas for a broadside. The old English nobleman's declaration behind the garden hedge rings again in his ears: *Let the Dutch Beggars be our navy for the time being.* This close advisor to the Queen of England is cannily happy to let the dissident Dutch nobles and their ragtag men 'o' war roam freely off the coast of England harrying Spanish and French shipping. A proxy navy from the Netherlands serving the Queen of England in her fight with the Spanish-Habsburg Empire captures Jonas' sense of irony. It is the same ironic seed that grew into the Dutch blacksmith forging chain links for the people of the Low Countries in service to the Spanish occupiers.

Three hours pass. By candlelight, he studies his handiwork: the east and south coasts of England with concentrations of warships at Dover and Portsmouth in the Dover Straits, and Norwich across the North Sea from the port of Amsterdam. He sketches a cluster of ships in the waters off La Rochelle, France, where he knows a flotilla of Dutch privateers flourishes near the French Huguenot stronghold. He relishes his work on the square-rigged sailing boats, a far cry from his reluctance to engrave a seagoing vessel when he had repaired the map of the world several months ago. Now, with firsthand experience, he can illustrate with certainty the masts held aloft by shrouds on the port and starboard sides of a vessel, along with forestay and backstay rigging. On impulse, he draws the boarding of a Spanish merchantman in the Bay of Biscay, further mocking the Spanish-Habsburg Empire.

In letters that would reverse when printed, he titles the illustration: "*Het Engelse Marine.*" The English Navy. The banners that fly from the yardarms and masts depict the coat of arms of Willem van Oranje. He smiles, pleased to sail blithely into the treacherous waters of irony. He knows this is a more complex idea than his blacksmith forging chains. For he is mocking the English Crown who are penny-pinching and willing to use the Dutch privateers as their proxy navy, as well as the Dutch nobles, captains of the raider squadrons, who are being used, unwittingly, to the English Baron Burghley's ends.

Jonas has crossed a Rubicon in his mind, now bent on completing his project.

CHAPTER 67

London, 20 September 1570

Jonas continues to improve upon the design of his broadside. This morning, he meets Marcus Gheeraerts as usual. They walk to the Whitehall Palace where they spend several hours painting scenery for a court masque that will be performed in a fortnight. After the day's work, Jonas suggests Marcus join him at one of their usual taverns. On the way, Jonas casually wonders which of the London printers the master engraver thinks highly of.

"Richard Seres. John Day—very good. Henry Bynneman. Why do you ask?"

"I'll tell you after we have a draught."

In the tavern Jonas unrolls his mockery of England's covert support of the Dutch Revolt and asks Marcus Gheeraerts for his opinion. Jonas holds his breath while the old engraver suppresses a chuckle. Jonas lets himself smile at the first impression of his teacher. Then his tutor puts a hand across the illustration to shield it from being seen by anyone else. His voice drops to a whisper and his eyes narrow.

"Your technique is improving. Your sailing boats rival Hogenberg's. But you are most impolitic, Jonas. This is very dangerous if viewed by the wrong people. You mock both sides." Jonas becomes concerned that he has offended his tutor and he attempts to apologize. "Quiet," Gheeraerts admonishes. "You need to hear this. You can do cartography engraving if you put your effort into it."

Jonas hears the implied praise in his master's comment, and his cheeks flush, but the old engraver is not smiling. "But you venture into political incitement and you risk being caught up in a maelstrom if you are not more circumspect."

"Yes, yes," Jonas says, "I understand, but from the short time I've been here I see how, with every humiliation of the Spanish power, so many people who fled from the reach of the Iron Duke are excited to learn that the Sea Beggars make another successful raid on a Spanish merchant galleon."

Gheeraerts regards Jonas with steely intensity. "Headstrong foolishness." Tightness grips Jonas, and he holds his breath as Gheeraerts' whisper transforms into an accusatory hiss. The old man looks about the tavern warily. "You have a wit with your pencil, but you would need an army to defend you if you make an engraving of this and put copies into circulation. And I see that you want to, by the reversed legend. But the *Vater Guezen*— You tread a very thin layer of ice, my boy."

"I was going to ask you to suggest a printer," Jonas says, hesitatingly.

Gheeraerts frowns and his tone becomes even more pinched. "I would be building a gallows for both you and the poor English printer if I did such a thing on this side of the North Sea. This is better circulated at home, if at all."

Jonas looks at his drawing and nods, trying to mask his disappointment. "I understand," he says. "Thank you." His words feel like dust in his mouth. He quickly rolls the drawing into a narrow scroll, fighting an urge to cry. With unusually clumsy fingers, he ties two pieces of jute twine near each end with intent to replace the illustration in his leather pouch. He freezes in place. Jan Du Forché is leaning against an oak post, looking directly at him, a smirk curling his lips. He is alone, but his darting eyes take in the entire scene. Jonas wonders if his interchange with Gheeraerts has looked suspicious. *Of course, when Marcus covered the drawing, when he lowered his voice.* Jonas wipes his sweaty brow.

"I should get home. Thank you, Marcus, for being candid," he says softly.

"Of course, Jonas. I don't want anything to happen to my best student.

Du Forché has disappeared from view. Jonas sets some coins on the table where the tavern keeper maintains his accounts. He looks about and can see no sign of the Brussels spy.

"I'll stay and have one more," Gheeraerts says. "Good night, Jonas."

Jonas waves and leaves the tavern. He hasn't gone ten yards when Du Forché falls in step and, with practiced bonhomie, puts a hand on Jonas' shoulder.

"My young countryman, I hope your lessons with the good engraver from Bruges go well."

"Hmmm," Jonas mumbles, unconsciously gripping the leather packet at his right hip. His once-injured shoulder aches under the grasp of the intruder.

"You may not like me, Jonas Hoen of Antwerp, but I may prove a very valuable friend when the need arises. We need merely be civil with each other."

Every word chills Jonas.

"For example, when you work in the precincts of the Palace at Whitehall you may see something that may have no meaning for you. But you have eyes. If you care to share any tidbits, any trifles, I am always available to listen."

Jonas clamps his lips together to utter no rejoinder.

The spy continues. "My mother said I had big ears as a child. My father would box them regularly. That was his mistake. You see it was my great pleasure to denounce him as a heretic and save my mother. The Procurator for heresies in Brussels was a man of wondrous support til he strayed from the path. I informed his superior. I now enjoy *his* patronage. But I am boring you with my life history. Pray, Jonas Hoen, that you have a long history to your life as you find your way back to the Mother Church. I can help with many difficulties if you confide in a civil manner what you see and hear as you daub your paints and make the scenery look pretty for the Tudor Court, and the false Queen. You can always find me. I'm never far off."

Jonas is numbed with fear hearing the smooth-tongued spy urging complicity. His joints ache, as he walks keeping pace with Du Forché, whose hand has never left his shoulder, until he removes it in a flash and is gone. Stiffly, Jonas turns to see the young man retracing his steps toward the tavern. Unnerved, he leans against the wall of a tallow maker's shop. Jonas imagines himself like the dog he had illustrated, tail dragging in submission under the whip of the vengeful stableman. He turns homeward. He rages inwardly with heat like candle wax singeing his thoughts, followed by cold stilettos of sweat under his collar. Fury one moment, fear the next. He is shaken and fights to focus on the present moment as he walks the cobbled street after dark, wary of lurking cutthroats. *Proceed with my plan—find a printer who would put ink to the plate. Issue an edition of a hundred copies. That would show Du Forché—paper the walls where this spy for the Duke of Alva threatens Lowlanders. That would poke a finger in the eye of the Spanish king.*

By the time he walks up the stairs to the Coles' flat, more temperate thoughts prevail and he again hears Gheeraerts' warning that *I would endanger the printer as well as myself.* He struggles to fuel his rebellious frame of mind, but his sensible side imagines *I would betray dear Marcus Gheeraerts if I proceeded with my wild plan.* As he lets himself into the Coles' household, he is thinking of the innocent brother and sister arrested for murdering the Spanish soldier on the road to Mechelen. *I am helpless and to blame.* Feeling miserable, Jonas goes to his room and begins a letter.

Dearest Sofie—I can't wait to be back home with you. England is even more treacherous than our homeland. I love you so. I love you so.

When he puts down his quill he is sobbing.

He continues to ruminate. He links his guilt about the Mechelen brother and sister to betraying his friend and mentor, Marcus Gheeraerts. *That brother and sister will die even though I committed the murder. Do I want Marcus implicated in any way if I find a printer willing to risk the gallows?* His host family, the Coles come into his imagination also as losing favor with the British Crown. He thinks of the de Critzes, banished from the Tudor Court for his indiscretion. He imagines little James Cole begging on the streets like so many London urchins in rags, children of South Bank harlots. After an hour of self-recrimination, Jonas resolves not to publish his broadside in England. However, as a balm to his shattered plans, he flattens his rolled up illustration, and begins embellishing it with more detail. Two hours later he affixes the thin paper version of his illustration atop a waxed plate; and he begins scribing according to his sketch.

I will be prepared as soon as I get back to Antwerp, he tells himself thinking that he might have an outlet through Mark Anthony Coppens.

He quits work on his copper plate when the clock in the outer hall tolls three times. He has completed only the bare outline of the coasts and the detail of most of one ship facing Europe in the Straits of Dover etched into the thin wax veneer. He douses the candle and falls into an easy sleep, satisfied that he is working toward his goal, a plate extolling the Sea Beggars, the *Vater Guezen*, ready for printing once he is back in his homeland.

CHAPTER 68

San Francisco, Fleming Galleries, 10:30 a.m. April 14th 2016

Owen nods to three others in the faux art deco elevator as it creeps its way to the fourth floor. Even though he knows the map will be auctioned two or more hours into the proceedings, he arrives early to have one more look at the copper plate print, and also observe who else might be in the market for the image of the world, even in its compromised condition.

Inside the auction hall, he catches the eye of Matt Warburg who nods a greeting from across the room. The first gavel will not be struck for forty-five minutes, but already collectors, dealers, and enthusiasts for Western Americana and 20th Century first edition fiction mill about in the display area and in the corridors, cellphones in hand, deep in conversation with their clients, bankers, or spouses.

This auction attracts a disparate range of potential bidders. In Owen's experience, it is dangerous for dealers when many unknown bidders are on hand. Items sell for higher prices due to amateurs hooked by the excitement of a bidding war where the driving force is ownership or beating the competition rather than paying a reasonable price based on auction history or established values. As in a gambling casino, where the house wins on statistical probabilities, oddball sales such as this one become windfalls for the auction house.

Owen notices Rodney Pinkham. With bags under his eyes behind rimless glasses and worn elbows in his auction jacket, he works the edge of the crowd, shaking hands, talking with bookmen and collectors who think they have a special relationship with the old auctioneer. When Pinkham circulates away from the map, which attracts few onlookers, Owen pulls out his loupe and zeroes in on the lines that encircle the engraved sea monster. "JONAS HOEN," he reads upside down. He returns to the front desk, presents his card and registers with Cheryl Vasquez, who smiles and issues him paddle number 63. Owen tucks the bidding card into his catalog at Lot 256. Moments later he seeks out Matt Warburg, who is reviewing the catalog, marking lots that he will be calling as one of the two employees of Fleming's who alternate with Rodney Pinkham as auctioneers. Ian Carstairs, the son of a Harvard Club of San Francisco member, had recently been brought into the business, as heir apparent to the foundering enterprise. At past auctions, Owen listened closely to the patter of the well-groomed young man. While he looks the part of a young worldly-wise auction house executive, Owen detects that Carstairs' knowledge about literary properties and graphics is lacking.

According to Matt, Carstairs will auction half the catalog thanks to his sonorous voice and smiling persona, which briskly moves things along.

Matt is the most knowledgeable of the auctioneers due to his interest in literature and printed imagery.

Owen asks, "Hey Matt, what part of the catalog are you going to flog?"

"I'm the relief pitcher for Pinky—er, Mr. Pinkham. I pick up at Lot 110 and go to the break at 225. Ian begins Round Two, and the dulcet tones of Mr. P pick up again at Lot 375 to the bitter end."

Owen mentally notes that Ian Carstairs would be at the mic for Lot 256.

"Matt, without stepping over any lines, give me a sense of the competition?"

"I'll tell you the most interesting thing. The consigner doesn't really want to sell it." Matt lowers his voice so it is barely audible. "He tried to have it pulled yesterday, but Pinky strong-armed him with threats of lawsuits, blah, blah, blah. Owen, between you me, and the doorpost, this is my last auction. After I ship the goods to the winners, I am out of here. I don't mind telling you that there's a Horst Harmon, Prints and Graphics, been huddling with the Pinkster."

"Something being rigged?"

Warburg shrugs, his palms turned upward.

"Question," Owen says on impulse. "Could you handle a really big project, say a feature length film?"

"I sure could," Matt said unhesitatingly.

"Then another question. Why does Mr. Dijkstra want to pull the map?"

Matt looks around the gradually filling auction room. People take seats, greet other auction regulars and rivals for the books going on the auction block.

"Something about how his father's blood on the map is thicker than water. He was very upset with the boss—me too—after he laid a financial trip on the consignor about how much it would cost to pull it. This piece is going to go for a lot more than was estimated. There's more than one bidder who wants to get his hands on that map."

Owen hopes his face hasn't noticeably clouded over. He checks the time and smiles his thanks to Warburg. "Have a good auction. We'll talk again."

"You too, Owen. Good luck."

"One last thing. You mentioned a dealer named Harmon. Is he in the room?"

Matt scans the auction floor. "There he is, between Pinky and Ian." Matt nods his head toward the trio who are talking outside Pinkham's office. "You could follow your nose. He wears some godawful orange cologne."

Owen sees a red-faced, buttoned down man in a dark blue suit, coiffed graying hair, and an insincere smile. He listens to Ian hold forth about something, creating the illusion that he is completely wrapped up in Ian's story. But Harmon's eyes dart everywhere, even catching Owen's for the briefest moment.

"Thanks, Matt," Owen says. He enters into his smartphone search engine: "harmon graphics sf bay area." *Harmon Prints and Collectibles, San Francisco*, pops onto his screen. *Specialists in What You Need for Your Collection.* A San Francisco post office box and phone number are listed. More revealing than the message is the typeface. The "Specialists" line was printed in *Fraktur*, the German gothic font that originated in the early 1500s. Its popularity came to an abrupt halt with the end of World War II. Owen thought it was an odd font for an American graphics dealer to adopt as a descriptor on his Internet webpage.

Owen walks to the side of the room where he can keep an eye on Harmon. He taps in the number and watches Harmon fumble for his phone across the room. He sees Harmon excuse himself from the conversation he is having with the auction house personnel. Owen also notices that an overweight man, who looks like he came off the set of *The Sopranos*, follows Harmon with his eyes.

"Harmon Prints?" Owen asks, cupping the mouthpiece to cut out ambient noise of chatting bidders, as soon as the phone is at the man's ear.

"Yes?" A hoarse voice asks, with no hint of a German accent.

"I just read about a map that is being auctioned at Fleming's this morning. Would you be able to represent me in bidding for that map? It's an Ortelius, the only one in the auction, I believe."

Owen listens to the silence and watches Harmon making mental calculations.

"Perhaps I could help," the squeaking voice finally answers. "But I would have to know what your top bid could be."

"Forty-five hundred," Owen says, eyes glued to Harmon's physical language.

His whole body appears to shrug its shoulders.

"Oh, you are way under, Mister—can I ask who—"

"By how much," Owen presses, quickly. "I could go higher."

"You would have to treble your highest bid at the least."

"Ah, thank you. Too rich for my blood." Owen clicks off. He watches Harmon looking at his phone, and a moment later Owen's phone buzzes.

"Marsden residence. Who shall I say is calling," Owen responds in a voice summoning a British butler from some long ago motion picture.

"Mr. Marsden, please."

Owen waits a confused moment. "Sir, there hasn't been a *Mister* Marsden here for five years, and Mrs. Marsden is indisposed. Who shall I say called?"

"Oh, never mind, sorry to have—my apologies."

Owen watches as Harmon clicks off. He has what he needs. The selling price might go as high as $15,000. Someone, somewhere, was willing to pay that and it appeared that Harmon was representing that client. Had Owen upped his fictitious top bid to $16,000, would Harmon play both clients off each other? Owen needs to call Maurice Bregmann. He leaves the auction room and walks down the office building's fourth floor corridor, punching in the curator's private line. He stops at an alcove holding a wall rack of neatly folded fire hose. A classic brass nozzle grabs Owen's attention momentarily while the connection goes through.

CHAPTER 69

Corridor, Fleming Auction Galleries, San Francisco, 11:00 a.m. April 14ᵗʰ 2016

"Dr. Bregmann, Owen Spencer. I'm at Fleming's and I've learned some things. First, our authorized top bid is at least five thousand low. Something is odd. This map, the condition it is in, the third or fourth impression of the atlas—fifteen thousand is far over the line based on past prices realized for a print like this."

"I could wake somebody in Jerusalem," Bregmann offers. "What do you think it will sell for?"

"The competition seems to have a deep bank account. I would let your contact make that call. If this was only for the art value, the original low catalog estimate might have been a marginally fair price. In fact, fifteen hundred would have been high."

"I'll call Chaim. How long do I have before I call you back?" Bregmann asks.

"This won't go 'til approximately 12:30, say 12:10 to be safe. But there is another development. I've learned that the map's consigner wants to pull it from the auction. He tried yesterday but the manager browbeat him into leaving it."

"These things tend to get calamitous, don't they?" Bregmann sighs.

"Also, the competition's rep is named Harmon, Harmon Prints, San Francisco. Do you know him?"

"I'm afraid not, Owen."

"I'd better let you go so you can talk to your man. Meanwhile, I'll try Mr. Dijkstra. He was talked out of withdrawing his consignment because it could cost him for breaking his contract. Maybe a couple of thousand. I'll let you go. Call me safely up to twelve-ten with any new instructions."

Owen studies the fire hose nozzle. The scene shows a horse-drawn fire wagon racing down a street to a burning building. *Always a calamity.*

He does not see Harmon when he returns to the auction room. People are taking seats in the rows of metal folding chairs. He wanders over to Ian Carstairs, whose saccharine smile is glued to his tanned face. Some men's cologne perfumes the air. Owen proffers his hand, and says, "Ian Carstairs, good to see you again." Carstairs squints, thinking he should know who Owen is. Owen snaps a business card from the top of his deck and passes it to the customer relations' officer of the auction house.

"Ah Mr. Spencer," Carstairs intones with false bonhomie. He has not a clue as to who Owen is, despite past introductions.

"I see you know Mr. Harmon," Owen chats.

"Harmon? Oh, yes. He and Mr. Pinkham go back a ways."

"He rather likes that Ortelius," Owen says.

Carstairs rolls his eyes. "Yes, pretty damaged. I wonder what he finds so intriguing. No accounting for taste."

"Pleasure talking to you. Have a good auction," Owen says, stepping away.

"And what piques *your* interest, today, Mr. Spencer," Carstairs queries.

"Frederic Remington. You've got one or two of his prints. Do you know if he ever did fire wagon horses?" Owen asks.

Carstairs is noting, "Remington fire wagon horses," on the back of his card.

"I'll keep a lookout," he calls after Owen, who searches again for Matt Warburg. He circles to the entrance and manages to stand in front of Cheryl Vasquez, as a few stragglers come up after him to register and get bidding paddles.

"Hi, Ms. Vasquez. Can you buzz the back for Matt Warburg? Owen Spencer."

The dark-haired college student smiles and presses the extension in the employees' area. Matt emerges from the door marked "No Entry Except Employees."

"What can you tell me about Harmon?" Owen asks.

Matt's wrinkled nose registers his distaste. "About five years ago, shortly after I started here, Pinky decided to do a Nazi memorabilia sale. Lots of people came out of the woodwork for that one, including Harmon. Only other time I've seen him."

"Huh," Owen grunts. "Any reason he stuck in your mind?"

"Well, it was all pretty offensive to me," Matt says. "I remember a bidding battle between him and a woman representing a Holocaust research organization for some Wannsee documents. You know the Final Solution meeting in 1942? Harmon's client had the deeper pockets. I couldn't stop thinking that his bidding style was a short, jerky *Sieg Heil* salute."

"Huh," Owen grunts again.

"I won't forget that auction because Pinky engaged the woman in some banter and he asks what the numbers on her arm represented? 'I was in two concentration camps,' she says. And Pinky says, get this, 'Two! You must have been a bad one.'" Matt does a double take at the sheer stupidity. "What am I still doing here?"

"The best you can, Matt, like all of us."

"We go in five. Starting off, I'm the Internet guy. Good luck," Warburg says, tapping a knuckle on Owen's arm and walking to his desk with a large display.

Rodney Pinkham moves up to the lectern and a hush comes over the bidders.

"Ladies and gentlemen," Pinkham begins. As he introduces himself, and his staff, Owen steps into the corridor and phones Michael Dijkstra. He wanders down the corridor to the fire hose that had captured his attention earlier. The connection goes to voicemail and Owen requests that he contact him as soon as possible, ending with, "If you would like to withdraw the map from auction I may be able to help."

Owen's phone buzzes and for a moment he is elated that Dijkstra is responding. The call instead is from Patricia. "Hi, I thought I'd come up to see you get that map."

"Wow," he says smiling. "It's far from a done deal, Patricia. But I'd love your company, maybe combine it with a late lunch at the Modern."

"Now there's a winner," she says, lightly.

"You sound chirpy," Owen says.

"I got off the phone with a ninety-something who thinks I'm the bees knees."

"Oh, competition! I don't know if I can handle this, Patty. Just what line did Michael Dijkstra hand you?"

"It was mostly about you, Owen. He said you set a whole change of worldview in motion. How's them apples?"

"I can't wait to hear the details," Owen says, peering again at the brass etching of a horse in full gallop hurtling down a street with a driver cracking his whip as the house at the end of the street blazes.

"He thinks you're an 'A-One man.' His words. Says you remind him of his brother. 'Focused, insistent, and with a good heart.' What did you say to him on Thursday? When you came home, you didn't look like you walked on water."

"More like treading water. Did you really just speak with him?"

"Yes, he was on BART headed in for the auction."

"Wait a minute. You have his cell number?"

"Sure."

"Patricia, what is it? Last I heard he was thinking of pulling that map."

"Well, he's rooting like crazy that you bid and win."

"Oh boy," Owen says in a dejected tone. He tries to explain, "If it goes to auction it's not a slam dunk that the good guys win."

"Well, I'm coming to town, win or lose. Sounds like you need a buddy."

"Yeah, thanks for that. His cell number, what is it?"

Owen listens to dead air while Patricia checks her incoming calls list. Finally, she gives him Michael Dijkstra's number.

"What going, on, Owen?"

"Patricia," he replies, his eyes glued to the flaming building etched on the fire hose nozzle, "The house is on fire, and here comes the cavalry."

"At least what you say is not cryptic," she chides. Then she relents. "OK. Where shall I meet you, at the auction house or the museum? I'm in the car now."

"Come to Fleming's. If it's a bust I'll call you."

"I love you, *A-One man*," Patricia says.

"Thank heavens," he replies and hears her phone click off.

Owen checks the time and recalls how long-winded Rodney Pinkham can be early in an auction. He guesses not more than a dozen lots have been gaveled, so he still has plenty of time.

He punches in Michael Dijkstra's cell number.

"Yes?" Dijkstra answers.

"Sir," is all Owen can utter.

"Yes?" Dijkstra asks second time.

"This is Owen Spencer, Mr. Dijkstra. I'm at the auction galleries, and I would like to know if you have intention of pulling the map, because...."

"No, so I hope you will continue your interest, Mr. Spencer."

"Well my client is interested, but I want to assure you that you are well within your rights to withdraw your property right up to the moment of a gavel announcing a sale. You may be liable for some expenses on the part of the auction house, but you are well within your rights, and if you do not want to part with the map, there is absolutely nothing to stop you; *anything* Mr. Pinkham might have said to you to the contrary."

"He made it sound like I could be taken to the poorhouse by the courts," Dijkstra says, his voice bitter to Owen's ears.

"Mr. Dijkstra, I only want to assure you that the choice is completely yours until Lot 256 is declared sold by the auctioneer."

"Hah. What lot are they up to now? My train is pulling into Oakland."

"There are a hundred lots to go. You should be good until twelve-ten."

"Your wife is a charming person. You make a good couple. You remind me of my brother and his wife. I have been wrong about them for many years."

Owen smiles at the compliment, but does't follow Dijkstra's train of thought.

"Hopefully, I will be there in half an hour. Goodbye, Mr. Spencer."

Owen clinks his fingernail on the brass nozzle. "C'mon, Jerusalem," he roots in a whisper. *Stake me so I can bid for this thing.* Citrus cologne odor wafts down the corridor, followed by Harmon's voice. Owen presses against the wall of the alcove.

"*Ja, ja. Vijftienduizend euros, genoeg.* Should suffice, Herr Schroeder.... *Dank u...* Good to know.... Only if I need it. I will call when I have the winning bid. Ja, ja."

Harmon's voice is more distant, as if he had turned back to the auction.

Vijftienduizend Euros? In dollars? Owen scrambles to do a search on the Dutch word *Vijftienduizend,* finally finds, it and sees it means fifteen thousand. He then enters *Euros = USD* and gasps. Harmon has $20,000 to bid with. His mind bubbles with questions. *Who would gain if this map was denied a winning bid by Yad Vashem? Who else would want such an item? A rival Holocaust remembrance group? Was there even such a thing? An enemy of Holocaust remembrance?* Harmon has dealings with Nazi enthusiasts! Owen speed-dials Bregmann.

CHAPTER 70

London, Late October 1570

After Jonas decides to proceed with his Sea Beggars engraving, he spends the next two weeks working with Gheeraerts, painting scenery for a series of autumn Court Masques. Each evening, he continues work on his broadside. He has been walking home along the Thames embankment as the shadows lengthen to sketch with keen interest a French-built merchantmen. The Dutch privateers have modified such captured prizes, cut cannon-ports below topside decks, and prowl the shipping lanes for cargo-laden Spanish galleons in their relentless pursuit of bounty.

Before he takes leave of Gheeraerts' this Thursday, his mentor asks, "Will Susannah and I see you at the fête for Jacobus Coels on Sunday?"

"Oh, yes, yes. Elizabeth says I am invited, too." Jonas has been too distracted by his late night work on his *Sea Beggars* project to think very much about the feast in James Coles' honor. When he arrives home that evening he makes a point of asking Elizabeth Cole if he can assist in any way.

"No, no, dear boy," she says, lists in her hands. "But thank you for asking. If I think of something I will let you know."

Jonas sees the additional hired help carrying in chairs and tabletops to extend the event from the drawing room into the hallway. Tablecloths are being laid across wooden planks that hide the utilitarian sawhorses, to create a thirty-foot long table. Fifty or more guests can be wined and fed in one sitting.

He decides to take his evening meal at a tavern to escape the hubbub and avoid both the noise and chances of being in the way. On the second floor landing he passes Margery, puffing up the stairs with a basket of pewter table sconces and tapers to illuminate the enormous table.

"Big doings, eh, Master Jonas?"

"Would you like some help?"

Her mouthful of teeth flashes. "Oh, you. You could help me kill my goat of a husband. I do need a younger man. Would you help me pin proper horns on him?"

Jonas has long ceased to be embarrassed by Margery's ribald jokes. "If you let me sketch your beautiful smile, I will consider it."

Margery purses her lips to cover her unflattering feature. "You can be cruel," she says, pushing past him.

Jonas doesn't immediately dismiss her comment. "My apologies if I offended, Margery," he calls as she heaves her bulk up the next flight. But his amends fall on deaf ears. He holds onto the thought as he makes his way out onto the curving street and walks north into Leadenhall Street. *Cruel? Am I cruel?* His thoughts jump to the mocking display he had pantomimed to humiliate Du Forché. And he makes a further connection. His sarcasm in calling the Sea Beggars "England's navy," may also have come from that well of "cruelty." He wonders if Sofie perceives the same thing. *Oh, I couldn't bear that.* His introspection ends five minutes into his meal of a lamb pasty and a tankard of ale.

"What do you hear?" Jan Du Forché slides next to him on his bench.

Jonas' jaw clenches. "Not much to be learned painting cherubs and seraphim on canvas," he answers guardedly.

"Do these cherubs fly the Duke van Oranje's colors?"

Jonas nibbles at the crust of his meat pie and says nothing. He knows he can never joust with Du Forché's wit and double entendre.

"I have heard, because I know how to listen," the Brussels spy says, mocking and conspiratorial, "there is a certain young papermaker's assistant in Antwerp...." Jonas' ears prick up. A fury begins bubbling. He looks straight ahead at the laughing eaters at the other tables, while the voice at his left shoulder continues. "Who misses her friend, this girl does."

Jonas grasps the balled fist of his left hand with his right, as though in prayer.

"But he," Du Forché continues, "spends his time prettifying the Tudors' entertainments. What must this devout Christian girl think when her dear friend wastes his talents to support the excommunicated Queen of England's irreverence for the true Roman Church?"

Jonas hears his own voice pitching into a low, dangerous register. "A devout monk told me on more than one occasion that I had a fatal flaw. And it is this." With a sharp movement he rams his elbow into Du Forché's face. The spy falls to the floor, his feet kicking the table with a clatter of tankards.

"Your bloody nose suits you," Jonas says coldly.

"I will hunt you down, stupid boy," Du Forché says, blood spurting.

"Hey you. Out of here you damned Flemmies," the tavern keeper orders.

Jonas picks up his scrap of pasty and walks out of the alehouse. He waits outside for a while, ready to continue the fight, but Du Forché does not appear. He wonders if he did serious damage, but resists returning to find out. He makes for the Billingsgate dock; feeling puffed up and sickened at the same time. The coolness of the fall London night, the moon bouncing off the Thames, helps Jonas lose his queasiness. The slapping of halyard ropes of the moored vessels bowing and rising slowly on the deep-draught river brings his mind back to his *Vater Guezen* undertaking. He counts the shrouds on a sixty-foot square-rigged merchantman, and watches the pennants snap in the brisk breeze. A flock of squawking kites interrupts his thoughts and he begins shaping a plan to see how quickly he can return home. He has spent five months in London. The chill weather signals that he needs to rejoin his love. If vermin like Du Forché threaten him with information about Sofie, this is no place to be. He decides after the celebration on Sunday night he will ask the Coles about sailing to Antwerp.

With the release of the second Latin edition of the *Theatrum Orbis Terrarum* that fall, Sofie hears rumors that the succeeding printings may move to the Golden Compass print-works close to the Friday Market plaza. Gilles Coppens de Diest, declining in health, retains the title of publisher for the time being, but the Boekprintere Scheldt will expand its publication of other books with the newfound celebrity. The printing facility owned by Christophe Plantin, the Golden Compass, is better equipped to handle the more demanding schedule as print runs with textual material printed in various languages are agreed upon.

In October, Sofie is in a dark mood, missing Jonas and rebuffing the attentions of Joop Baldus.

"He's not coming back, you know," Joop needles. "He's gone for good to escape the gallows he deserves. A sweet girl like you should be taken care of by a real Fleming, not some orphanage cast-out, who runs from the law."

Joop has cornered her near the main stairwell, both her arms laden with a trencher of wetted paper. He presses his chest into the tray she carries and pins her against the balustrade of the stairs. She tries to squeeze by, but Joop's garlicky breath is in her face. She pushes violently against the sneering boy to no avail, then kicks her knee into his groin. He falls backward, pulling the heavy tray of moist paper out of her grasp. The trencher clips his mouth. He cries with pain and spits out a bloody tooth.

He is sprawled on the floor when Pieter Du Brul comes through the doors of the papermaking rooms, wiping his hands on a towel.

"Only trying to help her," Joop complains spitting blood on the top sheets of the paper.

"Liar!" Sofie shouts.

"Stop discoloring the paper!" Du Brul demands. "You have made a mess here for the last time, if I have anything to say about it. Sofie, back to the deckle room." He draws off the two sheets that show Joop's blood and hands them to Sofie. Then he pulls the trencher off Joop's chest, and strides into the printing hall.

Sofie regards Joop scornfully as he gets to his feet pressing his fist against his bloody lips. "You really are a mess of a boy," she calls as she turns her back to him.

Something sounding like "You'll be sorry for this," emanates from Joop's damaged mouth.

Sofie's shrugs her shoulders as she walks back to the papermaking hall.

> *Dearest Jonas,*
>
> *Joop Baldus has been sacked. That's the good news. The Boekprintere Scheldt has taken on several new commissions. A first edition with Dutch commentary replacing the Latin, will be published next year. Master Ortels has been preparing the text for the Low Countries version. But the cartography plates will be reused for these editions, and we will print the first Dutch run. Additional copper plates are being readied by Master Hogenberg and the Arsen brothers in their own studios for future editions to add to the original group of fifty-three. That's the news here, where I am working. But my real news is that I am heartsick. I miss you so. When can you come home?*
>
> *Your sad best friend, who loves you,*
>
> *Sofie.*

CHAPTER 71

San Francisco, Late Morning, Fleming Galleries, Noon. April 14th 2016

Owen's chest thumps as his call to Bregmann's phone rings while the elevator creeps down to the Kearney Street level. When doors open, his contact in Berkeley has still not picked up, so he assumes that Bregmann is on his call to Jerusalem. He steps onto the quiet street and looks toward the top of Telegraph Hill and then down to Market Street. He spies a tall, elderly man in brown beginning his walk up Kearny from Market. Owen calculates that his shambling gait would take Dijkstra ten minutes to arrive. Owen's phone buzzes.

"Maurice here, Owen."

"Before you say anything, you should know that Harmon's client is ready to go to twenty thousand. I heard him on his phone and he was assured fifteen thousand euros. I don't think the map is worth anything like that. If the value is placed on its artistic merit or as rare cartography, it's only a mediocre specimen."

"Yes, Owen, Chaim knows that. It is the bloodstain, the fault in the piece. A hate group fronted by a Max Schroeder in Utrecht, apparently—"

"Schroeder, yes!" Owen says, excitedly. "That's who Harmon was conversing with, not ten minutes ago."

"Yes. They have been listening in to conversations at the acquisitions office. The Schroeder-Berghuis organization has long been a Holocaust denier—that and anti-Muslim activism—a full-service hate group. They seek to discredit Yad Vashem's corroboration of Nazi atrocity, especially at the hands of the Dutch SS."

"Maurice. I'm on the street now. The consigner of the map is walking up from Market Street as we speak. He'll be here in a minute or two. I have already advised him by phone that he is completely within his rights to withdraw the map until a sale is gaveled 'sold.'" As Bregmann begins his reply, Owen sees an open convenience store across the street.

"Well, Chaim has given me a cap of twenty-five, including the buyer's fee. So I guess you could go as high as twenty-two since there's sales tax to figure in, too."

Owen continues to listen as he crosses the street, picks out a container of bottled water from the cooler and pays the sleepy-eyed attendant. He walks back across the street to intercept Michael Dijkstra.

Bregmann continues, "As for Mr. Dijkstra's position on pulling the map, we would like to talk to him no matter what he decides, especially regarding the commentary that his father wrote while he harbored Hetty van Aalt."

"Here he comes now, Maurice. Would you like to tell him that yourself?"

"Certainly."

"Hold for a moment, then."

Owen juggles phone and water bottle as he offers his hand to Michael who shakes it. Owen passes the water to him and waits for Michael to regain his breath.

"Thank you. A Lowlander like me, not used to so steep a grade," he gasps.

"Mr. Dijkstra, I have Professor Bregmann on the phone. He represents the client I spoke to you about when I visited on Thursday. Can you speak with him?"

Michael looks suspiciously at Owen and then speaks hesitantly into the phone. "Yes? This is Michael Dijkstra."

Owen watches Michael's face gradually relax.

"Yes, well I have not made up my mind yet about withdrawing it." Michael says. "But I'm close. I think I understand that you have interest in my father's diary during the occupation when the little girl lived there. Yes, I might show those pages to you after I am sure that no damage could be done to my father's name."

Owen watches Michael frown, as he loses patience with Bregmann.

"If I withdraw the map, I might like the whole book intact for my family since it has been so long our property." Michael looks at Owen. "But I still have some time to make that decision."

Owen nods and checks his watch and sees that it is noon.

"Here's Mr. Spencer again, Doctor."

Owen takes the phone.

"So, Maurice. Yes, we will proceed as noted earlier, and if Mr. Dijkstra chooses to pull the map, that is certainly his right." Owen raises his voice and looks into the Dijkstra's eyes as he makes his last point to once again assure that it is his choice. In an even louder voice, to make certain the old man hears, Owen concludes, "And I'm very aware that our client would treat the property with utmost respect."

Owen ends the call.

"Thanks for the water, Mr. Spencer."

Owen smiles. "You looked like you could use it."

"Shall we go up?" Dijkstra asks.

"Good idea. They'll be closing in on it soon."

"So let me ask you, please," Dijkstra says, as Owen presses the elevator button. "If you were in my position, would you let a sale go through?"

"I couldn't answer, sir. It depends on how badly you need the money, versus the intangible value you place in this map. It is your choice, and I'm not you."

His answer does not comfort the old man, whose expression verges on anguish, his conflict far from resolved. The doors open to the fourth floor.

"Whatever you decide about the map, I hope you will let Yad Vashem read your father's account."

"Hmmm," Michael mumbles, lost in thought.

Owen can read no meaning in his faraway gaze as they enter.

"Hi, Ms. Vasquez," Owen nods. "What lot are they on?" The dark-haired girl looks with concern past Owen. He watches Dijkstra smile at the receptionist.

"I hope I didn't upset you yesterday, Miss. I was not myself when I left here."

"That's all right," she says, relieved. "They're on Lot 245, Mr. Spencer."

Owen can faintly hear Ian Carstairs cajoling bidders to add another twenty-five dollars to a grouping of first editions.

"I'm going to take a seat," Owen whispers to Dijkstra. "Your lot should go in ten minutes, or so. Good luck to you."

Owen leaves Dijkstra pacing off to the side of the receptionist's desk, and enters the auction hall where he takes an aisle chair in the back row. He chooses well, so that the auctioneer has a clear sightline when bidding commences. He looks for the back of Harmon's head, but cannot locate the groomed spray of gray hair. *He'll show soon enough.* Owen watches Ian Carstairs gavel a lot sold for $130.

"Lot two forty seven," Carstairs intones, his winning smile flashing. "Oh, here's a beautiful group, Jim Thompson's first four novels, each a first edition... and one of them signed, in pristine condition...."

Michael Dijkstra weakly takes a corner chair in the receptionist's area, completely unsettled. He ruminates on a jumble of reasons to let the auction proceed to escape his crushing debt and an ill-formed concept of honor to keep his last possession of value intact for.... *For whom?* The conflicting thoughts exhaust him and the clock is ticking. He debates whether to take a seat in the auction hall or wait out one or two more lots before entering. Either way he feels like a schoolboy who needs an adult to help him make a decision. He is no closer to a decision of whether to let the bidding go on or pull the map. From his corner chair he sees Patricia Spencer hurry through the main door from the outer hall. She does not notice Michael as she comes up to the receptionist's desk.

"What lot are they up to?" she asks.

Cynthia Vasquez, listening through one ear bud to the proceedings in the auction hall, holds up her copy of the catalog and points at Lot 251.

Patricia breathes a relieved sigh and says that she is going in where her husband would be bidding shortly.

"Mrs. Spencer?" Michael calls softly.

A smile brightens Patricia's face. "Mr. Dijkstra. How are you?"

Michael's frown darkens. "Struggling.... My heart says stop the sale and my bank account says get as much as you can."

Patricia nods. "How would you live if you stopped the sale?"

Michael's mind shoots back to the near starvation days toward the end at Krümmel. And following repatriation, the lines for bread.

"I would get by," he says. "An old man can swallow his pride and eat... and be housed, I suppose. Thank you for asking that question."

Applause can be heard from the auction room. There has been a spirited bidding war over one of the lots. Patricia nods in commiseration and cocks her head in understanding of his dilemma. "Good luck with your decision."

Michael watches her disappear into the auction hall. His gaze falls on the receptionist, who smiles back at him as she enters the final selling price of the last lot into her catalog. A nameplate tells him the pretty young girl is Cynthia Vasquez.

"I hope you get a good price for your consignment. Almost there," she says.

Michael nods, rises, walks into the auction room and stands at the back. He catches Rodney Pinkham's gimlet eye peering from a desk to the side of the auction podium. The young associate is auctioning Lot 253, taking bids in increments of five dollars for a geological map of Placer County, California, dated 1893.

"The sacred and the profane," Michael hears a voice mutter in the last row toward the end on his right. The voice is high, rasping, one that he has heard before. A much bigger man sitting to his left grunts a guttural acknowledgement. Michael glances to his left. The Spencers are also seated in the last row at the opposite end. They stare tensely at the podium, Patricia with a steady hand on her husband's shoulder. Inexplicably, he feels his throat thicken with sadness and loss. The face of Rudi Müller from Krümmel darts across Michael's mind, posed with his wife and baby boy in a photo the German had kept. The photo of Pim, Gerdi and him, buried so long in his bedroom chest of drawers, appears behind Michael's closed eyes. Then a framed silver nitrate print rises in his memory of his father and mother, radiantly in love, taken when they were in their early twenties, the one that sat on their bedroom nightstand in Eindhoven. The welling in his throat becomes unbearable and Michael steps back out into the anteroom. Cynthia Vasquez looks up from the college text she has been intermittently studying. Her eyes ask if she could be of any assistance.

"Miss," Michael croaks, "have you ever rescued someone? Or something you had no idea was important to you until the last minute?"

The receptionist returns his intense gaze blankly.

"Of course. How could you know what I am talking about?"

The young woman's brow knits.

"I'm sorry," Michael says, backing into the auction hall again to hear Ian Carstairs announce, "Lot two fifty four. A lithograph of important anchorages for the San Francisco Bay Area and stretching all the way to Sutter's Creek and Sacramento by Cadwalader Ringgold." Phrases ring out from Carstairs' repertoire, "Important Gold Rush era map," "Shipping anchorages—made men millionaires overnight."

The bids ring up and Michael sees the composite map of the Carquinez Straits and several inset maps fetch $1,100.

"Lot two fifty five," Carstairs announces.

Michael cannot bring himself to sit down. He knows he will be a distraction if he paces. Pinkham eyes him from his desk. He presses himself against the rear wall, closes his eyes and wills himself to calm down. Finally, Carstairs' voice, calls, "Lot two fifty six. Late 16th Century, an important map, from the first Dutch atlas of the known world ever published."

One of the part-time assistants carries the sleeve with clear acetate to the front of the room. The overhead lights bounce a glare in Michael's eyes as he tries to look at the map, which he will never see again when the gavel falls. From his position, Michael barely sees the ragged stain left by his father's blood.

"This item has sparked a great deal of interest," Carstairs intones. Rodney Pinkham speaks smugly behind his desk, and urges a spirited sale. "Let me remind everyone that the phone lines are open, as is online bidding. The bidding for Lot 256 opens at six thousand dollars."

A collective gasp, followed by a hush, envelops the hall. Michael stiffens. *No turning back now.*

CHAPTER 72

Fleming Auction Gallery, San Francisco, 12:30 p.m. April 14ᵗʰ 2016

"Can I hear sixty-five hundred?" Carstairs asks, unable to mask his glee.

Michael is shocked to hear the first bid. That is enough to get him out from under three months of back mortgage owed. Not enough, but....

Pinkham, his phone to his ear, raises his hand.

"We have sixty-five hundred on the phone. Seven thousand," Carstairs says, nodding to the corner of the last row, opposite where Owen Spencer is seated.

The young man, who had helped Michael into Pinkham's office the previous day, raises his hand before his computer, responding to an online bid. Carstairs' quick eyes take in Matt's bid. "Seventy-five hundred from an online bidder."

An arm shoots up from the third row.

"Eight thousand, thank you sir."

Again Matt Warburg's hand goes up.

"Eighty-five hundred," Carstairs advises everyone, with anticipation.

The arm of the third row bidder waves again.

"We're up to nine, do I hear any more?" Carstairs asks.

Michael steadies himself by holding onto the back of an empty metal folding chair. This is unbelievable. How could the auction house have miscalculated so poorly what his map would fetch?

"Do I hear ninety-five hundred for this rare specimen, the first map of the world published in Antwerp by Abraham Ortelius from the first atlas commented in Dutch ever published?" Carstairs implores.

When no one bids, Carstairs asks. "Are we done?"

Michael sees a quick movement in his peripheral vision, again from the end of the back row. The brief hand gesture belongs to the neatly coiffed gray-haired dealer who had passed Michael in the building hallway on Friday.

"Ninety-five hundred," Carstairs booms, inviting more. "Ten thousand!"

Carstairs looks briefly where Owen Spencer and his wife are sitting.

"Can I hear eleven?"

Silence comes back to the auctioneer. It is clear to Michael that it is rare for a single Fleming's consignment to reach those numbers.

"We have eleven," the auctioneer says. "Now twelve."

The battle is on at the extremes of the last row. Spencer, to Michael's left, and the unknown dealer to the right, are locked in financial combat. Michael sees the penalties he owes the IRS begin to chip away with every thousand-dollar increment.

"Thirteen." Carstairs acknowledges the bid from Michael's right.

"Fourteen," he says seeing Spencer's nod.

"Fifteen thousand," Carstairs voice rises.

"Sixteen, we have sixteen, now seventeen, and eighteen."

Carstairs pauses, cocking his head. "Nineteen."

"Nineteen," Carstairs says again.

"Twenty." He acknowledges Spencer's bid.

The auction hall is still. Most attendees have never heard such rarified bids for such an object as the stained copper plate map.

"Twenty-one, and twenty two," Carstairs says, snapping his head from Spencer to the other bidder like a spectator at a tennis match. To Michael, Pinkham appears to be salivating. It is a horserace.

"The bid is twenty-two thousand," Carstairs says in a full voice, nodding toward the opposite end of the row from the Spencers' seats. His reddened face shows heart-pounding exertion. "Going once—"

Michael summons his full voice. "This map is withdrawn! I own this map and it is not for sale."

Pinkham shoots up from his desk and shouts, "You cannot do this Mr. Dike-Dike-sir!"

"I can and I am. This item has been withdrawn!"

The bidder who has gone to twenty-two thousand dollars on the right side of the last row rises furiously. "No," he shouts in his rasping voice and begins advancing on Michael. "You son of a bitch!"

Michael backs away, pulling vacant chairs into the path of the menacing man. The bidder is red-faced, sweating profusely through a radiating citrus odor. Quickly, Owen Spencer comes from behind Michael, and stands between the furious bidder and the elderly Dutchman.

"He's within his rights, Mr. Harmon," Owen says in a steady voice.

Most of the auction attendees are standing, some precariously on their folding chairs, to observe the confrontation at the back of the room between the presumed winner of the bidding war and the consigner who has withdrawn his property from auction.

The burly man who has sat next to the scowling dealer restrains him. But Harmon kicks at chairs in his fury. Michael surmises the burly man might have been hired by the high-bidder to protect his expensive near-acquisition.

Someone taps Michael on his shoulder. He turns to see the bearded young man who had gotten him water the day before and helped him to a seat in Pinkham's office. The young man is offering the sleeved map to him.

"Thank you, young man," Michael manages, and takes hold of the map. Michael reads the Fleming's nametag. "Mr. Warburg."

The room buzzes noisily with standing bidders; chairs scrape as Pinkham desperately attempts to gavel the room to quiet down. "Ladies and gentlemen, ladies and…. We will be taking a short break—say ten minutes—and then we will resume. We have half a catalog to continue. Please—please take your seats."

Owen touches Michael's arm. "Can we drive you somewhere? Home—anywhere you'd like."

Michael feels dazed. "What have I done?" He walks bewildered, with the acetate pressed against his side into the anteroom of the auction hall. People mill about, looking at him as a curiosity, a madman. He catches the eye of a smiling Cynthia Vasquez.

"You rescued it," she says, simply.

Michael breaks into a grin. A feeling of youthfulness, rarely experienced, not even as a boy, washes over him.

"Yes, thank you, Miss," he says.

Patricia Spencer hovers near him, as her husband quick-dials his cell phone, doubtless to give his client the news. Michael notices a smile playing on the lips of the graphics dealer. Across the lobby, he sees the bidder who thought he had won, frustration etching his face, and getting an earful from his sponsor. The bodyguard from a grade B movie drills Michael with steely eyes.

Patricia Spencer touches Michael's arm. "Mr. Dijkstra. This roomful of people knows you are carrying something worth at least twenty-two thousand dollars. Won't you accept a lift?"

"No, I wouldn't want to trouble—" he says reflexively.

"No trouble at all," she insists. "I'm glad you are happy with your decision."

Owen Spencer joins them. "Mr. Dijkstra, you and your map would be much safer in a car than walking to BART and riding out to Walnut Creek."

"You're very kind."

"I just spoke with Maurice Bregmann. He says the people who were trying to bid for this map are a neo-Nazi group, skinheads. Their leader is based in Utrecht. They don't want your father's story told. Now where can we take you? Home?"

Anger wells and Michael's fist curls. "That rabble? In Utrecht? Why would they object to…?" Michael stops speaking. *Hadn't he been furious that his father's good deed had cost him his life?* "I don't understand," Michael says, dully.

"When a hero like your father is discovered," Owen says, "Yad Vashem honors that person for risking their safety to save even one Jew, because precious few took that chance when the SS took over. Groups like these, skinheads, Nazis, anti-Semites, Holocaust deniers, racial purity nuts, hate it when publicity surrounding these brave people is published. Some will do as much as possible to squelch the facts of a righteous gentile's good deeds."

A feeling of nausea sweeps through Michael. He had never framed his father's act as heroic in all those years. He touches his brow. "I'm feeling a little lightheaded. I did not eat much this morning. Can we get something to eat, first?"

"Do you need something immediately, or can you hold out for half an hour?" Owen asks.

"I'm a little hungry, only. I could wait."

"I'm thinking of lunch in Berkeley. I would like you to meet Maurice Bregmann. He's the curator of the Jewish collection at the Bancroft Library. He'd love to see the map in person, even if we could not bid successfully on it. And he could explain what would be gained if your father's words were made public. If you would rather not see him today, we could do lunch without him, and take you straight home. We could arrange a more formal meeting in his office at the University."

They walked down the corridor to the elevator.

Michael fixes his gaze on Owen. "Forgive me if this sounds intrusive. I have a question for you."

Owen meets and holds his gaze. "Go ahead, Mr. Dijkstra."

"Since I have withdrawn this map from the auction you have lost your commission, yes?"

"Money was no object for the competition. They were desperate to supress your father's good deed. I would not have been successful for my client."

"But your commitment on my behalf—"

"Mr. Dijkstra," Patricia Spencer steps in. "Owen, may I?"

Owen nods as the elevator door opens. He presses L for lobby. As the car descends, Patricia says. "When my husband recognized that this map was the one my mother saw as the ten-year old girl your father saved, he was very motivated to help get recognition for your father's heroism. Owen and I have only gratitude for your father's sacrifice, because—well, here I am. My mother lived, and lived as freely as she could with all of her guilt about surviving while all around her was death and destruction of families."

Michael nods. Something about Patricia Spencer is so moving to him. His voice wavers. "Yes, take me to lunch in Berkeley, and I will speak to your curator friend, if you wish. Forgive me for my angry heart. It still has walls. They are so built up with fortifications that I lose my humanity and think the worst."

As the elevator doors open, Patricia takes his hand and presses it. Her eyes are tearing. Michael sees that his demons are not so different from hers.

They step onto the street as a loudly gunned engine shatters the moment. Michael, Owen, and Patricia abruptly turn to see a black Mercedes with dark tinted windows roll by slowly. The vanity plate reads U-B-R-A-L-E-S. The car continues up the hill, almost mockingly slow, and then quickly peels away, leaving burnt rubber marks on the asphalt. Michael's fingers tighten around the map. Patricia grabs both Michael's arm and her husband's. Michael recognizes a glimmer of fear in her eye that is familiar. He had been gripped by the same terror whenever the German corporal patrolled the aisle on the munitions factory floor.

"It's a short walk to the car," Owen says, ushering them up the street.

CHAPTER 73

London, Sunday, 28 October 1570

The day after he knocks Jan Du Forché to the floor of the tavern, Jonas spends most of his Saturday working on the broadside engraving in his room behind a barred door. He works methodically to get his images right. The graphics are interesting to look at, but Jonas knows that the real message is in the politically charged title of *"Het Engelse Marine."*

He asks himself again. "Am I really willing to bar a back door escape?" For, if he goes through with his title, he will be a *persona non grata* in England. The people giving him shelter and safety will be put at risk if it comes back that Jonas is the author of the incendiary broadside. The mockery is of both England and Spain. Furthermore, the Dutch privateers, who enjoy the privilege of safe harbors in England, could also take issue with the mocking title: England's Navy.

It is late in the day, and the festivities are beginning in a few hours, to celebrate James Cole's return to England.

Jonas works feverishly. His graver etches the words in reversed letters, *Het Engelse Marine* across the top of his illustration. He builds a cartouche made of ropes, deck cannons, and banners around his title. He continues the rope motif down both sides of the illustration and across the bottom to contain the quarto-sized broadside. He hears the first guests arriving, greeted by the Coles' children and Elizabeth. The day outside has darkened, and he takes a last look at his work by candlelight before wrapping his hand-drawn illustrations and the copper plate in a cloth that he buries in the bureau drawer along with his other illustrations.

Jonas washes and grooms himself. He dresses in his best clothes, pulls the chair away from the doorknob and douses the candle on his table. He freezes in surprise as he opens his door onto the festive hallway.

Mistress Joan Casterleigh immediately catches his eye. She has come through the door to the apartment on the arm of a wizened, palsied old man whose jaw seems to clack behind his scruffy gray beard and mustaches. *Was he her grandfather?*

"The Baron and Baroness Casterleigh," the announcing footman at the door, hired for the occasion, tells one and all in a sonorous monotone. *Her husband.* Immediately, everything about the dalliance the woman has created falls into place. The old man wheezes a cough and dodders into the hall supported by a walking staff. His stick-thin legs show off his baggy hose. Joan smiles with flashing eyes and shoots a sly glint in Jonas' direction. She then carries on to kiss Elizabeth on both cheeks. She is radiant in her finery of pale green silks. Jonas thinks better of retreating back to his room. But the surprises continue, for immediately behind the mismatched Casterleighs, the announcing voice intones "The Baron John Gillesford and guest." Jonas beholds the young noble who had saved him from a beating by the Culver Alley ruffians. A pretty woman in pastel blue brocade holds his wrist.

"Hello, young man," the familiar nobleman says.

Jonas bows, tentatively, uncertain how to react.

"Ah. No formality. I'm John Gillesford. Call me Jack. And you are?"

"Jonas. Jonas Hoen."

"No more trouble, I trust, with our friends from that stinking alley?"

"No, sir. I thank you again for your assistance."

"Joan, my sister, the Baroness Casterleigh—says you are the Coles' guest."

Eyes blinking uncontrollably, suddenly thirsty, Jonas says, "Yes," in a clipped tone.

"She says you are part of the serjeant-painter's crew to keep the sovereign's Court looking bright and snappy."

"Yes, sir."

"Jack."

"Yes, sir—Jack."

"Not Sir Jack. Just Jack."

"Jack," Jonas says quickly. Then he sees Joan drilling him with her eyes not ten feet away. Her smile makes her nostrils flare. She is enjoying his discomfort.

"Will you take some refreshment?" Jonas asks of both Jack and Joan.

"I must pay my respects to James Cole, and I am sure we will cross paths again tonight," John Gillesford says. "Joan, this is that Flemish boy, got into and out of a spot of trouble in the neighborhood."

At once, Joan and Jonas are only a foot from each other.

"Nice to see you here, Jonas. I think you owe me a sketch, now that I am wearing proper attire," she whispers hotly.

Jonas' face burns like a scorching hot poker.

"You color up so beautifully. I wish I could paint. I would paint your cheeks."

Jonas feels the blood gushing in torrents to his face.

"Later, perhaps you will show me your quarters. Just now, I need to greet some people. Isn't it wonderful to have such patrons as James and Elizabeth Cole?"

Before he can answer, she has turned away, her wide skirts swooshing like billowing sails. As Joan glides toward the drawing room, Susannah de Critz and Marcus Gheeraerts enter through the main doors. Marcus the younger runs ahead to young James Cole who immediately hurries him off to his room, doubtless to show off his new butterfly specimens. Susannah kisses Jonas' cheeks.

"Have you been drinking, Jonas? You look like a blooming rose."

"Not yet, but I am parched," he replies. "A sherris sack? Or malmsey? Elizabeth was excited that she could procure a cask of the Greek malmsey."

"Oh, a small draught of the Greek. Marcus will want his ale. Thank you, Jonas. Has anyone interesting arrived?" Susannah asks, with feigned curiosity.

Jonas hides his embarrassment by threading through several merrymakers to the corner of the hall where the bungs are tapped on kegs and liquids flow into goblets and tankards. Serving men and serving maids hired for the evening pour. He grasps two tankards, one of ale for Marcus, one of sack for himself, and a delicate goblet of the precious malmsey for Susannah and weaves through several chattering guests, some of whom he met when he first arrived that summer.

At the other end of the center hallway, a trio of Flemish musicians strikes up a simple repertoire of songs from Flanders, Brabant, and the Netherlands. The men play a droning sack pipe, a flute and a hurdy-gurdy, and a woman bows a fiddle and alternates with a plucked dulcimer. The music is played softly. It is clear that Elizabeth Cole intends to provide the expatriates and refugees sore-missed touches of home. At the same time, members of the British peerage who attend can hear the quaint airs and dances of James Cole's homeland.

The guests are a mixed group of fellow merchants like the Coles, importers of linens and fabrics, wall hangings and rugs, wines and spices, owners of a ships chandlery, a London creamery, a lens grinder, and sundry other Low Country exiles. They gather to pay their respects to one of the leaders of their community. Others, like the Gheeraerts and de Critzes are in the arts, a step or two ahead of the crushing laws imposed by the Duke of Alva.

Jonas notices how the British peers and their consorts tend to float in convoys of two or three couples as they circulate among the Flemish merchants. Indeed, he cannot help but observe that even Mistress Joan is looking at books of silk swatches prepared by James Cole at one end of the main drawing room. When not taking orders for the fine fabrics, that evening, his future will be bright with outings to his warehouses in the coming weeks by the peers who attend the English Court.

Gentlemen who have an interest in cartography visit Elizabeth's bedsitting room, where the Ortelius atlas is on display. Periodically, orders are placed with the hostess. Jonas observes Jack Gillesford emerge from the room where Ortels' sister is showing off the third completed color-limned book of maps. The peer makes straight for him even as he is in the midst of denying to Anent Willemzoom, whom Jonas met when he was refurbishing the Queen's Barge, that he knows anything of a broken cheekbone that a spy from Brussels might have suffered at a nearby tavern.

"Jonas," Gillesford interrupts. "Elizabeth says that you have much to do with the publication of the *Theatrum Orbis Terrarum*."

Willemzoom, who barely understands English, drifts back uncomfortably, leaving Jonas to speak with the English peer.

"I was an apprentice assigned to Frans Hogenberg to help bring the engravings into order for the publication."

"You are an engraver then, of copper plates," Jack Gillesford says, eagerly. "That's what I thought when I saw you waving about those plates to ward off that vermin. Are you accepting commissions?"

"Oh, sir, there are far more accomplished engravers here at this fête than me. Have you met Marcus Gheeraerts? A *master* engraver."

"Yes, I know his work. Animals—very good at animals." Jonas hears hints of disparagement in Gillesford's tone. "But show me a sample of your work."

It is all happening so quickly, that Jonas becomes swept up in Jack Gillesford's enthusiasm. His bubbling energy and sincere interest in Jonas' apprenticeship become infectious and Jonas' is fully engaged in the Englishman's flattering attentions.

"So, you must tell me all about what it was like to help produce that magnificent book of maps. But first, show me something you've done."

Jonas shrugs. "I have some work progressing in my room. Shall I bring it out?" Jonas had in mind the story of the horse, the stableman, and the dog. He then wonders if that is a good choice since Gillesford dismisses animal engravings. He has also made studies of sailing vessels, and can show a practice plate that displays his nautical drawing.

"A quick look, that's all. No need to disturb the guests. Show me some of your work."

Jonas drinks greedily from his tankard of ale. This expression of interest is happening so unexpectedly, so suddenly, he fights to sort his thoughts.

"Well, come, on lad. Don't be so shy about showing off your skills!" Gillesford's enthusiasm wins the day, and Jonas leads the young noble to his door despite a hint of misgiving.

CHAPTER 74

En Route to Berkeley, Afternoon, April 14ᵗʰ 2016

Patricia and Owen insist that Michael take the front passenger seat, which has ample legroom for his long frame. Seated, Michael is grateful to be off his feet following the tension-laden auction. Owen picks his way across Market Street and takes the on-ramp to the Bay Bridge and Berkeley. They have left Patricia's car on Kearney Street to be picked up later. Michael listens with interest as Owen calls Bregmann, who rearranges his schedule so that he can meet Michael Dijkstra for lunch directly in the Claremont District of Berkeley. Michael approves that Owen chose the location so he can easily drive him to Walnut Creek following their meeting.

As the car speeds over the San Francisco span of the bridge, Michael asks Owen how Bregmann has come to take an interest in the map. Owen explains that in his position as curator of Jewish documents and lore at the university, he is sometimes requested to act on behalf of Yad Vashem to aid in documentation. "When they heard about the map with the stain, it must have triggered an interest in getting the map because, as I understand it, claims have been made that your father acted heroically to save a Jewish girl in 1943-1944."

"From who?"

"I hope Dr. Bregmann can answer that question for you. If not, I'm sure he can find out."

Owen takes the Ashby Avenue exit after traffic snakes from the bridge onto the freeway. They drive in silence to College Avenue where Owen is able to park across the street from the Mediterranean restaurant he has booked at Maurice Bregmann's suggestion.

Before Owen steps out of the car he turns to Michael. "I'm sure Dr. Bregmann would love a glimpse of the map we failed to win at auction. You wouldn't mind showing it to him, Mr. Dijkstra, would you?"

Michael smiles. "After all I struggled, do you think this leaves my sight?"

Michael takes an instant dislike of Maurice Bregmann as the Judaica curator shakes hands with everyone. He is a balding man in his sixties with black-rimmed eyeglasses, a salt and pepper beard, and, for Michael's taste, a too ready smile.

"If you don't mind, Maurice, can we order first? I know Mr. Dijkstra is hungry, and so are we,"Owen says, waving the waiter over.

"Well, I'm sorry we didn't win at auction, Mr. Dijkstra, but I'm also very glad you pulled the map before the opposition could claim it."

Michael adopts a taciturn attitude and nods silently.

They order lightly from the lunch menu. Michael feels like he would really like to get home as quickly as possible so he thinks showing the map to Bregmann might speed the process.

"Have a look, then," Michael says, passing the acetate sleeve to Bregmann.

"Oh, I can already envision this," Bregmann says as his eyes trace the swath of dried blood over the right side of the map. "Your father's last act, recorded on this engraving—I can easily understand why you would not want to part with this piece. I understand also, Mr. Dijkstra that your decision to keep the map cost you handsomely, which would doubtless have provided some financial relief, if not balm for your loss." Michael makes an indecipherable grunt, acknowledging what Bregmann has said. "After a call from Owen, following the auction, I took the liberty of having a conversation with one of the benefactors of our collection. He is very active in support of Yad Vashem and, in fact, has discretionary funds at his disposal to help individuals who are in need financially. As you have indicated to me earlier, you would share your father's memoir of the time that he kept Hetty van Aalt safe from the NSB. In return, I am authorized to reimburse you for the loss of income for withdrawing your lot from the auction."

Michael cannot quite believe what he is hearing.

"No, no, it's nothing—I could not," he begins.

"Mr. Dijkstra, this is merely a token of thanks for helping to remember your father whose bravery in the face of the Nazi machine saved a Jew. It's not 'nothing' to Yad Vashem, and those they remember."

Michael sees Patricia begin to wipe a tear from her eye.

"He saved your mother." Michael says, in wonder.

"Yes," Patricia presses Michael's hand across the table.

He feels her warm touch and taps her wrist with his long, blue-veined fingers. "Amazing how people get connected," he says. He had cried so much the night before, more than he had been willing to allow himself to do in scores of years. He looks again at Bregmann, whom he had disliked so intensely moments before. That was not the case anymore. *Was it the money?* Michael asks himself. *No*, he answers in his mind. *I have made so many bad judgments; it is hard to accept human motives without suspicion.*

Michael removes his right hand from Patricia's grasp and extends it to Bregmann.

"I thank you, Dr. Bregmann."

"You're welcome, Mr. Dijkstra," the Jewish collections curator replies. "By the way, we use a reputable museum restoration expert who will be happy to sew this map back into your *Theatrum Orbis Terrarum* book for you, also part of our thanks."

"Can you tell me how Yad Vashem came to be interested in this map?"

"Documentation and more documentation about every facet of the Holocaust. It seems every stone they turn over, more and more comes to light. From what Chaim Rubikoff tells me—he's my connection with the Yad Vashem organization—we met at a conference in Amsterdam—your father's name came to light when the Anonymous Group—you know them…?"

Michael squints trying to remember. He had studiously avoided learning of anything that reflected the war years and he shook his head. Bregmann consults a page of notes he had written in a pocket-sized notebook.

"Forgive my butchering of the language—they were the NV, Naamloze Venootschap, 'Anonymous Corp—?"

"Ya, ya, I did not know them. I was never political but the words are *Naamloze Venootschap*," Michael pronounces in perfect Dutch. "For 'Anonymous Company' in English."

"They rescued two hundred and fifty Jewish children," Bregmann says, "Saving many from the Amsterdam ghetto, sending them to Limburg province."

"Eindhoven is the provincial capital. I never knew…." Michael says softly.

"You have a sister-in-law," Bregmann continues, consulting his notebook, "Gerdi Ten Broeck?"

Michael nods vigorously. "Good! They know about her!"

"Your father's heroics came to light through her testimony, and a researcher in Jerusalem made the connection with the Fleming Auctions catalog. A long and tortuous path, eh?"

"I spoke with her on the phone only this morning. Oh, 'tortuous' describes it,'" Michael says, sinking into remorse. Patricia puts her hand on his sleeve and he smiles a faint acknowledgement for her concern.

"I am tired. If you would be so kind, I would like that lift home."

Michael rises and wobbles as though his roller coaster ride of a day is finally too much for him. Owen helps support him with a hand under his elbow and the other around his back. Michael finds his legs. Bregmann has also risen and Michael extends his hand.

"Professor Bregmann, I would be honored for you to read my father's document. Perhaps Owen can bring it from my house and drop it off on the way back. If you need a translator, I can be at your service."

Michael feels Bregmann's firm grip tighten. He sees relief in the curator's eye.

"I apologize for my suspicious heart—" Michael begins.

"You have nothing to apologize about. I am just very happy that we will help bring your father's story out." Bregmann steps back and nods to Owen. "Thank you, Owen, and a pleasure to meet you, Patricia. This has been no picnic for any of you. He fishes into his breast pocket and hands Michael his card. "Mr. Dijkstra, please call about anything. It has been an honor to meet you. And I am eternally grateful that you kept this map out of the hands of the Schroeder-Berghuis Group."

Michael's head recoils as though he had been shot. His eyes blaze. "The *what* Group?"

"Oh, I thought Owen told you," Bregmann began.

"He said 'a skinhead group from Utrecht.'"

Bregmann fishes out his notebook and flips the pages. "Schroeder—partners with Dirk Berghuis, born to NSB., later Dutch SS—Diederik and Emma Berghuis, November, 1940."

Michael's knees buckle and Owen supports Michael, easing him into a chair.

"Their kid," Michael says in disbelief. "They had a kid." He looks up at the uncomprehending faces of Bregmann, Owen and Patricia.

"Of course. How would you know? His father. This Dirk's father was there when my father was shot. He may have even pulled the trigger, but he blamed his NSB partner, Rost—Henk Rost. His wife, Emma, was my father's housekeeper—she informed on the little girl. She said they had a child. This cannot mean anything to you, but this Dirk Berghuis is the kid of the people who looted my father's art after he was killed. Pim and I—I only have this map, and the book of maps, because my brother and I took it back from the Berghuises, that damned SS Black Policeman and his wife." Michael stops abruptly. "Good, he does not get his filthy hands on this map." Michael laughs uncontrollably. "Absurd, yes? Absolutely. Absurd. Owen, Patricia, this is a good one, this cosmic joke." Michael concludes with a giggle he cannot suppress. "I am ready to go home," he says with full voice, feeling much stronger. "Let's go." He picks up the sleeve that holds the map. He addresses the map like it was a living thing. "Saved again, old friend."

Owen shakes hands again with Bregmann and they walk to Owen's car. Moments later they are headed to Highway 24 for the quick trip to Michael's duplex.

CHAPTER 75

London, Lyme Street, Late Evening, 28 October 1570

Gillesford follows Jonas into his room. Jonas sets down the tankard of ale on his table and lights a candle and two wall sconces with a taper. The sounds of the gathering to welcome James Cole recede when he closes the door. With ample light, Jonas motions for Gillesford to have a seat at the table.

"You do all your work here?" The Englishman asks.

"Here and Master Gheeraerts' studio in Abchurch Lane," Jonas says, pulling out an armful of drawings, sketches, and copper plates from his bureau drawer. Jonas tries to put the image on top of his pile at the bottom of his paper stack. It was his first sample he had made for Mark Anthony, the blacksmith forging chain links.

"No, wait. Let me see that," Gillesford insists.

"Allegory. Do all of you Flemish fellows think first in allegory? This is very interesting, Jonas."

Jonas wonders what he means by "interesting."

"I'm still only learning my skills," Jonas says.

"New at it or not, that's a powerful image to contemplate. All those people—willingly going into chains. And those are Spanish soldiers looking on, aren't they?"

"Yes."

"You have the plate for this?"

"No, that was left in Antwerp," Jonas says uneasily.

"And who is this?" Gillesford points at his drawing of Sofie.

"Someone in Antwerp."

"Do you admire her? From this image I think you are smitten with her."

Jonas smiles. *How could he tell that?*

"Hello? What this?"

Jonas' heart clenches. Gillesford is holding the plate he had been working on. If Gillesford could read Dutch he would understand.

"The English Navy?" Gillesford reads the letters reversed in Dutch and translates, cocking his head and smiling.

"Very good, Jonas. Allegory again. This is so truthful. My nation has not yet committed finances to build its own navy. It holds off the Spaniards only while the Turks, your countrymen, the Huguenots, and the Protestant reformers tie Iberia's hands. Hah! That's William of Orange's coat of arms, isn't it?"

Jonas nods through a sharp pain that is developing in his neck.

"The privateer navy of the Dutch? Van der Marck and those brigands— what are they called—the Sea Beggars? Oh, Jonas. This is brilliant. *You* did this, yes?"

"Yes," Jonas says uncertainly. He has been so sure he is playing with danger that he doubts anyone will appreciate his broadside outside the Low Countries.

"England has to raise its own navy to full strength," Gillesford says. "Eventually, we will be at war with Spain. Your Beggars are like gadflies on the Spanish for the time being, but this broadside—this alerts us to how it really is. Do you have a printer in mind?"

"This could be very risk-laden for an English printer to undertake," Jonas says, repeating Gheeraerts' warning. He is torn between the prospect of an immediate edition, and the deep concern for the safety of his countrymen.

Gillesford looks at Jonas. "Are you really only seventeen years?"

"I'm several hundred years old if my dreams tell the truth."

Gillesford shrugs. "Would you like me to get this safely printed so there is no danger to the printer—or to you?"

"Yes," Jonas answers, unhesitatingly, his face in a broad grin. His quick response surprises him.

"What else have you got?"

Jonas flips a pencil sketch: a cavalryman beheading a priest.

"You have a very dark side to your art, Jonas."

"Yes," Jonas agrees.

Gillesford turns over the image of the horse, stableman, and dog.

"A dark side," Gillesford repeats. "But I'm guessing you have earned it. I want you to meet me on Monday on Fleet Street. Hold your nose crossing the Ditch and come to this printing shop. Eleven in the morning please. And bring that plate."

Jonas looks at what Gillesford has written on the bottom of his sketch for the broadside. North door, Sign of the Bible, Saint Paul's church.

"I have a meal to eat with the Coles. Very good meeting you, formally, Jonas."

Gillesford steps out of the room, the party suddenly very loud, then muted when the door closes. Jonas' head spins with what he has heard. Jack Gillesford, a member of the British peerage, has assured him that his broadside will be printed with no danger to the printer or himself. He sets about putting all of his work back into the chest of drawers when a soft knock taps on the door, and it swings open.

Joan Casterleigh, rocking side to side with a tumbler of wine, nearly tips over as she leans down to pick up another brimming wineglass. She kicks the door shut and leans against it, looking at the startled Jonas.

"What is so interesting about my brother that you spend so much of the evening with Jack?" Joan pouts theatrically and then smiles broadly. "Let's find out how lumpy is your bed. Come. We don't have much time. A 'starter' before dinner? Which will be served shortly. You must still take your time," she says, ever the teacher. "We will have to imagine Aretino's sonnets." She thrusts the wineglass into Jonas' hand and sets hers down on the table.

Flustered, Jonas presses his chair against the doorknob. But as he watches her turn and fall facedown onto the bed, her legs dangling over the foot, he is quickly emboldened. Pink ribbon-topped hose above her knees offer an inviting vee.

"Jonas, we do not have all evening," she says hugging his pillow. "Quickly, like Bacchus and Ariadne. Come, as Aretino says, '*Ma lasciam'ir le ciance.*' Let us be done chatting."

He is completely in the thrall of both Gillesfords.

CHAPTER 76

London, 29 October 1570

On the Monday after the fête for James Cole, Jonas walks the familiar route to Abchurch Lane in a drenching rain, buys sweets at the baker's shop, and knocks on Gheeraerts' door. He and Susannah de Critz share recollections of the festivity for Cole. Mostly he listens to her tidbits, as he had been otherwise occupied for much of the night. He gives the cakes to Susannah and tells her that he hopes he will be back later that morning, as he has business to attend to. Susannah flashes him a sly wink. "Might you be meeting the Baroness Casterleigh, then?"

Jonas flushes with embarrassment. He has suspected that the Antwerp-born girl with connections to the royal court created the arrangement with the baroness from Gillesford. "I have business with a man today, if you must know," Jonas replies. Little did his teacher's gossipy mistress know that this morning he is to meet with the baroness' brother, Jack Gillesford. Jonas' quickened breathing signals a feeling that he walks a dangerous path among people above his station. He squelches his concern by smiling as brightly as Susannah.

"Til later, then," he calls cheerily.

The copper plate barely fits in his leather pouch, and he touches the carrying case several times on his journey by foot. He realizes that if anyone were watching him he would appear suspicious as he walks the cobbled streets. On Budge Row, the lane reeks of rotted flesh and Jonas holds his breath. He passes a skinners shop where hides of deer and sheep are stretched on racks. The rendered fat from these animals is used in the manufacture of tallow candles a door away. "Fleet Ditch near the bridge," he repeats to himself as he heads toward Westminster. "Sign of the Bible, North door of Saint Paul's Church."

He crosses the Ditch, rank with odor, sewage draining toward the Thames. Soon he sees his destination with Gillesford and another courtier, several years older than Jack, greeting each other. Jonas slows and waves tentatively. Jack furtively signals for him to follow the two men into the print shop. When he steps through the door, oil-based ink puts him at ease, in the odor of comforting surroundings.

"Jonas, this is my friend, Francis, and this," Jack says, pointing to a harried apron-clad printer with thinning hair, "is John Jugge. Mr. Jugge has graciously agreed to do the job for us straightaway."

The printer twists his mouth in a perfunctory smile and nods, while Jonas pulls the plate from his leather bag. Jugge has barred the door and pulled a curtain over the thick glass window. The friend named Francis never lets his gaze slip from Jonas' face, and the penetrating stare undoes Jonas' sense of wellbeing. Ill at ease, Jonas passes the copper plate to the printer and forces himself to ask the man named Francis: "Sir, may I know your interest in this plate?" Jonas' voice quavers. The man's eyes seem to drive nails through him. The question hangs in the air unanswered.

Jack Gillesford smiles disarmingly and says, "Lord Walsingham has an abiding interest in the safety of our monarch and the monarchy. As do I. He likes the idea of raising an effective British Navy to defend our Kingdom. Your illustration—"

"It is very droll, young man," Walsingham interrupts.

Jonas has heard the voice somewhere. No smile creases the face or warmth comes from the words of the man named Walsingham. "You have an acid wit. Your William of Orange would appreciate it. Did he or his agents put you up to this?"

"No, sir. This is all my invention." Jonas speaks firmly for the first time. Is it the familiar odor and surroundings of the printing shop that gives him his voice? With a start, Jonas makes the connection. When old Lord Burghley and his confidant in the gardens at Whitehall Palace discussed the Sea Beggars—*This was Francis.*

"Your lordship, I assure you that no one from my country has made any suggestion to me on this. It is commonly known that the privateer fleet harries Spanish shipping. And I thought it a fitting idea—to—to illustrate the *Vater Guezen*—the Sea Beggars—as protecting, in their way, England's coast from—against—the Spanish. It is only a joke for my countrymen."

Jonas hopes his explanation will suffice. His knotted stomach betrays his fear that he would be caught eavesdropping on the conversation of the two English lords at the Whitehall Palace.

"How do you like our little island, young man?" Walsingham asks. "You've only been here since you docked at Billingsgate the second week in June?"

Jonas blinks, wondering how this man knew these details.

"I came to study my craft."

"With another Fleming who barely escaped with his life from our friend the Duke of Toledo?"

"Yes, Master Gheeraerts is my mentor in engraving copper plates."

"Does he approve this work?"

"No. He never saw this plate." Jonas answers carefully. "He does not want me to engage in anything that might—that might reflect...."

"Something controversial like politics or the Dutch Revolt?"

"Yes, sir."

Francis Walsingham smiles slowly. The confidant of the counselor to the Queen resembles Ortels, except for his dark beard, Jonas realizes. But this man has a look of iron in his eyes, unlike his benefactor in Antwerp.

The printer, Jugge, has been nervously setting up the rack, the *forme*, that will hold the plate, on his press. The two nobles, Jonas, and the printer are the only ones in the shop. The whole morning strikes Jonas as odd, dangerously clandestine. Jugge holds up the copper plate and asks, "Don't you want to sign it?"

Jonas is at a loss for an answer. In Flanders he needs to be entirely anonymous, as when he engraved his blacksmith forging chains for Mark Anthony Coppens. But he is in England, the nation that has given him refuge from the Iron Duke. Jonas leans on the heavy timbers that hold up the press. He looks at Jack Gillesford for a hint on how to respond. Jack looks at Walsingham who may have signaled something. Walsingham's smile is inscrutable.

"Why not, Jonas?" Gillesford asks. "It's good work, certainly. The vessels are handsome and the groupings well designed. If you are proud of this work and think it worthy, why wouldn't you affix your mark?"

Jonas thinks a moment longer. Jugge clears his throat. The printer's time is precious and he is on a schedule.

"If you give me a scribe, I will sign the plate," Jonas says, finally.

Jugge sets the plate on a well-worn tabletop and points at several scribing tools in a wooden stand. Jonas decides to incorporate the rope motif. On the final paper version from which he transferred the scene to copper, he quickly sketches his name in reverse, N-E-O-H S-A-N-O-J, turning the N, J, and S so they will print properly. He lengthens the hawser he has drawn so that the letters of his name fit between the outlines of the rope. On first view the name is barely discernible, looking like the crosshatched motif of the rope. Then he etches the plate freehand with the scribe. He follows using a graver for the triangular trough so ink reproduces his name on the printed-paper. The entire operation takes ten minutes.

"Time is fleeting," Jugge says, placing the completed plate face up in the forme. "My devil is on an errand with my father; will you do the inking?" Jugge points to the lampblack and varnish ink in a pot with a blackened fleece dauber beside it. Jonas inks the surface of the plate, then rubs the plate clean leaving only the inked troughs as Jugge attaches a sheet of dampened paper to points protruding from the linen tympan pad. Jonas folds the oiled paper mask, the frisket, over the paper, and then folds the tympan over the forme.

"Ready," Jugge calls, grasping the arm to turn the screw.

Jonas pushes the frisket along its track under the press. Jugge sets his legs and draws the spindle a half turn so the pressure of the press platen forces the ink on the plate into the paper. Moments later, after the pressman pushes the spindle back across to raise the press, Jonas draws the rolling table back to its beginning position and returns the frisket and tympan to their open positions. Jugge peels the printed sheet of paper. Jonas' startlingly wry-humored visual comes to life.

Het Engelse Marine proclaims the heading and the eye is drawn first to the battle mid-ocean in the Bay of Biscay where two privateers, cannons blazing, ravage a vessel flying the Spanish flag. Then the eye is drawn to the coast of England where groupings of several ships lay at anchor outside Dover and Portsmouth flying Willem van Oranje's coat of arms on their banners. Tiny figures move cargo. Longboats with cannonballs stacked in pyramids fore and aft are rowed from the English shore to the Dutch men 'o' war at anchor. The rope motif unifies the image and Jonas reads his name, visible at the end of one hawser.

Walsingham nods and takes the first image off the press from Jugge's hand.

"The Privy Council will want to see this," Walsingham says to Gillesford. He debars the door and leaves with the drying broadside. Jonas frowns at Walsingham's quick departure. *Why would the nobleman need the engraving to show to the Queen's Privy Council directly? What was afoot?*

Before he can put his question into words, the beaming Jack Gillesford effuses "Well done, Jonas and John, only ninety nine more to go, gentlemen."

They print one more and Jack Gillesford takes his leave with it. Jugge bars the door and he and Jonas print and set to drying ninety-eight more leaves of the broadside. With each new sheet, Jonas studies his design, his workmanship, and notes how he might better execute the angle of the ships at sea, the billowing of smoke from the sea battle, the relative ship sizes. His experience of etching sea-going vessels has until now only been admiring the maps of the Ortels project in which the ships under sail were merely decorative embellishments to show the artistry of the engraver. Here, the vessels are the focus, along with the eastern and southern seaboard of England, and the hints of the European shoreline. As he compares his own work with Frans Hogenberg's, he is a harsh critic of his effort. But here it is, his maiden voyage developing an image and a statement entirely on his own. And he takes pride of ownership.

Hours later, broadsides are strung across the shop's ceiling beams to dry. Jonas cleans and collects his copper plate. He pushes it into the leather pouch at his hip. The inky odor hangs in the air.

The printer wipes his hands with an oily rag. "Come back tomorrow before nine and you shall have your dry copies. Bring a suitable case please. Don't be late. All of this must be out of this shop before ten o'clock. If my father sees this I will be drawn and quartered." John Jugge takes the last broadside printed to its drying space. The ink glistens darkly on the still-damp paper. "I hope your neck is not caught in this rope, young Master Hoen," the printer says. "Be careful." The printer hands Jonas his copper. Jonas burnishes the surface with an oily rag and slips it into his leather pouch.

As he steps into the rain-soaked street, Jonas hears Jugge bar the door, just minutes before three o'clock. He has so wanted to create this broadside, but has also become aware that uses are being made of his effort that he had not intended. Why did Francis Walsingham race off with the first proof to the Queen's Privy Council? Jonas' joke has become a matter involving the rulers of Great Britain. Sweat moistens his brow. Jack Gillesford had encouraged him and paid John Jugge for his time. The whole process had been secretive. As Jonas crosses back into London from Westminster, the printer Jugge's warning rings in his ears. The Saint Paul's church bells knell three times.

Jonas walks into the neighborhoods where expatriate Dutch and Flemish live. It is in these precincts that he has planned to find suitable walls to post his broadside. These people would understand the humor of calling the *Vater Guezen* the "English Navy."

When he arrives at Abchurch Lane, he knocks on Gheeraerts' door but no one answers. He steps into the baker's shop and buys three of the small cakes as he realizes he had not eaten since breakfast. He continues to look for appropriate sites to display his broadside, and idly nibbles at the dry cakes, when he catches the eye of Jan Du Forché's intimate, the black-clad Juan Carlos, twenty yards away in Saint Clements Lane. He sees the Catalan draw a stiletto knife from its sheath. Jonas immediately regrets pummeling the Flemish spy, but this is no time for remorse, as the Catalan advances. Jonas stifles his inclination to take flight. He hastens his steps along Lombard Street toward home, but his fingers nimbly undo the leather case from his belt. The leather with the copper plate within might at least provide a shield against Juan Carlo's weapon. Several Londoners walk along the street and a dray cart pulled by a tired old nag clacks along. At the intersection of Lombard and Saint Clements Lane, Jonas quickens his pace and senses that the Catalan is closing on him. Jonas passes behind the dray so that he comes abreast of the horse, and as he darts in front of it—smacks it on the nose. The horse rears, surprising the driver. Juan Carlos, following close behind, is clipped by the horse's hooves and sent sprawling onto the cobbles. Jonas sprints toward Fenchurch Street, the furious driver cursing loudly. He turns into Lyme Street and races to the Sign of the Cock.

Taking the stairs by twos and threes, breathing heavily, and exhilarated by his narrow escape, he knows that his days in London must come to an end. If he does not leave, he may come to *his end* prematurely in a strange city at the hands of an assassin, either English or a tool of the Spanish king. He must meet with Elizabeth Cole.

CHAPTER 77

En Route to Walnut Creek, April 14ᵗʰ 2016

Owen speeds up Route 13 leaving Berkeley. As the car enters the northbound tube of the Caldecott Tunnel, traffic is still light and they travel the speed limit toward Walnut Creek. Michael apologizes to Owen. "I'm sorry this has not been a very profitable venture for you, Owen."

"Its not all about profits," Owen responds.

Outside Orinda, Owen draws Michael's attention to the hills. They still retain a green cast from the winter rains. In less than a month the grasses will be the color of straw on the hillsides. "The 'corduroy hills' these parts are called. I always marvel that the undeveloped bits have that rippled look, like the ground was formed following a topography map."

Michael notices what Owen is seeing. "I see that now. It *is* like corduroy. I rarely see the forest for the trees. Comes from living too much in my head. Everything must make such complete sense to me, and I dismiss the rest. Not a very smart thing. That reminds me, Patricia," Michael turns his head to the back seat. "How is that little boy with the big mouth I met at the park?"

"Ah, Mario. Mario Kinsella. You had a most calming effect on him," Patricia says, smiling. "I was ready to call in the school counselor, but on the trip home yesterday through the afternoon, he was focused, considerate, and thoughtful. Amazing what inventing the LED long-life bulb can lead to."

They banter on until Owen pulls off the freeway into downtown Walnut Creek and eases his way to Michael's townhouse.

"May I invite you in for tea," Michael asks, turning to Patricia. "I could show you the big book of maps your mother saw when she lived in our house."

Owen and Patricia quickly glance at each other in the rear view mirror and agree that a "No" is in order.

"You've had a trying day, and I'm sure you'd like to rest," Patricia says. She opens her backseat door to trade places with Michael up front. She also hands the sleeved map to him as he stretches to his full height on the sidewalk.

"Thank you both for your encouragement to do the right thing," Michael says, before finding his keys and beginning to walk up the stairs. "Oh yes, my father's commentary—come up and you can take the photocopy to Professor Bregmann. I want to keep the original for my family."

Patricia signals that she will remain downstairs. She leans on the fender as Owen accompanies Michael up the stairs. "That's odd," says Michael, as the outer door lock opens too easily. It was as if the door hadn't been locked. He badgers himself about his failing memory when a faint odor of citrus fills the air. It is what he had smelled when the dealer who lost out at the auction came charging along the back row in anger.

"The atlas—Gone!" Michael cries in agitation.

Owen sees that the book is missing from its usual resting place.

Michael is dumbly holding the sleeve containing the map he had rescued from sale, but the antiquarian atlas is missing. He steps quickly into the kitchen to see if, inexplicably, he could have moved it there. He hastens into his bedroom in a panic, and then fully realizes the Ortelius is gone.

"Owen! Someone broke in and it's stolen, the *Orbis Terrarum*."

Concern wrinkles Owen's brow from the first alarm. Michael does another circuit of his rooms. He keeps returning to the empty rectangle on the table behind the settee. Then he lurches to the dining room table where the empty bottle of Hennessey's and the cognac glass stand, mute witnesses to whatever had befallen. Michael is holding his stomach; it aches enough to double him over.

"Michael, can I help you? Are you feeling ill?" Owen asks.

"My father's words, the handwritten—also gone from the dining room table!"

"Michael! You must call the police."

Michael shakes his head in shock.

"You're sure it's missing, not misplaced—anything else missing?

"His words. My father's words, also stolen."

Owen uses Michael's landline to dial 911 and report the theft." Well, it *is* an emergency," he insists. "It's the owner's entire life. Michael, please talk to the police."

Owen is completely caught up in the drama, but a picture is emerging. The citrus cologne... *Harmon? Harmon!* He asks Patricia to come up. 'There's been a break-in," he says in as calm a voice as he can muster.

While Michael describes events to the 911 operator, Owen speed-dials Fleming Auction Galleries on his phone. He hears Cynthia Vasquez's cheerful voice. "Matt Warburg, please."

"I'm afraid he's at the podium, auctioning right now," she says sweetly. "They're at Lot 382, just before the break."

"Cynthia," Owen says, inwardly cheering that he had remembered the receptionist's name. "Are they breaking at 385 or are they going straight through? I know an unexpected interruption—"

"They will still break, but a shorter one."

"I'm asking you to do a huge favor for me. Please pass Matt a note even if he's in the middle of a bid. Ready?"

"Yes," she replies, and he imagines her pen poised over a three by five card or a pink "While You Were Out" message pad.

"Here's the note: 'Call Owen ASAP. Later is too late.'" He gives her his cell phone number.

"Got it. You're sure you don't want to wait a few minutes?"

"It's terribly important that Matt call me immediately after the gavel goes on Lot 385."

He hangs up and sees that Michael has gotten off the phone with the police.

"Because it's not in progress, they will be here sometime between this afternoon and Monday afternoon," Michael says, dejectedly. "I cannot believe such a thing. My father's testament of those years after Mama was killed—why would they want to take that too? They don't only want his blood—they want his words, his private thoughts. They are still the Black Police."

Patricia asks Michael, "Might your neighbors have heard anything?"

Michael sits dazed in a chair at the dining room table.

"What are their names? Perhaps they heard something."

"Johnson," Michael answers in a lost little voice. "I doubt it. They play their TV so loud they must be deaf."

"I'll knock on their door." She catches Owen's eye and he nods as she steps outside onto the landing to try the neighbors."

"That fellow who was bidding against us. Had he made contact with you?" Owen asks.

Michael looks up dully. "Yesterday morning, very early. I gave him a piece of my mind. Imagine calling at seven o'clock in the morning. That damned Pinkham...."

Michael again rails against the injustice of an auction house giving out the details of a consigner's residence.

"Michael you don't use a citrus cologne, do you?" Owen asked.

"No. But that's what I smelled, too, when I opened the door."

"Harmon," Owen says. Michael nods.

"I guess they're not home," Patricia says, reentering.

"Oh, they're home. They never go out, but they don't hear their own doorbell."

A few minutes later Owen's phone rings.

"Matt! Thanks for getting back to me. I need a street address for Harmon Prints."

"Wait, wait, what?" Matt's voice betrays annoyance with Owen.

"Matt. The short of it is Michael Dijkstra home has been burgled. His full Ortelius atlas has been stolen, sometime between when he left his house this morning for the auction and twenty minutes ago. Harmon's website only notes a P.O. Box in the City."

"You think Harmon...?"

"I would stake my life on it," Owen says. "Just following my nose."

"Oh," Matt replies, "Let me call you back. We're on a short break here."

"Yeah, Matt. Please go do what you need to do. But time is really of the proverbial essence."

Two minutes later Owen's phone rings again and Matt Warburg gives him Harmon's shipping address on Marland Drive in Hayward.

"Good luck," Matt's voice said. "You'll get the Hayward police on this, right?"

"Yeah," Owen says, without really hearing the question, and hangs up. He looks at the five digits of the Marland Drive address. He writes them down and hands the note to Patricia who looks at him blankly. "That's where I'm headed. If you don't hear back from me in say an hour, call the Hayward police."

"Are you kidding me," Patricia explodes. "You're not going there without me!"

"No," Owen says, firmly.

"You are not doing this alone!" Patricia insists. "Goddamn it. This is police business. Have you lost your senses?"

"I promise I will call the police when I know for sure Harmon has the atlas."

"You are not going to do this alone, Owen. I am going with you."

Owen looks at his watch. He anticipates an hour's drive to Hayward.

"Okay," Owen says with exasperation and a touch of relief. "You keep me doing the smart thing, okay?" He sees mostly fear in her eyes. "Michael," Owen says to the scowling man in the dining table chair. "We are going to try and recover the atlas. We'll call when we know something. If the Walnut Creek police come, tell them to call the Hayward police to check out this address. Owen sets the Marland Drive address in front of Dijkstra who nods dully. "Let's go." He takes Patricia's elbow.

In the car, Owen enters the Hayward address into his GPS and sees that the drive time estimate is 49 minutes.

"Do you have a plan?" Patricia asks as they speed onto the freeway onramp.

"Get the atlas," he says grimly.

"Sounds like a plan," she shakes her head.

"You're the brains of this operation. You'll think of something," he says, merging into the traffic flow.

Her eye-roll is not lost on him.

CHAPTER 78

London, 30 October 1570

Jonas rises uneasily early on the day after the printing of his engraving. Sleet had slapped the windows most of the night and the temperature had dropped.

He is supposed to collect his broadsides from Jugge's print shop, but after his fitful night he wonders if he dare return to the Sign of the Bible. He imagines being thrown in irons, dragged into a plot hatched by Walsingham and Gillesford so that the Queen's Privy Council can use his satiric illustration to go to war with Willem van Oranje. He fears he could be a pawn in a more deadly game than he ever envisioned. On his third middle-of-the-night awakening, he had begun packing his traveling bag.

After the hall clock strikes seven that morning, Jonas walks down the hallway to Elizabeth Cole's bedsitting room. The Cole boys have galloped off to school. The girls are in the care of a nanny in the playroom and James Cole has gone to his warehouses on Thames Street. Jonas knocks softly and is admitted. By Elizabeth Cole's look she knows he is in distress.

"I have to leave, return to Antwerp, the sooner the better," Jonas says, fighting an unexpected urge to shed tears. "I have done some foolish things."

Elizabeth Cole gives him her full attention and Jonas relates his interactions with Du Forché and Juan Carlos, and then with Gillesford and Walsingham.

When he mentions Walsingham's name, she rises as though pricked by a tack. Her eyes burn through Jonas, who presses on, describing the broadside and his meeting with Walsingham at the printers. She paces, deep concern on her face.

"Walsingham is a powerful, dangerous man. You will not go back to the print shop this morning. I'll send Margery's husband. Get some ale and bread in the kitchen and send Millie to me. How many sheets of the broadside?"

"Ninety-eight."

"Not so many. The Sign of the Bible at Saint Paul's North door, you say?"

Jonas nods and walks slowly into the kitchen. He directs Millie to speak to Mrs. Cole. By his grave look, she may have thought she was being sacked.

Francis silently pours ale and puts several cakes on a plate for Jonas. He, too, is off-balance. Jonas' long face is a banner proclaiming, "Be careful this morning."

He takes his food into the hallway and nibbles in a numbed stupor at a side table. He has turned his folly over to Elizabeth Cole and hopes she will give him direction. But butterflies in his stomach rival young James' specimens when they could still flutter.

After he eats as much as he can, he returns the tankard and plate to the kitchen and knocks once more at Elizabeth Cole's door. She bids him enter. She is finishing a letter, which she folds and hands to Jonas.

"You will take this letter to my husband at his warehouse on Thames Street. Enter through the alley. He will get you passage to one of the provinces and then you will find your way back to Antwerp. You will seek out my sister, Anna. Abraham has too much on his mind. Let her guide you from there. Oh, Jonas—if you have a genuine care for your precious Sofie, you will make safer decisions about how you conduct your life. In the meanwhile, do you owe anything to Marcus Gheeraerts?"

"Only my thanks. Our accounts are balanced."

"Take a half hour to write your goodbyes then." Jonas hears a catch in Elizabeth's voice. "I will make sure they are delivered. Leave your bag outside your door for Francis. He will take it to the warehouse. Margery's husband will deliver your broadsides to the warehouse if he can. If they do not arrive, be especially grateful that he went in your stead."

Jonas shoots her a fearful glance, but she continues.

"When you are ready to leave, see me one more time." She stops speaking, rises and hugs him. "Oh, Jonas."

He breathes in her comforting scent but cannot choke back the lump in his throat. She kisses him on the eyes, moist with sadness. She turns him toward the door. Jonas cannot speak for fear of opening a sluice gate of weeping. He walks down the hall to his room, adds the last copper plates and illustrations to his traveling bag, and sets it outside his door for Francis. He takes up quill and paper and writes.

My humble duty remembered, my dearest Sofie

I will be home before you know it.

From my room in Lyme Street, London, this 30th of October, 1570, your assured loving — J

My humble duty, dear master James

Here is my feeble attempt to draw your Turkish butterfly. You are a bright boy to whom I wish a soaring future on butterfly wings. Make your parents proud. I pray you remember my duty to your good mother.

This with my kindest commend to you, wishing you all happiness, I rest, your friend this 30th of October, 1570, London

Jonas Hoen

After my very hearty commendations dear Marcus,

Words cannot express my gratitude for your efforts to help me master the craft. I wish only wonderful things for Young Marcus and Mistress Susannah. I hope one day we may share a tankard in a Bruges alehouse.

Here is a pencil study for an engraving I had hoped to make of you, Susannah, and little Marcus. Forgive my inexpert attempt.

Indebted to you for your pains taken for me, I bid you farewell. With affection

from my room in Lyme Street, this 30th of October, 1570,

Jonas Hoen

After heartiest commendations, dear Elizabeth

My debt to you can never be repaid. You have provided safe haven and unflagging basis for my success in London. I offer my deep apology for the shortcomings I have shown in my stay here, and sincere wishes that my intemperate behaviors be soon forgotten. You have saved my life. I wish you and your family the blessings of a bountiful future.

With the remembrance of my humble duty unto you, I take my leave from my most comfortable room in Lyme Street this 30th of October 1570,

Jonas

He folds and addresses each of the letters, then withdraws from its safe place at the back of his bureau the remainder of his coinage amounting to four English sovereigns, and deposits it in the leather case that Mark Anthony Coppens had given him. He draws on his woolen cape and soft cap and knocks one last time on Elizabeth's door. She takes his proffered letters and lays them on her desk.

"If I can do anything at all, at any time for you—" Jonas begins.

"Please, get home safely," she whispers. She presses him to her and he hears the rustle of her silks, smells her rosewater scent and he kisses her warm cheeks. She has been crying and her face is flushed. He swallows hard and steps back. Elizabeth forces a smile, and he has a remembrance of his mother's face when he was a child going with his father for the first time to deliver a wagonload of milled barley.

Impetuously, Jonas presses his fingers to his lips and waves to Elizabeth as he had done when he was eight with his mother. He turns and walks quickly down the back stairs to the garden and the lane to his left that will take him, he fervently hopes, to safety and a return to Sofie in Antwerp. The chilly day bites at his face. He sucks in the cold air with deep breath, hunches his shoulders and walks briskly in the direction of Thames Street. Tolling bells announce the noon hour.

CHAPTER 79

London, 12:30 p.m., 29 October 1570

James Cole reads his wife's letter. Jonas slowly backs away from his desk and looks about the enormous warehouse. Bolts of silk, boxes of trimmings from floor to ceiling, line the walls. Cutting tables with colored silks create three long aisles where several women with shears measure lengths of the precious fabric. Massive doors opening onto Thames Street allow two dray wagons to occupy the loading area. Several warehousemen reading from a wooden plank with chalk markings locate and order pick bolts of silk from various shelves. They use ladders to climb to the higher levels and load one of the wagons. With the recent arrival of several cargoes from Turkey, James Cole's inventory is brimming.

"You were not followed, I trust?" James Cole asks sternly, traces of his Flemish origins audible in his English.

"I was very careful," Jonas replies, trying to modulate his voice so it would not reverberate in the draughty warehouse.

"Not so careful, according to my wife," Cole rejoins, snapping Elizabeth's letter onto his desk. Jonas hangs his head. He notices that his traveling bag leans against the stout table and a muslin bag is open with one of Jonas' broadsides on top. Cole points at the bag of engraved sheets. Jonas expects a tongue-lashing. Surprisingly, James Cole, nee Jacobus Coels, bursts out laughing. Jonas watches, confused. Cole taps the legend, still guffawing "'Het Engelse Marine.' Your wit is dangerous, young man," he says, regaining his sterner tone. "We really must get you off this island before you do more damage to our community."

Cole presses fingers to his graying temple and looses a sigh. Puffs of steam breath pass from his lips into the air. "In the six o'clock hour tomorrow morning, you will leave on a dray with two of my drivers. They have deliveries in Stratford, Hornchurch, Chelmsford, and Colchester before they detour twenty miles…" Cole pauses a moment to make his point, "…out of their way—to take you to Harwich. There, you will wait for the Dutch merchantman mastered by Captain Vandeven."

"Oh, the *Tortelduif*," Jonas says recognizing the Captain's name.

Cole presses on, annoyed to be interrupted. "Do you have money? You will need some for lodging until the Captain puts into the port at Harwich."

"I have four sovereigns, sir."

"Ah, good. Here is a loan of another five." Cole tosses a sack of coins to Jonas. "If silk goes out of fashion, I shall need you to repay it. Otherwise, do not consider it a debt. But I want five of your engravings in exchange."

"As many as you like, sir." Jonas says, surprised, and now wondering if a smile was appropriate.

"Good. Those men are loading bolts of silk. They can use your strong back. Sleep on that pallet in the corner tonight. Cheese, sausage, and ale are in the cupboard." Cole removes five of the broadsides from the muslin bag, thinks a moment, and removes three more. Jonas cannot help but grin with every extra gift.

Jonas bows and moves his bag to the straw mattress. Then he joins the workmen and is pleased to hear the Dutch tongue again. They speak English, but fall easily into their native language. James Cole returns to his desk and goes over accounts with an assistant. Jonas works until eight o'clock that night. The orders for bolts of silk have been sorted into thirteen bundles, each one wrapped in burlap sackcloth and sturdily tied with jute twine. They load the wagon according to the order of delivery towns, the last destinations on the bottom and the first three topping the heaped bolts.

"Stratford in West Ham, Hornchurch, and Chelmsford where we will overnight," says the young man, Henrick, in guttural Flemish, his irritation evident. "Then to Colchester where we waste another twenty miles to deliver you in Harwich," he complains. "And it is likely to snow tomorrow. Then we backtrack all the way up to Ipswich before we return. You must be someone very special, Jonas."

"At least he's going home. It's too dangerous for me," says a swarthy dark-curled boy not much older than Jonas, named Emmanuel. "How come you are going back to Antwerp?"

"To be married."

Hands pound Jonas on the back and laughter peels as they finish tying down the load. Jonas dwells on the image of Sofie, stifling her tears at his departure and her written words beseeching him to come back to Antwerp. The other workers depart, leaving Jonas with a candle lantern. In the flickering light, he looks at a display of flowers made of brightly colored silks, doubtless to tempt visiting ladies of the peerage who trade and provide custom at James Cole's warehouse. A nagging plays in the back of his mind that he has no gift for Sofie. He investigates the display of silken flowers to discover that it is made up of multiple sprays of silk floral petals sewn onto thin wire to form hair combs. He imagines Sofie's jet-black ringlets and envisions the perfect spray of pale daffodils delicately arranged like a tiara on her hair. He removes the trifle from the presentation, and with minor rearranging, leaves the display as complete looking as he found it. He slips the purloined flower tiara into his bag between his garments to protect the delicate piece. He withdraws five copies of his broadside from the muslin bag and lays them face down on a corner of James Cole's desk—in payment.

Jonas bundles up as best he can against the raw night. He sleeps fitfully on the straw mattress. Visions of the steel-eyed Francis Walsingham looking through him as though piercing his brain, jumble with Jack Gillesford's grinning face. Gillesford's sister, mouthing, "Yes, yes," eyes rolling upward, transported, mixes into his unsettled sleep. He bolts upright and sees himself in chains awaiting execution for defaming the Queen's Navy. *How can I be in such a clammy sweat on such a cold night*, he wonders, shivering, fully dressed.

In the darkness of the early morning, one of the older warehousemen opens the doors and hitches two massive dray horses from the stable across the road to the loaded wagon. Jets of steam blow from the horses' nostrils and dissipate in the morning air. Thrilled that he will be leaving England, Jonas feasts on cheese, sausage and ale for his morning meal. He jams the muslin sack of broadsides into his traveling bag. He joins Henrick and Emmanuel on the wagon seat, and Henrick snaps the reins to begin the trip to the county of Essex on the Great East Road, first cut in Roman times. They are headed north to Stratford by six-thirty.

As the dray jostles over the cobbled streets, Jonas wonders if he will ever be in London again in his lifetime. He would have liked to show Sofie the marketplace at the Royal Exchange, which is to be completed within the year, and taken her to the parks and gardens of the Whitehall Palace. He abruptly stops his fantasy as the caustic look of Francis Walsingham thrusts into his heart like a dagger. He is leaving town like a whipped dog. This advisor to the Queen's Privy Council is not likely to forget his slighting of the English Navy. *Why did I sign my name to the broadside?*

The first wet snowflakes of the morning fall onto the backs of the horses as the road winds to fields north of London. Henrick curses next to him. Jonas draws his woolen cloak tightly about his shoulders and pulls his cap over his ears. The chill November day accuses him of stupidity. Why has he acted so precipitously to get his broadside printed and lose his warm bed with the Coles? *I have so much yet to learn.*

CHAPTER 80

En Route to Hayward, Mid-Afternoon, April 14th 2016

"Owen," Patricia gasps, as their car races south on Route 680. "What if he's armed or that—that *gorilla* at the auction is with him?"

Owen cannot help smiling at her term for the Harmon's bodyguard. "We could pound our chests, I guess," he says, making light of her concern.

"Don't you do that," Patricia retorts. "He's terrifying. What are we doing?"

"Patricia, please calm down. We're not going to do anything stupid."

"It's already stupid."

Owen, driving in the fast lane, looks in his rear view and side mirrors and weaves his car into the right lane searching for an adequate shoulder. He pulls off and hears the whoosh of afternoon traffic passing them. Occasionally the car shudders when the wind shear of the passing cars is close enough.

"Sweetheart, I'm not a fool, and I promise I won't do anything that will endanger us. But I really do want to get that book back for the old man and, for Bregmann, the documentation his father wrote. I'm sure we can do something besides wringing our hands."

Patricia relents and nods. Owen pulls into traffic again and accelerates.

"Okay. Let's find a way in then," Patricia says. She pulls her smartphone out of her purse and enters the house number on Marland. A real estate company website shows an overhead map of the tract house's location and some detail, including a street view.

"Wouldn't want to live there," she comments. "What's the name? Harmon?"

She goes to another site that lists people who live at that address.

"Harmon. You need to buy an app to get the full first name. 'H. Harmon.' Says, two residents. For a dollar we can discover more detail about the people who live at that address. For forty dollars we can find out what underwear he prefers."

"See how far we get with the cut rate."

"Oh, Owen. It's on the market! And there are 23 photos of the interior!"

"Find it on mine, too," Owen says, passing his phone. He picks up speed and checks his mirrors for lurking highway patrol. Patricia clicks on the links to bring up the realty promotional shots of the Marland Drive address.

"What does he want for the house?"

"Five hundred-ten thousand. He bought it for six hundred seventy in 2007."

"Not such a shrewd businessman."

"He's a criminal. Owen, I don't know if Harmon does this regularly, but he broke in and stole Mr. Dijkstra's property. We're in way over our heads."

"I don't think this guy is a professional."

"But what about his whatever, *gorilla?*

Owen cannot help smiling again. "I love it when you talk criminal."

"We're not going in without the police."

"They won't let us anywhere near the place."

"That's good, that's good," Patricia insists.

Owen turns onto Mission Boulevard as the car's GPS system advises and then onto Central Boulevard. As the satellite-directed voice says "At Marland Drive turn left," Patricia turns off the auditory guidance. They roll past the black Mercedes-Benz parked nose-first in front of the garage. The "UBRALES" vanity plate chills them as it had earlier. Owen continues up the block and comes to a stop near a similar 1960s era tract home. The street is devoid of foot traffic. The hillsides are already parched to a weedy, dull yellow.

"Okay, is there a dispatch number for the Hayward Police?" Owen asks.

Patricia says, "Got it. Shall I call?"

"Yes, a woman's voice might get a quicker response."

"Hello? My name is Patricia Spencer. My husband and I are parked near 15471 Marland Drive." She repeats the number. "The occupants there have stolen—just burgled—a valuable book of maps from the 16th Century and important historical correspondence. They robbed a duplex in Walnut Creek and we have followed them down to this address. Please send some officers because my husband and I don't want to get hurt by these people."

Owen smiles at Patricia's approach.

"You will? Good, we'll be just up the street in a green Toyota. Yes, we'll stay in the car. Yes, out of sight." Patricia continues to respond to questions, name and address of the complainants. "No, I don't know if they're armed. But one looks very tough, like he could be."

Within minutes, a Hayward City Police utility vehicle enters Marland Drive.

"Stay here," Owen says.

"Not a chance," Patricia rejoins and together they walk toward the police car, which is stopped outside the Harmon address.

"There's a man named Horst Harmon…." Owen begins.

The clean-cut young officer says, "Yeah, that's what we have. But you need to go back to your car. This could be dangerous and back-up is on the way."

Patricia tugs Owen's sleeve."

"I can identify this book," Owen says retreating very slowly. And there are about twenty pages, also stolen. They are handwritten in Dutch. The owner of the book is a man in his nineties. He filed a report with the Walnut Creek Police Department two hours ago. Officer, there may be two men."

"Let's see what he has to say. Back to your car now, please." He speaks into his collar-communicator. "Going in to talk to the subject, over."

As the police officer walks around the side of the house to the stairs that lead to the main floor, Owen trots gingerly toward the garage double doors that face the street. Patricia hesitates, then follows Owen. They hear the officer knocking, saying loudly, "Hayward Police, we need to talk. Please open up, Mr. Harmon."

No response. Owen looks at Patricia, both still at street level. They hear the electronic peep and see the lights flash as the Mercedes door is unlocked in the driveway. The garage-door mechanism begins tilting open.

Owen sees Harmon crouching to race to his car, the massive brown book of maps under his arm. As he runs for his car, Patricia screams. The central casting mobster follows on his heels. Owen lowers his head and plows into the knees of the lover of citrus cologne. Both go sprawling into a patch of lawn and Owen wrests the Ortelius atlas from Harmon's grasp. Owen twists as he falls, and the book never touches the ground. His shoulder is on fire, however. Patricia spots two manila envelopes that fly out of Harmon's jacket side pocket. She snatches the envelopes, noting one is thinner and lighter.

The Hayward Police officer cuffs Harmon as two more police cars arrive, sirens wailing. Harmon's accomplice raises his arms and goes to his knees in a practiced manner. The other responding officers handcuff him.

"I thought I told you to stay in your car," the young officer bellows.

"This is important," Owen says from the ground, tapping the antique atlas. "And documents of great historical value, too. And he was getting away."

Harmon glares furiously, his hands tightened behind him.

"He means these," Patricia says. She passes the packet of original onionskin pages to the officer and moves swiftly to help Owen up. Blocking the officers' view, she presses the photocopied set into the inner breast pocket of Owen's jacket, chastising him nonstop. "Look you've ruined this jacket. We'll never get the grass stains out. Why did you not listen to the officer?"

Owen gets up painfully, and passes the folio book to one of the police just arrived. "Officer Meltzer," Owen says, reading the cop's brass nametag. "This stolen property belongs to Michael Dijkstra in Walnut Creek. Those documents, too."

Meltzer looks at the original arresting officer, who nods. Harmon and his associate are locked in separate squad cars. The book of maps and Herman Dijkstra's written record go into the rear of the arresting officer's vehicle.

"Holy cow," a female voice calls from within the garage. "This place is like Hitler's bunker." A policewoman walks out of the garage speaking into her communicator. "Yes, lieutenant, you're gonna want lots of visuals at this address." She addresses the Spencers: "Folks, please follow us to the station, we're going to need your statements. Walnut Creek is sending their people down, too."

In the car, Owen removes the photocopied documents from his pocket and cocks his head at Patricia in question.

"These could be tied up for weeks, maybe months in some evidence locker," she says authoritatively. "Have you never watched *Law and Order*?" Owen nods and smiles as he slips the envelope under his seat.

He calls Michael and learns that the Walnut Creek Police will drive him to Hayward to identify the stolen property. Two and a half hours later, when Michael arrives, he looks haggard, but smiling. He even has brought the well-traveled map of the world he rescued at the auction to demonstrate how it is part of the stolen book of maps.

Nearly four hours later, Owen and Patricia are on the freeway to Berkeley.

"Your jacket is ruined. Don't you want to stop at an ER for your shoulder?"

He reaches under the seat and withdraws the envelope of photocopied notes. "I want to put this in Maurice's hands and jump into a hot bath at home," Owen says, exhausted. "Enough excitement for a lifetime, eh?"

"Who knew my hunk of a husband was such a crime-stopper?"

"Me! I always knew it." Owen laughs. "Elementary, my dear Miss Marple."

CHAPTER 81

En Route to Harwich, England, 30 October 1570

The air turns less bitter as the dray rolls out of Chelmsford for the last twenty-four miles to Colchester. The skies pour a steady rain. *Do not give in. Do not give up.* Jonas hears words from long ago. But Emmanuel opens a cheerful conversation.

Henrick, handling the team of horses, sinks into a sullen silence, while Jonas and Emmanuel chatter as though they had been friends for years.

"Pannekoeken. With honey sugar. That's my favorite. Yours?" The dark complexioned boy smiles broadly, teeth showing brightly behind olive colored lips.

"You're sure you're Dutch?" Jonas asks innocently. "You look like you could be from the south, Spanish or Moorish, even."

"Why are you so interested?" Emmanuel asks quietly. He seems not to want Henrick, handling the horses, to hear any of the conversation. Jonas sees Emmanuel's tautly drawn face and hears the concern in the boy's question.

"Forgive, me, please," Jonas whispers. "I can't help but take note of these things. I see someone and I wonder what it would be to sketch them. I see you and I am already thinking about how to do the crosshatching on a copper plate to suggest your coloring. It is rude of me, and I ask your forgiveness."

Emmanuel softens. "Nobody I know ever wanted to make a picture of me."

"You would make a good subject, Jonas says. "If we weren't on such a bumpy wagon, I'd try to draw a likeness."

"Hmmm," the boy says appreciatively and then falls silent.

The steam-snorting horses pull the wagon into the outskirts of Colchester, the roads slushy with mud-darkened snow. Carts and cattle driven on the road splash through puddles and both horses kick up roadway mud to spatter the boys' cloaks. Thatch-covered daub and wattle houses and stone and brick structures appear as they leave the farmlands behind and enter the manufacturing town.

"Look. You'll think you are in Flanders in this part of town," Emmanuel prattles, pointing to the Lowlands architecture with timbered walls. "Ten or eleven Flemish families have set up shop here in the weaving trades. We will drop our load at Ringer's before we head up to Harwich. They got here earlier this year, the Duke of Alva nipping at their heels. Protestants," the boy adds, Jonas thinks, unnecessarily.

Jonas and Emanuel off-load three of the burlap-covered packages of silk bolts at a building that looks quite new. Henrick hangs bags of oats over the ears of both horses and they munch while he relieves himself in a cesspit behind the building. Inside, several men kick treadle-powered shuttles to weave the spun wools. Seven women are spinning yarn from heaps of raw wool from recently shorn sheep.

"Good, the manors have been awaiting these bolts," an elder of the family says to Emmanuel in Dutch. "Can you stop for some cider?"

"We have long miles ahead of us this afternoon. Thanks."

"Good journey, then. And be happy you are here and not at home. Many towns may drown in the storms. I fear the Scheldt will take thousands of lives."

"Antwerp?" Jonas asks agitatedly.

"Zeeland will be worse," the elder says. "Thousands will die. Livestock, too."

The two young men return to the dray, now only half full of deliveries. Jonas' brow creases with fearful concerns for the safety of Sofie. His survival of the flood a few years before gives him a perspective he doesn't think his new friend has. As Henrick urges the team east toward the port town, Emmanuel continues chittering to Jonas. "I get homesick for Groningen. But if the Duke of Alva keeps driving out Lowlanders, we will have ample numbers here in England to keep me from losing my mother tongue. We are called *strangers* here; I warrant *they* are the strange ones, these Englanders. But I will admit, it is safer here. You must be deeply in love to go back to marry."

"I am. Yes." Jonas falls silent. His mind churns with thoughts of Sofie. He cannot get her mischievous smile out of his mind. He tries by thinking of the Baroness Joan Casterleigh and her lascivious smirk. Immediately, he casts her out of his consciousness and replaces her with Sofie's flushed cheeks when she is excited. He imagines her holding his face and kissing his lips. With his eyes shut, soon they are sharing the warm moist touching of their tongues. Jonas opens his eyes, and feels the sloppy wetness of the falling snow whipping his face. Emmanuel continues to hold forth, now on how the Dutch provinces are so much more hospitable than life in exile in England.

The dray continues only a few hundred yards from the town of Harwich. The odor of the sea has filtered inland and he can smell the salt marshes and the wetlands in the crisp late afternoon. In the waning light, Jonas sees ships' masts at the end of West Street. He looks for the lodging house called The Three Cups where Jacob Cole had instructed him to take a room and wait until Captain Vandeven's merchantman sails into the harbor. It could be two or three days. The Sign of the Three Cups inn appears not far from quayside at the sea end of West Street.

"Do you think there is room for one more?" Emmanuel asks as Henrick slows the team of horses.

"What?" Jonas asks in surprise.

"I hate England. The food is terrible. I need to return to Groningen. There. I've said it."

"You can't do that," Henrick says, shrilly. "We have all these bolts to deliver!"

Jonas has gotten off the dray and collected his travel bag. He watches as the two young men argue and finally hears Henrick shout, "Get off, then, filthy Christ-killer. Go back and I hope the Spanish cut your Jew dick off before they burn you."

Emmanuel hops down and stands next to Jonas. They watch Henrick angrily turn the team around and head back toward Colchester. "Where will you stay the night?" Jonas calls. But the angry Henrick is too furious to answer.

"He will find a rock somewhere," Emmanuel says. "His kind live under rocks."

Jonas regards Emmanuel who shrugs under his cap and cloak. "I came here with less than this," he says. "I have more than two guilders in English coin. I return home like a rich merchant."

"Aren't you safer here?" Jonas asks.

"There is no 'safe' anywhere. Some say we have been chosen to wander alone. If you don't want me with you just say so, and I will find my own way."

"No," Jonas blurts immediately. "You're fine company. And if we have time to wait before the boat arrives, I will make a drawing of you."

"Let's find out if they have a room for us, then," Emmanuel says, and they walk into the tavern bristling with drinkers. Jonas seeks out the innkeeper and is informed that no rooms are available until Monday, when an English merchantman is embarking for Hamburg. Jonas' dark look tells the story.

"Follow me," Emmanuel says, mysteriously. Jonas steps into the darkening day a step behind his new friend. "She lives on an alley near here. Ah, it's Friday."

They pass cottages in narrow lanes and barking dogs raise an alarm as the two strangers thread past, crunching the recently fallen snow.

"Here we are," announces Jonas' new companion. They are standing outside a tiny wood and wattle house. The last rays of the daylight are fading and the interior glows faintly by candlelight. Jonas looks a through the dark casement window to see an old woman with a shawl over her head in front of two candles. She is mouthing a prayer with eyes closed and drawing her hands to her forehead as though bringing warmth from the flames. Emmanuel nods knowingly as she completes her incantations and knocks on the door.

"Good Shabbos, Grandmother."

The wraith of an elderly woman cocks her head. "Who are you?" She asks in the Essex English dialect.

"My name is Emmanuel van Aalt and this is my friend, Jonas Hoen." We cannot get a room at the Three Cups until Monday. We are waiting for a boat to take us back to our homeland in the Low Countries. Can you give us shelter until Monday? We will not bother you."

Jonas listens, his mouth agape. She nods and points to two chairs near the wall. Emmanuel nods to Jonas and they bring the chairs to the table while the woman fills plates with a stew from the pot suspended over the hearth.

"Wash your hands," she instructs. Jonas follows Emmanuel's lead. He knows the ritual. He fills a cup with water and pours it over the top and palm of the right hand into a bowl to receive the water. He does the same with his left hand and says: *Barukh atah Adonai, Eloheinu, melekh ha-olam*. The woman passes a cloth and he dries his hands.

When Jonas follows suit, Emmanuel again recites the prayer.

"Hebrew," Emmanuel says in explanation to Jonas. Nothing more is said, and they eat in silence.

After their meager, but hot dinner, the woman says, "Sleep well." She retires to her bedroom.

"Is she your grandmother?" Jonas asks.

"No. But it's good to have community." Emmanuel says, banking the embers in the hearth. They make up beds with their cloaks.

CHAPTER 82

Harwich, 5 November 1570

"There, there it is," shouts Jonas, recognizing the lines of the *Tortelduif* at the end of West Street. Emmanuel follows close on his heels, thumping down the timbered wharf. Captain Vandeven scowls at both young men. After a negotiation, Emmanuel will pay for his passage by helping to load, secure and offload on arrival thirty bales of bays woolen fabric and another thirty of felt, all manufactured by the Dutch-in-exile of Colchester. Jonas' fare has been prepaid by James Cole. The brusque master of the vessel minces no words with Jonas. "I regard you as mad, so if you do anything amiss on our trip to Holland—why do you want so badly to return when you fled in such haste not six months ago? Nearly half the country is underwater now with that damned storm, anyway."

"To be married," intrudes Emmanuel. "Jonas is going back to be married."

"Ahh. You would be in far worse trouble if her father catches you, eh?"

Jonas decides a sheepish look would end any further conversation and he affixes one on his face.

"Aha," the sleuthing sea captain says, satisfied that he has gotten to the root of Jonas' problem. "Do consider a seafarer's life, young man. You have the makings."

"Thank you, sir," Jonas replies, and nothing more is said.

As though anointed by Captain Vandeven's words, Jonas weathers the crossing easily, with no sign of seasickness. Emmanuel, on the other hand, spends much of the voyage miserable, hanging over the rails. Jonas and his new friend, Emmanuel, hold tightly to cleats, lines, and rails during two and a half days riding the swells on the North Sea. Each is lost in his own thoughts as the crew ties up at a quay in the Port of Amsterdam on the Amstel River.

The city is not as busy as Jonas' remembers Antwerp, but it is a cosmopolitan port, nevertheless, merchantmen laden with freight and goods from many nations. Amsterdam is still firmly in the camp ruled by King Philip of Spain. Spanish troops are less of a hostile presence. Business and trading are in the air. Most of all, Jonas is happy to be back where Dutch is spoken universally.

He assists Emmanuel in stacking the Colchester woolens in a small warehouse nearby. When they are done, Jonas eyes a tavern across the quay. "Come, Emmanuel. I will take you to supper." Over ale, soup, and bread, Jonas learns more about Emmanuel who is completely forthcoming.

"Two years ago my father bought a farm near Groningen. My family is still on the land. Back maybe ten years we moved from Aurich, in Westphalia, to escape the zealots who wanted to shed Jewish blood. Then, in Groningen I got into some trouble with a priest who demanded that I convert and that's why I fled to London. But my father is ailing and my brothers and sisters are too young to run the farm, so at my mother's wishes, I return. More cousins from Aurich also plan to settle near us so we won't be so isolated."

As Emmanuel speaks, Jonas wonders why Emmanuel has chosen to be so vulnerable. On impulse, he asks, "Why are you a Jew?"

A curious smile crosses his new friend's face. "That's like asking 'why were you born?'"

"You mean you are a Jew because your parents were Jews?" Jonas asks.

"I was taught the prayers by my father and grandfather. My mother observes the laws for keeping a Jewish home. When I return I will observe the rituals once again. I will be loyal to my people."

Jonas feels a wistfulness that has awakened in him. He has no original family to return to—only Sofie if she will still have him.

"My father writes that they feel safer in Groningen than they did in Westphalia. Perhaps that is true for the time being. It is part of my loyalty to return home. And that priest has been sent abroad; makes it easier for me to return."

"I will miss your company," Jonas says.

"One thing—I want to say," Emmanuel summons his words slowly. "If life gets too dangerous in Antwerp, we'll make room for you on our farmstead. Just ask for Emmanuel van Aalt when you get to Groningen."

Jonas cannot imagine that he would ever need to take his friend up on his offer. Their food arrives and they eat a meal heartily, especially Emmanuel who hasn't held down his food for nearly three days.

CHAPTER 83

Oakland, Early Evening, April 14th 2016

Driving north from Hayward, Owen and Patricia arrive at the curator's home in the Oakland Hills and are immediately served brandies by Phyllis, Bregmann's smiling wife. She insists that they join the Bregmanns for dinner. "Maurice says that you have a lot to discuss, and from what I hear you have had a harrowing adventure."

"Not how I expected to spend our Saturday," Patricia laughs.

"His property is safe?" Maurice asks.

"Yes." Owen replies. "These guys were taken into custody by the Hayward police for possession of stolen property, but they may face charges in Walnut Creek for breaking and entering where the book was reported stolen."

"I'm so glad the old fellow gets to reclaim that heirloom," Maurice says.

"Actually," Owen says, creasing his brow, "the atlas and Herman Dijkstra's original sheets of comments will be retained as evidence."

"Oh, no—insult to injury." Bregmann says, sadly.

"The legal process will grind slowly," Owen adds. "It may be some time before Michael sees his property. Two Walnut Creek detectives drove him home from Hayward after he identified the book. The inside cover shows a genealogy of his family on his mother's side dating back to 1576. A Captain Vandeven of Rotterdam was the first owner. I have a snap of the inside front board. The atlas came into Herman Dijkstra's possession when he and Marthe were married in 1916."

"You say *fifteen* seventy six?" Phyllis Bregmann asks, in awe. "The diaspora was flinging Jews in every direction at that time."

"I have this for you, Maurice." Owen lays the folded photocopies of the commentary pages on the coffee table before the curator and his wife. "The originals are with the Hayward police. But you have this, thanks to Patricia's quick thinking."

"Good, good," Bregmann says, beaming at Patricia.

"Here's what's so curious—Patricia and I were debating this all the way up from Hayward—Michael said his father's commentary and these copies were not with the book, but on a table across the room."

"We think that Harmon knew about these documents, too," Patricia says.

Owen adds, "If the people who were behind Harmon's bid at the auction had access to your conversations or data transmissions with Chaim Rubikoff, they would have known about the commentary. I remember you saying this morning that a line at the Yad Vashem acquisitions office is not secure."

"So you think—?" Bregmann asks.

"The police have Harmon's cell phone and his computer and they can trace any interactions he may have had with the Schroeder-Berghuis group."

"We're speculating," says Patricia excitedly, "that Harmon wanted to steal the atlas and break it up to offset his lost commission when Mr. Dijkstra removed the map from the auction. And since he knew that the commentary was valuable to this group in Europe, he walks across the room and snaps up both the originals and the copies."

"Michael Dijkstra says that nothing else was taken," Owen adds.

"On Monday, I will call in a favor from Professor van Groot to do a quick translation on these sheets." Bregmann says. "I will call Mr. Dijkstra to fill in anything that needs clarification. Refills?" Bregmann asks, clapping his hands eagerly. "I also have some interesting news for Patricia."

"I'll get us some nibbles," Phyllis says, rising and going into the kitchen.

Bregmann pours more brandy as he speaks. "While you were chasing down desperadoes in the wilds of Hayward, the grinding wheels of the research division of Yad Vashem have come up with a confirmation." Bregmann's twinkling eyes make him look like a cherubic, albeit bearded, New York Mets fan, one who has a sense that his pitcher was on the verge of throwing a no-hitter. The adenoidal rumble forms these words: "Patricia. According to various records, you are the sole survivor of the van Aalt family who resided in Haarlem, the Netherlands. When your family was uprooted and deported for annihilation, a collection of art pieces was stolen from your mother's family apartment building. The short of it is that this art consists of some three hundred copper plate engravings by an obscure engraver named Jonas Hoen."

The words crash like Chinese symbols in Owen's ears. They blot out any intelligible words coming from Bregmann's lips. Owen discovers he is standing in disbelief, having jumped up unconsciously from the settee he had been sharing with Patricia. He feels her hand tugging at his wrist.

"Hoen?" Owen asks. "*Jonas Hoen?*"

Bregmann is confused by Owen's outburst.

"Yes. That is the artist's name," Bregmann continues, trying to regain his train of thought. "Once the claim for recognition of Herman Dijkstra had been put forth by the woman who rescued Hetty—"

"You say that an artist named Jonas Hoen—Patricia! The engraving of the horse, the dog—JH"

The wind is going out of Bregmann's sails, as he tries to right the ship. "You see the van Aalts, whose heirs might wish to pursue restoration of any stolen or looted art—"

"Maurice?" Patricia asks, tentatively. "Are you saying that a collection of copper plates engraved by this Jonas Hoen has been located and traced back to my family's ownership?"

"Precisely. I know it's good news, but the shock you are registering…."

"Are you ready for a long story, Dr. Bregmann?" Patricia asks.

CHAPTER 84

Amsterdam, 6 November 1570

Jonas Hoen watches Emmanuel van Aalt disappearing into the Amsterdam afternoon, now on his way to Groningen. He becomes aware how very alone he is. Across the quay, the swollen Amstel River is alive with water traffic and squawking curlews overhead. Afternoon light lengthens shadows from the cloudy ceiling above the river. The cries of the birds deepen the emptiness he feels. Jonas orders another tankard of ale and tries to decide how best to make his way to Antwerp and Sofie. The snowy weather when he left London for Harwich had turned into bitter rainstorms that battered the coasts of the Netherland provinces and ports all along the Scheldt River. After a few drafts of the smoky ale, he finally thinks he will find passage by way of the North Sea. He crosses the cobbled street to the dock to inquire of Captain Vandeven who is leafing through the ship's manifest seated on a stool on the stern castle deck. The ships master is in a good mood and casts a smile toward Jonas. "Come aboard," he offers. "I can't help noticing that you look grown up since you first set foot on this old girl in Antwerp last summer. You look like a man to me, now, not a callow boy running from the city with his tail between his legs."

"That's very kind of you to say so, sir, but can you say when you will be heading south again for the Scheldt River?"

"Not for some time. Next is Hamburg and then back to Bremen before we put in here at Amsterdam again. The ports along the Scheldt are still sunken. They will repair the dikes but it will be many weeks, before we venture to Antwerp. As I said when we left Harwich I could use a hand if you want to sign on."

For a moment, a familiar way home, even if weeks away, appeals. But visions of Sofie struggling, the Scheldt River at flood stage, intrude. "I will find a land route. Thank you for your kindness," he says, shaking the weathered captain's hand, and shoulders his leather travel bag.

He walks from the docks toward the Dam in the central district. He is aware that he is now surrounded by people moving like a river in the direction of the Dam, speaking excitedly about "the heretic." A disturbing sight meets his eyes. Two peasants unload a cart of tree branches in the central square. He has seen the remains of such a pyre before in the market plaza in Antwerp. A heretic burning is planned. Several steel-helmeted pike men observe as burghers gather. Across the square a woman is being bound to a ladder. He looks away, repulsed by the preparation for her brutal execution. Amsterdam is a stronghold of Habsburg-Catholic domination enforced by the Spanish crown.

Near the row of guildhalls, he sees several wagons loaded with lumber. He approaches the driver of the first in line who is feeding the four stout oxen.

"I am going to Antwerp. I can pay."

"I go as far as Utrecht," the driver says. "I'm leaving as soon as she blows up."

"What?" Jonas asks, thinking his ears deceive him.

"That Anabaptist across the square."

A roar of voices rises. Jonas follows his pointing hand. Two men are carrying the ladder bearing the bound and gagged woman to the center of the square where the branches have been set ablaze. "They know how to punish blasphemy in this city," the driver says. "The priest at the Nieuwe Kerk says they have filled her Anabaptist mouth with gunpowder. Climb up here for a good view." Jonas numbly climbs onto the wagon in time to see the ladder being raised at one end and the poor gagged woman toppling onto the flames still bound to the rungs and rails.

"Imagine if this was done in the night," the driver says. "Explosions—much more exciting at night."

Jonas never hears the vaunted explosion, but the crowd of onlookers surrounding the burning does, for a loud cheer carries to where Jonas, sickened, turns away. He thinks of Anent Willemzoom, the Anabaptist boy he met scraping paint from the English Queen's Barge a few short months ago. At least Anent was safe in England. The tongues of flame leap skyward, through billowing black smoke. A hush overtakes the crowd. Ten minutes pass as the eerie sacrifice is done. Jonas watches the onlookers walking away from the charred pyre. Wisps of burnt flesh odor waft past. The pike men, with their lances pointed upward stand by as weeping women and grim-faced men, the heretic's family, keen into the afternoon. Jonas is transfixed by the macabre aftermath. Cinders and charred bits swirl in the wind as the afternoon breeze picks up.

Lost in thought, Jonas takes a seat next to the driver. *Was it another ill-considered mistake? Dare I think I can come home without repercussions?* He turns again to see the scattering soldiers, the good burghers of Amsterdam safe another day from a now dead woman burnt to death and her tongue blown up for not recanting her Anabaptist beliefs. The driver snaps his whip to begin the journey to Utrecht. The heavy freight of mahogany logs, unloaded from a Spanish galleon, bears Jonas toward the Scheldt and Sofie. The disturbing thought that he must record this event on a copper plate drills through his mind as the laden wagon jostles over the cobbles. He envisions the ladder being tilted upright before plunging the hapless woman onto the flames. *Nightmares, these are the things that nurture nightmares.* Jonas tries to erase the scene he has witnessed, but the images are too powerful and they overwhelm him.

The driver is saying something, but Jonas is imagining how high to pitch the ladder, how broad the pyre of tree branches should extend, and the height the flames should reach. He considers if Mark Anthony Coppens would countenance such a scene for a pamphlet decrying the intolerance. The wagon dips as a wheel rolls across a hole and he is jostled by the chilly reality of his return to the Lowlands.

He focuses on appearing a devout Catholic. He draws on homilies taught at the abbey to keep the driver occupied. If heresies were punished as he had just seen, he must speak carefully. But the poor Anabaptist woman pitched onto a pyre in the Dam Square for not recanting her beliefs is etched deep into his unconscious. He shakes the distressing event from his mind by reminding himself of why he has come back. Sofie in Antwerp—seventy-five leagues after Utrecht.

CHAPTER 85

The Road into North Brabant, 26 November 1570

The damage from the floods is far more extensive than Jonas had expected even nearing a month since the Day of All Saints storms on the first of November. The breached dikes leave water flooding the roads, causing progress to be frustratingly slow. The annoyed teamster drives the mahogany-laden wagon east trying to avoid large swaths of sunken lands, adding many days to the trip. The muddy roads are also awash with displaced people whose homes and lands have been washed away in the deluge and aftermath of the North Sea surge.

Finally, Jonas hoists his heavy leather traveling bag over his shoulder and leaves the surly teamster and his wagon bogged down in a watery ditch to take his chances on foot. The general devastation of the land brings forth his deepest anxieties. The farther south Jonas ventures, the more fearful he becomes. Stories of drowned villages along to the Scheldt River only increase his fears for Sofie. Jonas finds himself on the road with many flood victims. He pulls his cloak tightly about him, hitches his bag over his shoulder, puts one foot before the other, and falls into line behind families trudging along the track.

"Where are you bound?" Jonas looks up sharply. The voice is harsh, with north-country accents, similar to Emmanuel's. He turns to see a man in a farmer's straw hat behind him. A wild grey and black beard, like an oval frame, emphasizes his clean-shaven face, his eyes above sagging skin bags looking like small black stones set in the yellowing whites.

"Antwerp," Jonas says. "And you, where are you bound, sir?"

The stranger seems surprised by the question. "Any place dry and tolerant."

Jonas looks past the stranger, who is followed closely by two little girls, perhaps four and six, their dresses spattered with mud.

"Do you mind if we walk with you for a while?" the stranger asks.

"No, but I am desperate to get home," Jonas replies, hoping the man will understand that he cannot be delayed.

"We can walk as fast as the road allows, can't we, girls? My name is Erasmus. The little one is Anneke and the older, Josepha." Josepha affects the hint of a curtsey.

Jonas offers his hand to Erasmus. "Jonas."

"You wouldn't hurt us, would you?" Anneke asks. Jonas struggles to answer her surprising question, but she continues, "Because we are not Catholics?"

"Anneke," Jonas says, "I would not hurt you for any reason."

"Hush, now, Anneke," Erasmus chides. "Save your breath for walking. We have a great distance to go, yet."

They cross into the Duchy of North Brabant, and the land seems drier, most of it is several feet above sea level. As they press on, Jonas learns that Erasmus and his family are fleeing persecution in the North, where the established Church vigorously prosecutes heretics, especially Anabaptists. Erasmus, a Mennonite, is an easy target for brutalization.

"Momma was killed with an axe," Anneke says, devoid of emotion.

"Yes, an axe swung by a Spanish-Hapsburg constable," Erasmus adds bitterly.

"Erasmus," Jonas cautions, "We are walking into the teeth of the Spanish Netherlands. Have a care about how you and your little girls speak. The town before us is Endehoven. When I was last in Antwerp, a garrison of Spanish mercenaries billeted within its walls. First, Willem van Oranje, and then the Duke of Alva—I do not know who controls it now. Be careful, Erasmus."

Jonas knows that after the south gate of Endehoven, he needs to travel thirty leagues due west to Antwerp. He can walk it in three days, two if he hurries.

As they pass through the north gate of Endehoven, several Spanish-helmeted troops confirm that the town is under the control of the Duke of Alva.

"We must pass quickly and quietly, Erasmus," Jonas says, hastening the little girls to walk more quickly. "Erasmus, can you carry them? Little Anneke, at least?"

Wordlessly, Erasmus catches up his four-year-old and sets her on his right shoulder. He picks up his sack of belongings and begins walking quickly toward the wide road that looks most like it will lead to the south gate. Jonas takes up Josepha's hand and follows quickly on Erasmus' heels. They are walking through a market square, venders calling out their commodities.

"I want a piece of bread," Anneke says from her perch on her father's broad shoulder. She holds Erasmus' head fast, pressed against the askew straw hat.

"We still have some. We will eat when we are on the road again."

"Look at the breads," Anneke complains. The odor of fresh-baked bread is everywhere. "And fruits. I'm hungry."

"Anneke," Erasmus warns, looking about nervously at several passersby eyeing the foursome with curiosity, suspicion, or scowls, "We must walk a little more before it is—before we can stop—safely." He races on. "Did I ever tell you the story about the little fisher boy...." Jonas hears the story of how Jesus told his disciples where to fish. Erasmus seems to grasp at straws and speaks rapidly with lengthy intrusions of invented detail to keep Anneke entertained and her hunger at bay, as Jonas veers off to one of the bread sellers and pays for a loaf and a small round of cheese. He tears off two pieces of bread, hands one to Anneke, and the other to Josepha. He stuffs the remainder into his travel bag. Meanwhile, Jonas keeps up the pace, only slightly slowing when Josepha tires and begins dragging on the arm attached to his once damaged shoulder.

"Josepha, stop pulling," Jonas says sharply.

"I can't run so fast as you walk," she complains. "Father, he makes me run and I want to stop."

Erasmus whirls about so angrily that Anneke is caught off guard and knocks off his hat. His eyes seem wild to Jonas. "What kind of God allows a brute to swing his axe and take my children's mother from us?" Erasmus looks at Jonas fiercely, a though he were to blame. His outburst attracts attention not only from staring burghers and vendors, but two Italian soldiers who approach the four strangers, hands on their sheathed short swords.

"Merely passing through," Jonas says in his native Dutch, but the pair, recent recruits to the Duke's mercenary army, barely twenty-years-old, are from Calabria and do not understand his tongue. One of the pair puts a hand on Erasmus' chest to make him stop. Instinctively, the Mennonite kicks the solder in the groin, nearly toppling Anneke. The struck soldier sprawls backward cursing in Italian; the second pulls out his sword. Jonas, laden with his traveling bag and Josepha's pulling hand, pushes Erasmus with his chest. Oddly, he remembers Aretino's call for an end of banter before lovemaking and he bellows it for the Italian soldiers to hear. "*Ma lasciam'ir le ciance.*" In Dutch he shouts in Erasmus' ear. "Let us be done chatting."

The fallen Calabrese is moaning, holding his genitals, and his compatriot, after a moment of indecision, kneels by his fallen comrade, and curses in their native tongue. Jonas looks over his shoulder and continues his accelerated pace, pressing Erasmus to get to the south gate of the town.

But as they pass through the portico to the road leading away from town, Erasmus calls belligerently to a Dutch castle warden resplendent in the red pantaloons of his office and helmet tied by red ribbon at his throat. "You murderous cur, you protect the pope but know nothing of Christ's teaching."

The bearded soldier squints at the mad-seeming Mennonite. To Jonas, he appears to be deciding what to do about the shaven-faced man with unkempt locks, holding a little girl on his shoulder and a burlap sack of his worldly possessions.

Jonas addresses the guard, who holds his arquebus and fork stand by each hand, leaving no free access to his sword or the powder horn lashed to his belt.

"Heed him not, sir," Jonas intercedes. He has lost his wits along with his wife and is in desperate straits. His two children, motherless, would be without anyone if harm should come to their father. He is just passing through and quits Endehoven for Liege. Please take no notice of what he says.

"He knows nothing of good works and service to others," Erasmus roars. "But he will kill—"

"Hush brother!" Jonas snaps. "Have a care for Anneke and Josepha."

Erasmus stops his tirade. Jonas addresses the guard. "Thank you for paying no attention to this distraught father. He is a farmer whose fields were flooded.

His mind cannot cope with the tragedy. He means you no disrespect." Jonas pushes Erasmus onto the roadway. "We have several leagues to go today, good Erasmus."

But Jonas has made up his mind. He must abandon Erasmus if he is to get safely to Antwerp. They do not go more than twenty paces when Jonas releases Josepha's hand. He reaches into his leather bag and pushes the remainder of the loaf of bread under the wild man's arm and the round of cheese in his sack. He roots in the pouch at his waist and pulls out several stuivers, which he presses into Erasmus' hand. "A more selfless man would not quit you today, as I do. But in my heart I am no Christian. I see too many religions to think that one provides an answer." Erasmus stares at Jonas as though he has just discovered that the cocky boy he had befriended is mad. "Goodbye. May your fortunes turn for the better."

Jonas strides down the road passing travelers and carts moving in both directions. Within minutes, he puts enough distance between him and the sad little family to focus completely on his next steps. *Find Sofie. Ask for her hand in marriage. Work at his trade of engraver, hopefully through the good offices of the De Diest printworks, or possibly Christophe Plantin's Sign of the Golden Compass.* He resolves to ask Anna Ortels for her guidance as Elizabeth Cole has suggested. His plan evolving, he covers nearly six leagues of his journey toward Antwerp before the shadows lengthen and he seeks a place to lay his head.

CHAPTER 86

Palo Alto, April 21ˢᵗ 2016

Owen's shoulder pain has abated from his Hayward heroics, and he and Patricia enjoy a welcome thaw in their relationship. Their teamwork in rescuing Michael Dijkstra's map has put them on a course of reconciliation. Except...

"Not another word about it, Owen. I am not in the least interested in having a restitution of plates from people I never knew."

"All right, all right," he says helplessly.

Anything to do with her mother's family murdered in the Holocaust brings on a torrent of anger from Patricia.

He does not raise the issue again, and assumes his outsider status as it relates to Patricia and her mother, Hetty, a boundary he cannot cross without becoming hopelessly embroiled in her angst. He concerns himself with his business and she with her classwork.

Today he has returned from an Ocean Street print gallery in Carmel-by-the Sea, having delivered a collection of Rockwell Kent maplewood engravings to a long-time customer.

Owen has scored a decent commission by fulfilling a request to scout and obtain work done by Kent whose iconic illustrations for Moby Dick helped define a style for American illustrated books in the 1920s and 30s.

He listens to his office answering machine and scratches notes in his day planner for the next two weeks.

One of the messages is intriguing, an apology from Sandra Bergen, Peter Phelan's personal assistant. She had been caught in the middle of an absurd phone discussion a week before the Ortelius map auction drama, when the hi-tech magnate wanted assurances that a purported contemporary engraved portrait of Johannes Gutenberg was the only state ever printed.

"It was engraved a century after Gutenberg lived," Owen recalls saying to the assistant, which drew in Phelan himself in to tell Owen he had it on "good authority" that the engraving was contemporary to the great printer's life.

Owen had doubted the veracity that it was genuine, let alone the state of printing for which there was no documentation.

The apology is not from her boss, but Sandra Bergen, who says she recognized that Phelan's tone was "snarky" and that he overstepped a line. As she put it in her phone message, "I was embarrassed to talk to you that way. It was very unprofessional. I hope you will forgive me."

Owen takes a note to respond to her apology, then checks email.

Among the notices and spam is a response from the Berlin print seller he had contacted.

Dear Owen

Alas, I have no way of knowing the state of the print for this Gutenberg portrait. I would guess sometime after 1580, based on the paper, of French origin. It looks to be one of the Paris papermakers.

The original plate was certainly metal, probably copper. Sorry I cannot tell you more. It is simply not known.

Owen, I believe I know you from a bookseller conference in San Francisco a few years ago. We had drinks at a Fraenkel Gallery reception that week. I offer you best wishes.

Heinrich Stössel

P.S. If you have continued interest in an early Gutenberg portrait engraving, I know of an exceptional small plate being offered in Mainz.

Owen puts the name to a face and recalls a friendly dealer who seemed to have stepped out of a Wagnerian opera, blond, flecked with gray, like Owen, in his forties. In San Francisco, they had talked about a shared love of Akira Kurosawa and his samurai swordplay movies of the 1950s. "Eastern westerns," Owen had joked.

"Each frame, exquisitely composed, samurai precision," Stössel replied in his German-tinged accent.

"Yes, razor-sharp images." Owen recalled Stössel laughing at his pun.

Interesting, Owen thinks, rereading Stössel's note. He wonders if anything might be gained in further communication with Peter Phelan. He grimaces at the thought. Can Sandra Bergen be sounded out?

Owen's reply to Heinrich Stössel requests a photo of the "exceptional" plate, and notes how much he had enjoyed his conversation at Fraenkel's.

Early in May, Owen is in his garage office, marking potential prints in a catalog for a client in Las Vegas. It is Wednesday, his night to fix dinner. In the kitchen, he turns the rack of lamb in the marinade he has concocted.

When he returns to his desk, he opens his email to a string of communications with the Berlin print dealer, Stössel. A new mail has come in. This one includes a JPG file of a portrait, delicately etched, no more than four inches tall, showing the capped head, shoulders, arms, and hands of a bearded man in his forties. Owen blinks to be sure he is seeing correctly. The figure is holding a composing stick of moveable type. This is not any ordinary typesetter. The print seller is onto something very special. The lines are precise, simple, and elegant. The graceful effect is familiar but Owen cannot pin it down. The print reveals no signature of the artist. As distasteful as his dealings with Peter Phelan have been, Owen feels a surge of adrenalin at the possibility of uniting a collector with something he wants desperately.

He copies the JPG image and attaches it to a text to Sandra Bergen with whom he hasn't yet communicated since her apologetic phone message.

> *Dear Ms. Bergen*
>
> *I want to thank you for your call regarding our phone conversation with Peter Phelan. I fully understand the difficulty inherent in such a communication.*

Owen stops typing his message, noting that it is addressed to Bergen's work number. He decides to delete the JPG and end this note as follows:

> *Best wishes, and thanks again for your call.*
>
> *Owen Spencer*

He clicks Send, then addresses a second email to Sandra Bergen on her company email and attaches the JPG file.

> *Dear Ms. Bergen:*
>
> *I am advised that the original of the attached image, and more important, the original copper plate that fathered this engraving, may*

be available through a German dealer with whom I am in contact. If Peter Phelan has an interest, please advise.

Yours faithfully,

Owen Spencer

An hour and a half later Peter Phelan's voice is on speakerphone. "I am interested."

Owen's head swims with possibility. He strains to maintain a poker-voice. "I may be in Germany in a month's time and can take a firsthand look," he says. "This will not be cheap, I promise you."

"If this has legs, let me worry about the cost," Phelan assures. Owen hears no hint of snarky in his tone. "It looks like very nice work."

CHAPTER 87

Antwerp, 1 December 1570

The Our Lady's Cathedral bells strike eleven. Friday morning finds Jonas crunching the frozen ground behind the Boekprintere Scheldt. A fluttering of nerves scrambles his digestion as he wonders how Sofie will receive him. He passes the wooden deckles and water barrels dusted by frost, and tries the door. It unlatches to the familiar odor of the papermaking rooms. Master Du Brul's reddened face breaks into a wide smile as he casts a sidelong glance at Sofie, back turned, sorting linen rags. Jonas sets down his pack. She turns as though to say something to Du Brul and cries.

"Oh, I hoped, oh, I hoped—" The rest is smothered by a kiss, Sofie—feet off the ground—wrapped in his arms.

"Jesu,—does this mean I have to get someone new to take Sofie's place?" Du Brul asks, half mocking. "We have five books to prepare next month."

But Jonas hears not a word. His thoughts are only that he is finally home in Sofie's embrace. Words begin but only turn to giggles. Jonas' fears evaporate; he has cast his future where he wants to be, no matter the consequences.

Jonas climbs the stairs to the second floor chamber of Mark Anthony Coppens. He presents the printed broadside, "Het Engelse Marine," but sees Mark Anthony's brow wrinkle nervously. He chuckles at the wit, but he shakes his head. "Very humorous, but open to misinterpretation," the young man says waving his spectacles. "If we were a nation, the Sea Beggars would be our national treasure. Suggesting that they are England's Navy is easily misconstrued and you would be looked on with suspicion in these provinces. Do you understand me?"

Jonas nods slowly. It has been his worst concern about the broadside, and within moments of their meeting, Coppens has proven his fear well founded.

"Yes, I do understand," Jonas, crestfallen, admits.

"But your wit, your skill—very evident. I am glad to say Master Gheeraerts' tutelage has proved very beneficial, Jonas." Coppens assumes a conspiratorial tone. "Do you have plans of where to work, yet?"

"I was hoping for a position here. Failing that, I have been advised by Master Ortels' sister in London to seek advice from Madame Anna Ortels.

"Let us see how it may be possible for you to rejoin us at Boekprintere Scheldt. Can you return at three o'clock?" His query is welcome. But a stab of recognition of Mark Anthony's encouraging tone makes Jonas uneasy. Despite assurances from the publisher's son, his work as a propagandist for the Dutch Revolt had been betrayed not six months earlier.

"Jonas," Coppens says earnestly, "I am now more responsible for other publishing projects at Boekprintere Scheldt, as my father works on new editions of the *Theatrum*. We have work for your excellent skills. A compendium of human bones, for example, under the guidance of a physician here in Antwerp. I need to discuss this with my father, however, to assure your safety. I will explain later."

Jonas looks quizzically at Mark Anthony who gives him a reassuring smile.

Almost immediately, the Boekprintere Scheldt becomes Jonas' principle employer, but things are not straightforward. "Your name may not appear on our records as Jonas Hoen." Before Jonas can reply, Mark Anthony says: "We can hire you as a member of the Guild of Stationers in London. But we need a usable name."

Jonas blinks at the matter-of-fact manner Coppens employs. "Confusing, yes, Jonas—I understand." He removes his glasses to slow things down. "I am racing as usual, my words like a scattering of arrows. Forgive me, Jonas. Here are the facts."

He explains that the Procurator for Heresy in Antwerp has issued a "find and catechize" order for Jonas Hoen based on a complaint by Nicholaus Bockel. "That's right, Bockel, the worm planted in our limners' studio to spy on us."

"Catechize?" Jonas asks, bewildered.

"Yes, to examine you on Christian dogma—a ruse of the procurator's office. It would not go well for you," Mark Anthony says, shaking his head. "If Jonas Hoen has no presence here, no issue exists. Nicholaus Bockel is in Ghent, making his mischief there. He will have no knowledge if you work here under another name."

"So if I were to become, as if by magic, someone named—Jonas Smit, or Johannes van Brabo, say, or Jos Graveur. "No, not 'Graveur,'" Mark Anthony says after considering. "Could raise some eyebrows. Van Brabo would suffice. Johan van Brabo? Johannes van Braab? Why not?" The young Coppens writes down the possibilities. I like *Johan van Braab*. Simple. Johannes sounds grandiose."

"But if the Guild of Saint Luke asks the Stationers' in London—" Jonas begins.

"Johan van Braab, freeman, I am pleased to inform you that your four-pence fee for the right to publish your broadside, *The English Navy*—printed by John Jugge—yes? Your fee will be sent on the outbound tide tomorrow, to be entered in the Stationers' Register, Peter's College, in the City of

London. Next week my father will inform our Guild of Saint Luke that we have brought on a freeman in good standing with the Stationers' Guild in England."

Jonas tilts a dubious nod at Mark Anthony's words.

"My father has standing. You need not fear." Jonas remembers when he had heard similar words about his anonymity for the illustrated forger of chains to protest the hundredth penny tax. But he is flattered that the son of the publisher wants him so badly that he would stretch the truth with the Antwerp guild.

Mark Anthony continues: "Come to my father's chambers tomorrow at eight o'clock to meet Doctor Brudo. He will have a bone to pick with you." The young man breaks into gales of laughter as Jonas wonders why. "For—forgive—forgive me, Jonas," he gasps between chuckles. "We have a commission to publish a book—of the human skeleton. The sketches by the doctor's father are of bones. But the son has arranged for our engraver— you—to work from real specimens. Bones exhumed from flooded lands— unidentified—except—to the physician's eye." Mark Anthony extends his hand. "Welcome home, Jonas. I'm sure Sofie van Alsing would love to see you for dinner tonight. And you are welcome to stay in your old room until you get settled." Jonas is warmed by the sincerity of his offer.

Coppens' voice drops to a whisper. "Next week, after you begin Doctor Brudo's undertaking, let us talk about how we can progress on loosening the Iron Duke's grip on our lands."

Jonas is surprised and pleased by the tickle in his breast on hearing Mark Anthony's words.

CHAPTER 88

Antwerp, Evening, 1 December 1570

Sofie hears the tap on her door and feels a quickening in her cheeks. She has dabbed lavender scent on her wrists. She steals a quick glance in the looking glass on her bureau, touches a stray ringlet fallen from her starched cap and opens the door.

Jonas' clothes still smell from his long trek to Antwerp, salt, ox manure, mud, even smoke from the horrific burning of the heretic on the Dam Square. He enters, his hands behind his back. Sofie restrains herself from crushing him in her arms, but inhales his odor and smiles. He presents his left hand, holding something wrapped in a scrap of linen. She takes it, staring into Jonas' eyes. She has difficulty pulling her gaze from them. She caresses his cheek and enjoys him closing his lids as a smile plays at his lips.

"What is this?" she asks, unfolding the linen. "Oh," she gasps at the delicate beauty of the silk flora tiara Jonas has brought from Jacob Cole's London warehouse.

"Try it on," Jonas says.

She tugs off her cap and poses before the small mirror, folding the wire comb beneath her tresses. She turns to Jonas to see him approving. "You make these silk daffodils look even more beautiful, Sofie."

"You are the sweetest boy. You make me feel so special." She touches the tiara of flowers. "Where will you stay this evening?"

"Mark Anthony says I can use my old room tonight."

"Come with me," she says, pulling his sleeve. His left hand comes from behind his back. "I have brought a lamb and mushroom pasty to share, if you are hungry."

"Will you always provide for me?" She laughs, making light of the moment.

"To my dying breath."

"Don't speak of dying, please. Not ever. Come downstairs with me. You need to bathe." She snatches up a bar of soap, a soft bristled brush and a towel. She pulls on Jonas' hand. They quietly descend to the first floor. The pressroom is silent and the hallway is in dark early evening shadows. She pushes open the door to the warm furnace room, and pumps once on the bellows to activate a lick of flame. Within moments she has lighted several wall sconce tapers. Jonas adds peat to the embers, while she carries a pot outside to a wooden barrel, breaks the thin coating of ice, and fills the kettle. The fire is roaring after a few thrusts of the bellows, and the kettle hisses from a hook over the flames. Together, they drag in a large copper bathtub from the adjoining washroom. They fill two more kettles with water and suspend them over the fire, all the while Sofie chattering as she leans a chair against the door latch to assure privacy. 'Tell me about your journey that makes you smell so, and tell me about England, and the English girls, and London, and about Master Ortels' sister—and—everything. I want to know about it all. I can't describe how I've missed you. I feared you would find some English girl and I would be gone from your life forever."

She accompanies her torrent of words by undoing his outer garments. She hangs his well-worn yellow leather jerkin that had belonged to Willem Booten, and gives him a knowing nod of how he came to be wearing the vest, replacing his blood-spattered doublet. She loses not a step, however and pulls his begrimed sweat-stained linen shirt above his head. "And you will also tell me if you have any hesitancy in coming back to me. If you do I will drown you like an unwanted rodent." She unties his breeches and pulls them down, taken aback by his hardness. Jonas quickly hides his erection with his hands. She pulls off his mud-spattered hose and points to the tub. She pours the first kettle into the tub and watches Jonas' toes curl as the water is hotter than either of them expects. His flag shrivels with the shock.

"Sit," she orders and Jonas gingerly folds himself onto his haunches in the copper tub, as she adds the other kettles and sees his body relax in the hot water. She soaps his upper arms, lingers on the slightly concave shape of his left collarbone, and scrubs his torso with the soft bristled brush. She washes his hair and pours newly drawn warm water from the heating kettles.

"You must never leave me again," she whispers.

That evening they lie on her small bed, legs enfolded facing each other by candlelight, holding hands. Jonas drinks-in Sofie's beauty; she wears the tiara of silk flowers and nothing else. She beams and he is aroused. She ventures a tentative touch.

"I must talk to your father." Her frown makes Jonas rush on. "I can barely think of anything beyond holding you, giving you pleasure, and making babies."

"I like that part. But you can hold me and we can make babies without my father," she rejoins.

"We should have his blessing."

"He cares nothing for me. But you do and that makes me very happy. Forgive me if I am still afraid from that day in the wood. That brute—"

"You must always say if you do not want me to—us to—for *any* reason even *no* reason. I will abide your wishes because I want only to make you happy, not sad or angry with me." Jonas strokes her cheek and lips. He hesitates, and traces the aureoles of her breasts. *Slowly, slowly*, Jonas reminds himself. She leans into him and they kiss so naturally Jonas has a sense that they have known each other all their lives. She urges him to move quickly but he slows to a measured pace. He employs many of the small touches that he has learned at Whitehall, teasing, caressing, nuzzling and nibbling. But it is Marcus Gheeraerts' voice he hears in his thoughts, ...*lovingly, like a woman's body you are touching...slowly...make the art...come to your touch.*

Sofie, radiant, puffs with quickened breath and dabs at her sweat-moistened face. "Oh, Jonas," she utters, flushed in his arms. "I had no idea," she giggles. "So scared—since that day in the woods. You take away my fear." She snuggles and luxuriates in his grasp. He crushes her softly to him, each delighted with their lover.

Later, after fretful objections from Sofie, they agree that Jonas will ask her father's blessing for their betrothal.

The next day, Jonas sits at the worktable Frans Hogenberg had used in the engraver's alcove. He sketches human bones at multiple angles, labeling the features of the bones using Andreas Vesalius' *De humini corporus fabrica* as a reference, but working from samples delivered by the physician-author of a new compendium of skeletal studies. The wood engravings of the Flemish born Vesalius make Jonas wonder why try to improve on the extraordinary precision of his dynamic imagery.

Doctor Manoelo Brudo is an olive-skinned Sephardic born in Antwerp, the son of a New Christian, Asher Brudo. His father had adopted the name Denis Rodrigues in Portugal after renouncing his Hebrew heritage at his heresy trial in Lisbon. The elder Brudo had been burned in effigy but he had chosen baptism and Christianity rather than certain, painful death. However, he had not renounced Judaism for the Catholic precepts. He practiced his faith in secret. Antwerp provided tacit, unofficial sanctuary and the crypto-Jews survived within their community while the heresy trials in the Low Countries focused on Reformed Christians.

The forty-year-old son of Doctor Brudo presents Jonas with age-darkened pages of notes and illustrations that his father had drawn nearly half a century earlier. The discussions usually are about the subject matter of the book, but occasionally Jonas indulges his curiosity about the Inquisition in Portugal, patterned after the Seville burnings and *auto-de-fé* acts of penance. "Much misery," Brudo says. "My father had healed a member of the royal house and was fortunate to escape such persecution, but he was forced to repent his faith." Jonas is reluctant to press for more, as Brudo offers no further details.

Later, while comparing the elder Brudo's notes to the trove of bones his son has brought to the printworks, Jonas stares at nothing for several moments. He hears the haunting cries of a man claiming to be falsely accused by the Spanish Inquisition. He tries to shake the sound of the plaintive wails, by busying himself with the array of bones Brudo has amassed. "I want our readers to view these specimens from as many perspectives as you can sculpt on your plates. A quarter turn reveals how tendons attach to muscles. You see?" Brudo twists a bone to show how facets on the bone accommodate the complex soft tissue connectors.

Jonas sketches arrangements of the bones to reveal as many of these facets as possible. He is particularly taken with bones the doctor has cut into, revealing the hard honeycombed interiors within the long bones of the arms and legs. This will require more work from Jonas to adequately illustrate cross sections. But he learns, as usual, that his first perception of something bears little resemblance to what is the deeper reality. Most of the bones are not bleached white, but mottled brown, from unidentified remains unearthed by the flooding the previous month. These artifacts put him through conflicted feelings—that he is tampering unnaturally with once living people—that he is providing a service to the physicians' profession—that he is guilty of desecration of sacred relics. *Could any of these bones be my mother's or father's?* He handles the bones very carefully from then on.

Jonas meets with Doctor Brudo on several occasions in the Jewish Quarter of Antwerp to discuss his progress. The section is relatively rundown to the naked eye, less desirable and often flooded in stormy weather. He observes many of the occupants of the quarter who share few physical traits in common. Many are dark-skinned like his friend Emmanuel with Semitic features; others look nearly like his father, fair-skinned and of European stock. Religious Jews wear beards, sidelocks, and kepis. Almost all carry books on their way to their modest temples, far less ornate than houses of Christian worship. He notices furtive looks when they pass him on the street. He realizes they remind him of how he had felt walking the streets of London. Always a "stranger" a "Flemmie," not quite full-fledged as a native. When he attempts on one visit to sketch a religious Jew in the street he is shooed away. "No graven images! No idolatry!" He apologizes, hoping to learn from Doctor Brudo how he gave offense.

On his own, as he begins work in earnest, Jonas sketches and sets up groupings of articulating bones. On the morning that he arranges the neck bones for illustration, he is seized by memory of the Spanish mercenary in the wood. While fitting the cervical vertebrae together on his workbench, a deep sadness for Sofie and anger for the Spaniard intrudes. A pounding heat in his temples returns him to his rage-filled leap onto the back of the rapacious brute. "Life is God's gift. Never take another man's life," Brother Thomas had insisted. In his haste to save Sofie, he broke the commandment.

Was he justified? Brudo has explained that blood supply and nerves run through the narrow vertebral foramen of the spinal column. Jonas gains his first understanding of how he had paralyzed the mercenary to cut short the brutal act with his twisting burin.

As he carves the images of bones onto his copper, he creates a second series that he returns to in his free moments, showing his graver at various angles severing the neural sheath running through the atlas and axis vertebrae. On one of these, he adds a skeletal hand grasping the tool. He hides these in his growing collection of sketches and plates.

Recalling his plunging stroke and vengeful crunch of the bones quickens his breath. He chases the last remnants of guilt by knowing why he was victorious over the rapist. "I have avenged Sofie," he whispers.

Jonas' lovemaking with Sofie that night is especially tender, all-consuming.

Sofie's father is a forbidding man whose eyes narrow when he regards Jonas.

"How can you support my daughter? You are barely an apprentice. She has wild ideas—needs a strong hand, and look at you." The man's sneer follows his appraising look at Jonas' physique, which tilts slightly due to his shoulder injury. "You cannot control her. She needs an iron grip to keep her in harness. Why is your body so tipped to the left?" Sofie's eyes implore Jonas to soldier on.

He summons a firm voice. "I have fruitful prospects at Master de Diest's printworks. I am the chief engraver for a book that analyzes the human skeleton. I shall be illustrating every bone in the human body. My work has already begun, sir, and I am assured a journeyman's rating at the Boekprintere Scheldt. Master de Diest's son, Mark Anthony Coppens, and Master Du Brul, Sofie's warder, vouchsafe me. I am strong despite my injury as a boy, and I will take very good care—"

"And a bride price?" Jonas' eyes open wide in surprise. He has been negligent, he realizes with horror, as a smile curls on his future father-in-law's face. Jonas turns to take in Sofie, whose head is shaking "no."

Her voice echoes her nod. "No Father. That is not fair to me. I choose Jonas. He does not need to buy me from you."

Jonas watches the smile on her father's face change to dark menace. "How do you propose to honor me by assuring you will not lead my daughter into penury?"

"I am an able guildsman in the engraving craft," Jonas objects. "We will get on. You notice, sir, I do not ask for a dowry. Do we have your blessing?"

Sofie's father, unused to being challenged by a youth, sputters unintelligibly then dismisses his daughter. "Go then, you irreverent girl. Couple with this whelp, but never return to my house. Make his life miserable, as you have made mine." Her father stamps his foot as though to shoo away a miscreant.

Jonas turns to Sofie, who rushes to him, broadly smiling. "I am free, finally."

Jonas shakes his head, perplexed. "Why does he—?"

"Hate me?" She glowers at the bitter man. Then she smiles, a weight lifted from her. "Since my birth. Mother died and I survived. He has never forgiven me." Her dismissive clarity, seals Jonas' understanding that they will marry. As they take leave of her father's residence, Jonas cannot stifle his joyous laughter. "What's so funny?" Sofie asks, catching his infectious giggle.

"You make me so incredibly happy. I love you so."

Entwined in each other's arms, they walk intoxicated by their joy through the streets of Antwerp. Between shameless kisses, they plan a walk to the Benedictine monastery to arrange their nuptials. "They will be busy with the new orphans taken in after the floods," Jonas says. "But the Brother and Maria de Vries will help us."

They marry in a simple ceremony two months later with the abbot officiating, two of her siblings in attendance and Pieter Du Brul and his wife along with Mark Anthony Coppens and his wife. Doctor Brudo and his family had also requested to be present. Brother Thomas, Maria de Vries and her daughter's family, several monks, and a few of the orphans who knew and appreciated Jonas also attend the nuptials.

Sofie's father had declined. "Thank heavens," she says.

Some months later Doctor Brudo confirms that Sofie is with child.

CHAPTER 89

Palo Alto, Mid-May, 2016

Owen hears Patricia's car arrive after a day of teaching. He closes his laptop, and greets her in the dining area. She has brought in the mail and absently opens a letter, then drops the printed pages on the table with a look of annoyance. When she sees Owen, she scowls. "My damned principal, Marge Bloom, says in a memo, 'state budget cuts have ended any hope of professional development for experienced teachers in the coming year.'"

"She sent a letter?" Owen asks, thinking that's what she had been reading.

"No—something from the Dutch—something," she says dismissively, pushing the Netherlands postmarked envelope and correspondence toward him on the table. She begins to unpack her rolling book bag, and pulls out a fistful of student essays.

He scans the letter and smiles. It is formal notification from the Dutch Restitution Committee in The Hague.

"This is great news, Patricia." Owen begins paraphrasing from the letter. "With proper identification, you can claim the art—looted from your family's home in Haarlem in the time of the Nazi occupation of the Netherlands.... Process... simplified by the support of Yad Vashem researchers who confirm extermination of the van Aalt family after deportation to Westerbork and Auschwitz."

Patricia shrugs in Owen's direction.

"I don't understand, Patricia. This news affects you like it was simply another annoyance, a Marge Bloom memo." He sees her mood darkening from storm clouds to full-blown gale.

"I don't need this now, Owen. They're long dead! I'm not going to get worked up over what was taken from those poor people."

"But they were your grandparents," he says, incredulous. "If your mother were still alive—"

"I'm so busy with a damned in-service training next week, I've got recommendations due on curriculum next Thursday, the principal has her head up her behind, I've got to tally my kids' grades for Monday, and I have a parent-teacher conference with a family of knuckle-draggers," she snaps. "I don't even want to think about something that happened in the middle of the last century."

"I really don't get you, sometimes." Owen is furious. *Are you crazy? Heartless? Don't you even care?* "Patricia, listen to me," Owen tries again. "Some people have to litigate for decades with governments and museums to get back what was looted and belongs rightfully to the survivors. Often they are not successful. Now, a government agency is saying 'We know this was stolen from your grandparents. It is rightfully yours.' And you blow it off?"

Patricia waves the multiple binders at him. "I have thirty-five student papers to read and I need to make up a final exam for my classes. I can't even begin to think about a trip to the Netherlands. Who says I even want to go?"

"Patricia," Owen growls.

But her voice rises shrilly. "I'm going to get a pink slip like every other teacher in the school and not even know until August that I'm going to be rehired. How can I think about the cost of a plane ticket to Europe?"

Was that it? He snaps the letter on the table. "The district sends out pink slips every damned school year. And you're always rehired." He pauses, trying to remember the arguments she was making. "If it's really about the cost of the plane ticket—Don't worry about a damned plane ticket. We *can* afford it. Patricia. You've earned a vacation. I'll handle the travel. The letter says we can take possession of the plates looted just by going to Den Haag. A vacation," he pleads. "Extraordinary museums, and *Amsterdam*, for crying out loud, the Rijksmuseum, Van Gogh, Kröller-Müller, nearby. The Van Hals—a hundred museums and galleries. And if they get boring, windmills, cheese factories, Delft plates."

She laughs mirthlessly. "Sure. The museums would be fun," she says offhandedly. Owen hears no energy in her comment.

"Please, Patricia, I know you've got end-of-term pressure, but surely a trip to Europe afterward—" he continues to pitch her on the vacation combined with business-related arguments, trying to sound upbeat. "I want us to get over to Mainz in Germany. See if I can look at this copper plate a German dealer knows about, visit the Gutenberg Museum."

"Of course," she says with mock weariness and a circular wave of her finger. Owen hates her sarcasm. "I'm trying to make it through to the end of the school year," she says, fingers grasping the air.

"Okay, concentrate on what you need to. But I'll start looking at flights."

Patricia silently picks up the stack of papers she must grade that weekend and leaves Owen holding the letter from the Advisory Committee for Restitution.

In the days following, what remains of Owen's spontaneity with Patricia takes a backseat to making sure he doesn't ruffle her feathers. "There's a new Coen Brothers' flick in town," Owen says on Saturday. "Give yourself a break from grading and we can get sushi."

Patricia pushes her reading glasses up on her brow and waves her blue pencil at him.

"How about a drive to Half Moon Bay, hike the cliffs, dinner at the Fish Trap," he pursues.

She turns with annoyance, eyes blazing. "You're trying to make nice, but it suits your schedule, not mine," she says testily.

"Jesus," Owen complains, throwing up his hands. Patricia returns to her desk in the back bedroom to continue correcting essays. Owen tries to read a novel he is only half interested in, and his mind wanders. After the recovery of the atlas for Michael Dijkstra, Owen has fallen into the naïve belief that, magically, the wounds that her Holocaust-damaged mother inflicted on her daughter would heal. He sees that such thinking is a foolish pipedream.

But he still does not feel strong enough to speak of his concern, to suggest that both of them go into counseling together to try and find ways to mend their marriage. They continue a polite rather than passionate relationship. Goodnight kisses become passing pecks. Owen fears that, like dripping water laden with limestone, the residue of their estrangement will harden into bars to keep them completely separated emotionally.

On Sunday night, he tries to broach the subject with Patricia. "I think I would like us to go into counseling," Owen says as firmly as he can manage. The entire subject frightens him. The more entangled in his feelings of fear that his marriage is slipping down an impossible slope, the more his palms sweat, and his brow burns.

Her head is shaking slowly at first and then rapidly. "No," she says in a clipped voice, and then again. "No! Maybe after the term."

Her reply is like a barrier, rather than an invitation to discuss at another time. He stammers through a tight throat. "I'm—I'm hitting a wall with you. As much as I love you, I'm losing what being a couple used to be. We're brittle with each other, sometimes polite, not even friendly."

Patricia winces, as though she is feeling the same, but she shakes her head again drawing a line in the sand. "We can talk about this in June."

"Well, I need to talk to someone for myself," Owen says. Patricia says nothing.

On Monday, Owen makes an appointment with a licensed marriage and family counselor whom he had seen years before when he and Patricia had hit rocky shoals after their third anniversary. The first available slot is nearly a month later.

In the third week of May, Owen gets a midweek call from Michael Dijkstra.

"Hello, Mr. Spencer—" Michael begins.

"*Owen*, please, Michael. After all that we have been through, we can be less formal."

"Yes, of course," the old man says with a chuckle. "I want to discuss something with you and your wife. Do you have a moment?"

"Of course. But Patricia, I'm sure you know, is teaching at this hour."

"Yes, I wanted to sound you out before I called your wife."

Owen pushes the circular for a San Francisco print gallery opening to the side of his desk to avoid distraction.

"Dr. Bregmann has made good on his very generous offer." Owen searches his memory for what Michael could be talking about.

"Thanks to a benefactor in his community, I can afford a trip to Holland."

"I'm glad to hear that, Michael," Owen says, smiling, now remembering Bregmann's offer at the Mediterranean restaurant in Berkeley.

"More good news—the lawyers for that Harmon are settling for a lesser charge and my atlas is back in my hands," Michael reports. "I also am having the map that I removed rebound in the atlas, with Professor Bregmann's help. This book should stay intact with the family."

"Good news, indeed," Owen says, genuinely happy for the Dutchman.

"The short of why I am calling," Michael continues, "is that I intend to spend time with my sister-in-law and I wonder if Patricia would like to meet her. Gerdi has told me she would be thrilled to meet Hetty's daughter."

Owen shakes his head in wonder, thinking about synchronicity. "We were talking about a trip, part business, part pleasure, to Europe. When do you go?"

"A soon as possible. I surprise myself every day, these mornings when my eyes actually open."

Owen laughs. "Patricia's school year ends soon and then she has another week for administrative stuff, cleaning up her room, you know. Right now she's swamped with end-of-school-term stresses and is—well—resistant to a trip to Europe at the moment. I'll try and talk to her tonight. I'll call you tomorrow."

"Thank you again, Owen."

"Thank you, too." Then a thought comes to Owen. Patricia and the old man had hit it off so well ever since they had met in San Francisco. "And—and, Michael, if Patricia needs encouragement to go, may I have her speak with you?"

"Of course, any time."

Owen ends the call and looks at the array of catalogs, openings, and correspondence on his desk in the cramped garage. Then he replays his conversation in his mind and concludes that he is asking permission for Michael Dijkstra to close the deal, as it were. *She'll listen to him and not me. At least she'll trust him, if not me. What the hell! In any event, we'll get to the Netherlands.* He scratches his chin, feeling half a day's stubble sandpapering his fingers. *Is that what is so annoying to Patricia? A need to have someone else run interference for me while my agenda is really to cajole her into a trip to Europe?*

Owen tries to hold on to the elusive thought—the idea that he has difficulty being direct with Patricia, that he thinks he has to protect her from what he wants. A childhood incident flashes in his memory. He had withheld telling his mother the truth as an eight-year-old. Not because he was guilt-ridden over his theft of library books, but that he wanted to shield her from the experience of disciplining him. He stares at a portrait of Whistler's mother, tacked on the garage wall covered with gallery postcards. Was that the same dynamic with Patricia? Did he fear saying what he wanted because he needed to save her from *her* uncomfortable feelings?

Instead of trying to trace his insight, Owen becomes entranced by the possibility of meeting Michael's sister-in-law. The more he allows himself to be drawn into events seventy years earlier in Europe, the more fascinated he becomes. But he can't avoid the questions, *Will Patricia come around? Will she have as deep an interest in meeting Gerdi Dijkstra as me? Or am I alone in this?*

Utrecht, the Netherlands 2 June, 2016

"Meet me at Zocherpark," Gerhardt Schroeder says into his phone.

Less than an hour later, Dirk Berghuis shakes Schroeder's hand as he slides onto the park bench. "Good news. This Bergmann professor in Berkeley—his phone hasn't been swept for spy apps. That Ortelius atlas the Jews in Jerusalem wanted? The one that butterfingers Horst Harmon lost? "It's on its way to Holland."

"No!" Berghuis whispers in surprise.

"The old man, Michael Dijkstra, will be visiting his family to gift them with the atlas.

A smile forms on Dirk Berghuis' face. His off-centered eyes make the result chilling. "Ohhh," he effuses. "You have no idea, Gerhardt. When the government shipped my father to New Guinea for collaborating, I was raised in a home for kids like us. He was stuck at hard labor with the *koelies* and *niggers*. My mother humiliated by the neighbors for years. It was fucking hell. When my father told how he and my mother were ratted out by those Dijkstra brothers, I vowed vengeance. Will you help?"

"Heil," Schroeder says quietly, with a languid raise of his wrist, "Hitler."

CHAPTER 90

Antwerp, Boekprintere Scheldt, March 1571

Jonas adds tiny strokes to a scapula when Mark Anthony stops by his workbench with a noble dressed in black velvets. He rises and bows, perceiving aristocracy.

"Jonas—er—Johan van Braab, this is the Vicompte Maurice de Villiers. Join us in my chambers."

Jonas covers his work with a cloth and nervously follows the two men up the main staircase. Mark Anthony offers the most comfortable chair to de Villiers.

"The Vicompte is here on behalf of Willem van Oranje, "Mark Anthony says. "He is of a like mind as we—the Duke of Alva and the Council of Troubles have become a burden that the provinces must throw off."

Jonas appears neutral. Inwardly, he sees Sofie's drawn brow and fearful eyes. She would have grasped Jonas' hand and made him flee Coppens' chambers.

De Villiers' speaks Dutch with a French accent. "The prince's words beseech eloquently of all those who despise injustice and religious intolerance. His words carry the fight to the Iron Duke and his armies. King Philip has sent sadistic overseers of the Inquisition to punish anyone who strays from the Catholic iconic excess in favor of the more sober precepts—Luther, the Huguenots, John Calvin. The Iron Duke is barbaric! If you have ever seen their brutality—"

"Monsieur de Villiers," Mark Anthony interjects, "Jonas has witnessed exactly what you speak of in Amsterdam's Dam Square when the Inquisition exploded the head of an Anabaptist woman for not recanting her faith."

"Then you know. Mark Anthony assures me that you are an engraver who shares our fight."

Jonas nods solemnly. It is not how Sofie would want him to respond.

"Good. We require artists to decorate our pamphlets—your work on the hundredth penny tax—eloquent in its simplicity—you are to be commended."

Jonas' face burns with embarrassment for the praise.

"Mark Anthony has the text for a new effort which we hope will provision another strike against the Duke and his hordes. I leave you two to realize our goals."

Jonas and Mark Anthony stand as the Vicompte rises. Mark Anthony escorts the Prince's emissary downstairs. He gestures for Jonas to remain in his chamber.

Here it is, Jonas thinks. His heart is behind an effort to help. *But Sofie....*

"You look troubled," Mark Anthony says. "How can I set your mind at ease?"

"How do I assure Sofie I won't need to run for my life again?"

Mark Anthony's shoulders drop. "In times as these I would be deluding myself and you to deny the danger. We will take every precaution, use an outside printworks; several do just this sort of thing. You will not sign these plates and you can disguise your style—" He stops abruptly. "If you cannot, Jonas, after a conversation with Sofie—that will be the end to it. I can ask others—and this does not reflect on your work here, the plates for Doctor Brudo's ossium studies. But let me know tomorrow so I can pursue another engraver for the Vicompte."

Jonas anticipates a confrontation with Sofie over something that he wants very much to do. That evening, Jonas cradles Sofie's small but growing belly. "Do you wonder what kind of world this little baby will grow up in?"

"I fear for our future in the Spanish Netherlands," she replies soberly. "Just today a soldier insulted me when I was buying bread at the square."

"Must we not take steps, even small, baby-sized steps, to rid our shores of these vermin? Willem van Oranje—"

"No," Sofie cries.

"Shh," Jonas says, "I know you fear for us. But turning away when we are threatened only makes the insult worse. I think of the Prince van Oranje like I do of Brabo, cutting off the evil Antigoon's offensive hand. When our baby is born, is all that we can imagine for this child—a cowering future under the Spanish boot—?"

"Our newborn must not have a father rotting in a dungeon for sedition," she cries.

"This is not easy for me to say, I have a secret I never told you," Jonas stammers. "When I was five years old, I played a joke on Jeltje, my sister, who was told to watch me while my parents worked in a rainstorm. I tricked her, ran into a field, and then hid from her. She went—far—far into a second pasture—when the dike broke. I was safe in the cottage while the flood washed her to her death." Jonas' voice fails him. He fights through it. "I have felt responsible for her drowning and always known that I must atone for what I had done. It means I must fight for what is right. It is the only way I know I am atoning for my guilt."

Sofie looks long and hard at him and sighs, "I ask only—do you promise to keep yourself safe?"

"Yes! And more importantly—to keep you and our babies safe."

"All right, what do you and Mark Anthony Coppens have in your stew pot?"

Most of Jonas' income is derived from his commission on the book of human bones by Dr. Brudo. But he augments his means by creating plates of arachnids for a book to be published the next year by the Plantin printworks.

The assignment had come following a conversation with Abraham Ortels in which Jonas related how the cartographer's young nephew, James Cole, was entranced by butterflies. "He's a bright, enthusiastic little boy, very much loved by his parents," Jonas had reported. "Your sister's husband brought young James a handsome specimen from Turkey, with which he was quite taken. When I had to leave so hurriedly, I sketched the butterfly and gave it to him. He's a special boy."

The pride in his nephew that issued from Ortels' face seemed far more genuine than the acceptance of kudos for his cartographical achievements.

"Christophe Plantin will be publishing a study about insects, spiders and the like. Would you like to submit some drawings for his consideration?"

And like that, Jonas Hoen had entree to an interview with the publisher of the Sign of the Golden Compass.

"I hate them. They make my skin crawl," Sofie complains, covering Jonas' sample sketches of arachnid varieties with a dishtowel. After Jonas had received the commission, spider-like symbols, webs, black widows, ticks, and scorpions crept into his illustrations decrying the Spanish Occupation. Antwerp's burghers were taxed to pay for the building that housed the troops who kept the Brabant pacified. They daily saw the progress on the fortified castle, The Citadel, with moats fed by the River Scheldt to surround the pentagon-shaped walls, under construction since 1568. Impending permanence of the Spanish presence on the river is lodged in the hated structure. It would replace Het Steen as the courts and site of carrying out heretical "justice."

Mark Anthony Coppens is thrilled with Jonas' new visuals as the Dutch Revolt begins to percolate. Coppens shows Jonas a copy of a pamphlet titled *The Harangue* by close allies of Prince Willem seeking funds to continue to pursue military engagement. It uses a parable from the Old Testament to raise funds from merchants, landowning aristocracy, exiles, and Reformation churches. "Each of these groups feels the lash of extortion in paying yet another tenth penny tax on corn, meat, wine, and beer to the Spanish Crown to maintain the occupation troops," Mark Anthony declares. He points out a passage to Jonas:

> *We read that King Saul, when he would free the men of Jabez from the pagan Ammonites, hewed a yoke of oxen in pieces, and sent them as tokens over all Israel, saying, 'Ye who will not follow Saul and Samuel, with them shall ye be dealt even as with these oxen. And the fear of the Lord came upon the people, they came forth, and the men of Jabez were delivered.'*

> *Children of the Netherlands, you have here the same warning, lest God's wrath, descend upon your heads. You may say that you are banished. Tis true: You may say you have been robbed of all your goods; yet many still have something remaining. You say that you have given much already. Tis true, but the enemy is again in the field; fierce for your subjugation, sustained by the largess of his supporters. Will you be less courageous, less generous, than your foes?*

For a reprint of the pamphlet to circulate in the provinces of Brabant and Flanders, Jonas creates a copper plate showing a series of spider webs choking the cities of Antwerp, Mechelen, Ghent, Bruges, Eindhoven, and Brussels. For the last, he adds a large scorpion to symbolize the hated Duke of Alva presiding over the stadtholders' Council of Troubles, named by the Dutch the Council of Blood. The Duke created this body to coerce Dutch stadtholders to conduct his reign of terror, prosecute the Spanish Inquisition, and approve taxes to pay for the occupation. This humiliation of nobles and ordinary burghers infuriates both Catholics and Reformers. Citizenry floods France, England, and the German states to the east, in attempts to avoid the heresy courts, torture, burning, or financial ruin.

"Soon buying sausage will make us paupers," Sofie complains. "These pennies, the butcher's wife says, tally up, and force them to leave Antwerp."

Jonas nods absently, stippling the shadow of the scorpion across the web that covers the Brussels hall of prosecution where the councilors, stone-faced, meet with the Iron Duke and his lieutenants.

"You're not listening to me," Sofie says.

Jonas hears the warning in her tone, and puts down the graver. "I hear everything you say, Sofie. I know that the Butcher of Brussels forces our stadtholders to squeeze every last stuiver from our larders. Short of taking up arms and dispatching the Iron Duke, I am doing what I can to rid the land of the lice that infest it." He picks up his burin again and scrapes the excess copper from his plate.

Dissatisfied that he has signaled no more to say, Sofie turns away to hide her anger. Jonas expels a sigh. He puts down his graver and takes her in his arms. "I will try to join the engraving group working on the Polyglot Bible—the *Biblia Regia*," he scoffs. "If I can slip into the good graces of Señor Benito Montano, there are many initial capitals that need etching for the fourth book." Jonas shakes his head at the irony. "The Spanish king's bible," he mutters. "Monsieur Plantin bends his knee to the brutal Catholic Philip to keep his position in the Spanish Netherlands. But—where there is opportunity…."He trails off, envisioning the fat-lipped censorious pedant, Montano, wandering among the drying leaves of the *Biblia Polygotta*.

Sofie's body softens in his arms.

Jonas' broad smile erupts immediately. He kisses her fulsomely and immediately envisions himself gaining favor of the Spanish theologian sent to Antwerp by Philip II to oversee the polyglot bible project. By joining the group preparing the bible, he can command a few more Spanish ducats to ease Sofie's fears *and* glimpse the passage in the original Hebrew quoted in the money-raising pamphlet by Prince Willem's supporters. He sketches King Saul ordering a yoke of oxen butchered, and portions sent throughout the Holy Land to terrify wavering believers against betraying the Lord for the pagan worship of the Ammonite gods.

"Beef. We must have a good cut of beef tomorrow night," Jonas announces. "And tell the butcher's wife she will not have to pay the tax too much longer."

Sofie giggles at her brash husband.

"Besides, do you not need your strength since you are eating for two? Yes. Red beef."

CHAPTER 91

Palo Alto, May 25th 2016

Owen checks several airline travel sites to compare prices, as he has done for a week, and sees the best one yet. He selects a late-June departure, and, while the online calculations are being computed, he calls Michael Dijkstra in Walnut Creek, who agrees that that date would be a good option.

While printing the confirmation of itinerary, he realizes the flight is a day before his first scheduled counseling appointment. A moment later the concern that Patricia would not welcome his news flies through his mind. But they are closing in on the completion of her stressful end of class year, and so he hopes she will be receptive. He pushes away thoughts that she might not fulfill his hopes.

Later, in his office, he becomes preoccupied with a client's request to locate Hiroshige woodblock prints from the *Fifty-Three Stations of Tokaido* editions. He burrows into his laptop in an online eBay bidding exercise, and completely forgets to share the news of the airline ticket purchase during dinner. Later that evening, after Patricia has gone to the back bedroom to correct final papers, Owen realizes he has not told her about the flight he has booked. He gathers the itinerary from his printer, takes a deep breath, and comes back into the house. He wonders if the crunch under his shoes are eggshells.

"I did it, Patricia," Owen says lightly. He holds up the printed itinerary. "KLM, to Amsterdam, direct. Shortest time available, eleven hours—non-stop."

Patricia does not take the printed itinerary. She looks at Owen, eyes blank.

"Decent price, late-next month. School's over. Europe!"

"I don't think so," she says, gripping the sheaf of papers she is marking up at her desk in the spare bedroom. "And I don't like this kind of—of end-around the kids call it on the football field. When you figure out how to ask for what you want, we can talk. Right now I'm kind of busy?" She riffles the schoolwork at him and slaps the papers on the desk.

He closes his eyes to fight the fire that is kindling. "Patty, I said I would take care of the tickets." He tries to keep his voice nonchalant.

She slams the desktop with her fist. "No. Refund those tickets, or at least mine! You can go if you want to," she snaps. "Make your damn connections with your print dealers—but not me. I don't want to be anywhere near Amsterdam."

Damn. Why do you make this so difficult? Simmering anger rises. He breathes deeply to keep calm. "Patty. You need to see this thing through. The Dutch government has some property that is rightfully—They've gone to—"

"I don't care about whatever trouble somebody has gone to," she retorts. "I don't want to pick over old bones of people I never knew. Why can't you understand that?"

Owen's face reddens. "It's like you are stuck in some—some goddamned pity pot." She is about to reply, but Owen's words roll over her. "You have really shut me out of your grief, like—like it's none of my business. Well it is my business." Owen's throat feels strangled. He thumps the desktop, angry enough to hit something. He sees fear in Patricia's eyes, but he needs to say his piece. "You can take as long as you need to mourn your mother, but I'm feeling buried under your grief, too. Since your mother died, I feel like she's moved in with us." His words hiss like white heat. "You've taken on all of her fears and they are like the elephant in the room."

Patricia's face contorts as if struck. "That's a little brutal, Owen."

"It terrifies me to confront you like this, Patty, because I keep showing up as the enemy." His voice chokes with tears and pleading. "I may blunder and be imperfect but I swear, since Hetty died, you have taken on all of her terrors, and I feel like I have to shut up all the time to avoid setting you off."

"Just because I don't want to go to Holland?" Her voice quavers.

"That's right." Owen gathers strength. "Exactly right. When we went there—what ten, a dozen years ago—it was you and I, not your mother, too, and we had a great time. You throw it at my feet that I'm only interested in doing business. That's not true. You're blowing smoke to hide your terror of going where your mother had such an awful time. It's not seventy years ago. Its now."

Patricia turns away from him. "You have no idea. You can't even begin to know what goes on for me."

He leans on the edge of her desk with both hands and pleads, "Tell me, Patty. Please." He presses the desk edge until his knuckles whiten. "If you shut me out—shut me out because—it's so scary for you—we're stuck in the same loop. Please, let me know what's going on for you. I promise I won't try and fix it. I want to be here for you. But if you push me away and push me away, how can I? Please, Patty. I'm begging you to let me be here. Your mother doesn't have to like me. I doubt if she ever did. But I married you, not her."

"She doesn't trust you." Her voice rasps like a file scraping steel.

"Patty, she's dead," Owen whispers. A terror grips him. "And I hear you speaking like she's in the room with us."

"I mean she didn't—that's the word, *trust* you. She said you would abandon me, get lost in your world." Owen winces at her words. *She was poisoning the woman I love.* "Go to cocktail parties with rich women and powerful men, 'plutocrats,' she said. 'Leave me by the side of the road.' That's what she thought."

His mother-in-law's face, disapproval evident, flashes. He speaks in measured tones, "Is that what you think?" She is silent. "Patty. Is that really what *you* think?"

"No."

"Damn right, *no.*" Owen snatches the answer sheets Patricia has been correcting and lays them on her desk. He draws up a chair and takes both of her hands in his. He locks his eyes on hers and every time she tries to look away he squeezes her hands to bring her back. "I swear I will never abandon you. I will never put any person before you. I'm in it for the full ride, wherever it takes us."

She is nodding through a mournful moan. "I am so scared of going back there. I know it's not reasonable, like it was me, not my mother. Me."

"I'm right here," says Owen in a steady voice. "I don't want to lose you, Patty."

Patricia's cries are like a young girl's keening. He kneels to one knee, holds her close, and sees his shirt dampening where her tears fall. His heart feels full as she sobs. He strokes her hair, damp with perspiration, and kisses her salty eyes. He holds her until she eases and then he gently takes her hand.

"You promise nothing will hurt me if I go?" Patricia asks.

"I'll make it as safe as I can," he whispers. *Be resolute* "I'll be there with you every inch of the way." He squeezes her hand again.

"There are terrible people, like that Harmon and his gorilla. Awful people."

"Yes, there are." *Be resolute for her, Owen.* "But I'm here and will be with you."

She dabs at her eyes with a tissue. "I'm a mess," she half-laughs....

"You're nothing of the sort," he reassures.

"Okay. I'll go, but you stay close." She shudders back another bout of tears.

"You're my girl. I'll keep you safe." Owen cups her face between his hands. Patricia looks into Owen's eyes with a trust he has not felt from her for a long time. He expels an involuntary whoosh of breath. Wisps of her hair blow in his breeze and his lips brush hers. He holds her hand until she releases his fingers, smiling shyly. Then her face darkens again. "I'm still really scared," she whispers.

"I know," he says.

CHAPTER 92

Jonas and Sofie's Hoogstraat Apartment, September 1571

After dinner, Jonas draws random lines on a sheet of paper while Sofie rocks their daughter to sleep. Thinking back to the journey from London to Harwich. He writes on another sheet:

My dear friend, Emmanuel,

With hopes that this finds you well, and your family prospers—

I have intended to write often but beg forgiveness for being consumed by so much here in Antwerp. Sofie and I married December last and the fruit of our union is a little girl. Our daughter is Liesbeth, so-called to honor Mrs. Coels, wife to our silk merchant benefactor when we were both resident in London. Mrs. Coels is also the sister of Abraham Ortels, my patron here in Antwerp. I regard you, too, Emmanuel, as a pathfinder along life's way and treasure the memory of our brief adventure and return to our homeland, troubled though it is. I merely want to mark that it has been, and always will be, a great comfort to know you. I wish you good harvests, farmer.

Yours in friendship, Jonas Hoen

He returns to his sheet of scribbles and begins adding lines and squiggles. Soon it is a sketch of two boys sitting on the seat of a wagon laughing as a sleeting snow rains down on them and the rumps of two horses in the foreground.

A month and a half later, he receives Emmanuel's reply.

We are exhausted bringing in the crops, but want to respond to your letter before time slips away. I enjoyed our escape from London together and the passage on the Tortelduif—well, not so much the rolling ocean. The union with your Sofie heartens me. I too, have married and hope you will someday meet Rachel. We have a child, a little boy, and another on the way, too who, G-d willing, will join us to till this land with our family. All about us, hopes abound of lifting the yoke that presses. Last year the Vater Guezen raised our expectations that the Spanish boot will be pinching the wearers. We think all of Groningen will be united with the Prince van Oranje soon.

Your picture of two young men huddled against the English weather brings me joy. Rachel can barely wait to meet you.

In friendship and hope that you can find your way to our barley fields,

Emmanuel

Hoogstraat Apartment, Antwerp, November 1571

Jonas comes home wielding a rolled up proof sheet of the map titled *Germany Inferior*. He chucks his toddler, Liesbeth, atop her head as she whimpers at Sofie's feet in their kitchen of their Hoogstraat rooms. The child giggles and Jonas wraps Sofie's torso in his arms and nibbles behind her ear. "I like your neck, like a swan's."

"We swans may look pretty, but we are mean tempered, as you know," she hisses, swinging the ladle in a wide arc.

Jonas ducks, then uses his rolled up map in a mock duel. "Look, the new edition is in Dutch," Jonas announces, unfurling it so Sofie can read the descriptive text on the verso. "Not Latin, like the first two editions—the commentaries on every map, rewritten for us. Master Ortels...." Jonas shakes his head slowly and speaks the cartographer-scholar's name with wonder and respect.

"He has always terrified me," Sofie says. "Even when he was so helpful to arrange our farewell when you fled to London."

"And me. Fearful that I would displease him," Jonas owns. "But if I shine, I owe it to the sun that man radiates—And you, of course, my hissing swan."

She locks him in a viselike hug and kisses his mouth until Liesbeth at their feet wails for the lovers' attention.

In the late afternoon, a week later, the printworks' large format press stops. While Jonas is at work on an illustration of foot bones for Doctor Brudo's book, a grim Mark Anthony enters the engraver's area with the copper plate of *Typus Orbis Terrarvm*, his finger on the sea monster Jonas had created the previous year.

"The plate has cracked where you made the fix last May. We need only eleven more usable imprints to make for the Dutch language run."

Frowning, Jonas holds up the plate to see the fracture where the copper is thinnest. He worried that the metal would crack after the many impressions the plate would undergo when he originally melted the section following the sabotage. The paper sheet of the reduced Mercator projection shows a jagged smear of ink where the copper had failed.

Unlike the frantic first edition repair, Jonas takes calm charge of the rework. He asks Mark Anthony if he would like a full-masted sailing ship similar to the first decoration. "I can do up a beautiful galleon or man o'war," Jonas says, half in jest.

Mark Anthony smiles through his upset. "One sea monster, exactly as in the Latin editions to get us through this Dutch run of two hundred and seventy-five."

"I need you to send someone to Hoogstraat, to tell Sofie 'do not wait up'— if you want this on the press tomorrow morning. Six or seven hours at the minimum."

"Good man. I'll send an apprentice to tell her of your emergency mission."

Flashes of the fraught moments the previous year play in his mind. *Oh, I would so like to improve my effort on this copper plate.* But he tamps down his drive for perfection to deliver a reasonable facsimile. He must get the furnace up to heat, enough to melt copper. After he reignites the flame, Jonas returns to his worktable and measures the rectangle he will need to remove from the fractured plate. He locates the small drill, narrowly tapered fine tooth saw, and a cache of copper shavings. He fashions a mask out of pasteboard to cover the entirety of the map face and assure he does not nick any of the copper. With deliberate turns of the drill, he incises four holes. Using a steel straightedge as a guide, he saws out the piece of ocean with the water-spewing sea monster; a "dragon" he recalls Ortels naming it. He clears all burs and cuts a rectangle slightly smaller than the segment he has laboriously removed. He returns to the furnace room and tests the tip of the hot poker on a piece of scrap copper. With the map side face down on the oak table, he sets the replacement rectangle into the plate, presses burred copper shavings into the seams, and breathes a sigh of relief as if to say "So far, so good." Hands wrapped in chamois, he runs the tip of the short poker over the seams and feels the blistering copper fusing the bits together. Beads of perspiration drip onto his work. He turns over the plate and masks the entire engraved map except for the new rectangle and an eighth of an inch bordering the new piece. He repeats the cauterization of the copper on the back, splashes water on his work and touches a successful fusing.

He returns to the engraver's area to duplicate the section down to the hundreds of stipple marks, and the form and detail of the lizard-like leviathan. He engraves at the table used by the estimable master, Frans Hogenberg. He looks up at where he used to sit with his back to the warden, learning the rudiments of his craft mostly on his own. In his exhaustion in the predawn hours, he thinks *Who am I. I must work here under an assumed name—Johann van Braab—A nobody, a fiction.* His mood turns dark.

At one o'clock in the morning, his worktable ringed by candles, he adds the slash marks that suggest the edge of the shell that tethers the beast. In a jolt of rebellion, he turns the plate, not from the vantage a viewer might study the map but from an upside-down position. He adds minuscule strokes so that his name—*my real name*—is discernible across the slash marks if someone searches with unusual attention—in the required reverse order; they read first S-A-N-O-J, then N-E-O-H.

Eleven imprints of this map in the first Dutch edition of *Theatrum Orbis Terrarum* will bear the name of the engraver of the Mar Di Indi leviathan.

Almost all of the Dutch language Ortelius book of maps sell out quickly.

Early in 1572 the Dutch Revolt receives a devastating blow, the expulsion of the Vater Guezen from English ports by Elizabeth I. But on 1 April, the Dutch privateers, seeking ports to berth their 25 warships, invade the lightly defended city of Den Briel, near Rotterdam, and repel Spanish attempts to retake it. Budding national pride sweeps the Dutch and Flemish populace, the Hoens included.

A few months later, the elderly Gilles Coppens de Diest takes his last breath at his cluttered desk and succumbs to a massive heart attack after months of ill health. His harried son, Mark Anthony, takes on the full job of running the printing house. He pulls back from his activities that support the revolt.

As the completion of The Citadel looms at the eastern edge of the city, Jonas creates an illustration for an engraving that imposes a six-legged tick over the five guard towers. He titles his work *Bloedzuigende Tick—Citadel van Antwerpen (Bloodsucking tick—the Antwerp Citadel)*. But Mark Anthony dissuades Jonas from publishing it, as the authorities would descend on all the local printing houses.

Meanwhile, emboldened by the belief that the tide is turning against the Spanish occupation, Willem van Oranje raises an army of German mercenaries to assist the French in casting off the shackles imposed by the France-Spain alliance. The Flemish, the Dutch in revolt, Willem the Silent, and, especially the Hoens, are to discover such optimism is unfounded.

CHAPTER 93

KLM flight to Amsterdam, Late June 2016

Patricia stretches her cramped body and raises the window shade. She looks across at Owen still asleep in the aisle seat. Across the aisle, Michael Dijkstra's head is pressed against the glass looking out over the Dutch countryside, becoming visible as the jet reduces altitude. Patricia nervously gnaws a hangnail. She tries to breathe deeply as the other passengers stir and the captain's voice announces that they will land in half an hour.

Owen stirs awake and extends and presses his hand on Patricia's. She brushes his rough cheek and scratches his five o'clock shadow. Across the aisle, Michael waves at her with a deep, contented smile on his face. *He is coming home*, Patricia thinks. *I am stepping into an abyss. Can I handle this?*

Aleida Dijkstra-Heershop, Gerdi's eldest daughter, collects Michael, Owen and Patricia from their transcontinental flight and bundles them and their bags into her gray Peugeot sedan after they have cleared customs.

Michael is astounded his niece's resemblance to his mother, Marthe, the last time he saw her alive, in 1940. Dress and hair styles, of course, are different, but Aleida's eyes recall Marthe's. The kind acceptance for Michael ends there, however.

Aleida is trying hard to sound cheerful and welcoming, but Michael also hears implied resentment that must have filtered through her upbringing regarding the brother who was rarely spoken of, never communicated with, and who had weighed on her parents as a mystery no one could explain.

"I'm happy to finally meet you, Uncle," she says unconvincingly as they speed toward Amsterdam. Even her voice has touches of his mother's timbre in Michael's memory.

"And me, you," Michael replies, glancing at Aleida's profile as she drives toward the city. "I'm afraid I missed seeing you back when I last visited in the '90s."

"You had a big row with them, didn't you?"

Michael tugs at his collar, unhappy with the memory and turns to Owen and Patricia in the back seat. "Aleida is talking of that big falling out I told you about, Owen, when I first met you." Having delivered the background to his American friends, he falls silent.

Aleida picks up the ball, however, and tosses it to Patricia.

"My mother is so excited that she can have a visit with you, Mrs. Spencer."

Michael is grateful the focus has switched to Patricia. Despite several phone calls with Gerdi, his abiding guilt over how he had acted toward Gerdi through the years is far from dissipated.

He hears Patricia's tension in her voice. "Yes, me too."

In that moment, Michael wonders for the first time if it is such a good idea for him to have arranged for Patricia to meet Gerdi. But his sister-in-law, with full energy in her voice, had insisted that if at all possible, Michael must present the invitation. Grateful to have been welcomed back, Michael would have made every attempt to satisfy Gerdi's wishes. A plan is set in motion for Patricia and Owen to be dropped at their hotel in Amsterdam. They will sightsee, rent a car, conduct some business in the city of Den Haag, and go to Soest, Gerdi's assisted living residence. Michael had not persisted in asking about "the business" earlier on the flight when he perceived that Patricia shut down the topic.

The city buzzes with tourists as Aleida drives Patricia and Owen to their hotel near Dam Square. Patricia and Aleida, both educators and similar ages, have a spirited conversation once she turns her attention from her awkward attempts of speaking with Michael. Aleida is a director of a school for students with special needs in Haarlem. In their chat about that city, Patricia reveals that her mother had been born there. Outside their hotel, Michael tells the Spencers he will call them later that day and they gratefully acknowledge Aleida's lift from the airport.

CHAPTER 94

Amsterdam, En Route to Soest, 27 June, 2016

Aleida's charming demeanor, on display for the American visitors, evaporates. She and Michael are silent in the car, on their way out of the city center, dodging tramcars for the trip east to Soest. The quietness in the car is oppressive.

Michael clears his throat to break the roar of the charged silence. "I am sorry to put you out like this, but that is how your mother insisted we come in to town. We could have taken public transport."

"Uncle," Aleida says sharply, casting a sidelong glance at him.

Michael steels himself for recrimination.

"I can't begin to tell you how depressed you made my father." Her voice is pitched the same as his mother's had been when she was fuming. "And I assure you that if you upset my mother in any way, I will drive you right back to the airport."

Michael nods. "I have a lot to atone for, Aleida. I am here begging forgiveness." He closes his eyes, miserable to put into words these truths.

By the gears grinding as she pulls the Peugeot onto the motorway, Michael doubts if she believes him. Still, they are bound for the town of Soest, and Gerdi.

"Can we at least be civil?" Michael asks. "I have learned so much in the last two months about what is important and what isn't. This couple we dropped off, the Spencers—Owen, shows up trying to learn about a map—you will see later the map I mean. And this leads me to meet his wife who is alive today because your mother saved a Jewish girl in the bad times, who became the mother of the print dealer's wife."

Michael sees his niece is listening, but focused on the road. "You look so much like our mother, Aleida. I don't mean to embarrass you, but Pim and I had the most beautiful mother. And you have her face. I'm sure Pim must have said something when you were growing up."

"Stop buttering me up," she demands.

Michael chokes back his impulse to defend himself, and clamps his mouth shut. Finally, Michael hears the scowling woman speaking in a quiet voice, thick with memory. "He used to tease me in my last years at university. He would hold up a snapshot of your mother from the twenties, sometimes, and say, 'Look Aleida, you are back from the grave to torment me for having been such a bad kid.'"

Michael laughs, imagining his brother saying such a thing, typical of his take-no-prisoners sense of humor. "He *was* a bad kid. And I got blamed a lot for stuff he did because I was such a—what everybody calls today a *nerd*." Michael realizes he is chuckling. "We had a good time back then. And then the war...." He trails off remembering how he learned of his mother's death in the Rotterdam bombing. He broods with the familiar sense of loss that has swept over him like a shroud since he was fifteen. The numbed feeling persisted, until he tried to auction the Ortelius map of the world.

"Aleida," Michael begins. An unexpected steel band tightens and makes his words catch. He is remembering his brother's broad, irrepressible smile. "I hope you—you had a good time growing up with your father and mother. I would have a hard time believing you hadn't."

Michael sees her shrug, and then smile briefly, thinking of something that confirmed his suspicion. It is the first time she has smiled since she dropped the Spencers at their hotel. Then her face becomes hard and drawn. "The worst was when he died. You probably never smoked, did you?"

"No," Michael acknowledges. "Was that it? What killed him?"

"Emphysema." Michael hears her struggle to say her words. "Big and strong his whole life. Until the last five years; a slow decline, then complications with lung cancer, tuberculosis."

"He took it up after. He never smoked in Eindhoven." Michael's mind plays a clip of his brother, racing downfield to receive a pass, dribble, and hook it like magic for a goal against the Rotterdam Feyenoord. "He was a fine athlete. You know, Pim met your mother at an Ajax match in Amsterdam."

"I know," she laughs. "My brother Herman was always so upset when he would show the Eindhoven colors at Ajax matches."

Michael laughs softly, and then goes silent again. He is enjoying himself listening to his niece. "This may sound like a stuck record, Aleida, but I apologize again for my absence, for shunning my family, for not sharing even a piece of my life with you when I went into a kind of self-imposed exile."

"My mother says—again and again: 'we can't change the past, only the here and now.' But I don't forgive so easily." Aleida casts a swiping glance at Michael. He struggles not to fall into depression under her continuing attack. The windscreen reflects the sun in her eyes as she drives east, and she tilts the visor to avoid the glare. Michael decides to endure the glare as a show of penance.

Michael sees a road sign noting ten kilometers to Soest.

"Is your mother in good health? She seems vigorous on the telephone. I hope it is not an act."

"She genuinely looks forward to seeing you in person. As for her health, her mind is sharper than mine. But I can out-walk her if I put effort into it. For ninety-two years, she is amazing. I think she had to call in some old favors to even get into this residence complex. She really requires very little assistance. But they have a lift there to visit friends and she doesn't need to climb three stories to open her front door. Still, she misses the energy of Amsterdam. I think that is why she wants to see the American, Patricia, so she can give her a tour."

Michael nods, but adds nothing. He knows from Gerdi's phone conversations that her interest in Hetty's child goes much deeper than serving as a tour guide.

"It isn't so often," says Michael, with newfound understanding, "that an old person can glimpse how an act in their youth can have such a resonance. Your mother's courage in the Anonymous Group, for example."

If Aleida understands his meaning, she does not acknowledge it.

As they draw close to the turnoff, Aleida speed-dials her cellphone and speaks to her mother. She looks at Michael's pensive face. He hears her say, "Yes, he does remind me of Daddy." Unexpected warmth rolls over Michael.

She clicks off. "I will take you to your hotel. It is a short walk. When you are rested, mother wants you to come over." Her tone is abrupt as the reserve has crept back. She does not offer her hand to Michael as he collects his luggage. He is disappointed. *Still, she didn't kick me out of the car and strand me on the side of the road. I hope we can be friends, at least.* A nagging voice tells him he deserves her rancor. He is guilt-stricken, now knowing how his brother had suffered through respiratory disease.

As he rolls his suitcase and carries the atlas in a canvas shoulder bag into the hotel on Birkstraat, he takes no notice of the black Audi parked across the street. Michael checks in. The desk has a message from the Spencers saying they had rented a car and might drive down to Den Haag, but that they expected to be back later that afternoon.

The trans-Atlantic fight and emotional ride to Soest with Aleida leaves Michael exhausted.

He asks the desk for a two-hour wake-up and collapses in the bed for a nap. The starched cleanliness of the hotel sheets lulls him quickly to sleep.

CHAPTER 95

Benedictine Monastery Near Antwerp, 23 September 1572

The familiar voice peals like a mournful church bell in Jonas' ears. *Por què estàs aqui?* Oh, how his head aches. He cannot open his eyes but explosions of light burst behind his eyelids. He hears the same voice that bedevils his nightmares. *I am Eduardo Orellano, and I am Christian as God is my witness.* But his was only one of the voices. A woman's cry—his mother's—implores, *Go home, Jonas! Listen to your mother. Go Back!* The nagging voice of his sister, Jeltje, long dead, cries. *We don't need you here!* She wails. *You can see—we have no room here for you.* The gruff voice of his father, rippling through water, demands. *Go home. It is not your time yet!* And then again in Spanish, an old woman's voice: *Ve a casa. Escucho al tu abuela. Regresa.* And his sister again, *If you die, who will remember me?* In that moment he sees every facial feature of his sister, Jeltje, when she was eight years old.

"Don't die! Oh, sweet Jonas, please don't die!" Sofie pleads, heard as though she were speaking through skeins of sheep's wool. Jonas struggles to open his eyes. Only his right eye parts wide enough to let in light.

Early that Saturday morning, Jonas, with one-year-old Liesbeth on his shoulders and Sofie, two months pregnant with their second child, have set out on the Mechelen Road to walk the two leagues to Brother Thomas' monastery. They will celebrate their first year of marriage with the man who had saved Jonas from floodwaters when he was eleven, and again at sixteen, hunted by Spanish troops.

But now, all of Flanders and the Brabant are unsafe as the Duke of Alva's armies drive the horsemen and foot soldiers of Willem van Oranje, into full flight. Willem's retreating German mercenaries and Walloon partisans race east toward the German duchies to escape the Spanish onslaught. In their retreat, the hired armies abandon once-captured cities and towns in France, Flanders and the Brabant. Meanwhile, ravening Spanish troops, unpaid for months, ransack and loot anything of value from the hapless burghers, no longer protected by the Oranje armies. These wanton massacres, looting, and rapes are called the "Spanish furies," all sanctioned by Don Federico, son of the Duke of Alva.

The frustrated fighters for Prince Willem van Oranje are also eager to turn anything they can steal into coin since their wages, too, have not been paid. Many of these soldiers, recruited in the German provinces, are rabid reformers, ready to shed Catholic blood and loot iconography which, they insist, debase sober Christianity.

Maria de Vries is chucking baby Liesbeth under the chin when Brother Aristide, robes flying, bursts into the cook shed. *"Soldats, mercenieres Alamands!"*

Brother Thomas springs from the bench at the table and races outside, followed by Jonas. Breastplate-clad mercenaries in Willem van Oranje's colors, half a dozen with arquebus firearms, cross the field driving two of the elderly monks and several of the orphans before them. The soldiers push the too slow Brothers to the ground and continue across the courtyard toward the monastery chapel.

Jonas runs back to the cook shed and shouts for Maria to bar the door. Then he follows Brother Thomas, who is trying to intercept the lead German mercenary.

The soldier runs past him and four more follow into the chapel. Brother Thomas shouts for them to stop but they disappear into the church. He attempts to enter. But a soldier carrying a jeweled chalice roughly thrusts him back out. The wooden statue of Saint Benedict, carved over a century before, is heaved onto the ground outside. Two of the soldiers emerge from the library, and throw several illuminated manuscripts, one of which Jonas had helped illustrate, atop the statue. They use burning tapers to ignite the old books.

Brother Thomas shouts, "No, you must not," and tries to wrest a taper from a soldier. A second soldier cocks the igniter lock on his weapon. As he is about to fire, Jonas launches himself at the arquebus to upset its aim. He grasps the barrel the moment it fires with a deafening roar. The ball misses Brother Thomas and buries itself in the earthen brick of the chapel exterior. The furious soldier swings the brass-studded stock against the side of Jonas' head. He collapses in raging pain.

"Don't die! Oh, sweet Jonas, please don't die!" He can hear Sofie's cries only through his right ear. His left hisses unrelenting, blood pounding in his temple. He smells acrid smoke from a fire. But words will not form in his mouth. Through his right eye he sees Sofie's distraught face. Now he is jostled and in the arms of Brother Thomas who carries him indoors. He can feel the planks of the kitchen worktable under him. A hand cradles his throbbing head. Through his right eye he sees Maria de Vries pass tiny Liesbeth to Sofie.

Sofie is crying for Jonas not to die when Maria takes charge. "Sofie, put peat on the fire. Then go outside and fetch me several leaves of the comfrey plant, the one with pink flowers. Bring a handful. Quickly, girl!"

He feels the sting of cold water on the pounding left side of his face and skull. He hears Brother Thomas repeating again and again. "He saved my life, Maria. You tend him, well."

"Brother, the salve on the shelf, please," Maria says quietly as she daubs at his battered head with cheesecloth and ointments. He smells peppermint and lavender. Maria repeatedly presses and coaxes his injured flesh to recuperate. "Oh this will do the deed. Yes, we'll slow the bleeding. This will stop it and—Brother Thomas, please press his cheek together, while I make a plaster. You will be right and bright as sunshine, Jonas, don't you worry."

Somewhere in the room, Liesbeth begins crying. Jonas tries to raise himself.

"No, no, no," Maria insists, forcing him back down. "You must lie still. Ah, good, Sofie. Give me four of the biggest leaves and we will make a bandage of them."

Liesbeth cries turn to whimpers. Maria's efficient skills are working. The raging fire on the left side of his face now feels cooler.

"Sofie!" Jonas cries, able to speak at last. "Are you and Liesbeth safe?"

"Yes, yes," comes her reassuring voice, and Jonas might have smiled if the pain had been less on his left cheek and brow. He feels the tiny fingers of his daughter tickling the right side of his face, and he smiles a crooked grin.

Jonas reaches for Sofie and she clutches his right hand and kisses it.

"Aghhh," he cries.

Maria opens his fingers to see the raw burn and char on his palm where Jonas had grabbed the arquebus barrel as it fired. "We'll have that feeling right in no time. Brother Thomas, that salve again, please."

Jonas feels the ointment of comfrey root applied as gently as Maria can to his damaged palm.

"Brother Thomas?" He asks in trepidation.

A big reassuring hand unfolds on his chest. The monk's voice is strong and resolute. "You saved me, Jonas. You are hurt because you saved my life."

"Good. We have saved each other," Jonas says with relief.

"God's work," Brother Thomas says softly.

Jonas emits a rueful grunt. But then he softens. "Are they gone? Did they destroy everything?" Jonas asks.

"Only the trappings. They left. We are all alive and we carry on."

Jonas feels his head swaddled in the comfrey leaves, and wrapped in gauze. The odor is foul. "Maria. This smells terrible."

"We will cook the leaves a bit in water and it won't be quite so bad when we change the poultice."

Jonas is captured by exhaustion. He exhales fully for the first time since he had been battered. On his intake of breath, he sinks into a reverie and recalls the cacophony of voices moments after the blow was struck. The voice from his inner hell—Eduardo Orellano—that one, he recognizes immediately. But the others—his mother, father, and sister—never before have they emerged from their watery graves to address him. And the grandmotherly voice in Spanish—was that for him, too?

"They told me to stay alive." Jonas tries shifting to find Sofie. Through his right eye he can see her rocking Liesbeth and nibbling her lip to keep her composure. "My mother, my father, my sister—they told me they had no room for me where they were. They told me to go back. My sister was beautiful."

His words exhaust him. He sinks into a helpless, discomforted doze. Unspoken, he ruminates, *How will I provide for my family?*

CHAPTER 96

En Route to Den Haag, 27 June 2016

Aside from driving a manual shift car in a foreign country with unfamiliar road signage and conventions, Owen's anxiety is heightened by Patricia's edginess in the passenger seat. "Careful," she says in a clipped tone as they turn off the A44 onto to the Scheveningen-Den Haag exit ramp and circle a roundabout, looking for the right road. Her underlying current of tension crackles since they had arrived at the hotel desk too early for check-in. Owen proposed that they get their business in Den Haag done and return to their hotel room later.

"I just don't feel quite ready for this," Patricia complains, when Owen suggests they take care of what they came to the Netherlands for, reclaiming the looted art. "It feels like sifting through old bones in a cemetery."

"Okay, sure. No rush," Owen replies, masking his disappointment. "But since we're too early for our room, let's head over to the Rijksmuseum, or get a bite."

"Well, maybe, just to get it over with," she waffles, scanning the hotel lobby. "A ride down to the coast might be fun." Owen hears the agitation in her tone.

"Patricia. We can take this as slow as you want. I can hear your anxiety."

"I'm not anxious," she says, too quickly.

"Good," Owen says in a soothing voice.

"I *am* anxious," she admits wearily.

"Of course, who wouldn't be?"

"Owen, stop treating me like an identified patient."

He stifles an angry rejoinder. *Oh, dear God, let me not say the wrong thing.*

"Go ahead, book a car. The man at the desk can connect us to the—'whatever it's called.'" She fishes in her purse for the letter with phone information, and shows it to the desk clerk while Owen goes to the concierge's kiosk to request a rental car.

The tension in their Opel does not abate as they struggle to find their way out of Amsterdam and onto the A10. Owen tries to familiarize himself driving in kilometers instead of miles per hour to stay within the speed limits as they motor over the unfamiliar roadways. Patricia sits tight-lipped through the journey.

Owen parks the sedan, and asks a policeman if he is in a legal space. For one hour, only, he is advised, and he and Patricia walk up the stairs into the orange brick building, housing the secretariat of the Advisory Committee on the Assessment of Restitution Applications for Cultural Value and the Second World War.

"Mouthful, huh? You okay?" The tightness in Patricia's jaw is evident to him.

She cracks a smile that leaves her face as quickly as it has formed.

"If you need time here to powder your nose or anything, I'm with you, Patty."

A smiling administrative assistant brings them coffees in Delft cups in a waiting area ringed with minuscule oil paintings dating from the 17th and 18th Centuries. The plaster scrollwork and marble floors suggest they are in a museum.

"Wouldn't this be a nice anteroom to Principal Bloom's inner sanctum?" Owen asks, trying to keep the mood light.

The door to an office up the corridor opens and an official in a black woolen suit, who nervously introduces himself with a name that ends with "boom," shakes hands with them. He asks for Patricia's passport and returns to his office. Owen shrugs and smiles. Patricia acknowledges him with a quizzical raise of the eyebrows.

"Michael's niece seems really hospitable," Owen says, striving to maintain a conversational tone.

"Yes, to us," Patricia says, "But did you notice she said nothing at all to Michael the whole time driving into town. I think there's bad blood there."

"They do give the passport back, don't they?" Patricia asks, half in jest.

"It's like, 'Papers, please,'" Owen whispers, affecting an old movie line, complete with European accent. The joke falls flat as first Patricia and then Owen remind themselves where they are and why they are there. Seventy years earlier this building was run by Dutch Nazis, whose strings were controlled in Berlin.

"Not so funny," Patricia comments.

"Not funny at all," Owen agrees.

They sip their coffees. Owen makes a nervous tour of the room's mostly workman-like oils of farm scenes, windmills, sluice gates, and bridges. He watches Patricia's eyes close as though she were in a yoga class concentrating on breathing. Then Owen's left upper eyelid quivers imperceptibly. It is his nervous tic, a rare occurrence, but one that told him to pay extra special attention. Patricia has now stood up pausing before a few scenes showing townscapes with rising church spires.

In this moment, Owen feels very alone. Patricia stares with unseeing eyes at a 200-year-old oil paint landscape. Owen moves over to her and puts his hand lightly on her shoulder and squeezes. She grins with a smile he had not seen in months.

"I was thinking of Esperanza Reyes. She once drew a picture from a photograph her parents had of their village church. Now why did I think of her?"

Owen presses her shoulder again. "Let's hope she's having a good summer vacation." He checks the time and sees that they have only 15 minutes left in the parking space. At that moment, the official, beaming broadly, opens the door to his office and beckons them in. Owen reads the door's nameplate: Jet Leuwenboom.

CHAPTER 97

Antwerp, January 1573

Jonas endures the most discouraging months of his life as he slowly recovers; his maimed palm prevents him from holding a burin. The burn ravaged tissue, nerves, and sweat glands nearly to the bones of his fingers, thumb, and palm. His ability to earn a wage at his trade has been compromised. Only after he realizes that his left hand has become adept at filling in for his right—pulling up his breeches and a hundred other banal acts he took for granted—does he consider that he might train his non-dominant hand to learn new skills. Four months after the attack by the rampaging mercenaries, he begins to teach himself to use his left hand. Frustrated, he is short-tempered with Sofie, herself enduring a difficult pregnancy in her sixth month. Even Liesbeth hears his anger with himself, too, for having to be a beginner again. Bedeviled by his slow progress, he gives up trying to grasp a graver. Failing to execute a smooth line, he falls into a deep depression.

While Mark Anthony has taken over his father's position at the printworks, he continues to translate, edit, and proofread much of the literary output of the printworks. He brings on other engravers both for jobs Jonas might have done, and for the pamphlets and broadsides he again clandestinely takes on in support of the Houses of Oranje and Nassau as they guide the fitful Dutch insurrection.

In-house papermaking is again required, as more projects come under the Coppens imprint with the success of the Ortelius editions. To help her family stay out of penury, despite her pregnancy, Sofie returns as the warden of the apprentice girls for Pieter Du Brul's papermaking section. Exhausted when she comes home evenings, Jonas tries to not appear self-focused. But his sense of uselessness is hard to conceal. He fights off headaches and puts on a cheerful face to care for Liesbeth while Sofie brings home a reduced income. He prepares meals, changes his daughter, and learns how to sew with his left hand. One day, Sofie brings home a kid glove with a layer of lamb's wool to cushion the deep tissue on his right hand. The pain is gone, and Jonas attempts to sharpen his ability to do precision work despite the scarring and nerve damage.

The previous year, he had taken, as partial payment for his work as an engraver for the Coppens enterprise, an untinted copy of the first Dutch edition of the *Theatrum,* one of the last off the presses. While Sofie oversees the young girls in the papermaking tasks for Master Du Brul, Jonas at home begins to mix colors and learn to limn the maps and front matter using his damaged hand. He works methodically to master the crafts of creating washes and contrasting colors to make the maps rise off the page. When he feels he is ready, he begins coloring his copy of his Dutch vernacular edition. He learns how to steady his grip, and apply the brushes to assure a fine line and incrementally thicker features on the surface of an engraved map. Even as he chafes at being forced to regain his skills, he learns patience by trying first to master the color scheme of every map. He tries to think like Abraham Ortels, focusing on every coloring detail of his title page. Little by little, he masters the techniques and then applies his colors. Using the maneuver Elizabeth Ortels Cole had demonstrated, he finesses the centerline gutter of the double-folio maps by arching the spine of the book so that the maps look like they had been limned before they were sewn into signatures. The work is painstaking. However, it refocuses his energy to the art at hand. Sofie compliments him on the superior product he is creating.

After just a few months, Jonas takes up engraving again, with his gloved right palm providing the etching force. His strokes are more elemental. They do not display the ease he achieved under Marcus Gheeraerts' tutelage; the results are brasher, more like his earliest work, as in the image of the blacksmith forging chain links. He perseveres and regains his former skills. At Sofie's urging, Mark Anthony Coppens invites Jonas back to the Boekprintere Scheldt to illustrate the familiar legend of the Roman soldier Silvius Brabo cutting off the extorting arm of the giant Antigoon and hurling it into the River Scheldt. The text is written by Mark Anthony and presented like a tale in *Aesop's Fables*; the four-page allegory creates a subtle invocation of the power of a hero to protect the people of Antwerp against an oppressor.

Soon, Jonas illustrates stories. Reynard the Fox outsmarts Felipe the Wolf, from stealing all the chickens in the farmyard. Another story personifies the Netherlands as a lion with a Spanish thorn in its paw, looking for a Daniel to alleviate the pain. A boy named Willem fights through his fears to remove the thorn.

Nearly a year after the mutinous German mercenaries had raided the Benedictine monastery, Jonas manages to restore his credentials, still under the name Johan van Braab, as the house engraver for the Boekprintere Scheldt. Thanks to Pieter du Brul, Sofie continues to work as the warden to the apprentices. The children are quartered in a corner of the larger papermaking room where Sofie can tend to their needs while she supervises the four young girls who are learning to make rag paper.

After months of overcoming his limitations, Jonas notices Sofie persisting in caring for him. One Saturday morning, in their Hoogstraat flat as they watch their children playing with small bean sacks in a corner on the floor, Jonas says, "It's as if you've had three children, now."

"Yes," she says slyly, "but you were the easiest to squeeze out into the world." She twists his chair at the table around and climbs onto his lap. "You gave me life like the mother and father I never had. You give me love like my mother could not and my father never gave." He feels her shudder with emotion. "Love me always, Jonas, with the love I bear for you."

She presses her head into his face. He sniffs her hair, and his mood is lighter than before the day he was burnt and clubbed. He rises and carries her to the bed. The children do not notice that their parents have moved; they chitter like birds as Liesbeth plays a game of tossing and catching bean sacks with one hand for the giggling Marcus.

CHAPTER 98

Den Haag, Restitution Offices, Early Afternoon, 26 June 2016

Owen's tension is palpable and he notes that Patricia, too, has nervous fingers that finally grasp his hand. They take chairs in front of an enormous glass covered desk topped with papers, including a lengthy official document that Leuwenboom refers to repeatedly. The official draws a deep breath.

"I am pleased to confirm that our records show that you, Mrs. Spencer, are recognized as legal heir to the four cases of copper plates engraved by the etcher Jonas Hoen, stolen from Emmanuel van Aalt, a Jewish pharmacist living in Haarlem, with his wife Frieda and his family, which included your mother, Hetty van Aalt, the sole known family survivor of the German Nazi occupation of the Netherlands."

Owen presses Patricia's hand as he ends his declaration. She squeezes back. "Emmanuel and Frieda, my grandparents," she says to Owen in a small voice. "I never knew their names." She seems dazed.

Leuwenboom looks down at his papers., embarrassed by even the trifling show of emotion Patricia allows to seep through.

Patricia regains her full voice, "Forgive my ignorance, sir, but this engraver, Hoen? How did this man's art come into my family's possession? We have no records at all, as my mother barely escaped with her life as a child."

"We only know..." Leuwenboom says, drawing out his words until he comes to the passage in the recommendation document, "Ah, here... 'In the provenance prepared by the Origins Unknown Agency, the B-G-H, it is stated that Mr. van Aalt was domiciled in a house in Gasthuissingel in Haarlem. This report is based on a post-war statement by Cornelius Antoon, the former landlord. He attests that in 1932, when the van Aalts took up residence, they requested to transport four cases of copper engravings to the rooftop shed. According to his deposition, the plates were in the family's possession since the 1600s.'"

"Sixteen hundreds—" Patricia repeats in wonder.

"Four cases," Owen says, breathless.

"Would you like to inspect these pieces?" Leuwenboom asks, obviously enjoying being the bearer of such news.

"Yes, yes," Patricia replies, caught up in the excitement.

"Our auto, a black rental downstairs, we were assured that we had only an hour's grace time—" Owen begins.

Leuwenboom holds up his hand. "Not to worry. My assistant has already posted permission for unlimited parking through the day. Follow me, please," Leuwenboom says, rising. "We are happy to help arrange transport of the property if you haven't yet handled such details." He leads the couple down some steps to a freight elevator at the back of the old building. "I suggest a partial container, given the weight. The Port of Rotterdam is only half an hour by *vrachtauto*—truck."

A jumble of questions about how to ship such a trove back to the States rattles through Owen's mind. But Patricia's hand clenching his makes him realize she is trembling. He wraps his fingers around hers and kisses her fingertips.

The doors of the padded elevator open on an immense basement. Leuwenboom speaks in Dutch to a stocky man wearing an apron and a knit cap. He hands him authorizing papers and they walk along rows of artworks, furniture, and statuary on palettes, some immaculately housed and some less well cared for.

"Are these all stolen from Jews?" Patricia asks. To Owen, her voice sounds little girlish. She is barely holding it together. The mausoleum-like basement has sent her into a very tender place. Owen takes her right hand and cradles his left arm around her back. They could have been walking in a cemetery.

"Not everything. Unknown origin in many cases," Leuwenboom says looking straight ahead. "We have been cataloging for years and trying to find the owners and their survivors. It is a huge job. The Nazis made a mess. Here we are."

They stop in front of four footlocker-sized wooden cases sitting on cracked, scuffed palettes. Leather straps, dried with age, secure the cases with brass buckles.

Patricia gasps when she sees the aged wooden cases. She is crushing Owen's fingers. "Like caskets," she utters involuntarily. "Children's caskets."

He feels Patricia shudder, wracked by unshed tears. "Sweetheart," he whispers, trying to strengthen her for her ordeal.

"I think we will have to arrange safer packaging for these lockers," Leuwenboom says, oblivious. "Aalbert," he gestures for the custodian to provide access to one of the containers. The leather straps crumble under Aalbert's fingers as he unhooks the buckles. When the lid is folded back on rusted hinges, they see several rows of plates on edge, separated from one another by yellowing muslin. Owen's eyes widen at the care taken to preserve the plates. Patricia lets out an audible sigh. Owen sees her relief that it is only a multitude of copper plates. Her eyes reveal to Owen that she has been unsure of what she had been expecting.

Owen reaches in, withdraws a plate and shows it to her. Copper oxidation shows green on the dull surface, but they can both discern the etched clarity of human bones: the bones of the arm extending out to the bones of the fingers across the top of the plate; below, the underside of the same bones in the other direction.

Patricia flinches as soon as she sees the plate, as though she was thinking of death and dismemberment. Owen tries to reassure her. "He must have made a living illustrating medical books," Owen imagines aloud to Patricia.

"Oh. That's all right then," she says, relieved.

Owen reaches into one of the other rows and he sees that it is an image of a woman who appears to be hand painting an engraved map. He twists his head and tries to transpose the letters on the cartouche. "Gallia," he says. "This woman is tinting a map of France. Our Mr. Hoen had some talent. And he knew mapmaking."

Patricia's demeanor softens. "She looks very capable, this map tinter."

"It's signed, too. He must have liked it," Owen adds.

Aalbert opens the cover of another case. The top layer is an array of proof sheets on rag paper, engravings, portraits, maps, anatomical studies, and sketches.

"Oh, my," Patricia utters, surprised by the disorganized collection of paper.

Smiling at the extent of the plates and hand-drawn sketches, Owen holds up several pencil drawings, including early and later versions for an engraving that shows boats off the coasts of France, Spain, and the English Channel. Another print shows a monk piercing a nobleman with a knife in the doorway to a castle. The words "Herman de Ruyter" appear prominently on the engraving. Owen declares, "Patricia, you will have the honor of introducing the world to one Jonas Hoen who engraved copper plates four hundred and fifty years ago."

Patricia is smiling now, as she takes title to her grandparents' legacy.

Owen turns one more sketch over and is startled when he sees the reworked image of what looks like a Komodo dragon, cinched down on a plate. "Patricia!" Owen gasps. "This sea monster is on the Ortelius map that Michael consigned."

She turns to Leuwenboom, and assumes full ownership. "We would like to take the paper engravings and sketches with us. Can we manage that?"

"Of course. We need simply do a manual accounting of the images. And the plates?" Leuwenboom asks, tilting his head toward the crated copper.

Patricia shrugs to Owen, ceding him the responsibility.

Owen addresses the Dutchman. "You have a suggestion how to ship the hardware. These images will give us the scope of the contents of the cases."

"Of course. Collect the paper prints now, and then come back upstairs and we will get the release forms ready."

"Aalbert, thank you," Patricia says, shaking hands with the custodian.

The stocky man tips his cap. Owen shakes his hand as well, and begins to load his arms with perhaps three hundred sheets of engravings and sketches easily accessed from the second wooden case. As Patricia slips her arm into the crook of his elbow for the elevator ride to the main floor, Aalbert motions for Leuwenboom to draw near, pointing at a form affixed to the back of one of the crates printed in German with several lines scrawled in pen. The two converse in Dutch, and then Leuwenboom accompanies Patricia and Owen to the elevator.

"I didn't know this," the official says, "but Aalbert points out that these cases of copper were headed for a smelter in Germany—found by British troops in a railroad shed near Bremen with other bronze and brass stolen from Holland."

"Oh, my God," Patricia says.

"Very fortunate," Leuwenboom adds as they walk to his office. "The cases were bound for the Rammelsberg smelter in Saxony. Luckily, it was side-tracked."

They listen closely as Leuwenboom answers their questions and Patricia signs receipts for what they will take home by plane, now bundled neatly in a cardboard box. She authorizes Leuwenboom to arrange for packaging of the cases to be shipped by container to Oakland, California. They learn of the customs duties they could expect to pay and how to proceed to transport the restituted artworks to Palo Alto.

On the drive back to Amsterdam, Owen grasps Patricia's hand several times and she rests endearing fingers on his neck. They talk about the artwork, but spend more time going over the rush of feelings awakened by these events.

"Mother said, 'Never let them know you're Jewish.' That's what rang in my ears in that basement, over and over. All those pieces once belonged to people who were uprooted, most murdered. 'Unknown origin,' he said. Jews. It didn't matter if they worshipped or not. They were defined as no good. Scapegoats to slaughter. I thought my heart would burst when I went into that basement. Maybe it did. It broke open. Emmanuel and Frieda were their names. Mother never told me her parents' names—not that I asked. I colluded with her, to keep it all secret."

"Nice names," Owen said. "I wish I knew them."

"Me too."

Keeping his eye on the road, he touches her cheek.

CHAPTER 99

Antwerp, 2 November 1576

Jonas and Sofie raise their children in their Antwerp flat as the forces of the Inquisition and the Dutch Revolt skirmish and erupt throughout the Lowlands. Willem van Oranje continues to rally and in 1573 the Spanish King replaces the Duke of Alva, who cannot contain the restive provinces, with Luis de Requeséns y Zúñiga. The war is bankrupting Philip II's nation, however, and the massive mercenary *tercios*, the battle formations of the Spaniards, go without pay for long periods. Their anger is often taken out on the cities hosting their garrisons.

On this day, Jonas sketches the river traffic at the quay where the *Tortelduif* usually berths when in port. He is preparing a book for the Boekprintere Scheldt commissioned by a merchants' group extolling the deep-water port of Antwerp. He sketches a sailor climbing the rigging of a French barque. The new and hated Citadel of Antwerp under the brutal command of General Sancho d'Avila, once head of the Duke of Alva's bodyguard, hovers in the background with its formidable walls, turrets and guns looming over the port. Jonas shifts his gaze to ground level but he is seized by terror as he sees four familiar forms striding along the quay from The Citadel; he shrinks behind a wood piling. Unmistakable, even some hundred and fifty yards away, Jan du Forché, the spy he had struck in the London tavern, deep in conversation, walks toward him, flanked by Nicholaus Bockel, the red-haired agent for the heresy procurator on one side, Joop Baldus, his flyaway straw hair in the gusting wind on the other, and the Catalan, Juan Carlos, whose jaw looks like it had been kicked by a horse, alongside.

Jonas feels trapped, draws a sharp breath, unsure of his next move, when the quartet turns up a lane toward the Antwerp City Hall on the western edge of the Grote Markt plaza. Jonas edges around the piling and sees them duck into an alehouse, the disreputable Seamens' Fists. With these footloose in Antwerp, he fears a day of reckoning. Panicked, he turns toward home but looks downriver for a moment and sees in the distance the familiar bowsprit and lowering sails of the *Tortelduif* as she makes her approach on a light breeze. He pauses only a moment as a plan hatches in his mind. It will be half an hour before she is made fast at the quay, so he sets a rapid pace, picking his way through narrow lanes and alleys to Hoogstraat, checking over his shoulder that the spies are not in sight. He pulls up short when he sees Sofie hurrying toward him, little Marcus in her arms and Liesbeth grasping her skirt.

"I saw them—I'm sure—at the Grote Markt—that false friend, Bockel. Nicholaus Bockel," she says breathlessly. "Joop Baldus and Nicholaus together."

Jonas is about to acknowledge that he, too, has seen them with the spies who dogged his tracks in London, but he asks, instead, "Did they recognize you?"

"Yes, I'm sure, and Joop made this sign." She does a slicing gesture at her throat, as her voice pitches higher in fear. "He was staring at the children."

"It is not safe in the city," he says, thinking aloud rapidly. "You must go directly to Kloosterstraat, the house of the Ortels. Ask to see Anna Ortels. Beg her to have their man—Antonius is his name—drive you and the children to Maria de Vries at the monastery at the earliest possible moment. Say that her sister Elizabeth told me if I ever needed help—" he breaks off. "Wait for me there, with Madame de Vries or Brother Thomas. Do not go back to our rooms." Jonas kisses his children and hugs Sofie. "We will be safe, but go now, I will bring clothes for you and the children."

After the briefest moment of indecision, Sofie sets off in the direction of Kloosterstraat. She uses a back alley to wend her way to the Ortels' neighborhood.

Jonas speeds along a footpath, rather than city streets, to his house. He takes the back stairs by twos. He has a plan. He fills his travel bag with changes of clothing for Marcus, Liesbeth, and Sofie, and a few bits for himself. He rummages in a cupboard for the guilders he knows has been saved out. He shakes his head ruefully at the paltry sum of three guilders; then he spots the first Dutch edition of the *Theatrum* he had so carefully colored. *Passage!* Moving quickly, Jonas hefts the book of maps, takes one last look around his rooms, stops abruptly—hurriedly gathers his burins, the paper illustrations, proof sheets, and copper plates he has engraved. The size and weight of the output gathered is formidable. With strength fueled by nervous fury, he fills a burlap bag, staggers under the weight of the atlas, his carrying bag, and his artistic output, and slowly picks his way down the stairs to the narrow alley behind his street. He progresses slowly, but steadily, toward the river.

Huffing, Jonas sets his burdens down as the *Tortelduif* ties up. He sees Captain Vandeven speaking to a mate who organizes the removal of cargo. Several merchants with bills of lading stand by ox-drawn carts as the first of the goods is trundled down the gangplank. Two men wrestle several large crates to the quay, and Jonas hops onto the gangway, holding the book of maps under his arm.

"Greetings, Captain…."

Vandeven squints in the afternoon light and circles Jonas so he is not looking into the low sun to the west. "Bless me, young man. It is you, isn't it? I see you somehow got here from Amsterdam. Married, eh? Five years nearly, eh?"

"Yes, Captain, and I am hoping you will meet my family very soon. I need to move my wife, my little ones, and me to Groningen—for a new opportunity. Might you be sailing up that way in the near-time?"

Vandeven cocks he head, but his frown changes to a wry smile. "Sooner than anyone imagines." Vandeven's voice drops to a soft whisper, "I don't want to alarm you, if you do not already know—but the Spanish garrison quartered in that Citadel is hanging by a very slim thread. They haven't been paid in months. The galleons that carried the paymasters' gold florins were forced to shelter on the English coast in the bad weather last week. The word on the wharf in London is that the English queen is counting four hundred thousand Spanish florins these days. Those tercios in The Citadel will be very angry when they learn of it. So we'll catch the afternoon tide tomorrow and sail out of these waters—"

"Tomorrow!" Jonas gasps. "But that is perfect. Can you take my family and me with you? Two children—under five years. I only have this to pay for our passage, and three gilders," he says, passing the *Theatrum Orbis Terrarum* to the Captain. "In Dutch, the commentary, not Latin," he adds. But the captain is already captivated. He turns several pages and looks at Jonas with incredulity. "I tinted this copy, myself. I hope it suffices for my family's passage."

"This is admirable, young man—I did not know you in this light—and in understandable Dutch!" Vandeven runs a hand through his beard. "Very well," he says, extending his calloused hand, which Jonas shakes. "You must all be aboard by three o'clock tomorrow. There must be no delay—do you understand?"

"Yes. May I bring aboard some of our belongings now? It is not much."

Vandeven nods and calls over his shoulder, "You know your way to the quarters. Not much for a woman and two children," he says giving Jonas a moment to opt out.

"They can't wait for the adventure," he lies.

Vandeven smiles, quickens his pace to oversee the cargo delivered quayside, and then carries the limned book of maps to his cabin. He calls to Jonas. "You colored these charts?"

"Yes, sir."

"Then you must sign this work for me, young man, when we have a moment."

Jonas, his heart lighter, drops down to the quay, then carries his burlap sack and traveling bag below decks.

CHAPTER 100

Soest, Netherlands, Late Afternoon, 26 June 2016

Michael's hotel room phone wakens him from a deep sleep. He dresses and picks up the canvas bag holding the gift for his family, the first Dutch edition of the Ortelius atlas, complete with the map he had tried to auction. At the hotel desk he asks directions to the assisted living residence. "Only a ten minute walk, sir," the clerk says offering a photocopy of the area streets with a purple marker showing his path. He begins to follow the map, and hears a door car open across the street. A burly man in this thirties with a shaven head in a short sleeved golf shirt, muscles rippling, begins to shadow Michael some ten yards behind. When Aleida had driven him to the hotel,

Michael had seen a florist's shop nearby. Michael stops suddenly and turns around remembering that the florist is behind him. The man almost trips trying to stop his forward progress. Caught completely off guard, he looks angrily to his left and right, then turns around and heads back to the Audi where the man in the driver's seat with an odd face sits rigidly. Michael finds his behavior curious. "Are you lost, sir," Michael calls out in Dutch. "I have a map."

The stranger laughs a high-pitched titter. "Map!" He quickens his pace to the passenger door and shifts his weight uncertainly while the driver of the car stares straight ahead.

Michael shrugs. He follows his impulse and continues to the flower seller's. He buys a dozen white tulips. He has a very early memory of his mother explaining, "A white tulip for forgiveness." The Audi has driven on when he emerges from the shop. He follows the map the hotel clerk had drawn and sees by the signs in the complex that Gerdi lives on the ground floor of the 150-apartment compound. He knocks on her door and beholds the white haired matron that Gerdi Ten Broeck has become in the years since he had first met her in 1939. He next sees the flat of her hand flying in an arc that catches him on his left cheek. He staggers under the blow and holds fast to the doorjamb to remain upright.

"Pim made me promise to smack you hard if I ever got the chance. So I have done it, and now I hug you, my long lost brother-in-law." Gerdi wraps her arms around his torso and squeezes with all her might. Michael shudders with emotion in her grasp.

"Oh, Gerdi, I deserve that smack and worse," Michael says through teary eyes. "You still pack a wallop. You must take better care you don't break bones in your hand."

She takes the bouquet of tulips he has brought and arranges them in a vase with water. The kitchen area is convenient to her sitting room and he sees double doors leading to a modest garden outside. He gingerly touches his smarting cheek. A moment later she emerges from the kitchen with an ice pack and a towel.

"Before it swells up. They're very concerned with elder abuse around here and I don't want a bad reputation."

Michael laughs despite the feel of her hand hitting his cheekbone. He presses the coolness of the icepack to his jaw. "I can see where Aleida gets her spunk."

"Pim. She was always Pim's favorite."

"I swear she made me think my mother was sitting next to me in that car," Michael says, shaking his head.

"Yes, some resemblance in certain lights. Sit, some schnapps? Peach brandy?"

"Yes, of course." Michael watches as Gerdi pours a generous glass of brandy for each of them. He finds himself smiling, seeing the vivacious woman of his young years whom he had vilified so in his haste to blame someone for his father's death, now slower, of course, but still crisply in charge and a picture of mental acuity. His cheek has stopped stinging, and a test of his jaw reveals no lasting damage, so he puts the towel and icepack on the coffee table. Michael drapes his long frame comfortably in the settee.

"I am so pleased you could get Mrs. Spencer to see me. Of all the children I've helped, the memory of her mother has always stayed with me—such a scared little girl. You and I, Michael, we survived one of the worst times, and we have a lot and a precious little to show for it."

"You can't say that." Michael insists. "You were recognized. I hope Pim told you. When we were being processed out of a DP camp across the border, a Dutch resistance fighter from Arnhem, knew who you were. Offered Pim big congratulations on getting married to you."

"Yes, we did what we could and it was a drop in the pail."

"You and Pim—you fought back, at least. You saved people. I was shaking with fear that he would be discovered damaging ack-ack shells."

"Yes, but you helped create light bulbs that don't burn out every ten minutes. You improved the world."

Michael waves off her compliment. "Not the same as saving children."

"Michael!" The old woman raises her voice as though to shake him. "You saved Pim for me. He told me he was knocked senseless by a bomb blast. You dragged him into the forest and revived him in a stream. He said if you had just run off, he'd have been shot the next day. Don't you understand?"

He shrugs out of habit, then raises his hand. "I see. But I was terrified."

"Of course you were." Gerdi touches her hand to her temple, brushing a stray wisp of white hair. It seems connected to a memory. "So was I, every minute. And even after, til you two came back safely. Every mission. Every child. I could barely take a full breath in those years." Michael sighs, again overcome by the enormity of Gerdi's willingness to reconcile. "So when can I meet your other children and their families? I have something for them." He nods at the canvas bag.

"The weekend. What's that?"

"Father's old book of maps," Michael says.

Gerdi's eyes moisten as soon as he says the words.

"His blood was all over the book. They shot him at that side table where he kept the map book displayed. Blood everywhere."

"Yes. You can still see it on the map of the world." Michael says quietly. "It should go to your son—Herman, since he was named for Father."

Gerdi nods.

"The one caveat is that—if the organization in Jerusalem, the Holocaust people, wants, it can display this book when it inducts my father in their Righteous Among Nations ceremony. But the book is our property."

"You'll meet Herman and his family on Saturday. Present it to him then."

After a pause, Gerdi asks: "So, Michael, besides inventing lightbulbs, what have you been doing since we saw you last? When was it? In the early nineties, yes?"

"Just physics. Light-emitting diodes," he laughs. "One foot in front of the other. And being stupid about investments." He changes the subject. "How do we arrange the week we have?"

"First I want to see Patricia, tomorrow. I hope she is free." Gerdi says. "And I have something for her."

When Michael leaves, he asks that Gerdi keep the atlas for Saturday.

CHAPTER 101

Antwerp, Afternoon, 2 November 1576

The tolling bells of Onze-Lieve-Vrouwekerk signal four o'clock as Jonas, eyes scanning the streets for the spies, raps on the rear door in the alley behind the Ortels' residence. After an interminable wait, a scullery maid opens the door a crack.

"Please, Miss, can you tell me, has Antonius taken the trap with a woman and two children to the Benedictine Monastery on the Mechelen Road?"

The maid, oozing terror, says, "I cannot say. My mistress has forbidden—"

"How long?" Jonas interrupts, putting his foot between the jamb and door.

"Not ten minutes—" she blurts, then puts her hand over her mouth.

Jonas begins at a trot to the north gate, but slows as he realizes he may draw attention. He decides to save his breath until he has cleared the town walls. He adopts a normal pace, not a moment too soon. Juan Carlos, chatting with a gesticulating Spanish musketeer, is scouring the streets from behind his crooked jaw. Jonas has slowed his walk to a lazy amble and will pass within twenty feet of the Catalan. Jonas rubs his brow as though he has a headache as he passes abreast of Du Forché's comrade–in–arms and takes note of the Catalan's dagger, still sheathed. He passes undetected and has gained ten yards toward the city gate when he hears. "*Hola!* I know that walk. Stop! *Alto!* "

Jonas bolts as if he were a horse feeling the lash of a whip; he charges ahead for the last street that nestles beneath the north wall of the town. Juan Carlos shouts in rapid Spanish, and instinct tells Jonas that the mercenary has been ordered to fire. He cuts erratically and hears the sizzle of the matchlock sending its charge down the barrel. A moment later, the street roars with the report of the pellet being fired, and a zinging ricochet off the curving city wall ahead. In his second of relief, he hears screams of two women on the street. Dogs bark. Doors slam shut. He continues to zigzag but realizes it could take up to a minute for the soldier to reload. He straightens his path, knowing Juan Carlos, with his dagger, is close after him. *How close?* Jonas turns to see him unsheathing his weapon twenty feet behind on a dead run.

A runaway donkey, terrified by the arquebus blast, is coming up quickly behind Juan Carlos. In a split second, Jonas stops abruptly and races back toward Juan Carlos at an angle that will draw his attacker into the path of the onrushing donkey. As Juan Carlos raises his dagger to send it flying at Jonas, the crazed animal sends the Catalan sprawling to the ground. His knife skids toward Jonas who leaps to it and sails it over the north wall. Juan Carlos lies dazed in the road. Jonas sprints, now chasing the donkey toward the Northeast gate. His heart thumps, but he has made it. The thought flashes that he owes his life to terrified horses and donkeys. Jonas wonders *Did Brabo have the same thrill when he slung Antigoon's forearm into the Scheldt?*

Two musketeers on the afternoon watch step into Jonas' path.

"They're starting to kill each other," Jonas cries, points at Juan Carlos barely regaining his footing. The uniformed soldier follows with his loaded long gun.

The musketeers trot toward Juan Carlos as Jonas passes through the Northeast gate of Antwerp and immediately cuts across farm fields on an angle to intersect the Mechelen Road. His lungs burning, he sees the trap pulled by the trotting horse. He cuts through another recently harvested field, which puts him in the path of the rig.

"Papa!" Liesbeth calls.

Jonas leaps onto the trap, crying through deep gulps of air, "Thank, you, thank you, Antonius." He hugs his family, regains his breath, and explains most of what has just happened, leaving out the pursuit and escape from Juan Carlos. He concludes, "We are going on a big sailing ship tomorrow; won't that be fun?" He signals to Sofie that all is well and he will explain later. "Has Antonius told you the name of his horse?"

"No-oo," the children say jointly.

"His name is Salty," Antonius says.

"Tell them why the horse has such a funny name."

"Did you notice the speckle of white on Salty's face and withers?" Antonius begins. The children are rapt. Liesbeth asks if the horse's face tastes salty.

"The *Tortelduif* sails tomorrow and we must be aboard by three o'clock," Jonas explains to Sofie.

"Where are the children's things?" Sofie asks.

"Already on board."

Before Antonius leaves them at the track that leads onto the monastery grounds, Jonas scrawls a note to take to Anna Ortels. In it, he warns of the likely mutiny of the Spanish garrison, summarizing what Vandeven had reported to him.

Later, Brother Thomas, Maria de Vries and her daughter, Godlieve, listen, transfixed and horrified by Jonas' account of why he and his family must leave. He saves for last Captain Vandeven's warning that a soldiers' mutiny is imminent and that Antwerp will be hugely dangerous in the coming days.

"These spies," Brother Thomas asks, "have they seen you?"

"One has seen Sofie, but by now they all will know that I am here."

"And you need to be on board Captain Vandeven's merchantman—"

"Tomorrow afternoon," Jonas confirms.

Across the cookhouse, the children's giggles pitch high as they play a game of pickup sticks with two of Godlieve's adolescent girls.

"Do you have money for your journey?" Brother Thomas asks.

"Three guilders only. That's all I could find," Jonas says.

"We have seventeen more at least. Where did you look?" Sofie asks, annoyed.

"We need to devise a plan to get you safely aboard," Brother Thomas says, stopping further discussion. "We must somehow get your guilders and anything else you can carry from your rooms. Let us decide how to proceed so you stay out of sight. Tonight, you will stay here." Pointedly, he says to Maria, "The less anyone knows, the better."

CHAPTER 102

Soest, Netherlands, 30 June 2016

Patricia suppresses a queasy sensation on her walk from the hotel on Birkstraat to Gerdi's apartment. She assured Owen that she is fine and is looking forward to talking with the old woman about her mother. But now a familiar dread knots her stomach. They had met briefly the previous evening when Michael took Patricia and Owen to meet Gerdi. Patricia observed Gerdi trying to find the nine-year-old girl she had saved in the features of her face. They had conversed quietly, Patricia describing her career as a teacher in California. "You speak English so well," Patricia says. "I'm afraid I can't speak a word of Dutch."

"Not to worry, my dear. When my husband and I owned a café, many customers were from the States, England, Canada. Please save tomorrow for a visit. I have a day planned that might answer a few questions if your mother never discussed things with you," Gerdi says. "Let the boys entertain each other and indulge me for one day."

Patricia forces a smile. "Of course." Her heart beat like tympani. "That is very generous," she says in a voice that sounds like a squeak.

"You're sure?" Gerdi asks. "I don't want to put you through anything you really do not—"

"I'm a big girl," Patricia says through a wincing smile. She hopes desperately she doesn't sound like an eight-year-old.

At ten o'clock the next morning the smiling, aged woman invites Patricia in.

She cannot help but be charmed by Gerdi; at once frail and robust with snow white hair in layers framing her face. She wears a sedate navy blue dress and no makeup. Her papery facial skin and neck are lined, crinkling when she laughs or frowns. Patricia can read the full emotional spectrum in Gerdi's eyes. She is completely transparent. Just now, she smiles slyly. "I have thought of this moment ever since I learned from Michael, that Hetty van Aalt had a daughter. Please, sit down. I have some refreshment. But first, I need to ask, would you *like* to see where your mother lived when she was a young girl, before the awful time?"

A clutching hand seizes her throat as she realizes the old woman means the flat in Haarlem. She still feels raw from the experience earlier in the week of seeing the looted art. She can tell by Gerdi's expression that Patricia's distress is evident. "No need, no need," the old woman assures. "I can see this raises deep emotions."

Patricia's fingers fidget with a cocktail napkin she has absently picked up from the coffee table. The twisted paper matches the vortex spinning in her stomach. She laughs nervously to stifle her rising panic and breathes deeply to push through. "Yes, deep emotions, but it is time for me to come to grips—grips with these feelings. Forgive me, I realize that I haven't even thanked you for helping my mother escape her family's fate."

"Some of us, we couldn't help—*but* help. You know?" Gerdi says. Patricia notices a catch in Gerdi's voice. The old woman reaches out a hand and slides next to Patricia on the settee. Patricia holds her hostess' warm wrist and they embrace. They hold each other for a long moment.

"If you feel up to a trip to Haarlem and Amsterdam, I just need to call Aleida."

"Certainly. Go ahead," Patricia replies. She looks at the furnishings of the modest apartment, hearing the Dutch phone conversation that Gerdi carries on with her eldest daughter as a charming background gabble she does not understand. She helps herself to a cup of Sumatra coffee and nibbles on cheese and grapes.

"Good," says Gerdi, rejoining Patricia. "Aleida will pick up my younger daughter, Michelle, and together, the four of us will take a tour." Gerdi cocks her head as she looks at Patricia.

"What?" Patricia asks with a nervous laugh.

"I have some things to give you. They were your mother's. In the rush to get Hetty placed with one of the Jewish agencies, this was left at her last safe house." Gerdi opens a mottled brown folder on the coffee table and withdraws a quarto-sized sheet of paper folded in half with a crisp centerfold.

Patricia looks apprehensively at the age-darkened paper. *What would this reveal?* With some trepidation she takes the sheet from Gerdi and opens it with more care than necessary.

"She kept this tucked in a favorite book, *The Mystery of the Angora Cat*. That book was lost in Eindhoven, but you may be able to find a copy somewhere."

Patricia devours it all. *Mother had a favorite book! Mystery? Angora Cat?*

"This old engraving—she packed it in her personal bag when she left the flat in Haarlem. I think there was one other, of a dog and a horse."

She immediately remembers the engraving Michael Dijkstra had given her at their first meeting. Patricia's hands tremble. *Why is it terrifying to know what mother treasured so—that she took it into the unknown with her?*

"She told me she found these engravings in an old trunk in the attic in Gasthuissingel and they were her favorite pictures."

The attic! She had gotten into the engravings!

Patricia looks closely at the plate. A boy, two years old she guesses, is standing on pudgy legs pointing at a butterfly just out of the grasp of an older girl with a ribbon in her hair. She lay on the edge of a blanket. The girl is smiling and appears to be calling to the boy. The clean, crisp lines and crosshatching make for a charming scene of toddlers at play. Then Patricia's hand shakes as though an electric current shot through it. She sees the initials "JH."

Through labored breathing, she says excitedly, "The trunks—filled with copper plates and engravings like this. Owen and I saw them in The Hague. They were stolen from the rooftop shed. Owen says 'Thank God, they were not turned in to be melted down for the copper.'" She looks again at the picture. "Mother must have loved this picture. What's this say?"

Gerdi squints to read the Dutch inscription. *Marcus en Liesbeth bewonderen het vlinder.* "Hah! Marcus and Liesbeth admire the butterfly—or perhaps— 'marvel at.'"

"Marcus and Liesbeth," Patricia repeats in wonder. Patricia can now fill in some of the story for Gerdi. "This artist was Jonas Hoen." She points to the engraving. "These may have been his kids. Owen and I will try to piece it all together when we get home. This engraver was linked with the family, we think. Oh, Gerdi. It is like opening a whole new life. My mother was so secretive. I wish I had known that she loved this engraving enough to take it with her. And what was that book? *The Angora Cat?*"

"'Het Raadsel van de Angorakat,' if I remember the title. The author was an American, I think." Gerdi squints trying to remember the details. "The cover was printed in a midnight blue and showed a fluffy black cat on the dust jacket." Gerdi shakes her head. "The things we think are so important.... Like me, the things we save. I have one more item for you, but only if you want it. When I found your mother squeezed against the wall of a building in an alley near the train station in Amsterdam, I cut this from her jumper."

Patricia digs fingernails into her palms. *With a knife? What did you cut?*

Gerdi opens the drawer of the coffee table and removes an old cardboard box. Trembling, Patricia sees several six-pointed Stars of David. Gerdi selects the one on the top in all its terrifying reality. The word "Jood" embroidered in black across the yellow star.

"This was Hetty's," Gerdi says softly.

A few loose threads hang from the yellow fabric, a child's marker for Dutch Jews in the Holocaust. Patricia feels like she is suffocating. She gulps mouthfuls of air. Her eyes blink trying to erase the mottled yellow star but she creates a strobe effect that intensifies the horror. Finally, she clamps her eyes shut. When she opens them and draws a deep breath she looks only at the threads hanging from the star that Hetty's mother—*Frieda*—had used to sew it to her jumper. The thread is green. This settles Patricia, oddly. *She wore a green jumper.* Patricia accepts the star. Then the ache in her throat begins and a welling tide of tears breaks and spills. She cannot speak, but her mother's warning, *Never let them know you are Jewish* pounds in her ears.

Gerdi's hands hold hers with the yellow star crumpled in Patricia's palm. She cries, as never before over the loss of her mother. She has shed a few tears, but never this fulsome, directed grief that no words express. Now, wrapped in the arms of the 92-year-old woman who had saved her mother, all the withheld sadness bursts in full measure. Gerdi layers tissues in Patricia's hands to catch her weeping. Over several minutes, as she surfaces from each deeper plunge to the depths of her grief, she feels lighter. When she regains her voice, Patricia says, "No child should have such tragedy."

"No. No one," Gerdi agrees.

"My mother never spoke about any of it."

"So you never knew." A distant look comes over Gerdi. "My kids never heard much about it from me or Pim either."

They are silent, holding each other when a knock on the door interrupts. "These will be my daughters. Are you ready for me to let them in?"

Patricia nods and takes a final swipe of her eyes with the dampened tissues. Aleida and Michelle enter and each kisses Gerdi. Patricia collects the engraving and the yellow star from the coffee table and drops them into her bag. She smiles and rises to greet Gerdi's daughters. Neither of them seems fooled by Patricia's adopted air of lightness.

CHAPTER 103

Mechelen-Antwerp Road, Midday, 3 November 1576

Two wagons jostle from the monastery track onto the Mechelen-Antwerp Road. The first, driven by Brother Aristede, carries Sofie, her children, Maria de Vries, and Godlieve. The children nestle against sheaves of grain stacked at the rear of the wagon. The women carry large baskets, as though they will attend the Monday market.

Two black-robed figures occupy the second wagon, also laden with wheat from the recent harvest. Brother Thomas drives the donkey, while Jonas, beside him, wears the musty robe of old Brother Bernardus, long-deceased. The odor of the garment reminds Jonas of the stuttering old limner who gave him instruction in illustrating initial letters in the scriptorium. But he takes comfort in the rough wool, another layer of warmth over his clothing in the chill afternoon. A little after noon, Jonas has difficulty convincing Brother Thomas that they must stop first at the Boekprintere Scheldt.

"But you say the printworks may be watched," Brother Thomas pleads "You must proceed to the quay while Maria and Godlieve retrieve furnishings and funds from your rooms."

"No," Jonas insists. "I must warn my friends that the Spanish garrison in Antwerp intends a mutiny. And let them know that Sofie and I will escape Antwerp, hopefully, before the firestorm erupts."

"Then let me deliver your message. It is too dangerous for you."

"I may never see these friends again. I must speak to them—tell Mark Anthony about the spies, especially Nicholaus Bockel."

The Brother is frustrated by his headstrong onetime student, but he holds his tongue as he slaps reins on the donkey's rump.

Gloom hangs in the air. Veiled looks on the faces of unpaid Spanish soldiers on the road into Antwerp tell the tale. In low tones, Brother Thomas reminds Jonas of the mutiny in Mechelen in the autumn, four years earlier. "Good Catholics," Brother Thomas laments, "their homes pillaged by Alva's army led by the Iron Duke's son, women raped—" Thomas recalls bitterly, "Troops of Prince Willem withdraw and innocent Flemish—Catholics, mostly—" The monk shakes his head, beyond words to describe the atrocities.

Jonas drives his point home. "You see, then, why I need to inform those whom I love of what may befall them."

Brother Thomas sighs, for he cannot disagree.

As arranged, the two wagons separate when they enter Antwerp.

Jonas enters the printworks at the rear door adjacent to the papermaking hall, while Brother Thomas hitches the donkey to a post.

A stunned Pieter Du Brul nods uncomprehendingly when Jonas pulls the cowl off his head. Jonas signals him to stay quiet and whispers that he must see Mark Anthony, preferably in Du Brul's domain, so that printers and others are not aware. The urgency is clear, and the master papermaker scrawls a note, folds it, and hands it to one of the girls to summon the young book publisher. "Keep silent and come back directly," he directs the bewildered girl.

Jonas, Brother Thomas, Du Brul, and Marc Anthony squeeze into the closet of a chamber that serves as Du Brul's office in the papermaking section.

"Imminent?" Mark Anthony asks, recovering from his surprise at Jonas in his monk's garb. "When word of Queen Elizabeth's confiscation of the florins finds its way here, General d'Avila may not contain his tercios within The Citadel."

"They may know already," Jonas interjects. "And here is more bad news."

He describes sighting the three spies and Joop Baldus the day before as they ducked into The Sailors' Fists alehouse. "Bockel, and two others who tracked me down in London, Jan Du Forché from Brussels and a Catalan called Juan Carlos."

Mark Anthony scratches notes on a sheet of paper. "Baldus, too, the rat." He is rapt in a calculation. On seeing Brother Thomas anxiously wishing to leave, Jonas offers his hand to bid goodbye to Du Brul and Mark Anthony.

"You must wait a moment," Mark Anthony insists. "You do not need to board until later this afternoon, is that correct?"

"Yes, and...?"

"You would like to get your own back, yes?"

Brother Thomas's brow clouds over.

"Remember when you engraved a copy of the Duke of Alva's coat of arms?" Mark Anthony asks, excited. "From his order decreed by the Council of Troubles for the hundredth penny tax? I still have that plate. Finally, we get to use it!"

Jonas, Du Brul, and Brother Thomas stare at the young publisher whose eyes flash. He continues to write, crosses out, and writes some more. "Pieter,"

Mark Anthony says, pointing to Du Brul. Spanish paper, octavo, two or three leaves."

Du Brul flips through a stack of blank papers, finally finds a quarto sheet of laid paper. "From a paperworks in Seville," Du Brul says as he folds and slices the sheet into two octavo leaves.

"Good," Coppens says distractedly. "Get one of the devils to moisten and prepare these for an imprint, Room 14. Lightly dampen just here." Coppens points to the center of the sheet near the top. Just enough for the coat of arms imprint of the Duke Fernando Álvarez de Toledo, Third Duke of Alva."

Energized by Mark Anthony's' excitement, Du Brul leaves with the papers, as Coppens whispers, "In half an hour's time, I will have written a note from the Iron Duke to his old friend, commander of his personal bodyguard when he so effectively decimated our lands with his butchery. General Sancho d'Avila, heir of the Iron Duke's mantle, will be cheered to receive these words. In your new profession of monk, you will easily gain admittance to The Citadel to deliver this letter, which, you will say was sent through the good offices of who?—Senor Benito Arias Montana—he who oversaw the Plantin printworks' *Polyglot Bible*—Benedictus Arias Montanus!" He looks at Brother Thomas. "Your order, I believe."

"Not an order, but a monastic community," Brother Thomas corrects, automatically. "Self-governing, not under the thumb of the Pope."

"The Rule of Benedictus is prayer and work in equal measure," Jonas explains, "not obeisance to Rome."

Mark Anthony shrugs, "I am properly instructed. But they won't deny you entry to The Citadel because you do not owe allegiance to the Pope—yes?"

Jonas notes a nod from Brother Thomas.

"Your work now, Jonas, will be to deliver a missive from the Duke of Toledo to the Antwerp Citadel commander, which came to you from the noted theologian, Montanus, yes? It will inform General d'Avila of the reprehensible actions by the false spies who have embezzled funds intended to pay the brave troops who enforce the Spanish directive of protecting the true Church from the corruption of the Reformation. These miscreants may be found taking refreshment at—" Mark Anthony checks his notes, 'Het Varenguezen Vuistje alehouse.' Ah, The Sailors Fists!"

Jonas hisses in mock terror. "The traitors! Embezzling King Philip's treasure!"

Mark Anthony smiles and concludes, "Wait here. I need to write this in the Iron Duke's hand with proper syntax. You will deliver the Duke's warning to the General."

He leaves Jonas and Brother Thomas speechless until they are alone.

"This is madness," Brother Thomas whispers.

Jonas nods, but he is deep in thought. "This is daring, yes."

CHAPTER 104

En Route to Westerbork, Haarlem, and Amsterdam, 30 June 2016

Patricia sits rigidly as Aleida drives the Peugeot. Gerdi and her younger daughter, Michelle, share the rear seat.

"First, I have asked Aleida to take us to Westerbork, just about an hour and a half," Gerdi explains from her seat behind Aleida. All of the conversation is in English. Patricia can easily turn to her but she opts to stare straight ahead, fearing what may be read on her face. "It was the transit camp where your grandparents were taken and your aunts and uncle when they were children. Razed to the ground now, but a monument tells the story." Patricia listens, controlling her uneasiness. *This is good. This is good.* Since she has learned the names of her grandparents, anything that makes them real means—*What does it mean? Not so cut off?*

"The camp was built as a place of refuge in 1939 for German Jews escaping Hitler," Gerdi's voice becomes bitter. "Most were allowed to enter the Netherlands. But the Germans invaded a year later. Starting in summer 1942, the Germans used this camp to deport Jews to Poland—Auschwitz and Sobibor."

Gerdi directs Aleida to park near the area where brown square stones of varying heights, representing the ages of the victims, memorialize the thousands of Dutch Jews who passed through Westerbork. Gerdi's betrays her anger. "A collection camp on the way to the gas chambers and crematoria in Poland." They step out of the car to walk near the stones. Then Patricia sees the stretch of rusted railroad track ending with broken and twisted rails bent skyward. She understands immediately that these tracks brought the victims to Westerbork and then carried them to their certain deaths in eastbound cattle cars. Gerdi is speaking again. "When the Allies liberated this place in 1944, they saved 900 Jews from deportation. But of course, it was too late for your family. I always think that those grotesquely bent rails are an apt reminder of the victory over the killing machine the Nazis had invented."

Patricia steals glances at Gerdi's two daughters. Michelle is clutching Aleida's shoulder. Something she has never considered before becomes clear to Patricia. These two women, close to her age, have also been sheltered from the Holocaust despite all the memorials, the Anne Frank House, the polished tablets and commemorating art. In a way they are not so different than she. Gerdi is acquainting her own grown children with the unforgiving details of the Nazi invasion of the Netherlands.

"You find this hard, Michelle?" Gerdi asks softly.

Michelle is slighter than Aleida. Everything about her is more fragile. "Awful," she replies. Then she hugs Patricia. "I'm so sorry for the dreadful things that happened to your family."

Patricia squeezes back in gratitude.

"Come Aleida, on to Haarlem," Gerdi says and they return to the car. But stones with the Star of David on each of the various sized markers have made an indelible impression on Patricia. *Children*, she thinks, *completely innocent children. My mother, alive, but her two younger brothers....* Gerdi's voice stirs her from her thoughts.

"In perhaps two hours," she says to Patricia, "we will come to the canal house across from the Frans Hals Museum, Gasthuissingel, where your family lived. Would you like to stop for a bite, first?"

"No. Not really," Patricia replies, aware of a knot in her stomach. "But if you would like—"

"We can eat later. Is that all right, girls?" Gerdi asks her daughters.

Michelle's voice is subdued. "I have no appetite, Mama." Aleida nods "No."

Owen and Patricia's room at the Birkstraat hotel is three doors down the hall from Michael's. After Patricia leaves for Gerdi's apartment, Owen taps on Michael's door to finalize plans for a sight-seeing trip to Huis Doorn, Kaiser Wilhelm's residence in exile less than half an hour down the road. Michael opens his door rubbing his darkened chin where Gerdi had made made good on Pim's request.

"What happened?" Owen asks.

"Just a love tap from a fellow I used to know. I'll tell you all after some breakfast, yes?"

As they walk to the elevator, Michael slows as he recognizes the bald pate of the heavyset man he saw acting so strangely the afternoon before. "Did you find your way?" Michael asks.

Owen goes on alert seeing the man's feral eyes. The man pushes by them with a scowl.

"Do you know that guy?" Owen asks.

"Yesterday on the street he seemed to be a little lost. I offered him use of the map the hotel man gave me, but he just seemed disoriented."

"Well, I would't want to run into him on a dark street," Owen says, half in jest.

"I've read there's a cafe near the Kaiser's manor, Michael says. "Can you wait breakfast for a half-hour?"

"Sure. If you're ready, I'm ready. I've called the desk."

As they step to the curb awaiting the valet to bring Owen's rented Opel, Michael emits a "Hmmmh," and taps Owen's arm to indicate the black Audi standing across the street. "That car," he says as the driver sends the dark-tinted driver's side window to the closed position. "That fellow was with that bald guy yesterday. Same car. His face is very familiar. Distinctive even to these old eyes."

Before Owen can reply, the Opel pulls up. He opens the passenger door for Michael to climb in and lingers to observe the Audi; the uneasy feeling he had on Kearney Street after the auction flits through him. Owen clicks Go on his smartphone maps app and they drive down Birkstraat toward the town of Doorn. He glances at his rear view mirror several times and sees the Audi pull onto the street. The coincidence flashes red for Owen.

Michael says, "I was never a fan of the Kaiser's, but believe it or not, Wilhelm was also a Prince of Orange, Holland's Royal Family since the Dutch Revolt. I've never been to the grounds, but they are beautiful I'm told."

Owen listens, but is distracted by the Audi tailing him. When they arrive at the carpark of the estate, they follow a map of the grounds to the cafe, overlooking the moat that surrounds the manor. Owen is hyper vigilant, but does not see the Audi enter the carpark.

They order coffee and dark bread with an assortment of toppings. The nearly empty dining area is a verandah, with a middle-aged couple sipping coffee at a table overlooking a pond with Dutch irises in full bloom on landscaped mounds. "That car you saw, the driver—you said he was what? Distinctive? Was that the word?"

"A little like a Dutch SS guy way back—crooked eyes—as I remember. This was not him of course. But definitely a messed up face like the guy Pim and I had a run-in with in Eindhoven at the end of the war. He and his wife looted our house. Stole the book of maps, too, back then." As if having conjured a specter, Michael's eyes widen, seeing precisely what he described. "Oh Jesus, it's like Diederik all over again." He rises, and Owen turns back to see the odd-faced older man screwing a silencer to the muzzle of his Walther automatic.

Owen pushes Michael to the side and in one motion sends a patio table chair skidding across the stone floor towards the gunman. The couple at the nearby table duck for cover and scream. The assailant, not at all agile, awkwardly backs against the railing overlooking the pond. He shouts angrily as he raises his gun. Owen's only weapons are more chairs, one of which he sends again toward the man who tries to aim his silencer-equipped pistol at Michael, shouting in Dutch over and over again, "Joodse minnaar klootzak, verdomde joden-minnaar klootzak." Owen only understands the word "Jood," screamed several times. The chair clatters against the assailant's hip, and he pitches himself half over the railing. Owen darts to a table with another chair and rushes at the gunman, the chair held like a battering ram. Before he reaches the man, sharp chatters of the suppressed weapon puncture the air, and .22mm bullets tear through the plastic fabric. Owen throws the chair at the man who tries to duck but loses his balance and flips over the balustrade and splashes into the pool below. Owen turns to see if Michael is injured. Dazed, but unhurt, the 90-year-old, white with fear, waves a hand signifying that he is alright. A waiter and a busboy race onto the patio. Michael speaks rapidly in Dutch and the waiter dials his cellphone. Owen has run to the edge of the grounds and sees the soaking assailant gain his feet knee-deep in water.

"Owen!" Michael shouts. Owen turns to see the head-shaved accomplice race across the green, pistol aimed in his direction. He dives behind a park bench. The bald man's weapon has no suppressor and three shots ring out loudly as the busboy and waiter take cover amidst the patio tables. Owen hears the waiter shouting frantically into his cellphone. Moments later, Dutch sirens wail above a new round of Glock gunshots. The skinhead gunman races to the assistance of the older man wading to the shore. And together they splash their way toward the green. Two white, blue, and orange motorcycles arrive first, then officers in a Volvo traffic unit, dispatched on the waiter's emergency call.

The assailants heave their weapons far into the pool and Owen takes note of where they land. The men raise their hands and are easily captured. The waiter quickly fills in the responding police on what transpired.

Michael, moving gingerly after his rough treatment provides details. He extends his hand to Owen, and Michael explains to the police how the American tourist saved his life. Owen points to a hillock of greenery in the pond and Michael interprets that the assailants' guns would be found nearby with an underwater search. The malformed face of Dirk Berghuis glowers with fury. His accomplice shakes his head as if to say "another fine mess you've gotten us into." Michael describes how these men stalked him on the street and in the hall of his hotel in Soest. He provides the Birkstraat hotel as his local address. Plainclothed officers interview the witnesses, taking statements from the waiter, the busboy, and the other diners. Michael translates Owen's account of them having been tailed from Soest, and the police drive off with the two suspects. Owen puts his arm on Michael's shoulder, and the two men hold each other's gaze, shrugging and silently sharing with gratitude that they had survived the hail of bullets.

The manager of the cafe, a nervous woman with excellent English, asks, "Cognacs, gentlemen? Gratis."

"Only if we can be served indoors and nowhere near windows," Owen replies. Michael nods. The manager flags the waiter who seats them inside at a small table. "Have you ever been shot at before?" Owen asks.

"No," Michael replies. "Only bombed, friendly fire. These guys? Not so friendly. That old guy kept calling me a 'Jew-loving bastard.' And you know something? I could get used to that. Hey, you're pretty good with patio furniture."

"I was always good with found objects."

Neither says another word until they are served.

For Owen, the numbing shock of being fired-on is only now beginning to wane.

"To life," Owen toasts.

"Proost. Your health," Michael says, clinking snifters. "Speaking of which, I don't think Gerdi needs to know about this excitement. She's a little old for this."

Owen stares at the 90-year-old and both burst into laughter.

CHAPTER 105

Antwerp, Cathedral of Our Lady, Early Afternoon, 3 November 1576

Sofie guides her two children into the cathedral, the Onze-Lieve-Vrouwekerk. She lifts them up to see art on the walls, but bypasses the grotesque depictions of martyrdom, and points out cherubs and angels for her children.

"Mama, why are we in here? The floor is cold," Liesbeth complains. Sofie seats them on a back pew and holds her children close.

"We will soon be on a sailing boat, but first we must wait for Auntie Maria," she says, pressing her girl close to her. "She is bringing your favorite doll."

After he stops at the cathedral to deliver Jonas' family, Brother Aristede drops off Godlieve and her mother one street away from Sofie and Jonas' flat on Hoogstraat. They agree that he will pick up everyone at the church shortly before the bells toll three o'clock. He steers his cart to the windmills near The Citadel to deposit his sheaves of grain for milling.

With their arms looped through the handles of empty wicker-baskets, Maria and Godlieve climb the staircase to the Hoens' flat, after a quick scan to ensure they are not followed. Once in, Maria collects the small articles, toys, and clothing that Sofie had enumerated, plus the seventeen guilders hidden in a crock at the back of the pantry. They also stuff bread and cheeses into their baskets.

But they have miscalculated their abilities to avoid surveillance. Nicholaus Bockel and Joop Baldus stand in the shadows of a weaver's shop across the street and watch the women enter the brick and wood building. Seeing the unfilled baskets, Bockel's suspicions take fire. He motions for Joop to remain on the street. He enters the building and listens as the women whisper and clack up the stairs to the third floor. He slips back onto the street and tells Joop to watch the front door while he takes up a position that gives him a view of both the front of the building and a side alley leading to another narrow alley parallel to Hoogstraat. He is convinced these women will lead him to Jonas Hoen.

In the cramped room off the papermaking hall at the Boekprintere Scheldt, the ink from the Duke of Toledo's crest is nearly dry. Mark Anthony waves the forged letter one last time, folds it, melts a dollop of sealing wax, and presses the small copper imprint of the Duke's seal into the wax. The seal is easily acceptable as real, despite the reverse image.

Mark Anthony's eyes light up. "I think General d'Avila will be very happy to receive this, as I have told him that a paymaster's armed column has also left Rome with Spanish florins to pay the troops since King Philip learned of the bad weather in the North Sea. Hopefully, that will delay a precipitous mutiny against Antwerp. And, of course, your spies are named as turncoats, apostates, who have embezzled florins for Willem van Oranje's treasons for years. Du Forché, Bockel, Baldus, and Juan Carlos—all identified by name."

Stunned, Jonas looks at the sealed message in his hand. "On your way, then," says Mark Anthony. You have a vessel to board after you deliver this. You have my most hopeful thoughts for the safety of you and your family." He grasps Jonas' free hand, pulls him close and hugs hard. Then he turns and leaves Du Brul's room.

"Pass on my love for Sofie, and your little ones," Du Brul says through tears that he struggles against. "You stay safe, young man, and keep your family safe."

Du Brul leaves the small room, but flips Jonas' cowl back over his head.

"You cannot do this, Jonas," Brother Thomas says.

"But I must, you see," Jonas replies and begins to leave. "I take this upon myself. If I do nothing to stop Du Forché or Juan Carlos—even Nicholaus Bockel, I will never feel safe enough to stop looking over my shoulder. And Joop Baldus threatened my children."

Brother Thomas finds himself nodding. "Very well. You are too headstrong for me to try to convince. But let us have a chance to succeed. At the least, I speak Spanish." Thomas snatches the faux letter. "Let me lead to deliver the message."

Brother Aristide walks his donkey and wagon through the narrow passage to the back entrance of the Hoens' residence. But Bockel has seen the young monk and his empty dray. He quicksteps down the side alley and peers around the corner at the women waiting with their laden baskets as Aristede draws near. The passage is too narrow to turn his cart around, and so the monk waits while Maria and Godlieve climb aboard and pack their baskets into the wagon. Maria rides next to Brother Aristede and her daughter sits on a blanket near the front corner of the dray.

"A red-haired man and his white-haired partner." Godlieve hisses, as her eye catches Bockel and Baldus trying to duck behind the alley, "Like Sofie warned."

Aristede clicks his tongue and snaps the reins to command the donkey. The beast bawls its complaint and lurches forward. Godlieve sees the furtive redhead duck back again and then stand brazenly watching the wagon enter the intersection. Godlieve looks back down the street but is shocked to see Bockel's accomplice emerge from a side alley just ten feet from the wagon.

"Mama," Godlieve screeches, tugging on Maria's arm.

Maria de Vries sees the red-haired spy and his towheaded friend and whispers to Brother Aristede. "Proceed to the cathedral. I will have a word with these two. Lieve," she snaps at her daughter, speaking quietly, but intently, "take the children and tell Sofie to stay in the church. I will find her."

Before Brother Aristede can slow to let her off, Maria alights from the wagon, stumbles, but regains her footing and, wincing, demands loudly of Bockel. "Why do you accost God-fearing women?" She does not wait for an answer but rapidly, in a rising voice to attract attention, rattles on. "I will call the watch to keep an eye on you both, young men." Several passersby pause to listen to the harangue. "This is a Christian city and if you are minions of the Evil One, we all bear witness." Maria sweeps her hand indicating the twelve or more burghers who now surround Bockel, Baldus and Maria. She addresses the crowd, "These lewd men press their attentions on godly women—can you imagine?"

Bockel feebly stammers, "This is a misunderstanding—" But Maria continues to fog his words. "I am old enough to be this boy's grandmother, but he presses—"

"Scoundrel," a woman of Maria's age snaps. Soon epithets fly from the mouths of incensed burghers. "Devil." "Possessed by demons." "Fornicators." "Shameful behavior." "Heretics!" "Sodomites!" "Call the watch!"

Bockel and Baldus try to run, but they are kicked and punched by a burly stableman and an incensed blacksmith. Burghers crowd about them as Maria de Vries turns and resolutely walks toward the cathedral spire two streets away. Her knee stings with pain from her jump off the wagon, but she soldiers on.

CHAPTER 106

Haarlem, Netherlands, 30 June 2016

As they motor into Haarlem in Aleida's Peugeot, Gerdi continues on her theme. "There, the museum across the canal," she says pointing at the classic, red-bricked building that houses the art collection. "When you look at a Frans Hals painting, you have to stand a certain distance away, nine or ten meters. Too close and his brush strokes make you think 'what an amateur.' But at the correct distance, those brushstrokes become precise, the perfect lines to give a photographic image. It's all in the distance, you see."

Patricia is touched by the elderly woman's instructions on how to view events. But, sitting in the front passenger seat, she feels like she is in slow motion fall from a very high place. She fears that dizziness or tears in her eyes will blur what she should be seeing. *Be strong.*

"The next street, Aleida. Park here, please." Gerdi's daughter eases the gray Peugeot into a space alongside the Kampersingel canal, across from a red brick row house, much like its neighbors on the street. Patricia follows Gerdi out of the car. Two painted black doors, one leading to the ground floor, and one for the staircase to the second floor, open at the street level. The bricks over each door and window fan out vertically, keystone style, creating a subtle arch. Wooden moldings, long ago painted white, had been added to the brick façade to break up the nondescript appearance. From the street level, Patricia can see a projecting wooden beam from which a block and tackle could be attached above the roofline. She imagines the four cases of copper plates slowly hoisted to the recessed attic in 1932 and then lowered to the ground as they were looted soon after the van Aalts had been taken.

Gerdi continues. "I learned that on the day of their deportation, the family was ordered downstairs from the second floor which they occupied. They each carried one allotted bag of clothing, personal articles. The vaunted Nazi machine failed, however, because the lorry that was supposed to be dispatched for Jewish families along the route never materialized. They and other families rounded up in Haarlem that day had to walk the twenty kilometers to the Stationsplein." Gerdi points down the street to the east. "Patricia. Are you all right, hearing this?"

Patricia has taken Gerdi's hint when she was speaking about Frans Hals' art, and allowed herself the distance to view events. She feels sturdy on her legs, but she has a death grip on her purse. Then she relaxes her fingers. "I feel fine, Gerdi," she says in a voice that she strains to control.

"Let us walk then," the old woman says, taking Patricia's arm. "Here along the canal, it is quite a charming stroll in normal times. Aleida, please follow in the car."

Patricia enjoys the view for a moment, seeing the grassy bank on the other side of the canal and the neat row houses, universally red brick, and art deco electric lampposts lining the street. The street curves, following the canal and Patricia imagines her mother clutching her cloth bag in one hand and holding her father's hand, her younger brothers hand in hand with her mother.

A moped with a loud muffler zips down the street past them, and Patricia shudders with the same awful sensation she'd had when she was on Dolores

Street in San Francisco two months earlier. She immediately understands the terror of her mother on La Cienega Boulevard when the police on their Harleys paraded, mufflers growling. She imagines uniformed Dutch NSB and German SS riding herd on the stream of Jews walking through these streets to the train station in Amsterdam.

Fear continues to grip her as they bear left on Flevoroute. They have walked less than five hundred meters. She turns to Gerdi. "I think my knees are turning to jelly. This is scaring me."

"Of course. We'll let Aleida take us the rest of the way." Gerdi waves.

Her daughter eases the Peugeot alongside them with Michelle in the front seat. "Sit with me in the back," Gerdi insists.

In the car, Gerdi directs Aleida, "Please follow this route as best you can." She hands Michelle a street map with a route marked with a yellow pen from Haarlem into Amsterdam. "It will be short by car," she adds.

They ride in silence. When they enter Amsterdamsevaart, Patricia pays close attention as Gerdi explains. "The streets begin to get congested as several hundred Jews, especially from the *Jodenbuurt*, the ghetto, are forced to converge onto the streets leading to the train cars for Westerbork. Their fear is overwhelming, as you can imagine. And then there are Dutch Nazis, hoodlums, who terrorized the deportees. Ironically they saved your mother on that day because Hetty was separated from her family by some of those thugs who pushed into the family and in the confusion she manages to hide in an alley just two streets from the train station."

Patricia's grasps an awful truth. Hetty's parents, Frieda and Emmanuel, lost track of their daughter in that moment. She imagines the frantic pleas that they must have made on the train platform and in the railcar bound for Westerbork. Falling on deaf ears of other deportees and their single-minded guards, other Jews gaining a few more months of life by working as a police force under NSB and German orders.

Gerdi says: "My group was anxious to save as many children as we can. One of the NV's operations was to shadow round-ups and help whoever slipped through the cracks. Aleida, stop here while I show Patricia where I found her mother."

Patricia feels a paralysis come over her. It is summer, 2016, and tourists abound as taxis and streetcars swarm over the train station plaza. But she is transported to a bleaker time. Her legs feel wooden as Gerdi opens the rear door. She numbly follows the old woman into a narrow covered passage leading to the inner courtyard for a group of flats.

"Just behind this gate—your wild-eyed mother, poor child, clutches her travel bag in shock." Gerdi's voice cracks with remembrance. "We could save so few."

Patricia takes shallow breaths as she looks at the wall where her terrified mother had pressed against the unforgiving bricks. She imagines her mother trying to make herself small to not be seen.

"I cut the Jood star from her jumper and told her she would be safe with us. She didn't believe us."

Of course, not—Oh, my poor mother.

"I was with two of my college friends, part of the Anonymous Group. I had to promise we would reunite her with her parents at the first opportunity."

But you couldn't. Patricia's tears well, as she imagines the scrawny-limbed nine-year old Hetty crushing her travel bag in her arms that holds her dearest material treasures.

Patricia hears Gerdi struggling not to become emotional through her recitation. The old woman's voice catches in her throat. "You should know that she was terrified to have me remove her star. She wanted so to be a good girl for her mother. For her father."

Yes. Yes. I know.

Gerdi continues. "'Mother said I would only be safe now if I wore the star,' she says to me. I tell her she would only be safe if she did *not* wear the star."

The voice of her mother pleads in her head. *What am I to do? Dear God, what must I do?* "Let her have it," Patricia implores aloud and feels Gerdi squeeze her hand in solidarity. She breathes shallow draughts of air hearing the firsthand account of how her mother was saved.

"Finally, she calms down and we got her eventually down to Eindhoven. Michael and Pim's father took her in. You understand," Gerdi says, putting her arm around Patricia, "I told this little girl that she must be an actor in a stage play where she lived with a kind old man who would call her his niece from Rotterdam. If she was a good actress she would be reunited with her family, I told her, in Eindhoven."

"Michael's father?" Patricia asks.

"Yes, Michael and Pim's father—Herman Dijkstra," Gerdi confirms. But her voice falters. "He was so—so brave to take this on." She pauses to try and collect herself. "He would have been my father-in-law if he had survived. When I found Hetty at his home in Eindhoven—oh, the blood—everywhere. More trauma for Hetty—oh, the damage that was done to everyone."

"We walked out of this alley in darkness to a safe neighborhood." Gerdi guides Patricia onto the street. The afternoon light hurts Patricia's eyes.

"I have one question for you, Patricia. I gave you your mother's star earlier and you took it. Do you still want it?"

"Yes. I do," she says in a steady voice. "My grandmother said my mother needed the star. My mother repeatedly would say, 'Never let them know you are Jewish.' It is important that I struggle with those conflicting messages. This piece of hateful fabric will help me remember."

Gerdi nods, smiles a crinkly grin, and squeezes her wrist.

"My mother, Gerdi?" Patricia asks. "Did she ever thank you?"

"Too much in shock. She seemed happier when I would check in on her in Eindhoven. But the hardening—the walls were already going up for her."

Patricia nods, and puts her arms around Gerdi. "I thank you—for her." Gerdi's body feels frail in Patricia's embrace. Patricia fights through her sobs to continue. "You are a heroine to me."

"I thank you too, for coming here. I know it was not easy." Gerdi says, over her own tears. The two women cling to each other a moment longer.

"Let's have a meal at the old restaurant Pim and I owned. The food is still quite good."

CHAPTER 107

Mainz, Germany, 2 July 2016

Owen, Patricia, and the Berlin print dealer, Heinrich Stössel, form a semi-circle around a white cloth-covered table in the modest living room of an elderly couple. They are in the downtown district of Mainz, near the Gutenberg Museum.

"Oh, my God," Patricia exclaims.

"Yes," Heinrich Stössel agrees.

Owen casts his eye on the tiny portrait. It bursts off the octavo sheet of rag paper with the same intensity as the famed Nine of Beasts and Three of Birds, the only other engravings by the Master of Playing Cards that Owen has seen firsthand. The portrait, only three inches, shows the presumed bearded likeness of Johannes Gutenberg examining a piece of type in a printer's wooden composing stick.

The engraving, pressed on a ragged-edged piece of handmade paper, is a deeply etched impression. The black ink is fading, entirely likely, given the unstable chemistry of early oil-based inks from the era of this printing.

Owen listens while Stössel and the old man and his wife, Herr and Frau Düssen, hold a discussion in German. The old man points to a wooden box with a hinge held in place with a tiny diameter dowel. He opens the lid with arthritic fingers and throws wide the oily rag revealing a rectangle of copper discolored by oxidation, mottled green ranging to orange. Through the multi-colored surface, Owen can see the reverse image of the printed plate.

He looks up to see Stössel's smiling gaze.

"I thought you would have an interest," Stössel says. "Frau Düssen has a dream of spending the rest of her years on cruise ships in tropical oceans. Herr Düssen likes the idea. And to finance it, he wonders if these two items can bring him their hearts' desire. Here is a copy of the family's records. They have been in Mainz since the thirteenth century. And on page two of these papers, it looks like a Gustav Düssen worked in the print shop that produced Gutenberg's bible."

"May I take some snaps?" Owen asks the old man. Stössel translates and nods to him.

He shoots three photos of the paper print, and seven of the copper plate. He moves the box to catch the light from various angles.

"May I?" He asks, indicating lifting the plate from its cradle.

"Ja, ja." the old man says, handing the plate to Owen. He feels the roughened surface and knows the plate can be cleaned up easily. Once the oxidation is removed, the copper plate could print many more impressions under careful circumstances. Owen lays the plate next to the paper print and photographs them together. He asks Stössel to lay his palm on the table above the two items to provide an indicator of size relative to the human hand.

Owen shoots snaps of each of the pages of documentation, showing the Düssens' historical lineage in Mainz.

"Heinrich," Owen asks, "do you agree that the Master of the Playing Cards was possibly the engraver of this portrait?"

"I wouldn't rule that out, Owen. This is not the work of a goldsmith, but an artist. Either the Master or one of his students, I would say. Look at the modeling, parallel verticals, no cross-hatching, just like his cards."

Owen signals to Patricia that it is time to leave. "Frau and Herr Düssen. Our pleasure to meet you," Owen says, extending his hand to shake with each of the elderly couple. Patricia also shakes their hands. To Stössel, he says, "Heinrich, I will text these images to my client and see if we can work something up. I would love to help this lovely couple sail in the Bahamas and the Caribbean."

Owen and Patricia take their leave with Stössel from the old couple's house.

"May we take you to dinner?" Owen asks Stössel.

"I need to be in Berlin by seven or my wife will serve Hamburger Heinrich. I will take a lift to the airport, if you wish to be of service. Half an hour."

"Done."

Patricia listens to Owen and Heinrich Stössel argue for twenty minutes of the drive to the airport about which was the better movie, *Roshomon* or *Throne of Blood*. For the last ten minutes, Patricia answers a barrage of questions from Stössel about why she prefers Northern California to Los Angeles. After Stössel shakes hands with both of them at the Departures sidewalk of the airport, they drive back to their hotel on the outskirts of Mainz.

Patricia puts her hand on Owen's knee and taps it. "You know your onions about copper plates, don't you?" Her question is rhetorical, as her voice hints an admiration and respect for his knowledge. "It was fun watching you work with Heinrich."

"I was hoping you weren't bored."

"Not at all. If fact, I hope you'll give some attention to a new collection of some very old copper that has come my way."

"You'll have my complete attention, Milady." She squeezes his knee.

As the lights of Mainz appear in the distance, she speaks again, her voice tinged with wonder and, Owen can detect, a residual dollop of sadness. "This has been some roller coaster ride, Owen." He touches her hand, still resting on his knee. "I've been thinking," she continues. "With all this talk about classic films, don't you think the story of the map and Gerdi's heroics would make a good movie?"

Owen looks at Patricia for a moment. He sees that she is in earnest.

"You must be reading my mind," Owen says, smiling broadly. "This is a story that should be told." On the drive to their hotel, they resolve to talk to Matt Warburg.

CHAPTER 108

Antwerp Citadel, 2:30 p.m., 3 November 1576

"Por favor, por favor. Perdóname," Brother Thomas strides hurriedly through the outer courtyard of The Citadel. Jonas follows close on his heels, trying to keep up in his ill-fitting sandals, and taking note of the Spanish garrison cleaning weapons, honing blades, cursing, whispering, or playing at cards and dice. "El Comandante D'Avila, gracias. I have a message for the commander," Brother Thomas announces in Spanish, never breaking his stride.

A tercio pike-man flips his thumb toward a barracks to the right.

The monk steps smartly toward the open doors. Several uniformed German soldiers with arquebus muskets and short-swords lounge uncomfortably outside a chamber with a cadre of four Spanish soldiers who stand ready, hands on hilts, while a loud-voiced Spaniard bellows within, "No le pido, Conde Eberstein. Te ordeno que se entrega la ciudad."

Brother Thomas stops abruptly and translates to Jonas as the authoritative voice speaks. "Count Eberstein is ordered to turn over the city."

"Traducir para que este idiota entienda. ¡No es una petición, es un orden!"

A Spanish translator in a monotonic voice speaks in High German. "It is not a request, but an order!" Brother Thomas looks at Jonas, who understands enough of the German to know they may be on a fool's errand."

"Tell him, absolutely not," Count Otto von Eberstein says in German.

The Spanish commander replies in a menacing tone.

"Aghhh," Brother Thomas gasps, in a whisper to Jonas. "Not good for the city. He knows about the English Queen's actions."

A grim-looking Count Eberstein stalks out of the chamber, followed by his adjutant. They stamp past the two Benedictines, the count muttering, "Look to my life, eh? He should beware for his, the idiot." The German soldiers fall in behind Count Eberstein as they march toward The Citadel gate.

Brother Thomas announces loudly in Spanish to be sure he can be heard within, "With respect, I have a message from Fernando, Duke of Toledo for General Sancho d'Avila."

The steely-eyed general, beard crisply cut, steps out of the chamber frowning and snaps the proffered letter from his hand. He fixes his gaze on the copper-tonsured monk. "How did you come by this?" General d'Avila demands.

"The King's emissary entrusted it to me, Senor Benito Arias Montana who functioned as the King's censor for the Hebrew text of the Polyglot—La Biblia Regia." The commandant nods, recognizing the name and the context of the Christophe Plantin project, sanctioned under the Iron Duke's tenure.

He turns his gaze to the seal on the folded sheet, breaks it and reads as he walks back into his chambers. The doors are closed by one of the guards. Brother Thomas turns and nods to Jonas to begin to leave. The doors are flung open, behind him and General d'Avila issues commands to the his adjutant.

Brother Thomas whispers the translation to Jonas. "Ten cavalry from the Catalan unit—"

The angry general continues in Spanish "and deliver them to me."

The adjutant sent to order the Catalan unit into action runs past Jonas and Brother Thomas, holding the missive with the four names, toward another barracks in The Citadel compound.

General d'Avila turns to Brother Thomas. "Gracias, Hermano."

Brother Thomas attempts to acknowledge the general, but he has already passed through the doors. Brother Thomas taps Jonas on his back to hasten their departure and whispers urgently, "He wants the spies—'deserters,' he calls them, brought here for proper punishment. And he wants the letter returned to him."

Back in the wagon they head toward the Scheldt quayside, and Brother Thomas explains that a detail of Catalan cavalry is ordered to the Seamens' Fists alehouse. "These Catalans have a bad reputation."

"What happened with the German count?" Jonas asks.

"The general ordered Count Eberstein to turn Antwerp over to him. He refused. I think there will be looting soon. It could be like Mechelen again, only much more bloodshed. You are fortunate to be on your way soon."

The cathedral bells toll the three o'clock hour just as Jonas sees the pennants flying from the *Tortelduif*, sailors hurriedly stowing cargo, preparing to sail.

"We should be on board by now," Jonas says, concern in his voice. Brother Thomas slaps the reins on his donkey's rump.

They see Brother Aristede, Maria, and Godlieve completing the offload of baskets from their wagon. Captain Vandeven hurriedly welcomes Sofie and the children on deck. Jonas peels the monk's habit over his shoulders. He undoes the sandals and picks up his hose and boots from the wagon-bed.

"My boy, please write when you are safe," the Brother says in a choked voice.

"Keep out of danger," Jonas replies. "And Maria, and all of you, thank you. I pray for your safekeeping."

Brother Thomas' arm lingers on Jonas' shoulder. He squeezes the monk's hand, alights and hugs Maria, claps Brother Aristede on his knee, and briefly holds Godlieve's hands before he snatches up the last basket of their goods. He takes a deep breath to stifle a welling lump in his throat at leaving his surrogate family. Then he smiles when he sees Sofie's tiara of silk daffodils on top of the basket and grins up at his family already on board.

Captain Vandeven says "Quickly, quickly. We are casting off. Rotterdam— tomorrow afternoon. Then Amsterdam and Bremen. We'll get you to Groningen somehow. A few minutes more and we shall have the tide."

He turns for one last look at the departing wagons and sees the unmistakable face of Juan Carlos who points at him with his three comrades from the lane before the tavern. They break into a run toward Jonas as he spins around to race onto the gangplank. Sofie has seen them also and she screams just as a clatter of cavalry hooves gallop down the quay. The ten Catalan horsemen pull up as the quartet of Jonas' attackers comes to a screeching halt. The Catalans know they have their prey and chase them toward the alehouse.

Jonas races to his wife and his children as his heart fills with the mix of remorse at leaving old friends to perilous events to come and exhilaration that they are escaping dangerous Antwerp. He pulls Sofie and his two little ones to the port side rail, grabs a rope ladder and peers two streets up the lane. The uniformed Catalans drag four men onto the street from the alehouse. One has a shock of red hair another a head of white straw. Sofie squeezes Jonas' fingers and she lets out a long sigh of relief.

Within hours of docking in Amsterdam, the Hoens learn that the Spanish garrison has sacked Antwerp and massacred thousands in three mutinous days begun the morning after they had sailed. Sadness overwhelms them. How did their friends fare? Did they survive? Mark Anthony? Pieter Du Brul? Andreas Grober? Dr. Brudo—others in the Jewish Quarter? Abraham and Anna Ortels? Even Antonius, the Ortels' driver springs to mind as Jonas envisions the garrison sharpening weapons in their fury over not being paid.

Ten days later, they stand before a farmhouse near Groningen and behold the grinning faces of Emmanuel van Aalt and his wife and children, Isaac and Ettie. "Thank God you and your family escaped and have found us," Emmanuel says.

Rachel embraces Sofie and pats Liesbeth's cheek. "Here, you are safe," she says, cupping young Marcus' forehead. The van Aalt's little boy reaches out to pull Lisbeth's hair. "Gently, Isaac, gently," Emmanuel chastens.

Jonas does not know what the future will bring, but he has an unmistakable sense that, for now, he has come home. Even with that comforting thought, he conceives of a broadside illustrating the mutinous troops spilling out of The Citadel and laying waste to Antwerp's citizens. His illustration of the Bloodsucking Tick—the Antwerp Citadel, would be the basis. He hopes he will have a quiet corner to turn his vision into a copper plate.

CHAPTER 109

Soest, Netherlands, 7 July 2016

Behind Owen, in Gerdi's living room, a chatter of voices, some English, some Dutch, fades into the background. He sips his beer and slips a yellowing mimeographed manuscript from its place on a bookshelf in an alcove. He is intrigued because he sees the name *John Steinbeck* on the front page with, he assumes, its title in Dutch above, *De vliegenvanger*. He wonders what the title means. He turns back to the room and again hears the laughter and banter. He smiles, as children run in and out of Gerdi's living room to her patch of garden where Michelle and Herman Dijkstra, Gerdi and Pim's son and second daughter, sit with their spouses, turning pages of the 16th Century Ortelius book of maps on a glass-topped table. Three giggling young cousins play a board game at another table outside. Patricia and Aleida chat in a corner of Gerdi's living room, engrossed in discussion of Aleida's school for children with special needs.

The elders, Gerdi and Michael, animatedly turn pages of a photograph album on the settee, pointing at snaps of Pim and Gerdi and their family through sixty years. Michael laughs and sighs at pictures of his brother and Gerdi with their children on vacations, family celebrations, and marriages of their grown children.

Pim and Gerdi's eldest, Herman, is in his mid-fifties. Outside on the patio, he swallows a draught of a beer, and examines one of the engravings in the big book of maps. He has the same bone structure as Michael, and a full head of blond-brown hair. He waves at Owen to join him.

"You are the expert here," Herman, the man who carries his grandfather's name says. "Please help us understand something about this map."

"Of course, Herman, if I can." Owen sits on a plastic folding chair next to Herman's pretty wife, Helga. "But first, can you tell me what this says?" Owen hands Herman the fragile mimeographed manuscript with Steinbeck's name on the cover sheet. "Ah, *De vliegenvanger*," Helga reads, smiling.

"Oh, your John Steinbeck.," Herman says. "That's not the real title. It was translated as *The Flypaper*, a good simile for the occupation of a country with a strong Resistance. This little novel is really Steinbeck's *The Moon is Down*. Father let me read it when I was twelve. If Mother had been caught with this, the bastards might have shot her on the spot. Reprinted by the underground, it gave Resistances all over Europe a blueprint on how to fight back, not that they needed it."

"Thanks," Owen says. "This is remarkable." He tries to imagine the Fleming Galleries handling a piece of literature like this. He doubts Pinkham would touch it. "So, what about this map?"

"Here is the map of Great Britain—Anglia, but it looks like somebody's pancreas or kidney. It's turned on its side, not North-South, but West-East."

"Yes,"Owen says, chuckling at the plate. "I think Ortelius wanted to get what we would call in the States 'maximum real estate.' So he turned the British Isles sideways to produce a map across the double folio sheet. This way, he shows more detail, topography and towns. Ortels had a great affinity for England and Wales so he gave it broad exposure. But it is not the view you would get from Google is it?"

"The painstaking detail...." Herman shakes his head in wonder.

"I can imagine how your father could spend hours looking at the engravings of these countries, and all the named towns and rivers and seas. Four and a half centuries later we have satellite images that get within a few feet of a house and you can even look inside the windows. Treasure this book of maps, Herman. It was an extraordinary undertaking in its day."

"You love this stuff, don't you?" Herman asks.

"My exuberance is showing, eh? Patricia thinks I get carried away."

"When I'm on a project I'm glued to the drafting table," Herman admits.

Herman's wife, Helga, rolls her eyes.

"Hard to strike a balance, sometimes," Owen leans back and drains his beer. In the living room Patricia laughs, still in conversation with Aleida. Michael now has a ten-year-old girl and an eight-year-old boy, Herman and Helga's younger kids, hanging off his knee and leaning over his shoulder. Although Owen's grasp of Dutch is nil, he is certain the nonagenarian is explaining how a diode emits light to his rapt young listeners. Beaming, Gerdi rises from the settee. She taps a coffee cup with her spoon. "Everybody, listen. Uncle Michael says he will consider moving here."

The two children hanging off Michael begin cheering. Michael is flustered, but smiling. Herman flips the pages of the book of maps and he, Michelle, and Helga rise from the outdoor table and converge on Michael, wide smiles on their faces. "Oh, please do more than consider it, Uncle," Herman pleads. Aleida is smiling too and walking to the settee. Michael catches her eye as though to ask permission. "Yes, yes!" Aleida says, unequivocal.

Owen's eyes meet Patricia's. She steps into the garden and they press against each other, hip to hip, enfold arms around the other's back. They watch, moved, as Michael wells up. Owen and Patricia hold tightly to each other and expel long-held breaths. Michael catches their eyes and puts a hand to his chest, smiling.

Owen looks down behind him for a moment at the map of the world with the sea monster anchored forever in the Mar Di Indi. He sees clearly the scratchings of JONAS HOEN helping to define the leviathan's perch. He squeezes Patricia to him and they can't help but smile broadly at the noisy family reunion before them.

— The End —

Dramatis Personae

The following character names may assist in the reader's understanding of the multi-century scope of this novel and its locales. If these characters are based on actual individuals, an asterisk (*) follows their names.

16th Century, Duchy of North Brabant, Spanish Netherlands 1560s-70s

Jonas Hoen, flood-orphaned miller's son, apprentice engraver

Joachim Hoen, his father, Vrouw Hoen, his mother, Jeltje, his sister

Brother Thomas, Benedictine monk, Jonas' mentor

Maria de Vries, cook for the monks and orphans

Godlieve, her daughter

Benedictine Brothers, Cornelius, Bernardus, Uwe, Aristede, Theo, and the Abbot

Orphans, including Willem Booten at the monastery

Spanish, Italian, Catalan and German mercenaries

The Duke of Alva (Fernando Álvarez de Toledo*), the Iron Duke, enforcer of the Spanish Inquisition in the Lowlands

Antwerp, Boekprintere Scheldt, etc. 1570s

Abraham Ortels (Ortelius)* cartographer, map seller, conceiver of the Theatrum Orbis Terrarum

Gilles Coppens de Diest*, master printer, bookbinder, publisher of the Ortelius book of maps

Mark Anthony Coppens*, his son, proofreader, translator, pamphleteer

Frans Hogenberg*, master engraver, principal engraver of the Ortelius cartography

Pieter Du Brul, master paper maker

Andreas Grober, master limner (colorist)

Apprentices: Joop Baldus, Ritsaert, Jan Grens, Sofie Van Alsing, Janine, Nicholaus Bockel

Anna Ortels*, sister to Ortelius

Antonius, servant of the Ortels'

Captain Jacobus Vandeven, ships master of the Tortelduif

Doctor Manoelo Brudo, Antwerp-born son of a Portuguese victim of the Inquisition

Vicompte Maurice de Villiers, representative of William of Orange

Erasmus, homeless Mennonite widower, father of two little girls

General Sancho d'Avila*, commandant of the Antwerp Citadel

Count Otto von Eberstein*, drowned in the Scheldt during the Antwerp Fury

London 1570 (Sign of the Cock lodgings)

Elizabeth Coels* (Cole) sister of Ortelius

Jacobus Coels* (Cole), silk merchant, husband to Elizabeth

James Cole*, their little boy

Marjory, housekeeper

Francis, cook

Millie, scullery maid

Marcus Gheeraerts*, Flemish engraver, refugee from Bruges, Jonas' tutor

Susannah de Critz*, Antwerp refugee, Marcus' mistress, Tudor Court retinue

John de Critz*, Tudor Royal Court, cousin to Susannah, on the Court's Serjeant-Painters crew

Jan du Forché, Juan Carlos—Spanish Inquisition spies in London

Anent Willemzoom, Flemish refugee in London

Baroness Joan Casterleigh, Queen Elizabeth's retinue, Whitehall

Baron John Gillesford, brother to Joan Casterleigh

William Cecil (Lord Burghley)*, principal advisor to the Queen Elizabeth

Francis Walsingham*, intimate of William Cecil in countering plots against Queen Elizabeth, later her spymaster

John Jugge, Fleet Street printer

Emmanuel van Aalt and Henrick, Dutch-in-exile young draymen, England

21st Century San Francisco Bay Area (Palo Alto, San Francisco, Berkeley, Walnut Creek, Hayward)

Michael Dijkstra, 90-yer-old former electronics engineer, survivor of forced labor munitions factor in Germany

Patricia Spencer, schoolteacher, daughter of Hetty Baron

Owen Spencer, her husband, a dealer in prints and art

Hetty Baron, nee van Aalt, mother to Patricia

Maurice Bregmann, curator of Western Judaica, UC Berkeley, Bancroft Library

Rodney Pinkham, book and print auctioneer, San Francisco

Matt Warburg, chief cataloger, auction house

Cynthia Vasquez, receptionist, auction house

Ian Carstairs, associate auctioneer

Horst Harman, print and Nazi memorabilia dealer

Hayward Police officers

Fourth graders, including Mario Kinsella and Esperanza Reyes in Patricia's class

21st Century Netherlands and Germany

Gerdi Ten Broeck Dijkstra, 92-year-old estranged sister-in-law of Michael Dijkstra, widow of Pim Dijkstra

Aleida, Michelle, and Herman, nieces and nephew of Michael

Jet Leuwenboom, Dutch Office of Restitution official, Den Haag

Aalbert, custodian of artifacts of unknown origin, Den Haag

Heinrich Stössel, art and print dealer, Frankfort

Gerhardt Schroeder and Dirk Berghuis, Dutch neo-Nazis

1940s Eindhoven, Netherlands and Krümmel Munitions Works, Germany

Herman Dijkstra, linen factory owner dispossessed by Nazi takeover, father of Michael and Pim

Marthe, his wife killed in the Rotterdam blitzkrieg

Hetty van Aalt, 10 years old, hiding in Herman's home, 1943-44

Gerdi Ten Broeck, fiancé to Pim, who rescued Hetty as part of an underground effort to save Jewish children

Diederik Berghuis and Henk Rost, Dutch SS officers

Emma Berghuis, wife to Diederik, housekeeper after Marthe's death

Michael, 17, and Pim, 20, sons of Herman torn from their jobs at Philips and shipped off to forced labor 1942

Rudi Müller, disabled German soldier working at Krümmel munitions factory

U.S. Intelligence officers, Dutch Resistance translators—Displaced Persons Camp, Duisburg, Germany

Eindhoven neighbors

Acknowledgements

I owe sincere thanks to those who supported my efforts in bringing this novel into being: My loving partner Rina; writers' group members Don Rothman, Dave Dodson, Joel Wallock, Tod Connor, and Dan Phillips; many teachers over the years, including Marie Minuto, Leo Lieberman, Marvin L. Seiger, Mildred Kuner, Karen Yamashita, Shellie King, David Sullivan, Lisa Simon, and Marcie Alancraig, in whose classes I developed my short story into early drafts of this historical novel.

I am grateful to the dedicated beta readers who cheered me along this five-year journey: my brother Arlin, Jim McKinney, Clifford Ammon, Michael Fligner, Paul Gabriel, Lewis DeForest Brown, Bonnie Barberini, Bryan Miller, Claire Tristram, Mark Budz, Marina Fitch, Paul Briscoe, Kim Jastremski, Geoff Lightfoot, Jim Jones, David Brick, Oskar Leuthold, Toni Taylor, and Ruth Pullman Cameron.

I owe debts of thanks to editors Karen Funk, Mindy Conde, and Natalie McDermott (The Crimson Quill), and novelist/editor Nick Brown.

Special thanks to literary agent Greg Aunapu for sharing his thoughts, to Stewart Tiley, Librarian, Saint John's College, Oxford, England, for giving me access on short notice to the library's 1579 copy of Ortelius' Terrarum Orbis Theatrum, and Timber Hawkeye, for bringing this book into print with a great cover design.

CPSIA information can be obtained
at www.ICGtesting.com
Printed in the USA
BVHW030920031019

560037BV00027B/43/P

9 781946 005311